MEMORY'S HOPE

A Medical Thriller Series Book 3

Chris Bliersbach

Smashwords

Cover design by: Tatiana Fernandez, Vila Design

CHAPTER 1

Jackie woke up, momentarily confused, to find herself in an unfamiliar bed. Memories of the prior evening flooded in, providing context, which helped orient her. She relaxed, comforted that the business portion of her trip to the Farrisport Inn in Maine had gone well and was giving way to weekend plans with Curt and his kids.

Jackie Deno, who formerly worked as a pharmaceutical representative for AlzCura Pharmaceuticals, and Curt Barnes, a healthcare consultant whose wife was brutally murdered by Darius Scott, first met serendipitously at the Farrisport Inn. Jackie and Curt and his two kids Caitlin and Cade had all arrived at the Inn's restaurant hostess station at the same time. Brittany, the hostess, mistakenly assumed they were a family. When she asked, "Table for Four?" it not only provided comic relief, but it caught Jackie, Curt, and his kids at a time when they desperately needed saving.

On that fateful evening, Jackie arrived in Maine, puzzled at how her husband Stu snapped at her when dropping her off at the airport in Buffalo. To that point, Jackie and Stu's relationship could only have been described as a fairytale romance come true. Inexplicably, that morning he said words that were now forever etched in her memory.

"You aren't going there for work. I know better. Don't lie to me. You're going to destroy everything."

She had first thought he was joking. But when he erupted in anger and drove away erratically, nearly hitting her as the car fish-tailed away, she knew something was wrong. Despite trying to call him multiple times that day, he never picked up. It was Jackie's first business trip after her maternity leave, and the guilt she had about leaving her 3-month old daughter Ashley weighed heavily on her. It was a perfect recipe for arriving at the restaurant that evening, angry, confused, and worried.

Curt had arrived at the restaurant in a similar emotional state. Calli, his wife of 10 years, had been murdered three months earlier. Strapped to their marital bed and burned alive by a crazed man who was later identified as Darius Scott, an unemployed 48-year old man from Barry, Maine. Darius had been taken into custody and placed in the Harlow Psychiatric Institute. Curt's hopes of finding answers to why he killed Calli diminished when Darius died unexpectedly two days later of liver failure and a massive brain aneurysm. On top of Curt's anger was an unrelenting concern for his kids. They were struggling with the loss of their mother. He had started to go to counseling sessions but was firmly ensconced in the anger stage of his grief the evening he first met Jackie.

With this as the backdrop and Caitlin and Cade pleading with Jackie to join them, they had agreed to have dinner together - a meal that would provide healing for all four. Unbeknownst to Jackie and Curt at the time, this accidental meeting would eventually bring them together for a dangerous crusade.

Jackie had returned from Maine to her home in Nora, NY, to find her beloved husband, Stu, dead in bed. Now, she was not only racked with questions about his outburst but grievously searching for answers to how her healthy, young husband could have died. It would be her job with AlzCura and Stu's autopsy results weeks later that would ultimately provide Jackie with answers and the impetus to reach back out to Curt.

Jackie's position as a pharmaceutical rep with AlzCura was focused on getting physicians in the Northeast region of the U.S. to prescribe the company's Recallamin vaccine. The Food and Drug Administration (FDA) had approved Recallamin for use in mild and moderate cases of Alzheimer's. Clinical trials had proven that Recallamin stopped the progress of Alzheimer's, and in some cases, even reversed its effects. Another clinical trial was underway to vaccinate younger people who had the so-called "Alzheimer's gene" to determine if Recallamin could prevent Alzheimer's altogether.

She was good at her job. So good that she garnered the company's Newcomer Award in her first year. Having lost her grandmother to Alzheimer's, she loved that the company and her position had such a noble mission. It gave hope to millions of individuals and their families suffering from the ravages of a disease that slowly extracted the entire essence of its victim, leaving only an empty shell. But all was not sunshine and rainbows as Jackie was to learn. Increasingly, the physicians Jackie met with, particularly Dr. Steven Caron in Central Maine, started voicing concerns. Specifically, the Recallamin vaccine seemed to be causing a higher prevalence of fatal adverse events leading to liver failure and brain bleeds.

When Dr. Jacobsen, who performed Stu's autopsy, told Jackie that her husband had died of liver failure and a massive brain bleed, it immediately struck a chord. Weeks later, the toxicologist reported an unidentifiable substance, ruled as "suspicious but inconclusive," had been found. This prompted the coroner to obtain records from Stu's physician's office visits. Jackie subsequently learned that on Stu's last doctor's appointment, he had received the Recallamin vaccine after genetic testing confirmed he had the Alzheimer's gene. She was devastated. She had recently learned of concerns about the Recallamin vaccine's safety but never thought to share this with Stu. Now she bore the crushing guilt that by not doing so, she contributed to his death. She never considered that Stu would make such a decision without consulting her. But he did, and now he was dead.

The final insult came shortly afterward when her boss, Cheryl Baker, Vice President of Operations at AlzCura, accused her of impropriety with a client and unceremoniously gave Jackie her walking papers. Along with her termination, she had to sign a strict confidentiality agreement that threatened legal action should she violate its terms. Jackie saw through the false accusation. She had become a liability. She knew too much and was too principled for the AlzCura executives' tastes. Instead of walking quietly into the sunset, Jackie fought back. She reached out to Curt, and together with DA Wydman and Dr. Caron, they met at the Farrisport Inn and formed the Table for Four - a crusade to expose the truth about AlzCura and Recallamin.

When Jackie returned home, her house had been broken into, and the ominous message, "Goodbye Baby," had been spray-painted on Ashley's wall. Later, when she asked a security company to assess her home for a security system, they found hidden cameras throughout her house, placed during the break-in to spy on her. A few days later, Dr. Caron's body was found hanging in his office, dead of an apparent suicide. Concurrently, someone had tried to pick up Curt's kids at school and left a menacing note on the door to his apartment. Within two weeks of the Table for Four's pact, it seemed clear that AlzCura was watching them and was not going to sit back without a fight.

With their resolve shaken but still committed to continuing their crusade to expose the truth, the Table for Four replaced Dr. Caron with Inspector Theo Adams. Theo had investigated Darius Scott's murder of Calli Barnes and was presently investigating Dr. Caron's alleged suicide. The evidence around Dr. Caron's death was starting to weigh in favor of someone assisting in his hanging. Compromising pictures of Dr. Caron with Margo, Jackie's interim replacement when she was on maternity leave, were found on his office computer. Files, including those of Darius and Elvira Scott, were missing, along with Norman Boulanger's patient record. All three had been part of Recallamin clinical trials, and all three were dead of the same causes - liver failure and massive brain bleeds. And perhaps the most damning evidence that Dr. Caron didn't commit suicide, GBH, the date rape drug, was found in Dr. Caron's bloodstream.

A new wave of terror, thought to be the work of AlzCura, would follow. In New York, Jackie's daughter Ashley was kidnapped. Someone had grabbed Ashley from her stroller in the park when an unidentified woman had temporarily distracted Jackie's mother. Fortunately, Ashley was found unharmed, laying at the feet of the Virgin Mary statue in St. Paul's Church a couple of days later. In Maine, someone broke into Celeste Boulanger's trailer and decapitated her dog, Sophie, leaving her head, Godfather-syle, on Celeste's bedroom pillow. Also found in the trailer was Leslie Anderson, the notorious Channel 5 news reporter, who had apparently been in the wrong place at the wrong time. Her slashed throat and partially-clad body testimony to a sexual assault and a brutal slaying.

Jackie stretched and thought about extracting herself from the hotel's comfortable bed. Lingering a bit longer, she reminisced about the dinner meeting the previous evening. The meeting had been emotionally challenging, especially for Celeste, Curt, and Jackie, who had to relive their losses and the horrors brought upon them thereafter. As challenging as it was, it succeeded in bringing new allies to the table to continue the crusade to expose the truth about AlzCura. It offered hope, not only to get redemption for Celeste, Curt, and Jackie's losses but ultimately to save countless numbers of people from the dangers of the Recallamin vaccine.

As Jackie left the warm cocoon of her bed and made her way to the bathroom to take a shower, Ashley stirred in her hotel-provided crib. Detouring to Ashley, Jackie greeted her daughter.

"Good morning, beautiful," she cooed.

In response, 9-month old Ashley smiled, held her arms out, and said, "Mama."

Ironically, the first time Ashley said "Mama" had been in the same park across from Jackie's house where she would be abducted a week later.

Jackie picked up her daughter, cuddled her a moment, and brought her to the bathroom, where she prepared Ashley to join her in the shower. As the warm water rained down on them, Ashley laughed and reached up toward the showerhead in what looked like an attempt to catch the water before it fell on her. Jackie's tears were hidden from her daughter as she recounted the magical moment in the shower with Stu at the Oasis Hotel & Spa in Arizona, where Ashley was conceived. Every experience she had with Ashley seemed to be bitter-sweet without Stu there to experience it with them. She was overjoyed when Ashley first said, "Mama." But broke into tears and collapsed in her mother's arms when she was hit with the realization that Stu would never hear his daughter talk. Now she wondered if every momentous occasion in Ashley's life would always have that bitter aftertaste.

After getting out of the shower, and while she was getting Ashley dressed, her phone rang, alerting her to Curt's call.

"Hi, Curt," she answered while trying to cradle the phone and continue to dress Ashley at the same time.

"Good morning, Jackie. How was your night?"

"It was," she began, only to have her phone slip and fall to the ground. Leaving Ashley half-dressed, she retrieved the phone.

"I'm sorry I dropped my phone. I was trying to dress Ash and talk at the same time. Both Ashley and I slept well. It must be the comfy bed and the fresh Maine air. You?"

"I slept well too after surviving Caitlin and Cade's interrogation after I got home."

"Interrogation?"

"Yes. The first question out of Caitlin's mouth was, did you see Jackie?

"Really?"

"Yeah, I thought it was because they knew I had a business dinner at the Inn. They always think of you when we go there. But then Caitlin said she thought she smelled your perfume."

"Busted!" Jackie exclaimed.

"Yeah, no kidding."

"What did you say?"

"I said she must be imaging things."

"Did she buy it?"

"I'm not sure. She said she still smelled your perfume this morning when she hugged me before getting out of the car to go to school."

"I'm sorry," Jackie apologized.

"I'm not. I enjoyed every second acquiring that intoxicating scent," Curt said, recalling their long, tender good-night kiss the previous evening.

"I did too, but I hope we haven't blown our cover," she said, sounding like they were covert spies on a critical mission. Curt and Jackie had devised a plan to surprise Caitlin and Cade with a weekend together at the Rockport Inn.

"I guess we'll see when we pick them up from school. When can I pick you and Ash up?"

"Can you give us an hour? We just got out of the shower."

"No problem. See you in an hour."

Hanging up, Jackie proceeded to finish dressing Ashley, who was happily babbling on the bed. She realized that for the first time in a long time, she felt genuine excitement about something. Yes, she had been excited when she got the job at Nora Community Hospital, but it meant she had to leave Ash every day. Every enjoyable experience she had since Stu died always seemed to have a downside. Their weekend plans bore no hint of such a drawback.

Finished getting ready faster than she had anticipated, Jackie killed some time by taking Ash to the toy store within walking distance of the Inn. As Jackie explored and occasionally presented toys for her daughter's consideration, Ash seemed unimpressed and disinterested. That is until she spied something she really wanted. Squirming and reaching over her mother's shoulder, she said: "Mama, mama" with urgency. When Jackie turned to see what had attracted her daughter's attention, she saw Monty Moose. It was the same stuffed animal that Curt and the kids had the hotel's front desk clerk deliver to her after their magical dinner together. Ashley had come to love her Monty Moose, but Jackie had forgotten to pack it for the trip. The joyous and contented expression on Ashley's face when Jackie handed her the Monty Moose was priceless. There was no way Jackie was going to leave the store without Monty Moose #2.

Returning to the Inn, Jackie got her bags, checked out, and held Ashley, who held Monty Moose, as they waited in the lobby for Curt's arrival. Curt breezed in and immediately spotted them.

"I see Monty Moose made the trip with you," he grinned, giving Jackie a hug and a kiss.

"Well, actually, he's an imposter." When a quizzical look came over Curt's face, she explained.

"Well, the kids will be delighted to see Ash with Monty Moose, imposter or not."

After loading Jackie's bags into the trunk and settling Ash and Monty Moose into the car seat, they drove North on the pine tree-lined freeway to pick up Curt's kids from school.

"So, what's object permanence?" Jackie asked out of the blue.

Curt's face reflected his momentary confusion until Jackie refreshed his memory.

"Remember? You picked us up at the airport, and when you made Ashley cry, you said it was stranger anxiety and that it occurs about the same time as object permanence."

"Really? You remembered that?" Curt said, genuinely impressed.

"I'm not just a pretty face," she laughed.

"I agree, and pretty is an understatement."

"So out with it. What's object permanence."

"You're amazing. Alright, object permanence. Object permanence is a developmental milestone where a child begins to understand that just because they don't see something, it doesn't mean that something doesn't exist."

As Jackie's facial expression communicated that she was pondering the concept, Curt tried to clarify.

"It's a theory a Swiss psychologist named Jean Piaget developed. To a certain age, babies can't understand that an object can still exist when they can't see it. If you leave the room, they think you're gone. Think about playing peek-a-boo. When you put your hands in front of your face, babies without object permanence really think you're gone. When you reappear, they're relieved because you're back. When babies get older, they know you're not really gone, but laugh anyway when you reappear because they just know you're acting silly."

"OK, I got it. Interesting," Jackie replied.

"You know, I'm not just a pretty face," he jabbed in response.

"Now, who's making the understatement?" she said as they

smiled and looked at each other with the knowledge it was going to be a great weekend.

Curt pulled into the school driveway and took his customary parking space to wait for Caitlin and Cade's arrival. Both Curt and Jackie were filled with anticipatory excitement. As they spied the kids exit the school and saunter toward the car, they finally realized someone was in the car with their father. In a flash, they both started to run. As Jackie exited the vehicle to greet them, Caitlin yelled with glee.

"I knew it. I knew it," her sprint culminating in an impressive leap into Jackie's arms.

"Oh, I missed you so much, Caitlin, and you too, Cade," as she released Caitlin and bent to embrace Cade.

As Caitlin and Cade piled into the backseat on either side of Ashley, their excited greetings and their strange faces caused a predictable response. Ashley began to cry.

"Stranger anxiety," Jackie and Curt said in unison from the front seat in a moment of levity before they sprung to action to console Ashley and educate the kids on why she was crying. Armed with this new knowledge, Caitlin and Cade did their best to calmly and quietly win Ashley over as they drove out of the school's parking lot.

"Are we going home?" Cade asked, always the one who needed to know what the plans for the future were.

"Nope, we're going to the Rockland Resort," Curt replied, to cheers that were abbreviated so as not to startle Ashley.

"For the whole weekend?" Caitlin asked, hopefully.

"Yep, until Sunday when we have to bring Jackie and Ash to the airport," he replied.

Curt knew that he needed to start managing their expectations around Jackie's visit to avoid potential drama on Sunday.

The hour-long drive allowed Caitlin and Cade to update

Jackie on school, their friends, horseback riding, and hockey. As Ashley started to get comfortable with the two new faces beside her, Caitlin and Cade transitioned to giving her attention, allowing Curt and Jackie to converse.

"So, what's tomorrow's lesson, professor?" Jackie asked.

"I'm thinking separation anxiety," he replied. "Sunday will not be easy."

"For you?"

"Well, yeah, me too, but I'm thinking about them," his head gesturing in the direction of the backseat.

"What about me?"

"I'm always thinking about you," he smiled.

Arriving at the picturesque resort on Penobscot Bay, they checked in to their private, two-bedroom, oceanside cottage. The cottage, nestled on a rocky outcropping a good distance from the resort's main building, came with the use of a resort golf cart. This immediately spurred Caitlin and Cade to fight over who would drive the golf cart first. Before Curt had an opportunity to referee, Jackie stepped in.

"No fighting, or I'm going home."

"We're sorry," Caitlin replied, speaking for her brother and ceasing their battle instantly. "Cade, you can drive it first," she directed at her brother.

"Thanks, Caitlin," Cade replied, giving his sister a hug.

"That's better, I think we let your Dad drive first, and then you can take turns later after we've unpacked and settled in, OK?" Jackie replied.

"OK," Caitlin and Cade responded in unison.

Curt, who didn't intervene in the scuffle, looked at Jackie with a sense of wonder, as if he was in some alternate universe. Who was this beautiful woman with the power to end what were usually epic battles between his kids?

"Perhaps I should be taking parenting classes from you?" he remarked as he took the driver's seat next to Jackie.

"Thanks, but I'm quite sure it's just the honeymoon period. Might as well flaunt it while I got it."

"Well, you just set a world record. What was that?" Curt asked rhetorically, raising the fingers on his hands as he counted the words. "No fighting, or I'm going home." Six words! I don't think they even hear my first six words when I jump into the fray."

"Seven technically," Jackie replied. "I'm is a contraction of I am."

"Oh, well then, smartypants, what took you so long to break up the fight?" he said as he took the driver's seat and released the brake on the golf cart.

Laughing, she leaned into his shoulder as Curt steered the cart down the path to their oceanside getaway.

"What is that?" Cade said, pointing to a long granite rock structure that extended almost a mile into the bay.

"That's called a breakwater," Curt replied. "It is used to protect the boats in the harbor. And do you see that house at the end?"

"Yeah."

"That's a lighthouse. We'll take a walk out there sometime this weekend, OK?"

Arriving at the cottage, an awkward conversation about sleeping arrangements ensued. The kids had not been privy to Curt and Jackie's prior agreement that the boys and girls would sleep in separate bedrooms. Instead, they must have assumed or perhaps wished that Jackie was their new Mom and Ashley, their new little sister. When they saw the first bedroom had a King-size bed and crib, they assumed that their father, Jackie, and Ashley would take that room.

"Dad, are we going to have to sleep in the same room?" Cade

asked in distress as he and Caitlin stood outside the bedroom with the two twin beds.

"Nope, Cade. You and I will take that room. The girls sleep in the Master over here," pointing in the direction of the other bedroom.

Relieved, Cade entered the room while Caitlin skipped happily to the girls' boudoir.

"Not bad," Jackie said as Curt's response averted a potential scene. "What was that? Fifteen words?"

"I'm not sure. I don't have that many fingers. I'm still not in the big league like you are!"

"Yeah, it's probably my halo effect," she said with an air of superiority.

"Undoubtedly. I always thought you were an angel."

"Awww," she said, walking over to where he stood to give him a hug that turned into a kiss while Caitlin and Cade were unpacking in their respective rooms.

"I love you, Jackie."

"I love you, Curt. Thank you for suggesting this. It's beautiful here."

"Eclipsed only by you," Curt replied, prompting another hug and long kiss that was only interrupted by Cade's appearance.

"Eww gross," Cade exclaimed, as Curt and Jackie separated as if they were two high school kids caught necking by one of their parents.

"What?" Caitlin asked as she rushed out of her room. Afraid she had missed something.

"They were kissing," Cade said in an accusatory tone.

"That's not gross, Cade," his sister replied. "That's what people do when they love each other."

"I think it's gross."

Meanwhile, as Caitlin and Cade debated the topic of kissing, Curt and Jackie grabbed their respective pieces of luggage and disappeared into their separate bedrooms.

The cottage was quaint, clean, and comfortable, but it was the view from the outside deck that was breathtaking. The cottage's proximity to the ocean not only gave guests an unobstructed picturesque view of the rocky coast and vast ocean, but the waves crashing into the nearby rocky shore caused a rejuvenating cold sea spray—a kind of natural spa treatment.

"I'm famished," Jackie exclaimed, realizing that she had not had anything to eat.

"Well, you're in luck. There's a great restaurant just up the path. Cade, you ready to drive us to dinner?" Curt asked, knowing it was a foolish question.

Cade took the driver's seat only to realize he couldn't steer and reach the pedals at the same time. They reached a satisfactory solution when Curt suggested that he would sit next to him and work the pedals while Cade steered.

"Thank you for letting me drive first," Cade directed towards Caitlin as they made their way up the cart path to the main building. "This is fun."

Successfully having navigated the short trek, they walked through the lobby and down the stairs to the restaurant.

"Table for four," the hostess asked, failing to see Jackie was carrying Ashley on her back in a baby carrier.

"Four plus a high-chair," Jackie replied, turning slightly to show the hostess who needed the high-chair.

Although they had only had one previous dinner together, it felt like they had been dining together for years. Caitlin, Cade, and Curt had relived this scenario several times when they would go to the Farrisport Inn. They would leave an open seat for Jackie and imagine she was there. The kids would even reserve a bite of their desserts for her.

True to tradition, Caitlin ordered Crème Brulee, and Cade ordered the chocolate cake with vanilla ice cream. This time, Jackie was able to sample each of their desserts for real. By the time dinner had ended, Ashley was asleep in her high chair and Caitlin, and Cade's eyes were at half-mast. This didn't prevent Caitlin from claiming her turn to drive the golf cart. Curt reprised his role as the pedal operator as Caitlin navigated the path. The sun was giving way to dusk with a full moon rising as they arrived at the cottage. Caitlin and Cade needed no encouragement to find their beds as Jackie changed Ashley's diaper and placed her in the crib. As the sun bid adieu behind the horizon, leaving the full moon in charge, Curt invited Jackie out to the deck for a bottle of champagne.

"What's the occasion?" Jackie asked, spying the bottle of champagne.

"What, being together isn't occasion enough?" he replied as they settled into the Adirondack deck chairs.

"I'm so happy, Curt. I haven't been this happy since," Jackie caught herself, not because she was uncertain but because she knew exactly when she had been that happy.

"Me too," Curt said, rescuing her from having to complete her sentence and popping the cork on the bottle.

"Stu and I had that same champagne on our honeymoon," she confessed, seeing the bottle of Moet Chandon.

"I think we are going to have many times when something reminds us of Stu or Calli," he said reflectively.

"I think you're right," she replied as Curt poured champagne into her glass.

"To Stu and Calli," Curt toasted, raising his glass towards Jackie.

"To Stu and Calli," Jackie replied as their glasses clinked

After each took a few sips and silently took in the view, Curt stood and offered his hand to help Jackie out of her chair.

Leading her to the deck's railing, he wrapped his arms around Jackie from behind as they looked over the shimmering moon-lit ocean, just a stone's throw away. They stood for a long time, wrapped in each other's arms. The only sounds being the rhythmic waves lapping against the rocks and the occasional haunting wails of loons calling to one another. Their content-ment didn't require words, they knew what they were feeling, and tonight, those emotions were too big for words. Whether it was the day's activities, the meal, the champagne, or rocking in each other's arms, it didn't matter. The combination had a somnolent effect. Walking back into the cottage with their arms around one another, they paused between the two bed-rooms and kissed.

"I love you," they said almost in unison, their laughter tem-porarily interrupting the romantic moment.

"Sweet dreams, angel," Curt whispered, referencing an en-dearment he had applied to her in an earlier conversation.

"Sweet dreams, professor," she countered as she turned to head off to bed.

CHAPTER 2

D A Wydman walked into AG Talcott's office the morning after his dinner meeting at the Farrisport Inn, excited to update him on the progress made towards determining AlzCura's culpability in multiple crimes. Over the past nine months, AlzCura's involvement had been implicated in no less than three crimes. Nailing down definitive proof to bring charges against the pharmaceutical giant had been elusive. Armed with the information that Jackie, Dr. Preston Slack, and Dr. Stephanie Mason had shared with him the previous evening, DA Wydman now had cause for optimism.

"Good morning, Will. Have you had your coffee yet this morning?" Attorney General Lewis Talcott greeted as he was pouring himself a cup of joe.

"I'm good, Lew. Thanks."

"You look like a man on a mission this morning."

"I am. I wanted to fill you in on what I learned last evening."

AG Talcott sipped his coffee and listened intently to DA Wydman's briefing on the meeting, which involved Inspector Theo Adams, Jackie Deno, Curt Barnes, Celeste Boulanger, Dr. Preston Slack, and Dr. Stephanie Mason.

"In addition to Dr. Caron's 13 patients in Recallamin trials who died of liver failure and brain bleeds, we now know that

Jackie's husband died the same way. Drs. Slack and Mason are also going to send us their list of patients that had adverse events to determine if there are any additional cases."

"That does sound promising. No wonder you're so upbeat."

"That's not all. Both indicated that Dr. Sheridan recently contacted them, saying there were errors in the abnormal liver function test results they originally sent. It looks like they may be trying to cover their tracks."

"That sounds suspicious. Did we ask Drs. Slack and Mason to supply us with the names of those patients?"

"You know what? No, we didn't. Good idea. I will ask Theo to contact them."

"I would recommend we have those patients retested by a lab other than the Regional Lab AlzCura uses."

"I'll let Theo know to suggest that."

"Anything else?"

"Yes. We got an earful about Margo. Apparently, she isn't going to win any popularity contests with the Portland docs. Jackie was none too impressed by her either. Theo is going to do an in-depth interview with all three in preparation for his meeting with Margo. If circumstances dictate, we may even have Jackie and the doctors present to witness Margo's statement."

"Well, that was a productive dinner meeting. Anything new on the murder of Leslie Anderson in Mrs. Boulanger's trailer?"

"No, but Theo tells me that Celeste is now staying with a friend. Apparently, that has thrown the media off her scent. At least temporarily."

"Yeah, I heard a reporter on the news last night mention they couldn't find her. Let's hope she stays put wherever she is. Good work, Will. Keep me posted, and have a good weekend."

"Thanks, Lew, you too," DA Wydman replied, unintentionally rhyming like a Dr. Seuss book.

When DA Wydman got back to his office, he saw that Theo had already sent him a list of patient names from Dr. Slack and Dr. Mason. He called Theo to see if the list included the patients that had abnormally high liver function tests that were allegedly due to erroneous test results.

"Hi, Theo. Thanks for the patient lists," he opened.

"Hi, Will. You're welcome."

"Say, I just met with AG Talcott, and he had a good idea. By any chance, did the lists you sent include the patients with abnormally high liver function tests AlzCura claimed were due to faulty test results?"

"I'm not sure. I'd have to call them and ask."

"Do that. Lew thinks we should have those patients retested with the specimens analyzed by a lab other than the Regional Lab AlzCura uses."

"I'll get on it right away. I can tell you that when I spoke to both doctors earlier today, they're highly motivated. Both of them have already decided to discontinue offering the vaccine."

"Really? That will get AlzCura's attention. We better be prepared for any potential backlash."

"Yeah, that will probably put Jackie right back in their cross-hairs big time."

"I'll give her a call and let her know," DA Wydman replied. "I think she knows what she's getting herself into, but what Dr. Slack and Mason are doing will hit AlzCura right where it hurts. They will not be happy."

"You know, Will, that makes me wonder if there are other doctors in Maine who are prescribing Recallamin."

"Good point. I'll ask Jackie when I call her."

The touch base completed, both set off to follow up on their respective tasks.

CHAPTER 3

J ackie awoke with a start, disoriented for the second morning in a row. Until Caitlin appeared in view to tell her what was now evident, Ashley was crying from across the room. Rubbing the sleep from her eyes, she trudged to the crib, her appearance immediately reducing her daughter's cries a few decibels. As Jackie changed Ash out of her wet diaper into a dry one, Caitlin looked on with interest.

"Can I hold her?" Caitlin asked.

"You can do more than that. Could you take care of her while I take a shower?"

Jackie's question made Caitlin feel as though she had been elevated to big sister status. While she was still 4 months away from turning 9 years old and had never taken care of an infant, she answered as if she had specialized training.

"Sure, I've taken care of Cade my whole life."

Entrusting Ashley's care to Caitlin, Jackie quarantined herself in the master bathroom and stepped into the hot spray of the multi-head shower. Jackie's figure had finally returned to its pre-pregnancy form. The jets of water pelted her toned body stimulating a memory of her honeymoon with Stu and the multi-head shower at The Castle in Buffalo. Closing her eyes and luxuriating in the full-body experience, her mind drifted. Eventually landing on Curt and how natural it felt to be in his arms the previous evening. Her loneliness without Stu and a re-emerging libido as the hormonal storms of pregnancy and childbirth subsided now fueled what felt like an unquenchable desire. How much she wished Curt was with her now. Holding her. Caressing her. The pulsating water, exhilarating at first, started to feel like unbearable torture, and she exited in frustration but determined to find fulfillment. Completing her morning routine and slipping on form-flattering jeans and an equally becoming top, she emerged from the bathroom.

"Whoa," Caitlin exclaimed, seeing Jackie's transformation. "You're beautiful."

"Aww, thank you, Caitlin. You are too."

"Can you teach me how to put make-up on?" as Ash beckoned for her mother and squirmed in Caitlin's arms.

As diligent and caring as Curt was, there were just some things a father couldn't help an 8-year old girl with, especially one who fancied herself as going on 18!

"I'd be happy to, but we'll have to ask your father first. Thank you for taking care of Ash."

Caitlin brightened and transferred Ashley back to her mother.

"Do you love my daddy?"

Caught momentarily off-guard, Jackie replied, "What do you think?"

"I think you do love him."

"Why do you think that?"

"You look happy together, and Cade caught you kissing."

"Well, you're a very smart young lady," giving her a hug and elegantly answering her blunt question without technically answering it.

"I'm going to see if Dad will let me wear make-up," Caitlin

said excitedly, jumping off the bed and scurrying out the bedroom door.

Jackie dressed Ashley and followed shortly after that to find Caitlin locked in conversation with her father on the living room couch. Curt did a double-take when he saw Jackie, his stomach doing its characteristic flip-flop. He was unable to take his eyes off her while he completed his conversation with Caitlin. Judging by Caitlin's enthusiastic reaction, Jackie surmised Curt had just given his daughter permission to learn how to apply make-up. Caitlin bolted from the couch and called to Jackie as she disappeared back into the bedroom.

"Daddy said I could wear make-up."

"OK, I'll be there in a minute," she replied, her eyes locked intensely on Curt. "You look like you've seen a ghost," she commented while putting Ash down to crawl around and explore.

"The most beautiful ghost I've ever seen," he replied, standing and closing the distance between them, not stopping until she was in his arms and his lips met hers. Instantly aroused, they kissed, hugged, and fondled, desperate to fill their deep emptiness. Awakened but hardly sated, they reluctantly tore themselves apart.

"I'm waiting," Caitlin called from the bedroom.

Curt and Jackie looked at each other, both recognizing that absent the children, the match they had just lit would have set them both on fire. A fire they would not have tamed until after they had both felt its explosive intensity consume them.

"I'm coming," Jackie called back to Caitlin.

Jackie could tell what Curt wanted to say just by the look on his face. She turned and purposefully worked it to tease him on her way to the bedroom. Halfway there, she paused briefly to glance back at Curt.

"Nice ass," he whispered.

To which Jackie smiled, blew him a kiss, and disappeared

tantalizingly through the bedroom door.

While Jackie gave Caitlin her first lesson in applying make-up, Curt went to check on Cade.

"Good morning, sleepyhead," he said as his son rolled over in bed.

"Good morning, Dad. Can I drive the golf cart today?"

Cade's ability to focus on one thing and one thing only was legendary.

"I think it is your turn, but before that, you need to take a shower and get ready. You can drive us to breakfast."

Cade didn't need any further encouragement. As Cade got ready and the ladies continued to primp in the bathroom, Curt made a cup of coffee and retired to the deck. The morning sun, the sea breeze, and the infinite ocean view, interrupted by only a few islands silhouetted in the distance, were like a healing salve calming an angry wound. His silent reverie was only interrupted when Jackie opened the door to announce Caitlin's transformation. As Caitlin stepped through the door, beaming from ear to ear, Curt couldn't believe the change in his daughter's appearance. He couldn't find the words to say.

"Don't you think she looks beautiful?" Jackie prompted.

"Stunning. Honey, you look like you're at least 12 years older."

At this time, Cade also made his appearance, and when he saw his sister, he was stunned.

"Jeez, Caitlin. You're really pretty," which was so far removed from the names he usually attributed to her that she wasn't exactly sure how to react.

Caitlin didn't have to say anything. You could see that her new appearance and her growing relationship with her surrogate mother, Jackie, had given her a boost of confidence. She carried herself differently, and for this, Curt was extremely grateful, if not a little uneasy, about his little girl growing up too fast.

"Who wants to go to breakfast?" Curt asked.

Receiving a unanimous vote in favor of breakfast, Cade got behind the wheel of the golf cart, and they made their way to the restaurant for breakfast. As they arrived at the restaurant, the hostess, in addition to seating them, handed them a sheet of paper with the resort activities for the day.

"Look, kids Explorer's Day Camp," Curt announced.

"What's that?" Cade asked, not interested in reading the description.

"It's from 10 a.m. to 2 p.m., and you get to do a scavenger hunt, collect shells on the beach, visit the lighthouse, do crafts, and play arcade games. You also get lunch."

"Will you and Jackie do it with us?" Cade asked.

"No, it's only for kids. We can't go, although it sounds fun," Curt said as he shot a glance towards Jackie.

"I'm sure it will be awesome, Cade," Jackie added. "What do you think, Caitlin? Do you think you could go and pick some seashells for me?"

Curt was beginning to learn to never under-estimate the powers of others in convincing your children to do things they wouldn't necessarily do with his encouragement. As Caitlin and Cade agreed, Jackie and Curt looked at each other, knowing they would be experiencing Explorer's Camp in an entirely different manner.

With breakfast behind them, they went and registered Caitlin and Cade for day camp and then let the two take turns touring them around the grounds on the golf cart until it was time for them to check in. As Caitlin and Cade marched off to their adventure, Curt and Jackie sped off with the cart to theirs.

Relocating the crib outside the bedroom and putting Ashley down for a nap, Curt and Jackie's three-hour exploratory journey began and ended in the shower. In between, they cuddled on the bed, alternating between verbal and non-verbal means of communicating their feelings for one another.

"Weren't you going to teach me about separation anxiety today?" Jackie asked, shortly after the third act of their play, as they lay beside one another.

"You mean you didn't feel separation anxiety just now when I rolled over here? Or the two previous times?"

"Oh, professor, I didn't know you were going to show me. I'm sorry, I'm a slow learner. Could you show me again? I'll do anything to get an A in your class," she added, in her best schoolgirl imitation.

"OK, young lady, but pay attention this time. We're not afraid to use corporal punishment in this university. If you don't get it this time, I may need to take my hand to your bottom," Curt scolded, imitating a venerable old professor.

Suffice to say, Jackie enjoyed and learned her lesson well as much as professor Curt was elated to infuse her with the contents of his curriculum. For Jackie, it was reminiscent of the playful relationship she used to have with Stu when he would talk about Betty Sue as foreplay to their bedroom activities.

Both were surprised when the clock indicated that they only had 30 minutes before they had to pick up the kids. Their second shower together was more functional than fun. After putting themselves back together, Jackie changed Ash. Curt returned the crib to the bedroom and made the bed to hide any hint of the gymnastics they performed earlier. Arriving at the pick-up spot just in time to greet the happy little explorers, Caitlin and Cade were bubbling over with enthusiasm as both talked over each other for attention.

"Slow down, one at a time," Curt finally interjected.

"We got you a bunch of shells, Jackie," Caitlin said as she and Cade revealed their bounty that filled half of a paper bag. As Jackie pulled out examples of cone shells, cowries, and whelks, she came across a piece of aqua sea glass.

"These are beautiful. Thank you so much," genuinely touched at the thought and the effort they had obviously put into their seashell collection.

"Look at this," Curt said, holding up a shell he pulled from the bag. "I think this is called an Angel Wing," handing it to Jackie. "How appropriate."

She looked like she was about to cry.

"Are you sad?" Cade asked, misreading the tears that had welled up in her eyes.

"No, Cade. Sometimes I get so happy, I cry," she said, pulling Cade in and giving him a hug. "Thank you both so much," she sniffled, pulling Caitlin in for her embrace. As Caitlin pulled away from Jackie's hug, she felt a tug on her hair, followed by Ashley giggling. Ashley, who was riding on Jackie's back, had grabbed Caitlin's hair during the hug and now was hanging on for dear life and laughing at Caitlin's surprised reaction.

"I think Ashley likes you," Curt commented as his daughter tried unsuccessfully to pry open Ash's little fist.

"She won't let go," Caitlin giggled, amused at Ash's tenacity.

"I have an idea," Jackie suggested. "Tickle her."

As soon as Caitlin began tickling Ashley, she immediately released Caitlin's hair and started laughing so hard that it made the rest of them laugh with her. It was just another special moment during a weekend that had already been filled with special moments.

Afterward, Caitlin and Cade took turns driving the golf cart and showed Curt and Jackie points of interest they had explored during their half-day at camp. Then returned to the cottage and played board games. Playing until it was dinner time when Curt made a suggestion.

"What do you say we make dinner here tonight?"

"What would we eat? There's nothing but a few boxes of crackers," Caitlin asked.

"I'll go out and pick up some lobsters, corn, potato salad, and we'll have a proper Maine feast."

"Yeah!" Caitlin and Cade shouted in unison as Jackie's face indicated she was just as much in favor of his idea.

"Do you mind staying with the kids while I go shopping?"

"Not at all. We'll have fun."

Curt, forced to be solely responsible for the food shopping and cooking over the last 9 months, had significantly increased his skill level at both. As he left to get the fixings for dinner, Jackie and the kids played hide-and-seek, which Ashley loved even if she didn't quite understand the concept of being quiet while hiding. Given Ashley's proficiency in crawling, Cade and Caitlin also had crawling races against Ashley across the living room. In preparation for dinner, they set the dinner table with Caitlin and Cade, educating Jackie on the proper implements and dishware required for lobster. This brought back memories for Jackie of the time she had brought lobsters back home to Stu after one of her business trips to Maine. She and Stu had been woefully inexperienced and ill-equipped for solving the problem of cooking and eating lobsters. While that night with Stu had been exceptional, as were most times with Stu, trying to eat had been an exercise in futility. She hoped tonight's dinner would not be as frustrating.

Curt returned, and while he and Jackie prepared the lobster and corn in the kitchen, the kids played with Ashley in the living room. Jackie confessed her inexperience with lobster by telling Curt the story of her dinner with Stu.

"That's OK, you'll be an expert by the end of dinner tonight," as he put the lobster pot on to boil the water. "Let's get the corn in some sugar water."

Jackie gave Curt a quizzical look.

"What? Did I say something bizarre?"

"No, I just have never put corn in sugar water."

"Oh, it's the best."

He described the process of taking the corn still in their husks and soaking them in sugar water for 30-45 minutes, and then grilling them.

"You can put them in the oven too, but since we have a grill out on the deck, we'll use that. Grilling is the way to go. Let's have a glass of wine," he suggested.

"Now, opening a bottle of wine, I can do," Jackie laughed.

They clinked their wine glasses and snuck a kiss in while the kids were busily involved playing before returning to dinner preparation. As Jackie was spooning the potato salad into a serving bowl, Caitlin called.

"Dad, Jackie, you need to come here, like right now."

The tone of her voice and the urgent demand had them dropping everything in the kitchen, thinking that there may be some kind of emergency. When they stepped out of the kitchen, they saw Ashley wobbling in a standing position with a determined expression on her face. As Ash looked up at her mother and the others in the audience, she lost her balance and plopped back down on her bottom.

"Oh my God, she's trying to walk, Curt," Jackie cried as tears came to her eyes for the second time that day. "Did you help her?" she asked Caitlin.

"No, she just did it on her own."

As if to prove Caitlin wasn't lying, Ashley tried to stand again. Succeeding, she stood for a moment and, with a studious look, raised her right leg only to be thrown off-balance and end up on her backside. Undaunted, and with all four now huddled around and encouraging her, she lifted herself up and this time succeeded in taking two steps towards her mother before falling forward on the carpet. Jackie picked Ash up and hugged her while the rest cheered. If the fall had hurt Ash, you wouldn't have known it. She smiled and laughed as if delighted by her accomplishment. For the next 10 minutes, while the water was heating to a boil in the lobster pot, they concentrated on Ashley's continuing efforts to walk. Pictures and videos were taken, and Ashley achieved a personal best six steps before Curt and Jackie needed to attend dinner.

When they returned to the kitchen, Curt pulled Jackie into a hug.

"Congratulations, Mom. Your little girl is growing up."

"Too fast," she replied as tears fell.

"He saw her do that from heaven, Jackie. I have to believe he did," he said, anticipating what was going through her head and heart.

His words were precisely what she needed to hear as she sunk deeper into his embrace. As much as she missed Stu, sharing this moment with Curt, who obviously knew what she was going through, was a blessing. She lifted her head, and their lips met in a long, tender kiss that resurrected all that was good and exciting about the moment they had just witnessed.

"So I guess today's lesson is cooking, huh, professor?" she asked as they continued preparations for dinner.

"Yes, and it's not just the corn that's smoking hot," as he turned the corn on the grill.

"Why, professor, do I detect you may have a hankering for little ole me?" she pouted southern belle style.

"Nonsense, dear girl. I'm an academician who values intellect over the base and lustful things. I'm not at all interested in your tight little ass, for instance, or those zaftig breasts, your luscious lips, those mesmerizing eyes, or your beautiful long tresses spilling all down that deliciously sinful body."

"I'm sorry, I must have misunderstood, professor. I was

going to suggest you might enjoy having me for your dessert."

Curt never thought that the mundane act of turning the corn would result in turning both of them on, but it did. Closing the lid on the grill, Curt pulled Jackie to him, out of view of the kids. He proceeded to take liberties by caressing and kissing the features that the professor had claimed no interest in. It was the evening's delicious appetizer.

Lobster dinner was a much more pleasant experience this time for Jackie, as Curt and the kids assisted her in the proper technique for disassembling the crustacean. The job was made significantly easier in that Curt had purchased soft-shell lobsters that required few, if any, implements to liberate the sweet, tender meat inside.

"I didn't know there were soft and hardshell lobsters," Jackie exclaimed.

"Yes, well, you're not alone. Most people outside of Maine don't know that," Curt replied.

Curt surprised the kids with their favorite desserts, delivered from the restaurant to the cottage, which allowed them to continue their tradition of sharing with Jackie. Ashley, who had achieved a major developmental milestone that day, was nodding off in her highchair.

As Jackie put Ash down for the night, the kids settled in to watch some TV in the living room. Curt took the half-drunk bottle of wine out to the deck, where he was joined shortly thereafter by Jackie, the two sinking into their Adirondack chairs to watch day fade into the night. For the first time that weekend, their conversation turned to the crusade against AlzCura.

"Don't get me wrong, Jackie. I am all in just as you are, but I can't help but be concerned about you."

"Thanks, Curt. I just don't see what choice I have. They stole my little girl when I wasn't even doing anything."

"I understand, but now you are doing something, and if they were involved in what happened at Celeste's trailer, I worry what they will try to do next. You live in AlzCura's backyard."

"What do you suggest I do?"

"I don't know. I just wish we didn't live so far apart."

His sentiment resonated with her, and both sat silently, pondering the statement. Despite their connection and the intimate moments they had shared, it seemed premature for either of them to consider moving closer to one another.

"What if the kids and I come and visit you in a couple of weeks?"

"I'd love that."

"Good. We'll do that then."

"Is this your way of dealing with separation anxiety?" she said, half-joking.

"Works for me."

"Me too. I love you, Curt," she said as she left her chair to sit on his lap.

"I love you too, Jackie," kissing her as she settled in.

Sunday came, and with it, the realization that Jackie and Ashley's visit was coming to an end. They went to breakfast, took a walk along the breakwater, packed up, checked out, and headed for the airport. Jackie and Ash's departure was not as traumatic as it could have been for Caitlin and Cade as Curt divulged their plans to visit Jackie and Ash in New York in a couple of weeks. With hugs and kisses all around, they parted, counting the days to when they would be together again.

CHAPTER 4

Monday morning, DA Wydman sat at his desk with 10 minutes to kill before he was to meet with Cole Minor, Jr. and Sharon Orendorf. Their meeting hoped to put a close to the complaints Elvira Scott had leveled against the Harlow Psychiatric Institute and the State's Medical Examiner's office. Realizing that he had not called Jackie, as he had promised Theo, he gave her a call.

"Good morning, Will," Jackie answered enthusiastically.

"Well, you sound in a good mood for a Monday morning."

"I am. I spent the weekend with Curt and his kids at the Rockland Resort in your great State of Maine."

"Oh, that's a great place. The wife and I go there for their Sunday brunch a few times a year. Not that I need 6 buffet tables full of food to get me to eat!"

"I know everything there was just great. Plus, Ashley took her first steps!"

"Oh my gosh, what a great weekend. Congratulations, and I'm glad you got to enjoy a bit of Maine."

"I did. Thank you. I assume you must be calling for something other than an update on my weekend, however."

"Ha, Ha, yes, you're right. Theo and I spoke late last week, and I have two things. First, we were wondering if any other physicians in Maine prescribe Recallamin besides the doctors in Dr. Slack and Dr. Mason's practices?"

"Not that I'm aware. AlzCura was thinking of expanding to the Bangor area, but I never went there.

"OK, good to know. This brings me to the second and more important reason for my call. Dr. Slack and Dr. Mason have voluntarily discontinued prescribing Recallamin."

"Really?"

"Yes. Our meeting apparently spooked them enough to make that decision. My concern is that once AlzCura catches wind of their decision, they may take out their anger on you. We're concerned about your safety."

DA Wydman's words echoed the conversation she had just had with Curt over the weekend. Hearing it again away from Curt and the idyllic paradise she was in over the weekend made his words feel more real, more ominous.

"Thanks, Will. That makes sense. I just don't know what I should do."

"What about that Officer you mentioned who was going to speak to his Chief."

"Officer Todd?"

"Yes, him. Maybe you and I can get on a call with Officer Todd and his Chief and work out some kind of plan."

"I can do that. He was going to text me after he spoke with his Chief, but since I haven't heard from him, I can give him a call."

"Do that and let me know. All of us here in Maine who care about you and Ashley will sleep much better knowing you're safe."

"Aww, thank you, Will. I appreciate your concern. I will call Officer Todd and get back to you."

"Have a great day, Jackie."

Hanging up, DA Wydman made last-minute preparations for his meeting with the representatives from the Office of Advocacy and the Maine chapter of the National Association for the Mentally Ill.

* * *

Inspector Adams, having secured the subpoenas to access the patient records in Dr. Slack and Dr. Mason's practices, made the 45-minute trek to Portland. In addition to the patients who experienced adverse events, he subpoenaed the patients with abnormally high liver function test results, AlzCura claimed were due to a lab error. The doctors agreed with DA Wydman's suggestion that the patients be retested at an independent local lab. Dr. Slack and Dr. Mason had assured Inspector Adams that they would ask their patients to come in for that purpose.

He arrived at Dr. Slack's Casco Bay Neurology Associates office mid-morning, anxious to potentially add to the evidence they already had on AlzCura Pharmaceuticals.

"Good morning, can I help you," asked the bubbly receptionist whose name tag announced her name as Amy.

"Good morning, Amy. I am Inspector Adams. I called earlier this morning."

"Yes, of course. Nice to meet you, Inspector Adams. I've set up space in our conference room for you to review the records. I assume you have the subpoena? I will need to copy that for our records."

He handed her the subpoena as she led him down a hall to a small conference room. The room had a wall of shelves brimming with medical texts, journals, and a section that looked like it was reserved for medical artifacts one would see in a museum. He took a seat by the stack of records that sat at the end of the table.

"I will let Dr. Slack know you're here. I'm sure he will want to stop in and see you."

"Thanks, Amy."

"You're most welcome, Inspector Adams. Would you like some water or coffee?"

"Water would be great. Thanks."

Before he got two pages into the first record, Amy reappeared with a bottle of water.

"Here ya go. Just holler if you need anything else," she said, placing the bottle next to him.

"Thank you, Amy," he replied, grabbing the bottle, cracking it open, and taking a swig.

Unlike the records he received from the hospital, these records had helpful tabs identifying different sections of information. He found the Vaccine Adverse Event Report System (VAERS) form under the tab "Other." In the case of this first record, the adverse event was not fatal and only required an office visit. He did note in the description of the event that the patient's AST and ALT levels were high. While he thought these levels were related to the patient's liver function, he was not sure and wanted to confirm this with Dr. Slack. Setting the first record aside, he grabbed the next record, just as Dr. Slack knocked on the door and made his appearance.

"Good morning, Inspector Adams."

"Good morning, Dr. Slack. Thank you for identifying these patients so promptly after our meeting last week."

"You're welcome, but that credit goes to Amy, who undoubtedly greeted you this morning."

"I'll make a point of thanking her. Quite a collection you have here," gesturing toward the wall of books and artifacts.

"Thank you. And this is just a sample. You might say it's the overflow from my study at home. My wife gave me an ultimatum, find someplace else to store them, or she'd donate them to a library. I'm a sucker for books and things associated with the great minds that contributed to the evolution of the field of medicine, with a bias towards neurology and psychology. I couldn't part with them, so here they sit."

"Interesting and impressive."

"Not the words my wife uses, but thank you. I find them comforting. We all stand on the shoulders of those who came before us."

"That we do."

"So, what can I help you with today?"

"I've only gone through one record so far," Inspector Adams began, handing the record to Dr. Slack. "I read the Vaccine Adverse Event Report and wanted to confirm that elevated AST and ALT refers to liver function."

"Yes, that's right. This is one of the patients that AlzCura claims had falsely elevated levels due to a laboratory glitch. I just received the letter from their Regional Lab Medical Director. Would you like to have a copy?"

"Yes, please. That would be helpful."

"It outlines the corrected lab values for four of the six patients you'll find in that stack. The glitch they had apparently doubled the AST and ALT levels, so you'll see the corrected values are exactly half of what they were originally reported as. They're still mildly elevated but not as concerning as the original values. You should find a notation from me on the corrected values in my notes and on the original lab report. Yes, see here," pointing to an entry in the Progress Note section of the record.

"That's helpful. Thank you. If six patients had elevated liver function test values, what will I find in the other records?"

"There are 16 records in all, so the other 10 represent a variety of adverse events, 4 of which are patients that succumbed to liver failure and brain bleeds."

"I noticed that the adverse event reports that didn't result in mortalities had evidence of being faxed to DHHS as required. I didn't see that same evidence for adverse events that resulted in death. I saw you faxed them to AlzCura, but not DHHS. Why is that?"

"AlzCura asks us to call them on those cases, and I fax them a copy. Dr. Sheridan indicates that they subsequently submit the reports to DHHS. Although now that I mention that, I have never validated that they have."

"Thanks. That is helpful. Roughly how many patients total have you treated with Recallamin?"

"Exactly 50 patients. I don't deal in rough estimates when human lives are at stake."

"I appreciate that. So that works out to," Inspector Adams paused, and Dr. Slack anticipating what he was thinking, answered.

"An overall mortality rate of 8%, but that's not the issue. The issue is that those 4 patients represent two-thirds of my Recallamin patients that have died - four of six. The other two died of what I would classify as more typical causes of old age and ill-health unrelated to liver failure or brain aneurysms. The patients with elevated levels, whether it's six or two, as AlzCura now alleges, combined with what I learned at last week's meeting, was more than enough evidence for me to suspend the use of Recallamin. I called Dr. Sheridan last Friday and let him know. I think Dr. Mason did the same."

"So, they know you've discontinued the use of Recallamin?"

"Yes. In addition to the statistics I just quoted, I also told Dr. Sheridan I hadn't received the letter on the corrected values from their Regional Lab as promised. I think that is what prompted my receipt of the Lab Medical Director's letter yesterday."

"Did you tell him about our meeting last week?"

"Heavens no. The data from my own practice was sufficient rationale. If AlzCura is as under-handed and retaliatory as it sounded from our meeting, I didn't want to put anyone in danger, especially Jackie and her daughter."

"Good, because that is a concern we all share."

"I assume you'll be visiting Dr. Mason's practice. You'll find that she has done the same thing. We talked about how to approach this."

"Yes, I was hoping to get over to Dr. Mason's practice this afternoon."

"Well, I won't keep you from your record review. Is there anything else you'd like to know?"

"Just one more thing. Let's talk about Margo."

"There's not much to talk about from my perspective. Margo didn't communicate my concerns to Dr. Sheridan and then tried to sell me on the Recallamin 3 trial expanding the use of Recallamin to younger patients. I had had enough, I ended the meeting, and that was the last I ever saw of her. Thank God for small favors."

"Did she have any contact with any of the other physicians in your practice?"

"No, but one of Dr. Mason's associates certainly did as you heard at the meeting."

"Well, thank you, Dr. Slack. You made my job infinitely easier to be as prepared and organized as you are. I should be out of here shortly."

"No need to rush on my account. I'll have Amy get you a copy of that letter from the Regional Lab Medical Director, and if you need anything in the meantime, have Amy track me down."

Inspector Adams, armed with the data that Dr. Slack had given him, did a quick verification review of the records. As he was finishing up, Amy knocked and popped her head in.

"I'm sorry to interrupt, but Dr. Slack asked me to get this to you," handing him a copy of the letter as promised.

"No apologies necessary, Amy. Thank you. And thank you for all the work you did to prepare for my visit. Dr. Slack mentioned that you deserved all the credit."

"Why, thank you, Inspector Adams. Dr. Slack is so great to work with."

"I can see why you say that. Many doctors don't give me the time of day. That was not the case with Dr. Slack."

"I know what you mean. Dr. Slack is way different."

"That he is. Thank you again, Amy."

"My pleasure, Inspector Adams."

Taking his leave, he grabbed some fast food and ate in the car as he drove cross-town to Dr. Mason's practice. Along the way, his phone rang, announcing Celeste calling.

"Hi, beautiful," he answered.

"Aww, you really know what a girl needs to hear,"

"I try. What's up?"

"Nothing. I'm just going a little stir-crazy. Except for last week's dinner, I haven't been off of this property for two weeks. Don't get me wrong, I love it, but without you and without Sophie," she started to cry uncontrollably.

"Oh, Celeste. I'm sorry," in an unsuccessful attempt to console her.

Her crying jag was interrupted only by occasional apologies for bothering him.

"You're not a bother, Celeste. Listen, I'll try to get home a little early today, OK?"

The call concerned and frustrated him. He knew that his phone intervention had been insufficient, and as much as he wanted to go home to comfort her, duty called. As he walked into Dr. Mason's Cumberland County Neurology Partners office, he knew that Celeste could not hold out indefinitely at his home. She would eventually have to move along with her life. He just didn't know how or if he could give her the amount of support she seemed to require.

Inspector Adams' experience at Dr. Mason's office was much the same as his visit to Dr. Slack. They had prepared the files for his review in a small conference room, the only difference being this conference room was adorned with pieces of artwork versus books and museum pieces. Dr. Mason's medical assistant gave him an orientation to their records, which were organized in much the same fashion. There were fewer files to review, and as he was summarizing his findings, Dr. Mason arrived.

"Good afternoon, Inspector Adams. Finding everything you need?" she asked, sitting down at the table.

"Good to see you again, Dr. Mason. Yes, I think I've been able to find everything that I needed in the records. One question, how many total patients have you treated with Recallamin?"

"We've treated 38 patients in total."

"So there are 12 records here with adverse event forms, meaning that 32% of the Recallamin patients had adverse events."

"Correct."

"I noticed that the adverse event reports that didn't result in mortalities had evidence of being faxed to DHHS as required. I didn't see that same evidence for adverse events that resulted in death. I saw you faxed them to AlzCura, but not

DHHS. Why is that?"

"The protocol for Recallamin is to call AlzCura when there is a death that may be related to the vaccine. They are responsible for submitting the information. I'm not a fan of the process, but there is no standard process. It all depends on how the study sponsor wants to design the adverse reporting process. And there are as many processes as there are study sponsors, it seems."

"Thanks. And did you recently get a letter from the Regional Lab Medical Director as Dr. Slack did?"

"I did. Yesterday. After I called Dr. Sheridan on Friday to tell him my practice would not be prescribing Recallamin in the future."

"Yes, Dr. Slack mentioned that you two had coordinated your strategy. I appreciate that. You didn't mention anything about our meeting last week to Dr. Sheridan, did you?"

"No. All I mentioned was that Dr. Slack and I had compared notes to arrive at our independent decisions."

"Good. So of the 12 adverse events, four were for elevated AST and ALT."

"Yes, and of those four, Dr. Muckland's letter claims three were erroneously high. An error in their lab system that he claims doubled the actual values."

"That's consistent with what Dr. Slack mentioned to me as well. And you're having those three patients retested, right?"

"Yes, I'm hoping we can get the results by the end of the week."

"If my review is correct, two of the Recallamin patients died from liver failure and brain bleeds."

"That's correct."

"How many Recallamin patients have died of all causes in your practice?"

"Four, so fifty percent are due to liver failure and brain aneurysms. I'm sure Preston shared his numbers with you. He's a whiz when it comes to statistics. I usually go by my gut more than statistics. I had concerns about Recallamin before Preston got me to look at the actual numbers. Then when we put our numbers together, it was pretty evident that there was a problem."

"Let's talk about Margo. You mentioned concerns at the meeting last week."

"Well, yes. I don't want to sound indelicate, but when someone uses an I'll let you fuck me if you use our drug approach with one of my doctors, I draw the line. Not the kind of science we use to select treatments for our patients, if you know what I mean."

"So she came right out and said that?"

"Not in those exact words. but she made it clear she was available for that type of transaction."

"Anything else that you can tell me about her?"

"Not really. Although I did have a rather odd conversation with Cheryl Baker, AlzCura's VP of Operations, a few weeks ago when she visited."

"Tell me more."

"She asked me about my concerns, and at the time, I couldn't remember Margo's name, so I just told her that I wasn't impressed with Jackie's interim replacement. She then said the name Alexis, which didn't sound familiar to me. Only to correct herself and say Margo after that. It may not have been anything, but I found it strange she made that error."

"Hmmm, OK. That is interesting. Did you ever learn Margo's last name, or did she give you a business card?"

"No, but then again, I wasn't hoping to ever see or call on her again."

"Understood. This has been very helpful, Dr. Mason.

Thank you for your time."

"Happy to help. Let me know if there is anything else you need."

Inspector Adams exited the office and called DA Wydman as he sped home to try and rescue Celeste from her emotional storm.

"Hi, Theo. What's up?"

"Hi, Will. I just completed my reviews and interviews with Dr. Slack and Dr. Mason."

"And?"

"And our case against AlzCura has gained some strength. Nearly 1 in 3 patients receiving Recallamin had adverse action reports, and both faxed their adverse reports involving death to AlzCura but not to DHHS. Get this, sixty percent, six out of 10 patient deaths, were cases of liver failure and brain bleeds."

"Wow. That does paint a concerning picture. What about the patients with elevated liver function tests?"

"There are ten patients between the two practices, and AlzCura claims that seven of those were due to erroneous test results. Both doctors have asked those patients to get retested. We should hear something by the end of the week or early next week."

"Do you think you'll want or need Jackie or the doctors in attendance when you interview Margo?"

"No, I don't think so. I am concerned about Jackie's welfare, though. The doctors contacted Dr. Sheridan last Friday and informed him that they were not going to be prescribing Recallamin anymore."

"Jeezum, then they already know?"

"Yep."

"Did the doctors say anything to Dr. Sheridan about Jackie or our meeting last week?"

"No, thank God. But given AlzCura's history, who knows if they've had someone watching her."

"I spoke to Jackie about working with her local law enforcement for protection. I guess I should call her back and let her know the urgency. So do you think you will be ready to interview Margo in the next few days?"

"As ready as I'll ever be."

"OK, I will have AG Talcott contact AlzCura and request that they arrange to have her appear for her interview in the next 7-10 days."

"Sounds good."

"Good work, Theo."

"Thanks, boss," he replied, ending the call.

CHAPTER 5

D
r. Asa Sheridan, AlzCura's Chief Executive Officer, sat bookended by Cheryl Baker, Vice President of Operations, and Chet Humphreys, Senior Legal Counsel. AlzCura's Chief Financial Officer was just finishing his report to the Board at its mid-year meeting.

"I'm concerned about our performance in the Northeast Region. Every other region of the country and our International divisions are meeting or beating projections. What are we doing or not doing in our own backyard?" the Board Chair, Dr. Simon Rosenthal, asked, turning his attention from the CFO to Dr. Sheridan.

"The weakness in the Northeast Division is largely due to a series of unfortunate events in the last quarter. Dr. Steven Caron, who had a very robust practice in Central Maine, committed suicide, and the hospital in that region has yet to recruit a replacement. We also lost the pharmaceutical rep for that Division this past quarter. We're in the process of filling that vacancy."

"So all fixable, you're saying."

"Yes, all fixable," Dr. Sheridan affirmed. Conveniently not addressing that two doctors in Portland had recently informed him that they were discontinuing the use of Recallamin.

"So, we should see a recovery when we review the financials at next quarter's meeting?"

"I'd like to think so, but it depends largely on the hospital's success in recruiting a replacement."

"Isn't Dr. Caron the physician we provided financial support to?" said Easton Arthur, another Board member.

"Yes, he was."

"What prevents us from doing a deal like that again? Instead of waiting for the hospital, we recruit a physician and support them to take over the practice Dr. Caron vacated."

"I thought about that," Dr. Sheridan replied. "If the Board is open to it, I will certainly pursue it."

"Anyone opposed to Easton's suggestion?" posed the Board Chair to the rest of the Board members.

"I'll take your silence as consent," the Board Chair remarked after no one spoke up. "Go for it, Asa."

"We will thank you."

AlzCura's Board Chair, Dr. Simon Rosenthal, was a former FDA Commissioner. He left his post as part of the mass exodus that naturally occurs in government leadership positions when there's a change in the White House. Although he still had connections at the FDA. Contacts that didn't hurt AlzCura's ability to gain favorable treatment for the company's ambitious research agenda. Like many government officials who move to the private sector, the pay and the equity grant he received from AlzCura was far more lucrative than what he made at the FDA.

Easton Arthur was Executive Vice President of Noreast Regional Bank, a large, business-friendly bank with a commanding presence in the region. Not surprisingly, AlzCura's bank of choice was Noreast. With Easton Arthur's support, they had been able to provide a tidy, forgivable loan to Dr. Caron. This greatly expanded his practice, and thereby, the client base eligible for the Recallamin vaccine. The arrangement had paid off handsomely for AlzCura. Despite practicing in the mostly rural central Maine region, Dr. Caron was AlzCura's highest vaccine prescriber per capita in the company. His forgivable loan criteria, based on the volume of Recallamin vaccine use, were met in two years, making him the most profitable physician on AlzCura's books.

After the Board meeting ended, Dr. Sheridan left feeling like he had dodged a bullet. That he also gained the Board's support to invest in finding Dr. Caron's replacement was the icing on the cake and a far better outcome than he had anticipated. The Board was typically ruthless when faced with any negative news, particularly adverse financial performance. Calling Cheryl and Chet into his office for their usual meeting after the Board meeting, he divulged what he had kept from them over the previous weekend.

"Sit down. I have something to tell you," he commanded while placing three crystal tumblers and a full bottle of Maker's Mark on the conference table.

"We have a major problem in Maine, and we need to fix it now, or the next Board meeting will be a blood bath."

Cheryl and Chet shared a look of concern, and Asa poured a healthy slug from the bottle.

"Dr. Slack and Dr. Mason called me on Friday to tell me that they have discontinued prescribing Recallamin."

"Why? I thought your call with them about the error in the lab values had talked them off the ledge," Cheryl asked, reaching for the bottle.

"Apparently not. They got together and compared notes. That and fuckhead Muckland not promptly sending them letters with the corrected lab values as I asked apparently caused them to lose faith."

"That means we don't have anyone in Maine selling Recallamin," Cheryl said, downing the contents of her glass and reaching for the bottle for another.

"What are our options?" Chet added, motioning Cheryl to send him the bottle after she poured her second drink.

"I say we not only take Easton up on his offer to support the recruitment and support for a physician in Central Maine, but we do the same in Portland. We will be able to suck Dr. Slack and Dr. Mason's practices dry as patients flock to a physician who can deliver care that cures or prevents Alzheimer's."

"What about Bangor?" Cheryl asked.

"You go up there, and if the physicians don't have an appetite to support Recallamin, we'll place a physician up there as well. The Board will not accept our excuses next time. We have less than 3 months to turn things around."

"What about expanding the Recallamin 3 trial to our other regions?" Cheryl proposed. "Right now, the trial is only operational in the Northeast. If we expand it to a few more regions, it would quickly and favorably impact the bottom line. The Northeast's financial picture may not recover by next quarter. Still, if we hit it out of the park on the overall financial picture, it could satisfy the Board long enough to give us time to recover the business in Maine."

"Good idea. Even if we were able to get physicians into Maine in the next few weeks, it would take at least a couple of months to build their practices."

"Do you think Jackie or Maine law enforcement could be behind any of this? And if so, what should we do about them?" Chet asked, finally able to wrestle the Maker's Mark away from Cheryl long enough to pour himself a drink.

"I don't think we have the luxury to worry about them right now," Asa replied. "Maine has our response to their letter. We're going to produce Margo, and unless we see erosion in Recallamin use in other areas of the region, I'm not worried about Jackie."

"I agree," Cheryl added.

"Sounds reasonable," Chet chimed.

"To saying go fuck yourselves, Dr. Slack and Dr. Mason," Asa announced, raising his glass towards his colleagues.

"To saying go fuck yourselves," Cheryl and Chet replied in unison, clinking their glasses and downing the golden elixir.

CHAPTER 6

T rue to his word, Theo Adams returned home early after his meetings with Dr. Slack and Dr. Mason to find the previously distraught Celeste in bed asleep. Beside the bed, he saw a prescription bottle. Picking up the bottle, he learned it contained diazepam (Valium).

"Take 1-2 tablets for anxiety. Do not exceed 8 tablets in 24-hours," Theo read to himself, noting that the bottle still had many pills. Satisfied that she had not overdosed, he closed the bedroom door, fixed a drink, and retreated to his favorite chair on the porch after starting a fire in the fire pit.

An hour and two drinks later, Celeste joined him on the porch, sauntering out of the house still a bit groggy from the Valium. Wearing nothing but what could best be described as a hint of underwear, she curled up on Theo's lap.

"I'm sorry I bothered you at work today. I'm better now."

"You're never a bother," he replied, kissing her and cradling her in his arms.

"I think I need to go back to work. I love it here, but without anything to do, all I think about is what I've lost and how much I miss you."

"I understand," Theo replied, not exactly sure how to raise the question about how her current living arrangements would have to change as well. At least until the completion of his investigation into the crimes committed against her.

"I don't know how I can ever move back into my trailer, though," she said as if reading his mind. "Maybe I'll sell it and just rent a place closer to work."

"You know I'd let you stay here if I wasn't involved in the investigation."

"I know, sweetheart. But I also know that you took a big risk bringing me here. I don't want to compromise your career or reputation. I can rent a place short-term, and when the time is right, and if you still want me, I can come back here."

"Sounds like you've been doing a lot of thinking," Theo replied.

"What else is there to do when you're not here to keep me occupied? Speaking of which," Celeste said as she shifted in his lap to face him while spreading her legs to straddle him, leaving no doubt what she expected him to do next.

* * *

Julie, DA Wydman's assistant, poked her head into his office to ask if he had a moment. Waving her in, she took the seat in front of his desk.

"What do you got for me, Julie?"

"I've been working on that meeting with Dr. Woodson Shearlow and Dr. Elizabeth Harder from the FDA's Center for Biologics Evaluation and Research."

"Oh, ya, what a peach of a guy!" he said facetiously, recalling the less than pleasant call with him about the adverse event reports.

"Well, his assistant isn't much better," Julie replied. "Every time I talk with her, I feel like I should be counseling her on finding a job that makes her happy. But getting to the point, they proposed a meeting next Friday morning at 9a.m., which works for AG Talcott and Inspector Adams, but not for you."

"What's the conflict?"

"You were going to take a vacation day. It's your wedding anniversary. If you can't meet next Friday, the next available date for them isn't until the end of next month."

DA Wydman planned to take his wife to Quebec for a long weekend at a French-style castle converted into a luxury hotel on the cliffs overlooking the St. Lawrence River.

"I don't want to push the meeting off until next month. What does the following Monday look like? Could I take that Monday off and change my travel plans a bit?"

"Let me check when I get back to my desk. If I can free up that Monday, do you want me to call the hotel and change your reservation?"

"Would you? I'd appreciate that. Your French is better than mine!"

"Oui monsieur. Je serais heureux de le faire," she replied, getting up to walk back to her desk.

"OK, I understood the oui monsieur, but what was that last part?"

"I said 'Yes, sir. I'd be happy to."

"You're the best, Julie. Thanks!"

As Julie exited, DA Wydman looked at his calendar and saw "Call Jackie" in the current timeslot. When he made that calendar entry a few days earlier, he didn't know that Drs. Slack and Mason had already informed Dr. Sheridan of their decision not to prescribe Recallamin. He hoped that the delay in giving Jackie a heads up had not allowed AlzCura to retaliate against her. Picking up his phone, he made the call.

"Hi, Will," she answered, just after putting Ashley in her stroller.

"Jackie, I'm glad I caught you. Is this a good time?" he asked, relieved that he had reached her, and she didn't sound distressed.

"Yep, I'm just about to take Ashley to the park."

"How's the cutie pie doing?"

"She's great, but I don't know if her mother has quite gotten used to this walking thing she's picked up," she said, laughing.

"It's a whole different ballgame when they start walking," he replied, reminiscing how much more attentive he and his wife had to be when his boys were Ashley's age. "Listen, I don't want to keep you long, but what I have to say is important. I'll make it quick so you can go and enjoy your time with your daughter."

"That sounds a little ominous, Will."

"I'm sorry, I don't mean to concern you. I just learned that Dr. Slack and Dr. Mason called Dr. Sheridan last Friday to let him know they both decided to stop using Recallamin. I know we previously talked about a plan to speak to Officer Todd and his Chief. This revelation bumps up the timetable for us to get that done."

"Hmmm, I'm not quite as anxious to take that walk to the park now. As it was, it was going to be our first time back there since Ash was abducted. I wanted to exorcise the demons, so to speak, but now I think the demons are winning."

"I'm sorry, Jackie. I don't want you to feel like a prisoner in your own house, but we can't be too careful, given all that has happened. Let's do this if you're willing. You call Officer Todd and see if he and his Chief can get on a call with us now or in the next hour. Then we can tell them the situation, see if they can employ any safety measures. Hopefully, you and Ashley can then go on your merry way to exorcise those demons."

"I can do that," Jackie agreed.

"Good. Hope to hear back from you soon then."

As soon as DA Wydman hung up, Julie appeared at his door.

"I was able to rearrange your schedule. You're scheduled for the Friday meeting, and you have Monday off. Hotel reservations have been adjusted accordingly."

"Thanks, Julie. You've saved my marriage for at least another little bit. Marge is a saint, but I'm afraid she would have turned into the devil pretty quick if I didn't make good on this weekend."

Meanwhile, DA Wydman's call was like a cloud that suddenly blocked out an otherwise sunny day for Jackie. With the planned visit to the park now postponed, she lifted Ashley out of her stroller and set her on the living room floor. As Jackie called Officer Todd, Ashley stood up and walked the few steps to the couch where her mother was sitting, trying unsuccessfully to climb up on the couch.

"Hi, Jackie," Officer Todd greeted as Jackie helped Ash up on the couch.

"Hi, Barrett. I'm sorry to call you out of the blue, but I just got off a call with my District Attorney friend from Maine. Remember how we talked about having you and your Chief speak with me and Maine law enforcement?"

"Yes, and I did brief him. I'm sorry, I should have gotten back to you. He's willing to get on a call."

"Well, there's been a development. The DA and I would like to speak with both of you as soon as possible. Is your Chief in, and would you both be able to get on a call now?"

"Let me check, Jackie. Can I put you on hold for a minute?"

"Sure."

As Jackie was on hold, Ashley now wanted down off the couch. Helping her daughter down, Ashley wobbled her way across the living room to a cache of toys. Selecting Monty Moose from the assortment, she wobbled her way back and plopped down by the couch.

"Jackie?" Officer Todd asked as he came back on the line.

"Yes."

"You're in luck. Chief Maxwell is available in about 15 minutes. Can you and your DA friend call into our conference line?"

"Yes, that would be great. Thanks!"

"I'll text you the conference line number, OK?"

In the interim, Jackie texted DA Wydman, who returned a text confirming he had received her message and conference line number. As Ashley busily held a conversation with Monty Moose, Jackie went to the kitchen to fix a cup of coffee. Shortly after entering the kitchen, she heard Ashley call her. Jackie walked back into the living room, and upon seeing her mother, resumed playing. Jackie went back into the kitchen to retrieve her coffee, only to have Ashley called her again. Returning to the living room, this time with her coffee, Ashley once again returned to playing. Jackie sat down on the couch, and all of a sudden, realized that the interaction she had just had with Ashley was related to Curt's lesson on object permanence. Smiling, she picked up her phone.

"I love you, professor," she texted.

"I love you too, angel," appeared a minute later.

"Chat later?"

"It's a date, ♥ ♥ ♥" he texted back.

The brief communication with Curt lifted the gloom that had settled over her since DA Wydman's call. She hoped that the conference they were about to have would put her mind further at ease. Calling in at the appointed time, Chief Maxwell opened the call, and after everyone introduced themselves, he began.

"Good morning, I'm Mark Maxwell, Nora PD, Chief of Police. Officer Todd has briefed me on your employment at Alz-Cura, Ms. Deno, and I am, of course, familiar with the criminal acts perpetrated against you. I understand that you and District Attorney Wydman have additional information for us?"

"Yes, thank you, Chief Maxwell. You can call me Jackie. I'll let DA Wydman brief you."

"Thank you, Jackie. And thank you, Chief Maxwell and Officer Todd, for making yourselves available on such short notice. As background, we are still investigating a suspicious suicide, a murder, potential fraudulent research practices, and other incidents here in Maine that implicate the possible involvement of AlzCura. More recently, two doctors in Maine contacted AlzCura to tell them they would no longer prescribe their Recallamin vaccine. Based on past history, I am concerned this may prompt AlzCura to retaliate against Jackie, and we were hoping that you could offer assistance providing some protection."

"Thank you for that background," Chief Maxwell replied. "I understand why you might think Jackie would be targeted, but wouldn't you also be concerned about the safety of those two doctors?"

"Good point. That is a concern that we in Maine need to address."

"And out of curiosity, if the doctors came to you asking for protection, what would you be able to offer them?"

"I hear where you're going with this Chief. I know that police resources are slim, no matter what jurisdiction you're in. We would likely increase the frequency of patrols by their homes and offices and suggest ways they could protect themselves personally."

"And that's what I'm prepared to offer in this case," the Chief replied. "We had increased patrols temporarily in your area in response to your daughter's abduction. We can increase them again for the next week or two."

"Thank you," Jackie replied.

"Yes, thank you, that's a start," added DA Wydman.

"Jackie, did you ever follow up with that Security company about installing a system in your home?" Officer Todd interjected.

"No, I haven't. But they sent me a packet that I haven't had time to review yet."

"Well, that would be a good place for you to start your personal protection plan," Officer Todd replied. "Most security systems have options to alert police dispatch and a panic button that transmits directly to us. I would choose a system that provides both of those features."

"OK, I can do that."

"Other things you should get in the habit of doing is always letting someone know where you're going and when you plan to return. When possible, have another adult with you when you go out. And obviously, avoid going out alone at night or going to unfamiliar areas of town." Chief Maxwell added.

"And you have my number, Jackie. You can always call me," Officer Todd offered.

"Thank you all for your concern. Let me practice your advice. I'm going to the park with my daughter and will return home in about an hour. How did I do?"

"Perfect," Chief Maxwell laughed. "I know our advice may sound basic, but most crimes are crimes of opportunity. Don't provide the opportunity, and most crimes don't occur."

"Are you comfortable with the plan, Jackie?" DA Wydman asked.

"Yes, thanks, Will."

Ending the call, Jackie finished her coffee and prepared Ashley once again for their trip to the park. Heeding Chief Maxwell's advice, she called her mother.

"Hi, Mom. Do you want to join Ash and me at the park?"

"I'd love to. Are you going right now?"

"Yep. See you there?"

"With bells on."

Fifteen minutes later, as mother, daughter, and grand-daughter sat in the sun on a bench in the playground, a patrol car appeared and made a slow loop around the park. Jackie's mother didn't notice the cruiser, but Jackie did. With a sigh of relief, she started to exorcise the demons from the beloved park she had played in growing up, hoping that her daughter would have that same opportunity.

CHAPTER 7

W hen Dr. Kathleen "Kit" Carson received a notice from AlzCura about a neurology practice opportunity in central Maine, she nearly jumped on the next plane out of San Jose. She was born and raised in the Bay area and loved much of what life had to offer in Silicon Valley. However, the skyrocketing cost of living, paralyzing traffic, and stifling regulatory environment had her disenchanted and ready to consider her options. Dialing the number at the end of the notice, she reached Dr. Asa Sheridan.

"Good morning Dr. Sheridan. This is Dr. Kit Carson. I'm a neurologist in San Jose, California, and I am calling about the opportunity in Maine."

"Good afternoon, Dr. Carson. Thank you for your interest."

The two talked at length about her training, experience, and aspirations. Dr. Carson shared the genesis of her nickname, given to her by her father. When Dr. Sheridan disclosed that the previous neurologist had committed suicide in the office, Dr. Carson was initially disturbed. However, the information he provided thereafter quickly eroded any concerns she may have had.

Dr. Carson was not only well-trained, but she was one of AlzCura's top Recallamin prescribers in the Bay area. Convinced that she would be a perfect candidate, Dr. Sheridan outlined the financial support plan that AlzCura was willing to provide through Noreast Regional Bank. The income guarantee, forgivable loan, turn-key practice, and Maine's lower cost of living were too good to pass up. She accepted the offer, and Dr. Sheridan indicated he would send her the contract. After signing the agreement, all Dr. Carson needed to do was gain medical staff membership at Dracut-Campion Regional Medical Center and move to Maine.

"I'll call the hospital's Medical Staff Office today," Dr. Carson replied.

"That's great. I'll send you the contract. We look forward to working with you."

After the call, Dr. Sheridan called Cheryl Baker to tell her the good news.

"I think we have our replacement physician for Dr. Caron."

"That's great! What's his name?" Cheryl asked.

"Her name is, get this, Dr. Kit Carson. Short for Kathleen. She's in San Jose. She's young, well-trained, ambitious, and sick of California's smothering regulatory environment. She's already a big prescriber of Recallamin, so I think she'll fit perfectly."

"That's what we like, young, ambitious, and not beholden to all the regulatory red-tape!"

"I need you to call DC Realty and let them know to expect Dr. Carson's arrival next month."

"Will do. By the way, I've booked a flight to Bangor next week to see if the Neurology practice up there will play ball."

"Good. In the meantime, I have Marketing putting out another notice for a Neurology practice opportunity in Portland. I also want you to start prepping Alexis for her appearance in Maine as Margo. I expect that Maine's AG will be contacting us soon, and I want to be sure she's ready."

"Are you sure you don't want to prepare her?" Cheryl joked.

"Oh, I've already been over there. You might say I've been whipping her into shape!"

"I'm sure you have, you dirty dog."

Ending their call, Cheryl called Dracut-Campion Realty, the company AlzCura had hired to manage the four properties that Dr. Caron's practice occupied. The hospital had contracted with a locum tenens physician and leased the offices temporarily—a move designed to retain the inpatient business that Dr. Caron's practice previously generated. Now with Dr. Kit Carson taking over the practice, Cheryl needed to have the property manager inform the hospital that their month-to-month lease would be ending.

That out of the way, Cheryl called her daughter and made arrangements to visit her the next day to prep her for the grilling she would undoubtedly have to endure in Maine.

CHAPTER 8

With no new leads on who perpetrated the horrific murder of Leslie Anderson and Celeste Boulanger, the Maine media was clamoring for stories. Something more sensational than the usual summer filler stories about the importance of protecting yourself from the sun and being attentive to your little ones around swimming pools.

Channel 5 had hired an attractive young woman to replace Leslie, but there was really no way to replace her. Leslie's replacement didn't have her experience, audacity, and larger-than-life personality. The station that had openly encouraged and flaunted Leslie's soft-porn news delivery changed its stripes out of some newfound sense of reverence or respect. Leslie's replacement dressed conservatively, and the camera never strayed to ogle her feminine assets. Her script lacked dynamism, bearing no hint of sexual innuendo that had been a mainstay of Leslie's reporting. Predictably, Channel 5's viewership dropped as quickly as a lobster trap in Casco Bay.

Celeste Boulanger, now nearly a month removed from the media firestorm she created, was ready to rejoin society. Upon Theo's recommendation, Celeste had contacted Attorney John Dryer to help her formulate an exit strategy from Theo's hideaway. In addition to her return to the public eye, she wanted to file a lawsuit against AlzCura for their role in her husband's death and subsequent break-in, animal cruelty, and the result-

Attorney John Dryer was well-known to the Maine media and the public in general. He had been Darius Scott's public defender until Darius' untimely death. Although Darius' case was brief and hardly a test of his legal chops, the notoriety Dryer gained from the case had translated into a burgeoning law practice.

Attorney Dryer had agreed to meet with Celeste at Theo's home, which proved to be a challenge in itself. The entrance to Theo's house was not well-marked. In fact, it wasn't marked at all. Except for the rickety gate that was not usually locked, it looked more like a trail for recreational vehicles cut into a forest of trees. You had to navigate down a mile-long bumpy and circuitous dirt road before you arrived at Theo's picturesque four-season cabin on a pond.

"Wow, Theo. I can see why this has been such a good hiding place!" Dryer said as he exited his vehicle and greeted Theo and Celeste, lounging on the porch.

"Welcome to paradise!" Theo exclaimed. "Can I get you something?"

"I'm good, thanks. But invite me out here on the weekend sometime, and I'd be happy to share a beer or three with you!"

"Will do, John. Thanks for coming out. This is Celeste," he introduced as she rose to shake hands the attorney's hand.

"Hi, Attorney Dryer."

"Please, call me John. Thank you for calling me. I'm so sorry for all you've been through. I hope I can help."

"Well, Theo swears by you, so I know you must be good at what you do."

"Thanks for that. I'll do my best. No pressure, huh, Theo?" he chuckled.

Theo and Celeste then outlined the goals they hoped to accomplish in engaging Attorney Dryer.

"First, Celeste would like to sell her trailer and move into an apartment close to where she works," Theo began.

"But I'm worried about the reporters. I don't want them outside my door all hours of the day and night."

"Selling your trailer and getting the apartment should be relatively straightforward. As for controlling the reporters, that's more of a challenge. One thing we could consider is a press briefing where I'd appear with you and potentially do most of the talking."

"That sounds interesting," Celeste replied. "What would you and I say?"

"The key would be to give them enough information for them to write their stories so they don't swarm your home but not so much as to compromise any lawsuit we may file."

"How would we do that?"

"Let's hold on to the answer to that question right now. I have to get familiar with your husband's death and why you and Theo think it implicates AlzCura Pharmaceuticals. Do you have a copy of your husband's medical record?"

"At the trailer."

"I can get it from the trailer for you," Theo offered.

"By the way, where did Norman work?"

"He worked as a forklift operator at the paper mill. Why?"

"I want to check on what benefits he may have had through his work. I suspect you have a big hospital bill staring you in the face. I just want to check on whether he had any life insurance or death and disability benefits that might be due to you."

"I never thought about that," Celeste replied.

"That's why I'm here, to help you think about those things none of us want or know to think about when we lose someone we love."

"Thank you, John. This means so much to me."

"No problem. OK, once I've had a chance to review the medical record and do some digging on Norman's benefits at work, let's meet again and finalize our plan. Sound good?"

"Sounds good," Celeste replied. "Thank you, John."

"My pleasure, Celeste. In the meantime, you two enjoy paradise!"

"We will," Theo responded. "And we'll have you out here some weekend for those beers."

"That would be great. Thanks!"

As Attorney Dryer's car disappeared around the corner on the mile-long driveway back to civilization, Celeste kissed Theo.

"Thank you for helping me. For the first time in a long time, I finally feel like my life is moving forward."

"You're welcome. You have done the same for me, Celeste."

"Let's go for a swim," Celeste suggested.

"The last one in has to take off all their clothes," he replied, jumping up and jogging towards the pond while peeling off his shirt.

After jumping in the pond, Theo looked back at Celeste, who was taking her own sweet time and using the path down to the water like her private model's runway. All that was missing was appropriate music to accompany her sensuous strip-tease. When she finally dove into the pond, he half expected to hear her body sizzle as she hit the water.

CHAPTER 9

When Cheryl Baker turned her car onto the street where her daughter lived, she didn't expect to see a crowd outside the apartment building. As she drove closer, she noticed some in the group were covering their mouths and looking away. Others were looking up and using their phones to record something of interest. When she saw what was attracting all the attention, she screamed. In her effort to exit her car as quickly as possible, she mistakenly hit the accelerator rather than the brake, propelling her vehicle into the back end of an SUV. The accident momentarily caused the crowd to turn their attention towards Cheryl, who flung her door open and emerged screaming tearfully.

"Stop looking. Stop looking. That's my daughter, you bastards! Stop," she shrieked while running into the crowd of people pawing wildly at those with cell phones aimed at the picture window where her daughter's naked body hung on full display. Blood covered the lower half of both her arms from lacerations as if she needed a backup plan should hanging herself not be successful. When Cheryl's attempts to stop their insensitive recording failed, she urgently pushed through the crowd towards the apartment building entrance. Only to be thwarted from entering by police officers who had just arrived on the scene.

"That's my daughter," she screamed, trying to push past

the officers.

"I'm sorry, ma'am. We can't let you go up there. This is now a crime scene."

Wailing, spitting expletives, and continuing to try and push her way past the officers, only earned her a time out in the back of one of the police cruisers. She looked on helplessly from the caged backseat, her muffled screams ignored by the ogling crowd outside the apartment building. Mercifully, officers finally pulled the drapes closed, ending the gruesome show. By that time, the videos and photos had already populated the Internet or been sent to local news outlets. Meanwhile, Cheryl decompensated in tears, unable to believe her baby girl was dead.

Shortly after, an ambulance arrived, followed by a Crime Scene Investigation team, and sometime later Detective Brent Farest.

"Whatcha got?" Detective Farest asked as one of the CSI agents met him at the door.

"Not sure. It might be a suicide, but she has welts all over her back and bottom like she's been whipped. We have a suicide note. The note suggests that she may have been involved in criminal activity. We thought you should take a look at it," said the CSI agent as he handed the note, now contained in a plastic evidence bag, to Detective Farest.

Taking the note from the agent, he read.

"Mom, I'm sorry, I couldn't take it anymore. When I had that baby, it just made me feel more inadequate than I already felt. Like I didn't deserve to live if I couldn't even take care of a baby. All I do is screw doctors to get them to use drugs. They treat me like shit, even Asa. The thought of going to Maine for that meeting is just too much. I'd rather be dead than go to jail or live my shitty life. I love you, Alexis."

Detective Farest looked up from the note and quickly

scanned the apartment.

"Hmm, I see what you mean. Is there a baby here?"

"Nope. We haven't found one thing that indicates that a baby ever lived here. No crib, no diapers, no baby stuff at all."

"What about drugs?"

"Nothing yet, but we haven't finished canvassing the apartment or her vehicle, assuming she has one."

"Is the medical examiner on the way?"

"Yep."

"OK, let me know if you find anything," as he turned to leave.

"Will do, Detective. Oh, by the way," the CSI agent added, pausing as Detective Farest turned back to face him. "Her mother is on scene. She's in the back of one of the police cruisers. Apparently, she got a little out of control when she couldn't come up here."

"Has anyone talked with her?"

"Not that I'm aware."

Thanking the agent, Detective Farest made his way out of the apartment and found the officers who had detained the mother.

"She's calmed down now," the officer began. "I just got done taking her license, registration, and insurance information. She ran into another vehicle, and I needed it for the accident report. I've got a tow truck on the way. Her name is Cheryl Baker. That's her daughter, Alexis, upstairs."

"Anything else?"

"She wants to see her daughter."

"Yeah, well, that ain't happening until after the Medical Examiner's office does their thing. Take her down to the station and put her in an interview room. I'll be down there soon. Have the tow truck bring her vehicle to the police impound lot.

She can pick it up there after I'm done with her. I'm going to interview some of these people that are still hanging around."

"Will do, Detective."

As Detective Farest went to canvas the few remaining looky-loos congregating outside the apartment, Cheryl was transported to the police station. As her blinding grief slowly transitioned to a clearer and broader realization of the impact of her loss, fear started to creep in. What if the pictures of her daughter were made public? What were they going to tell the Maine Attorney General now that they promised to produce Margo? She needed to call Asa but couldn't while riding in the back of the police car. She started to text him but then deleted the words for fear her text could become discoverable. By the time they arrived at the station, she had gone from deep despondency to high anxiety. She felt trapped and vulnerable. Not only due to temporary confinement but because she didn't know the answers to the barrage of questions in her head.

The interview room and the swill that was supposed to be a cup of coffee they gave her did nothing to reduce Cheryl's anxiety. The wait seemed interminable even though Detective Farest arrived only 10 minutes after she had sat down.

"Mrs. Baker, I'm Detective Farest. I'm sorry for your loss."

To which Cheryl could only nod as tears came to her eyes. "When can I see my daughter?"

"The medical examiner needs to do her investigation first. After that, you can visit your daughter," he said, trying to avoid words or phrases that would upset her any more than she already was.

"Mrs. Baker, I know this is a difficult time for you, and you must have many questions of your own, but I would like to ask you a few questions. Is that alright?

His question momentarily threw her. Did she really have a choice? What if she chose not to answer his questions? She quickly vetoed those thoughts, thinking that if she didn't co-operate, it would only raise his suspicions. Nodding her assent, he continued.

"Mrs. Baker, do you know of any reason why your daughter would have done this?"

"No," she blurted out in advance of a wave of sobs that prompted Detective Farest to move a box of tissues within Cheryl's reach. After she took a tissue and blotted her tears, Detective Farest resumed.

"Was she depressed? Did something happen recently to upset her? Was she worried about anything that you know of?"

"No. I just spoke with her yesterday, and she seemed fine."

"When you spoke to her yesterday, what did you talk about?"

"Nothing really. I just called to see if I could visit today."

"Was she in any trouble, financial, legal, or otherwise?"

"No."

"Had she ever tried to commit suicide previously, or did she ever make any suicidal gestures?"

"No. She was happy most of the time. Just the usual ups and downs."

"Did you visit her often? Did you have a good relationship?"

"I loved my daughter, and she loved me," Cheryl declared. Taking offense to his insinuation that their relationship may have been a contributing factor in her suicide.

Her sad tears were now turning to tears of rage.

"How could you imply," she began but couldn't finish as the combination of anger and loss caught in her chest to such a degree that she found it hard to breathe.

"I don't doubt that Mrs. Baker. I'm sorry, I wasn't trying to imply anything," he replied, trying to cap the volcano of emotion about to erupt as a result of his question. "I just wanted to know the nature of your relationship and the frequency with which you would visit."

His words served to loosen the tightness in her chest enough for her to catch her breath. Recovering, she warily formulated and gave a response.

"We saw each other as often as we could. Her job entailed quite a bit of travel. We were close. If she were depressed or had any concerns, she would have told me."

"From what you're saying, it doesn't sound like she would ever commit suicide. Do you think someone could have staged this to look like a suicide?

"What?" she replied in surprise. "No. I can't imagine either of those things. I can't believe she would commit suicide, and I can't imagine anyone doing this to her?"

"So she didn't have any enemies? Anyone who could have been mad at her? A husband? Someone she worked with?"

"No. She wasn't married. And no, I don't know anyone who was upset with her or that could have done this. Can I see my daughter now?" she pleaded as his continuous questioning was beginning to feel like Chinese water torture.

"Just a few more questions, Mrs. Baker. Was your daughter in an intimate relationship with anyone?"

"No."

"Did she have any previous relationship that may have ended poorly?"

"No."

"Was your daughter ever married? Ever have any children?"

"No."

"You mentioned she travels for work. What did she do for

work?"

Cheryl's radar alarmed, and she had to quickly find her tap dance shoes.

"She had a job in sales. She just got back from Europe."

"Do you know the name of the company she worked for?"

"I can't remember the company's name. It was a foreign-sounding name. Italian, I think."

"What did she sell?"

"She sold clothing and shoes."

"And what is it that you do for work, Mrs. Baker?"

She hadn't expected this question, and the pause between his question and her answer tipped him off to be suspicious of her response.

"I work from home. I'm a Day Trader."

"And your husband?"

"I'm divorced."

"OK, thank you, Mrs. Baker. I know you want to see your daughter. I will have someone come to escort you. Your car was towed to our impound lot. You can pick it up there when you're ready to leave."

Handing her his card and promising to be in touch, he left the interview room knowing he had been lied to. There was much more to the story than what Cheryl let on. He knew that the CSI team, the Medical Examiner, and further digging into the suicide note would provide him with the truth. Then he'd probably see why Cheryl felt she had to lie.

Detective Farest escorted Cheryl out of his office to a waiting area. A few minutes later, a technician arrived to accompany her to the morgue to see her daughter. Cheryl felt the cold, impersonal, and unwelcoming environment the moment she stepped out of the elevator. The narrow halls, cold concrete-block walls, marginal lighting, and a foreboding silence screamed death. Making an already uncomfortable journey that much worse as they approached a restricted-access door.

Cheryl shivered as the technician used his badge to allow them entrance. Her mind was reeling. She imagined a room of horrors – autopsy tables with dead bodies, the cloying smell of formaldehyde, and a bank of stainless steel cooler doors like some kind of sick Jeopardy board of death.

"I'll take Died Too Young for $1,000, Alex."

Then, the technician would open a door and slide out a body covered by a sheet. He'd pull back the cover revealing something that resembled, but in no way looked like, her very alive and vibrant young daughter.

Cheryl was about to turn and run when she realized she was in a warm, comfortably appointed anteroom with another door and curtained window. The technician invited her to sit down in one of the cushiony chairs.

"Ms. Baker, I know this must be very hard for you. I want to help prepare you and make this as comfortable as possible."

"Thank you," she replied, as the gruesome images she had been playing in her head melted away to reality.

"Your daughter is in the room behind that door. You have the option of either going in the room or staying out here and viewing your daughter through the window. In either case, we will only reveal your daughter's body from the shoulders up. We can reveal less if you wish, but not more. The room is cold, and some people find it difficult to be in there. Your daughter's appearance may be disturbing to you. If you choose to go into the room, I need to accompany you. We've had family members faint and injure themselves. I'd be there just for your safety. You may also choose not to view your daughter. Some family members decide when they get here that they'd rather remember their loved one alive. That's perfectly understandable and acceptable. Do you have any questions?"

"How does she look?"

"We've done the best we can to make her presentable. She does have bruises on her neck. I can just reveal her face if you'd prefer not to see the bruises."

"OK. Can I touch her?"

"You can touch her, but know that her skin will be cold and pale. The two most frequent times that family members faint are when they first see their loved ones or when they touch them. It's your choice. Do you have any other questions I can answer?"

"No, no, thank you," she replied in a daze as she replayed the last time she was with her daughter in her head.

"Do you want some time to think about your choices? I can leave and come back in a few minutes if you'd like."

"No, I think I'm going to remember my daughter as she was. Thank you for your time. Can you get me out of here?" she asked, now sounding like a caged animal that desperately wanted out.

The technician obliged by quickly escorting her out of the room and back to the lobby. In Cheryl's rush to exit the building, she almost bowled two police officers over. Realizing her vehicle was in the police impound lot only compounded her anxiety. About to explode, she reached for her phone.

CHAPTER 10

J ackie reluctantly got out of bed after a restless night of sleep following her call with DA Wydman, Officer Todd, and Chief Maxwell. Despite her knowledge of the increased police patrols in her neighborhood, she didn't feel more secure. In the middle of the night, she even moved Ashley's crib into her bedroom, hoping that having her daughter close would prompt sleep, to no avail. While Ashley continued her slumber, Jackie padded down to the kitchen to fix a cup of coffee. Taking a sip and settling on the couch, her phone rang. Not enthused about having to get up to retrieve her phone that she left in the kitchen, she grudgingly got up from the sofa. Seeing the name "Sunny" on her cellphone gave her a lift that no amount of caffeine could.

"Sunny! Oh my God, where have you been?" she answered excitedly.

"Hi, girlfriend! Since I hadn't heard from you, I thought I'd call you. How's life, and how's that little snugglebug of yours?"

Jackie had last talked with Sunny after losing her job at AlzCura and realized that in the ensuing two months, her life had been a roller-coaster ride from hell. She had much to discuss with Sunny, who had grown to be not only a friend but a confidante and savior since they first met on Jackie and Stu's honeymoon in Arizona. Jackie's first introduction to Sunny was from afar. Stu had left to get them drinks from the Ca-

76

bana bar while Jackie lounged poolside. Jackie remembered feeling a twinge of jealousy when Stu appeared to be enjoying his interaction with the petite, blond, bikini-clad bartender a little too much. Little did Jackie know at the time, but Sunny would eventually rescue her during the darkest hours after Stu's death. Jackie felt guilty that she hadn't been in touch with Sunny, and bringing her up-to-speed on her life over the last months was painful.

"Why didn't you call me? You know I would do anything for you?" Sunny asked, hurt that Jackie hadn't called her when Ashley had been abducted.

"I'm sorry, Sunny. I know you would, and I love you for that. I can't tell you how out of sorts I felt. It felt like my whole world had collapsed."

"I can't imagine. But thank God you got her back!"

Jackie subsequently told Sunny about her decision not to continue her job at Nora Community Hospital in favor of the crusade to expose the truth about AlzCura. She also told Sunny about her relationship with Curt and his kids and their recent weekend at the Rockport Resort in Maine.

"Every time I talk with you, Jackie, I feel like my life is moving in slow-motion."

"Don't knock it, Sunny. I'd like a little more slow-motion in my life. So enough about me, what about you?" Jackie asked, trying to transition the one-sided conversation.

"I'm glad you asked," Sunny began. "I'm thinking of doing my required internship in your neck of the woods."

"What? You're thinking of coming here?"

"Yep. I have to do a three-month internship in my field of study to get my degree. I thought maybe I'd do it there to get away from this 110-degree Arizona summer."

"Refresh my memory, weren't you studying criminal justice?"

"Yep, and the Buffalo Police Department has an opening. I had a phone interview yesterday, and now they want me to come out there for an in-person interview."

"Oh my God, Sunny. That's great. When are you coming out?"

"They want me to interview next Monday. So I was thinking about flying out Sunday."

"Why don't you fly out Friday? You can stay with me, and we'll make a weekend of it."

"I like your plan better than mine. You sure I won't be a bother?"

"Sunny, you will never be a bother. Besides, I need one of those drinks you used to make me. What was it called?

"The Baja Pineapple Grenade?"

"That's it."

"I'll see you on Friday then. I'll text you my flight information."

"I can't wait."

"Me either. Hug and kiss your little snugglebug for me."

Sunny's call re-energized Jackie, and hearing Ashley stirring upstairs, she bounced up the stairs, ready to take on the day. Her need for sleep a distant memory.

CHAPTER 11

C urt discovered that there was a downside to telling Caitlin and Cade about their plans to visit Jackie and Ashley in New York. It may have avoided meltdowns at the airport, but it sentenced him to daily interrogations thereafter.

"Are we going to New York this weekend?" Cade asked for the umpteenth time as Curt was driving them to school.

"Not this weekend, Cade."

"Why not?"

"I have to talk to Jackie and see when it would be a good time for us to visit."

"So why don't you talk to her."

"I will."

"Today?"

"Maybe," Curt said, exasperated by his son's persistent questions. Realizing that his frustration with the questions was the only reason he didn't give Cade the satisfaction of an affirmative response, he softened.

"I'm just as excited about going to see Jackie and Ashley as you are. I'll try to call her today, OK?

"OK," Cade relented.

Granted a temporary reprieve from Cade, Caitlin took over.

"When we go there, what are we going to do?"

"I don't know, Caitlin. What would you like to do?" he asked, trying to turn the tables so his kids were on the receiving end of the questions.

"Ride horses," was her predictable response.

"I don't think Ashley can ride horses yet."

"What can babies do?" Caitlin asked, successfully flipping the onus for a response back on her father.

"Your mom and I used to take you to the zoo and water parks when you were that age."

"Do they have a zoo and water parks there?"

"I don't know. I'll have to ask Jackie," he replied, happy to be pulling into the school driveway, signaling a definite end to their cross-examination was in sight.

After dropping the kids off, he decided to drive to his office instead of working from home. Loribeth Lacroix, the administrative assistant to Curt and his partner Sam Jackson, greeted him enthusiastically.

"Well, hey, stranger. It's good to see you here," she said, getting up from her desk and giving him a hug.

"It's good to see you, LB. Is Sam in?"

"No, he won't be in today. Did you need to talk to him?"

"No, I was just wondering."

"Well, I'm glad you came in. You have a stack of mail I was going to send you, but now you're here. Let me know if there is anything I can help you with as you go through it."

"I will. Thanks," Curt replied.

"Coffee's fresh. Can I get you a cup?" Loribeth offered.

"Thanks. I'll grab a cup myself," he replied.

Sitting down with his cup of coffee, he reached for the first envelope from the stack on his desk. Every time he tried to focus on the letter's contents, thoughts of Jackie would intrude. After getting halfway through a second reading of the letter, he gave up and called Jackie.

"Good morning, professor," she answered.

"Good morning, young lady," he answered.

"Pray tell, what gives me the pleasure of your call?" Jackie asked with southern belle formality.

"I thought, given your difficulty grasping the subject matter, I would call to set up some in-home tutoring."

"Aw shucks, and I thought I was grasping your subject matter just fine in our last lesson."

"Yes, well, it never hurts to practice, young lady. I think you'll find the subject matter gets much harder," he burst into laughter, unable to stay in character and continue their playful charade.

"I miss you," Jackie added after laughing with him.

"Not as much as we miss you, apparently."

"Why is that?"

"It seems like they haven't stopped asking me questions about when we are going to visit since the moment we left the airport."

"Well, let's set a date for your visit then. I have a friend visiting me this weekend. What about next weekend?"

"That could work. Who's your friend?"

"Why? You jealous?" she teased.

"No, should I be?"

"No. It's my best friend, Sunny, from Arizona."

"Is that Sonny with an O or Sunny with a U?"

"Sunny with a U. Stu and I met her on our honeymoon. She's coming up to interview for a criminal justice internship in Buffalo this summer. You'll have to meet her sometime. I'm sure you'd like her."

"Well, if she's your best friend, I'm sure you're right."

"Are you going to drive or fly here?"

"I hadn't thought that far ahead yet."

"Well, there aren't any direct flights, so door-to-door, it will probably take you about 7 hours if there aren't any flight delays. If you don't mind driving, it takes about 8-9 hours, depending on how often you stop."

"Wow, you've thought a lot about this."

"Well, I had plenty of experience flying there when I used to work at AlzCura. As long as it's summer, driving may be the way to go. Less hassle and cheaper, especially not having to pay for three airfares."

"Thanks. I'll probably drive then. The next topic I'm getting grilled on by the kids is what we will do there."

"I know one thing we'll be doing," she said mischievously.

"Thanks, now how do you think I'm going to be able to concentrate on my work?"

"Why, professor, is your subject matter getting harder already?"

They ended the call as they began it. Replaying remnants of their conversation in his head throughout the day, Curt got through the stack of mail but wasn't as productive as he had hoped. However, he knew that he was better prepared to answer Caitlin and Cade's inevitable questions when he arrived home.

CHAPTER 12

Rattled by her daughter's graphic and public suicide and Detective Farest's questions, Cheryl was in no condition to claim her car from the police impound lot. Finally, free from police presence, she pulled out her phone to call Asa.

"Keeping banker's hours today, are we?" Asa joked.

It was late morning, and he had noticed she hadn't been in the office yet. Cheryl didn't even register his greeting, nor could she appreciate his humor. Her mind could only think one thing, and it barreled out of her like a train without brakes heading towards a bridgeless chasm.

"My baby is dead," she sobbed. Before he could react, she spewed more words of pain punctuated by hiccuped crying. "It was horrible. She's dead. I don't know what to do. Come get me. Now!" she screamed her last word, drawing the attention of a few people within earshot.

"Where are you?" he managed to ask as tears welled up and he struggled to keep the contents of his stomach in.

"The police station," she blurted. "Hurry, please!"

"I'm coming," he replied, hanging up. Only to projectile vomit his bilious, half-digested breakfast across his desk before he could make it to his trash bin.

Unconcerned, he wiped the drooling remnants on the

sleeve of his $2,500 Armani suit. Grabbing his keys, he rushed out of the office and took the elevator to the parking garage. Jumping in his red BMW Zagato Coupe, he squealed out of the garage, breaking traffic laws all along the way. He was blind with grief, and his brain seemed disconnected from reason or any semblance of cohesive thought.

He had just been with Alexis two nights earlier. She had indulged him in a sadomasochistic fantasy, employing a cat o' nine tails whip, the sting of which was welcome during the throes of their twisted encounter. Both would end the evening with welts, which turned angry and painful the following day.

The immorality of Dr. Sheridan's relationship with Cheryl and her daughter and his bizarre sexual proclivities were known by a few tight-lipped people in the company. Or so he thought. The rumors across the organization were rampant. To this point, the knowledge and rumors had failed to adversely affect the workforce's sensibilities or the Board's faith in the company's leadership. AlzCura employees, particularly those in the upper echelons of management, were generously compensated. Even the lowest-paid positions paid significantly more than similar jobs in other companies. Profits pardoned many sins.

Turning into the police station parking lot, Asa saw Cheryl pacing. As he pulled up, she threw up her hands, flew open the passenger-side door, and stepped in, greeting him with a hail of expletives.

"What took you so fucking long. Alexis kills herself, and I'm stuck at this shithole police station. It smells like shit in here. Don't you ever clean your fucking car? God da..."

"Cheryl, I'm here. I threw up. Shut the fuck up," he screamed, interrupting her tirade as he punched the accelerator pedal burning rubber. His angry response and being thrown back in her seat from the burst of speed shut her up, and she dissolved into tears.

How he escaped the police parking lot without a citation was anyone's guess as he squealed his tires and sped off in front of the highest concentration of police cruisers in the city. Reaching into his suitcoat pocket, he pulled out a monogrammed handkerchief and handed it to Cheryl.

"Thank you," she softened and wiped her tears. Regaining her composure, she recounted the horror she had been through.

Asa could only listen and wipe his eyes when tears blurred his vision. Pulling into his private parking space in the underground garage, they exited. He swiped his ID badge to have the elevator transport them to the executive suite on the penthouse floor. As they stepped off the elevator, they saw a group of executives and their assistants clustered in front of a TV screen broadcasting the gruesome suicide story. As one of the assistants rushed to grab the remote to shut the TV off, the rest broke the huddle. Slinking back to their offices, like puppies cowering for cover after their owner discovers an unwelcome gift left on the carpet.

Cheryl and Asa were spared the garish news coverage. Though anyone who watched local TV news that day was assaulted by the videos and photos of the bloody, naked female body hanging in the third-floor apartment picture window. The newscaster's forewarnings of disturbing content and the blurred-out private parts of Alexis' dead body were the only nods to decorum.

As Asa and Cheryl marched to his office to fix themselves drinks, Chet Humphreys joined them, cringing at the sight and smell of the semi-dry vomitous on Asa's desk.

"I'm sorry, Cheryl," he said, grabbing a crystal tumbler from the bar and joining them at the conference table.

All she could manage was a slight nod and a tip of her glass in his direction before knocking it back and reaching for the bottle.

"I know this is the absolute worst time to try to talk about this, but time is not our friend right now," Chet began.

"What do you mean, Chet?" Asa asked.

"Every TV station is airing videos and photos, and her name is out there."

"What?" Cheryl asked, finally finding her voice.

"I don't know how they got it, maybe her landlord? A neighbor? Who knows, but it's out there. It won't be long until they make connections. If that weren't bad enough, I heard from Maine's Attorney General. He wants us to send Margo up there for an interview next week."

Asa groaned. "That's not good."

"I was interviewed by some Detective at the police station," Cheryl blurted out, responding to her increasing anxiety.

"Why? How?" Chet asked.

She recounted the story for the second time, made slightly easier by the alcohol, which was starting to anesthetize her pain and loosen her tongue.

"You need to tell me what you told that Detective," Chet exclaimed.

"I didn't tell him anything, really. I told him I work from home as a day-trader and that Alexis worked selling clothing and shoes for some Italian company."

"In that case, we need to scrub your name and picture from our public-facing website. We will also want to remove your name from company rosters and public reports. They will check the facts of your interview. We can't let them catch you in a lie."

"What kinds of questions did they ask about Alexis' suicide?"

"I don't remember it all, just the usual stuff," Cheryl slurred, downing her third glass of whiskey. "Was she depressed? Did she have any enemies or anyone who would want to hurt her? Was she married? Did she have any kids?" she rambled on.

"Wait, they asked you about enemies? And what do kids have to do with it?"

"I don't know why he asked so many questions. I just kept on saying no," as she started to tear up, yet still able to reach for the bottle to pour herself another drink.

Chet could see that Cheryl's ability to answer his questions thoroughly and reliably was being compromised by her emotional state and the rapid ingestion of alcohol. Turning to Asa, Chet expressed his concerns.

"Asa, the only reason they would ask those types of questions is if they have doubts that it's a suicide. They must have found evidence to prompt those questions." Turning to Cheryl once again, Chet asked, "Cheryl, did you go into Alexis' apartment this morning?"

"No. The police wouldn't let me in, those bastards. My own daughter and they toss me into the back of a cop car and leave me there to rot," she declared, her head swiveling as though she had lost control of her neck muscles.

"Did the Detective mention anything about a suicide note or finding anything in her apartment? Anything to lead them to believe that Alexis didn't kill herself?"

Cheryl's eyes were at half-mast, and instead of answering his question, she put her head down on the table.

"Cheryl?" Chet and Asa asked simultaneously with no response.

"I think she's passed out," Asa declared. "Let's get her over to the sofa, and she can sleep it off."

After moving Cheryl, they returned to the conference table, and Chet continued his guidance.

"I'm concerned that Cheryl's story won't hold up. For all

we know, that detective may have already done some preliminary fact-checking. The moment he finds an inconsistency, he's going to be all over her. If he learns she works here, he's going to wonder why she was trying to hide her association with us. It will not be pretty."

"What do you suggest we do? Fire her?" Asa asked incredulously.

"No, it's too late for that, and it wouldn't necessarily get us out of the woods. It would help to know what the investigators may have found in her apartment. When was the last time you saw Alexis?" Chet asked.

"Two nights ago, why?"

"I was hoping she may have shared something with you that would shed some light on why she did this. Did you see her at her apartment?"

"Yes," hoping the brevity of his response conveyed he didn't want to go into detail with the Chief Legal Counsel.

"Asa, I'm sorry, I don't mean to pry. I asked for two reasons. Since you were at her apartment recently and they're investigating this as a potential crime, they will likely find your fingerprints."

"That means they'll want to interview me," Asa replied.

"Right."

"And the second reason?"

"If there is anything you can tell me, it may help me determine how to approach this situation and protect our asses."

Asa refreshed his glass, took a sip, and reluctantly responded.

"You might say our activities got a little rough. Nothing she didn't fully consent to, mind you. But I'm afraid it may have left marks on her that could be misconstrued as evidence of an assault."

"That explains why they may think someone assisted in her suicide. You will probably need to own up to that if they interview you. Better to admit it and have them rule it a suicide than deny it and potentially raise suspicion that you may have been involved in her death. Is there anything else? Did she say anything? Or did she do anything that gave you any reason to believe she would commit suicide?"

"Nothing at all," Dr. Sheridan replied. "That said, I wouldn't characterize our relationship as one based on deep, philosophical conversations. I doubt she would have confided in me even if something was bothering her. How shall I say this? I think our relationship was a way for both of us to escape the depressing realities of life, not help each other psychoanalyze them."

"I got ya," Chet replied, amused at Asa's roundabout description of what everyone knew or suspected was a purely sexual relationship.

"What are we going to do about responding to the Maine AG?" Asa said, trying to transition away from the uncomfortable focus on his relationship with Alexis.

"That's a tough one. I don't think we say she died. They would want proof, and we wouldn't be able to produce it. If we tell the AG she's disappeared, they may not believe us and turn up the heat."

"Why not say she died and use Alexis' suicide as proof? We can make sure her obituary reads Alexis Margo Baker, and we wash our hands of Maine's request altogether."

"That would work if Cheryl hadn't told the detective that Alexis sold shoes for some Italian company."

"Oh yeah, I forgot about that."

"We have to assume that what the Buffalo PD knows may find a way to our law enforcement friends up in Maine. I also would be concerned that it links Alexis to us and who knows what Maine and now Buffalo PD have for evidence. It would just compound our problems. We don't want to shoot ourselves in the foot."

"I understand why Cheryl would lie, but it really painted us into a corner. It sounds like our only choice is to tell Maine's AG that Alexis disappeared and hope for the best," Asa posited.

"I think you're right. Do you want me to call the Maine AG's office and tell them that?"

"Yes, we might as well rip the band-aid off that one."

"OK. In the meantime, I better make sure we scrub our website of any reference to Cheryl. You might consider sending Cheryl on a long vacation out of the country when she wakes up. It would be best if she weren't around for the next few weeks."

"That will be difficult given what we have to accomplish to appease the Board by their next meeting. Right now, I'm more concerned about satisfying the Board than trying to anticipate what if anything will come of Maine's investigation or Buffalo PD's investigation of Alexis' suicide."

"I hear that, but we may need to pivot quickly."

"Pivot is my middle name, Chet," Asa laughed, raising his glass and draining its remaining contents.

CHAPTER 13

Detective Brent Farest hadn't wasted his time after he interviewed Cheryl Baker. The combination of the welts on Alexis' dead body, the suicide note suggestive of criminal activity, and his doubt about the veracity of Cheryl's responses had him on high alert.

Typing in "Cheryl Marie Baker" in the search bar produced too many hits to be helpful. When he narrowed the search to Buffalo and clicked on images, he got the desired results. There, in full color, was a picture of the woman he had just interviewed with the caption "Vice President of Operations at AlzCura Pharmaceuticals."

"Day Trader, my ass," he said to himself. "Now, what are you trying to hide, Ms. Baker? Could your daughter's reference to doctors and drugs in her suicide note have anything to do with AlzCura Pharmaceuticals?"

Typing in "Alexis Baker" narrowed down to the Buffalo area produced a surprisingly large number of photos and entries. None, however, matched the woman who was now residing in the morgue.

"A mystery woman," he said under his breath. Searching on "Alexis Baker" and "Italian Clothing" came up empty. So did "Alexis Baker" and "AlzCura."

"A ghost in a day and age when it's virtually impossible to

keep your identity off the interweb," continuing his internal monologue.

Navigating to AlzCura's website, Detective Farest clicked on the caption "Our Executive Team," hoping to find additional information on Cheryl Baker. The job title and job description under her photo didn't provide as much information as he had hoped. But it was the photo and name of the President and CEO that caught his attention.

"Dr. Asa Sheridan, President and CEO," he announced to himself. "I'd bet you're the Asa referenced in the suicide note, Dr. Sheridan. And now the plot thickens," he said aloud, continuing to narrate a story only he could hear.

When Detective Farest smelled something fishy, he was like a dog to a bone. He left his office and took the elevator to the basement, hoping that the Medical Examiner could provide additional information on the mystery woman Alexis Baker. As he entered the morgue, Dr. Twyla Potter was about to make the Y-shaped incision to begin the autopsy.

"Sorry to interrupt you, Dr. Potter."

"No apologies necessary, Detective Farest. You're just in time for your favorite part," she replied facetiously, knowing the Detective's aversion to seeing cadavers splayed open.

Dr. Twyla Potter was a rare breed in the medical specialty of forensic pathology that had its fair share of introverts, misfits, or otherwise socially challenged individuals. Instead, she was a gregarious, outgoing, free-spirit. When not conducting autopsies, she occupied herself with high-risk activities like skydiving, free climbing, and scuba diving, preferably in shark-infested waters. Her parents had wanted her to become a dancer in the model of her namesake, Twyla Tharp. To their chagrin, she found dissecting dead bodies and death-defying diversions more desirable than dance.

"I don't suppose you have much to tell me yet," Detective Farest commented.

"Au contraire, monsieur," she replied in French. "It's not often I see someone use two modes of suicide. She was obviously dead set on dying, pun intended. Sorry, bad pathology humor."

"What about those welts on her backside?"

"Not so fast, Sherlock. While she used two modes of suicide, it was the hanging that did her in. I estimate that she died about 12 to 14 hours ago between 1 and 3a.m. She did a commendable job lacerating her forearms vertically, which would have killed her if she hadn't hung herself. Most people slice their wrists horizontally, which rarely does the trick. It's a good way to gain attention but not a reliable method of suicide. As for those welts, they look a couple days old. There's no broken skin, and they don't look as angry as I would expect if she was whipped by someone who really had it in for her. To me, they look more like welts from sex play. I took vaginal, anal, and oral swabs. If she had unprotected sex in the last couple of days, the level of acid phosphatase from the semen should tell us if and when she had intercourse."

"Is there any evidence that suggests someone may have staged this as a suicide?"

"No. At least not yet. Her blood and other bodily fluid analysis may tell us if there's more to the story. At this time, I'm 95% sure this is a suicide. The lacerations on her arms were made from wrist to elbow. The laceration on her right forearm isn't nearly as deep as on her left. This would be expected for someone who is right-hand dominant. If someone else had lacerated her arms, they would typically be made from elbow-to-wrist, and the depths would be more consistent."

"Can you tell if she has ever had a baby?"

"That's an interesting question I don't usually get. Why do you ask?"

"She left a suicide note that mentions not being able to care for a baby, yet there was no evidence in her apartment of a baby."

"In that case, to answer your question, I should be able to tell if she's had a baby. There aren't any stretch marks, no tell-tale c-section scar, but my internal examination should provide a more definitive answer."

"Thanks, Dr. Potter."

"My pleasure, Detective Farest. Did you want to stay and assist?" she smiled, knowingly goading him.

"Well, aren't you so kind to ask? As tempting as your offer is, I'll have to pass," he replied facetiously.

Leaving the morgue, Detective Farest was called away to another crime scene, putting an abrupt end to the progress made on the mystery of Alexis and Cheryl Baker.

CHAPTER 14

Attorney Dryer turned onto the mile-long jostling and jolting dirt track that passed as the road to Inspector Theo Adam's secluded pond-side cabin. Now armed with the information he had gleaned from Norman Boulanger's medical record, he felt optimistic about taking Celeste's case. Shaken but not stirred, he pulled into a parking spot next to Theo's hideaway as Theo and Celeste stepped out of the cabin to greet him.

"How do you ever get in or out of here in the winter?" Attorney Dryer greeted them with wonderment.

"Slowly," Theo replied, laughing. "And sometimes not at all."

"Hi, Celeste. How are you doing?" Attorney Dryer said, greeting her more conventionally.

"Hi, John. I'm good. Thanks."

As the trio sat down in three mismatched foldable lawn chairs on the porch, Theo spotted a doe and a fawn down by the pond.

"Look there," he said in a hushed tone while pointing.

The three looked on transfixed as the doe and fawn approached the pond and began to drink. A Great Blue heron flew leisurely across their view, followed by a fish jumping and breaking the lake's mirrored surface.

"So this is what you do out here," Attorney Dryer remarked. "Choreograph wildlife to impress your guests."

"You caught me," Theo laughed heartily, causing the deer to look up briefly in the direction of the trio. Satisfied there was no threat, the doe and her fawn returned to hydrating themselves.

"Would you like something to drink?" Celeste offered Attorney Dryer, seeming to take her cue from the deer.

"I'm good, thanks. Are we ready to get started, or do you have more National Geographic moments for me, Theo?"

"We're ready, but I can't promise you we won't get interrupted," he chuckled.

"OK. First, the good news. I've reviewed Norman's medical record. Dr. Caron makes it clear that he thinks that Norman's engagement in AlzCura's Recallamin trial is to blame for his behavior, symptoms, and death. The bad news is that Dr. Caron isn't around to testify or expound on why he thought this. The other bad news is that we don't have an autopsy to provide clinical proof."

Theo worried that Celeste would only hear Attorney Dryer's bad news, quickly interjected. "Yes, and while I'm not at liberty to give details, I can assure you that we have plenty of other cases and autopsy results that will strengthen your case."

"If the State levels charge against AlzCura and make those details available," Attorney Dryer added.

"When the State levels charges and makes them available," Theo countered.

"And how can you be so sure?" Attorney Dryer questioned.

"You know I can't divulge the details. Let's just say the weight of evidence and the players we're bringing to the table have me convinced bringing charges is imminent."

"By players, do you mean the Feds?"

"Sorry, John, I can't say."

"Which is as good as a yes in my book. So this could end up being a class-action lawsuit?"

"Why? Are you anxious to run one of those TV lawyer ads that try to reel in clients?" Theo shifted to a TV announcer's voice, "Have you or a loved one been injured or died after taking Recallamin? If so, you might be entitled to compensation. Call the law offices of John Dryer immediately."

"Well, I won't hold my breath, but it would certainly strengthen Norman's case."

"What's a class-action lawsuit?" Celeste interjected.

"I'm sorry, Celeste," Attorney Dryer replied. "A class-action lawsuit is a lawsuit that is brought against a defendant that represents a whole group of people injured by the same cause. That group of people is known as a class. In your case, you might be part of a group that has lost loved ones due to the adverse effects of the Recallamin vaccine. That's how we get a class-action lawsuit."

"Thanks, I understand now. But how would it strengthen Norman's case?"

"Class-action suits collect evidence from multiple cases like Norman's, making it more difficult for the defendant to claim Norman died of other causes. Settlement amounts are much larger in class-action suits, and they typically require that the defendant change their harmful practices. It's a win for everyone except the defendant. The only downside is that class-action lawsuits can take years to get settled."

"What about selling my trailer and getting an apartment? Are we still going to do that meeting with media thingy?"

"Yeah, I've been thinking about that. I'm not so sure we should hold a press conference at this point. As for selling your trailer, I've talked with DC Realty, and they'd be happy to put your trailer on the market. It's going to need new carpeting throughout, I'm afraid, and some of your furniture will have to be disposed of."

"I'm already upside down with the hospital bill, and not working the last two weeks hasn't helped. Did you have a chance to check on Norman's benefits?"

"As a matter of fact, I did. And good news, Norman did have employer-paid life insurance equal to his annual income, which was about $35,000. I would also suggest we appeal the health insurance company's calculation of what they paid for Norman's hospitalization and what portion of the bill is your responsibility. If nothing else, it will delay your having to pay the hospital while protecting your credit. In the best case scenario, the insurance company agrees to pay a larger share of the bill. By the time you need to pay the hospital your portion of the bill, you have Norman's life insurance payment in your bank account."

"You're a life-saver, John," Celeste replied, tears coming to her eyes.

"Thanks, Celeste. Let's talk about getting you an apartment."

"OK."

"My law firm could rent an apartment and sublet it to you. Keeping your name off the lease, however, will only delay the media from finding out where you live. Or you could just rent an apartment yourself. As I see it, their interest in you is already giving way to other news stories. If and when we file a lawsuit, there will be a bump in media interest, but then I will be representing you, and they'll have to get their information from me."

"What if we moved Celeste's trailer to a lot closer to the front of this property?" Theo brainstormed. "There's a clearing about a quarter-mile in. It would take some work to run power, dig a well, and install a septic system. The narrow road and the ability to lock the front gate would greatly discourage the media."

"Oh, now I love that idea," Celeste brightened.

"What about access? Can you even get that trailer down that road?" Attorney Dryer asked skeptically.

"Getting it down the road won't be as much trouble as trying to shoe-horn it into the lot. I might have to clear some additional space."

"Well, in that case, moving your trailer there may be a good solution, at least until winter hits. What kind of car do you drive, Celeste?"

"Not one that will be able to get through the snow here, I'm sure."

"Well, you might just have to upgrade to a four-wheel drive," Theo suggested.

"Which I might be able to afford after I get Norman's life insurance."

"Well, if it's alright with both of you, I'll let you two figure out what you want to do about Celeste's living arrangements. I will get to work drafting the complaint and drawing up an agreement for your review Celeste."

Both Theo and Celeste voiced their endorsement of his proposal. While doing so, Celeste reached over to hold Theo's hand, feeling a sense of relief that life was finally moving in a positive direction.

"In that case," Attorney Dryer said, getting up out of his chair, "I'll bounce down the road, and you two can continue choreographing wildlife!"

Laughing, they said their farewells. Celeste had nothing against wildlife. However, she had other activities she wanted to choreograph to show her appreciation for Theo's idea of moving her trailer onto his property.

CHAPTER 15

Attorney General Talcott's assistant uncharacteristically knocked on his office door, interrupting the meeting he was in.

"I'm sorry, sir. There's a Chet Humphreys from AlzCura Pharmaceuticals on the line for you. He says it's important."

Thanking his assistant, AG Talcott then addressed the person in his office.

"I'm sorry, I need to take this call. Let's reschedule."

His office guest nodded and took his leave. Once back at his desk, AG Talcott notified his assistant by intercom to send the call to his phone.

"Hello, Mr. Humphreys. This is Attorney General Lewis Talcott."

"Good afternoon, AG Talcott. I'm calling about your request for us to produce our employee Margo for questioning."

"Yes, I left a message that we'd like to interview her next week."

"Yes, I received that message, and we had every intention of having her travel there for that interview."

"Had? Is there a problem?"

"Yes, sir. It seems Margo has disappeared. She hasn't reported to work, and we have been unable to contact or find her."

"Did she disappear before you told her about the meeting or after?"

"Before."

"So her disappearance wasn't related to concerns she had over meeting with us."

"No. We'll continue to try to locate her, and if we find her, we'll certainly let you know. We want to cooperate with your request."

"I appreciate that," AG Talcott replied. "Say, as an aside, we never got Margo's full name and contact information. Would you be able to supply that? We'd like to join your efforts to locate her."

"We'd be happy too. I'll have my assistant track down that information and send it to you," he replied, even though he had no intention of fulfilling the AG's request. Without the AG's written request, he had plausible deniability and could conveniently forget that the verbal request was ever made.

"Thank you, Mr. Humphreys. Let us know if you find her."

"We will," he said, ending the call and concurrently letting out a big sigh of relief.

Chet Humphreys wasn't a fan of making phone calls to highly-placed government officials. But in this instance, he hoped that expediency and a more personal touch might help to stave off the suspicion and increased scrutiny that having a person of interest go missing could provoke. He felt reasonably confident that he had accomplished that mission in his call with AG Talcott.

* * *

Attorney General Talcott hung up the phone, and before he

could call DA Wydman with the news he had just learned, his assistant called him over the intercom.

"Sorry, sir, but you're obviously quite popular today. A Detective Brent Farest from the Buffalo Police Department is calling. He says it's important."

"OK, send it in. When's my next appointment?"

"You've got 15 minutes."

Thanking his assistant, he picked up the call.

"Good afternoon Detective, this is Attorney General Lewis Talcott. How can I help you?"

"Good afternoon, and thank you for taking my call. We are investigating a recent suicide in our jurisdiction, and a suicide note left at the scene alludes to a meeting she was supposed to have in Maine. It doesn't say that her meeting was with law enforcement, but the note does mention that she'd rather be dead than go to jail."

Given the proximity of the Detective's call to the call he just had from Chet Humphreys, AG Talcott couldn't help but think this might be the answer to why Margo was missing.

"Interesting. What is the individual's name?" AG Talcott asked.

"Alexis Baker."

"Hmm, doesn't ring a bell. Do you have a description of her?"

"Mid-twenties, blond, about 5 foot 3."

"That description matches the young woman who is a person of interest in a case we're investigating, but her name is Margo, not Alexis. Do you happen to know where she worked?"

"Her mother reported she worked for an Italian clothing and shoe company, but I haven't been able to verify that yet."

"OK, well, our person of interest works for AlzCura Pharmaceuticals," AG Talcott replied, thinking the trail had gone cold on this being his person of interest.

"Alexis Baker's mother, Cheryl Baker, works at AlzCura Pharmaceuticals," Detective Farest exclaimed. "Actually, her mother lied to me and said she worked from home as a day trader, but I subsequently found her on AlzCura's website. She's their VP of Operations. Also, the suicide note describes that she, pardon my language, screwed doctors to make them use drugs. Could our Alexis be your Margo?"

AG Talcott felt like he had been hit by a lightning bolt. "Detective Farest, I think so, but before I get too far down the road on this, I think I should connect you with Investigator Theo Adams. He's been doing all the legwork on our investigation, and it would be best for the two of you to compare notes and confirm they're one in the same woman."

"I'd be happy to work with Inspector Adams," Detective Farest replied. "May I ask why she was a person of interest?

"Yes, of course. We found compromising pictures of her with a doctor who appeared to have committed suicide. The evidence we found at the scene subsequently raised suspicions as to whether the doctor's death was staged to look like a suicide. AlzCura Pharmaceuticals is also on our radar for a series of deaths that may be related to their Recallamin vaccine. We are scheduled to meet with representatives from the FDA next week."

"Thanks. That background certainly makes what she wrote in her suicide note more comprehensible. I will definitely coordinate our investigation here with yours. I look forward to speaking with Inspector Adams."

AG Talcott took down Detective Farest's contact information and promised that he would have Inspector Adams call him at his earliest convenience.

AG Talcott and Detective Farest felt buoyed by their conversation and discovery, even if it opened up a whole new set of questions. Why would Cheryl Baker hide the fact that she worked there? Why would her daughter work there under an alias? What had Alexis done in Maine that was so egregious that it caused her to commit suicide? And if these were one in the same individual, how could AlzCura's Chief Legal Counsel not have been aware of her death or choose to lie about it and say instead that she was missing?

AG Talcott poked his head out of his office and addressed his assistant. "It's one of those days. Can you reschedule my next meeting? I have to get DA Wydman and Inspector Adams on the horn right now."

"Will do," she said, unfazed by the fluidity of his schedule, which was more the rule than the exception. "Do you want me to get them on the phone and transfer the call to you?"

"That would be great. Thanks."

Taking a seat back at his desk, AG Talcott began to wonder if it was time to call in the calvary. That is, include not only the FDA but also the Federal Bureau of Investigation (FBI). It certainly seemed like AlzCura executives were running from or hiding the truth, which was never a good thing. While ceding control of their investigation to the Feds was never easy, delaying in doing so could allow AlzCura to shore up their defenses, or worse yet, destroy evidence. While Maine could bring charges against AlzCura, the State did not have the latitude, resources, or muscle that the Feds had. He knew a decision to involve the Feds was an extraordinary step. But it looked increasingly like this was an extraordinary circumstance. His deliberations were interrupted by his assistant patching him into the call with DA Wydman and Inspector Adams.

"Good afternoon, gentlemen. Thanks for dropping whatever you may have been doing to get on this call."

"Good afternoon, Lew," DA Wydman replied. "What can we do for you?"

"Well, it's more about what I can do for you," AG Talcott responded and went on to brief them about the information he had just received from Detective Farest.

"So, Theo, I need you to call Detective Farest back as soon as possible," AG Talcott directed, giving Inspector Adams the contact information. "Make sure that Alexis Baker is our Margo."

"Will do. I'm optimistic that it is. What Dr. Mason told me when I interviewed her now makes sense."

"What's that?" AG Talcott asked.

"Dr. Mason indicated that when she met with Cheryl Baker, she initially misidentified Jackie's replacement as Alexis but then quickly corrected herself and said, Margo."

"Ah, what would we do without the good ol' Freudian slip?" DA Wydman asked rhetorically.

"Well, we also have to give credit to Sir Walter Scott," Theo replied.

"How's that?" asked DA Wydman.

"Oh, what a tangled web we weave, when first we practice to deceive!" Theo quoted.

"I thought that was Shakespeare," DA Wydman added.

"OK, boys," AG Talcott interjected. "We may owe a debt of gratitude to psychology and Scottish poetry, but class is over. Let's get back on topic."

To which DA Wydman and InspectorAdams both apologized for going off on tangents.

"What I would like your help on is making a decision about whether we should meet with the FBI either separately or together with the FDA next week."

AG Talcott went on to verbalize the thoughts and rationale he had just before the call.

"Makes sense," DA Wydman said in support of the AG, "but the Feds don't always play well together. I'm not sure bringing the FBI into our meeting with the FDA would be constructive. On the other hand, meeting separately with them risks their acting independently, which isn't a good thing either. Tough call, boss."

"Yeah, and far be it for the Feds to accept us as facilitators of their inter-agency cooperation," AG Talcott added. "Let me do this. I have a friend at the Department of Justice. I can call him for advice on how to coordinate our efforts if that's even possible."

The crusade to expose the truth about AlzCura had taken a big step. Engaging the Feds would represent a giant leap. A leap AG Talcott wanted to ensure landed on terra firma and provide the leverage needed to bring AlzCura to justice. Not a leap that would fall short and let AlzCura off the hook as their crusade spiraled into the abyss of Federal bureaucracy and dysfunction.

CHAPTER 16

Sunny bounced more than walked through the airport security exit, her perpetually cheerful countenance on full display despite the 6+ hours of flights from Phoenix. "Hi, girlfriend," Sunny called and waved animatedly from afar as she navigated around a tottering elderly couple.

"It's so good to see you, Sunny," Jackie said as they embraced. "Is that all you have?" pointing at Sunny's carry-on.

"Oh, heaven's no. I'm so embarrassed. I packed like I was coming here for a month. Where's Ashley? I miss that little snugglebug."

"She's at my mother's, and she's not so little anymore."

As the two made their way to baggage claim, Jackie could hardly keep up with Sunny's pace.

"Jeez, Sunny, are you in a hurry to get somewhere?"

"It must be all my pent-up energy from sitting on those planes. And I'm excited to see you!"

Arriving at the baggage claim area, they talked excitedly about the weekend ahead of them.

"I'm famished," Sunny exclaimed. "A girl can't survive on pretzels alone. Can we go to that restaurant we went to last time I visited?"

"You mean, Danielle's?"

"Yeah, that's it. I knew it had a female name."

"Your wish is my command," Jackie replied, which prompted an enthusiastic hug from Sunny.

"You're the best. I'm so excited to be here. Just think what fun we'll have if I get the internship."

At that moment, a very large and very bright yellow piece of luggage dropped onto the carousel with a resounding thud.

"And Sunny's entire wardrobe makes its grand entrance," Sunny announced.

"Well, you certainly can't miss that," Jackie said, laughing. "And in your color too!"

"I'm going to be so embarrassed when I try to haul that monstrosity off this carousel. You might have to help me."

"Think of it this way, when you get that internship, you have already moved all your clothes here."

"Do they have storage units big enough here?" Sunny replied facetiously.

"You won't need a storage unit. You're going to live with me. I have plenty of room, and besides, your niece wouldn't have it any other way."

Jackie's offer of housing and christening her as Ashley's aunt made Sunny scream out in delight, attracting the attention of all those on their side of the carousel.

"Oh great," Sunny remarked, holding her hand in front of her mouth, "now everyone can watch me wrestle with Big Bird!" causing Jackie to erupt in laughter.

"You named your bag, Big Bird?"

"Of course. Look at it. What else would you call it?"

"I love you, Sunny. You haven't been here ten minutes, and you've already made me laugh so hard I've almost peed myself."

This caused Sunny to snort and erupt in laughter as Big

Bird passed by for another lap around the carousel.

"Oh, good. Hopefully, by the time Big Bird comes around again, at least half these people will have picked up their bags and left."

Sunny's wish came true, but the spectacle of getting her bag off the carousel never transpired as Jackie hefted Big Bird in one graceful motion. The shocked look on Sunny's face was priceless and caused Jackie to break out in laughter again.

"How did you do that so easily?"

"Leverage and nine months of picking up Ashley and carrying her around."

Jackie, at 5'9," was a full 8 inches taller than her petite friend. And while Jackie's years as a standout basketball and volleyball player were behind her, she hadn't lost the tone or the power in her legs.

"I've always hated tall girls," Sunny said facetiously, feigning a death stare in Jackie's direction.

"What did you say? I couldn't hear you from way down there!" Jackie baited her diminutive friend, causing another round of laughter as they rolled Big Bird out of the airport terminal toward the parking structure.

Arriving at Danielle's without dinner reservations relegated them to a 30-minute wait, which they choose to pass with a drink at the bar.

"Let's have Baja Pineapple Grenades," Jackie suggested. "Do you think they will know how to make it?"

"I doubt it," Sunny replied. "It was my own creation, but if the bartender doesn't mind, I could tell her how to make it."

No sooner were the words out of Sunny's mouth and the bartender, whose name tag read, "Shaylene," arrived and asked what she could make for them.

"Hi, Shaylene, I'm Sunny. Have you ever heard of a Baja

Pineapple Grenade?"

"Hmm, I don't know that I have. What's in it?"

"Melon liqueur, tequila, pineapple juice, Sprite, and grenadine served in a cored pineapple," Sunny recited.

"Yum, that sounds delicious. I'll be happy to make them if you walk me through it. They'll have to be in a glass though, we don't do pineapples in Buffalo."

As Sunny was leading Shaylene through the recipe, a young man stumbled over, positioned himself between Sunny and Jackie, and draped his arms around their shoulders.

"Where haf you two booties been all my life?" he slurred as Jackie and Sunny reacted in surprise. Before either could address the unwelcome visitor whose hands were slithering their way down to cup their breasts, Shaylene intervened.

"Beat it, Robbie! These are my friends, and if you don't take your hands off them, I'll cut both of your hands off," she threatened, reaching for a knife and showing him she meant business.

"Whoa, Whoa, awright, awright," he slurred, removing his hands and arms and backing away unsteadily. "I dint mean nothin' by it. They're jus so bootiful."

"And if you think I'm going to serve you, forget it. Now leave before I call the police."

As Robbie weaved his way out of the bar and out the door, Shaylene commenced making their drinks.

"I'm sorry," she apologized to Jackie and Sunny. "He's 86'd from every bar in town except the one just across the street. When they stop serving him, he tries to come over here," she explained, setting their drinks down in front of them. "They're on the house."

"Thanks, Shaylene. You didn't have to do that," Sunny replied.

"It's the least I could do. Besides, you taught me how to make a new drink!"

Fifteen minutes into their wait, Shaylene came by.

"You two are apparently quite popular. The two gentlemen at the end of the bar would like to buy you drinks."

As Jackie and Sunny turned to see who their admirers were, they saw two middle-aged men in suits. As they waved, Jackie and Sunny turned back to Shaylene.

"What's their story," Sunny asked, knowing from her own experience that bartenders generally knew their clientele.

"I actually don't know them, but I can tell you that both of them came in with wedding rings, which are now mysteriously missing."

At that moment, the digital coaster that the hostess had given Jackie lit up and vibrated, announcing their table was available.

"You can tell the gentlemen, thank you very much. Also, tell them we're married, and we love our husbands too much to accept their generous offer," Sunny said as she and Jackie stood to make their way to the hostess station.

"Perfect," Shaylene replied. "It was great meeting you two. Thanks for teaching me how to make your drink, Sunny."

"My pleasure, Shaylene. Here's a little something for serving as our bodyguard," Sunny said with a smile, laying down a twenty-dollar bill on the bar.

"You're too kind. Come back and see me again."

"I will. Us bartenders need to stick together," Sunny called as she and Jackie made their way to the hostess station.

Dinner was delicious, but Jackie and Sunny hardly savored or took notice of it, so immersed in their conversation about Sunny's criminal justice studies and the internship. Tempted by but eventually skipping dessert, Sunny made a suggestion.

"Let's go dancing."

"Dancing? Aren't you tired?"

"Heck no, I'm still on Arizona time. What's the matter? Has the tall girl lost her stamina?"

"Oh, we're going to play that game again, are we?" Jackie countered.

"Oh, it's no game, honey. This is war! Can't beat Petite!"

"Tall is better than small!"

"Oh, you're in trouble now, you gangly beotch."

"Oh, really. Whatcha gonna do? Punch me in the kneecap?"

Their competitive repartee had them laughing again as they left the restaurant. Needing to refresh their make-up and change into more appropriate clubbing attire, they stopped at Jackie's house. Sunny wrestled Big Bird up the steps to the spare bedroom. Twenty minutes later, she emerged in a v-neck ombre sequin mini dress accompanied by lace-up stiletto high heel sandals. The dress shimmered, its color transitioning from berry red on top to silver at the hem.

"How are you doing in there?" she called from outside Jackie's bedroom.

"I can't find anything to wear," she replied.

"Let me help you," Sunny said, striding into the room to find Jackie standing in the middle of the walk-in closet wearing only her underwear and a frustrated look.

"Oh jeez, Sunny. I can't go clubbing with you. Look at you," Jackie said in a defeated tone, her exasperation intensifying.

"What? Ms. Petite doesn't look good enough?"

"No, you look too good. I'll look like a frumpy old lady next to you."

"Oh, stop that. You're beautiful. I wish I had legs like those. Now let's find something for you to wear," she replied as she started to inventory Jackie's wardrobe.

"I don't know the last time I even wore a dress," Jackie sighed, paging through her selection of dresses.

"Then wear these," Sunny suggested holding up a pair of dress jeans.

"Jeans?"

"Dress jeans. I guarantee you, with those legs and that ass, you'll look better than fine, my tall amazon goddess."

"But what about a top?" Jackie asked, ignoring Sunny's compliment and still unconvinced about the jeans idea.

"Here," Sunny said, picking out a black darted sleeveless top with a wide-cut rounded hem and tulip back. "Put these on. I'll wait out here for the fashion show."

"I don't know, Sunny."

"Trust me," Sunny said, exiting the closet.

Two minutes later, Jackie emerged in Sunny's recommended outfit, along with a pair of black suede ankle strap heels.

"What do you think?" Jackie asked, though her face told the story. She knew she looked better than fine, just as Sunny had predicted.

"Girl, if I were a guy or gay, you wouldn't get out of this bedroom."

Jackie put the finishing touches on her make-up, and the transformed pair of femme fatales, heels clicking in syncopated rhythm, returned to Jackie's car.

"I don't even know of any dance places in Nora," Jackie remarked as she started the car. "We'll probably have to go to Buffalo."

"I'll find one," Sunny announced as she picked up her phone.

As Jackie navigated her car through town on her way to the freeway, Sunny scrolled through a directory of dance club options.

"Here's one. Club Merci'. It has four and a half stars and 150 reviews."

"Where's it located?"

"Pierpont Street in Buffalo."

"Hmm, I'm not familiar with that street. I wonder if it's a safe area of town."

"The pictures of the place look good. And besides, you're with someone who almost has her bachelor's degree in criminal justice. What do you have to worry about?"

"Yeah, I saw how well you protected us when Robbie tried to cop a feel earlier this evening!"

"I was just about to subdue him had Shaylene not pulled out that knife."

"Oh, OK, Officer Sunny, what were you going to do? Smother him with your double-barrel boobs?"

"A girl's gotta use what a girl's got."

"OK, OK, so you have great boobs. That's the one thing I can say about pregnancy. It made my boobs bigger. Now, why don't you give me directions to Club Merci', Officer Boobs."

"Take exit 19A. It's 3 miles away."

"Thanks. You know what?"

"What?"

"I consider you my best friend, and I don't even know your last name."

"There's a reason for that," Sunny replied.

"Why?"

"You're obviously not a very good friend," she said, laughing. "No, I'm kidding. I don't like telling people my last name, and my first name usually gets me by."

"What's your last name?" Jackie asked, intrigued.

"Day," Sunny replied, waiting for the inevitable response.

"Sunny Day?"

"There it is. The reason I don't tell people my last name. My parents thought it was cute."

"Well, I have to admit, you do brighten up a day, so if anyone deserves that name, it would be you."

"Aww, that's sweet, but I took so much grief for my name in grade school and high school, I came to hate it."

"Kids can be so mean. They used to call me Jackie Slay Me because my last name was Selaney."

"Well, I have to admit, you do make me laugh, and you're drop-dead gorgeous, so if anyone deserves that name, it would be you."

"Touche'," Jackie laughed at Sunny's payback as she changed lanes in anticipation of the exit to the dance club.

They could already hear the infectious bass beat as they approached the entrance to Club Merci'. Entering the dance hall, a beat drop and blinding laser lights pumped up the large Friday night crowd undulating like waves of humanity.

"Let's get a drink and find a table," Sunny yelled, barely audible to Jackie, only 2 feet away.

Their drinks procured, they orbited the dance floor, finally finding an available high-top table. As they were orienting themselves to the club and adjusting to the full-body assault of the music and lights, Sunny's attention was drawn away from Jackie.

"What are you looking at," Jackie yelled above the din.

"That delicious hunk of man over there."

Jackie looked beyond Sunny and saw a chiseled Adonis who was making his way in their direction. As he got closer, Jackie thought he looked somewhat familiar. When he all of a sudden called her name, she was shocked and panicked, still unable to place him.

"You know him?" Sunny turned to Jackie.

"Ah, I don't know," she replied before he was within ear-shot.

"Jackie, it's me, Barrett," he said, now arriving at their table. "Officer Todd?" he added when saying his first name failed to produce a look of recognition on Jackie's face.

"Oh, Barrett," she replied, "I'm sorry, I didn't recognize you without your police uniform. What are you doing here?" she asked but then immediately answered herself, "Duh, what a stupid question. Dancing, right?"

"Not yet, but I'm hoping to," he replied.

"Hi, I'm Sunny. I'm Jackie's friend from Arizona," Sunny cut in, unable to wait for an introduction.

"Hi, Sunny. I'm Barrett Todd," he replied, his face tele-graphing that he was clearly enamored by the zaftig, petite blond before him.

"Did I hear you say you wanted to dance?" Sunny asked.

"Yes, would you do me the honor?" he said formally, hold-ing out his hand.

"You don't need to ask me twice," she said, excitedly jump-ing off her chair and putting her hand in his.

"Love you, Jackie," Sunny called back as she marched with Barrett to the dance floor.

And just like that, Jackie was left alone at the table. For some, being left alone would have been uncomfortable, but for Jackie, it was entirely welcome. Taking a sip of her ginger ale and sitting alone amid the raucous crowd made her reminisce about the night she first met Stu at Carter's Bar. Stu was her Adonis, and that evening was the start of their extraordinary relationship. She smiled as she watched Sunny shaking her stuff and Barrett's surprising grace for a big, muscular man.

Jackie thought about Stu and wondered if Sunny and Barrett's meeting would have a similar fate. Similar in the depth of love, but hopefully not its premature and horrific end.

Sunny talked about Barrett all the way home from the Club Merci', but Jackie didn't need that as proof that her friend and the police officer had hit it off. Each time they came back to the table to take a break from the dance floor, their relationship seemed to have evolved. Although Jackie was approached by several men throughout the night asking if she cared to dance, she deftly deflected their offers. Except for one dance with Sunny and another with Barrett, she had been content to people-watch.

By the end of their weekend together, Jackie was exhausted. Sunny was an Everyready Bunny of energy. In addition to playing with Ashley and taking her to the park, they went shopping and went to dinner with Jackie's parents. Sunday after church and brunch at Momma's, Sunny convinced Jackie to take a road trip to her college. Jackie hadn't been back to South Temple University in nearly three years. The memories that their visit exhumed had an emotional impact she had not anticipated. More than once, Sunny found herself consoling Jackie, who would inexplicably begin to cry. What Sunny could not appreciate, but what Jackie ultimately came to realize was that she could not be there without being bombarded continuously by memories of Stu. Oddly, as emotionally wrenching and draining as it was, it brought Jackie a sense of peace.

Monday dawned, and Sunny took Jackie's car to Buffalo for her internship interview. Jackie was all too happy to do nothing but enjoy a cup of coffee and sit quietly at home. Only motivating herself to move when her daughter's increased confidence and ability to ambulate took her to places that Jackie considered beyond Ashley's capacity, like the stairs. Jackie could already see vestiges of her daughter's fierce determination and independence and knew that in a few years, she would really have her hands full.

Sunny returned in the late afternoon ecstatic to report that they had offered her the internship and was asked to start in two weeks. In celebration, Jackie invited Sunny and Officer Todd out to dinner at Rue Franklin in Buffalo's theatre district. The restaurant where Stu had proposed marriage to Jackie. While not as magical as the last time she had been there, Jackie could tell it was a magical night for Sunny and Barrett. It was no surprise to Jackie when Sunny said she would be riding home with Barrett. She was happy for them and understood they had a special connection.

The next morning, Sunny and Barrett picked Jackie and Ashley up to take Sunny to the airport. Big Bird and most of its contents stayed at Jackie's house as Sunny chose to use a much smaller carry-on that Jackie provided her. She would be coming back soon, and Barrett, Jackie, and Ashley looked forward to her return.

CHAPTER 17

Cheryl Baker woke up to find herself lying on the sofa in Dr. Sheridan's empty office. Disoriented and sporting a splitting headache, the ugly truth flooded back in. It had not been a nightmare. Her daughter was dead, and the last thing Cheryl wanted to be right now was awake, aware, and alive to feel the pain all over again. Still woozy, she stumbled over to the conference table. She picked up a crystal tumbler and the bottle of Maker's Mark. About to pour the rest of the bottle into the glass, she skipped the formality and chugged it. Only to have Dr. Sheridan breeze through the door to witness it.

"You know, I'm sure we could arrange to have that infused intravenously. It would be much more civilized and effective."

"Fuck you!" she said, slamming the empty bottle down on the table. "You're going to give me shit on the day my baby took her life? You're an asshole."

"I lost her too, Cheryl. And if you haven't noticed, we have a company to run, a Board that isn't happy with our performance, and law enforcement in two states that are nosing around in our business. I can't afford to lose myself in a bottle right now as much as I'd like to. So save it."

Before Cheryl could respond, he continued his lecture.

"You know what? Just go home. Go take care of arrangements for Alexis, and whatever you do, don't speak to the police."

"What do you mean by that?" Cheryl asked indignantly.

"Had you not passed out during our meeting with Chet earlier today, you would know that your not so little lies about where you and Alexis work has a good chance of backfiring. Right now, Chet is working on getting our website scrubbed of any reference to you. A simple internet search will blow your day trader cover story, and we'll have Buffalo PD crawling all over us. Not to mention, we now have to renege on our offer to produce Margo for that interview with Maine law enforcement."

"Why not just tell them that she died?" Cheryl offered, trying to deflect the heat of Asa's intensifying anger.

"You know what, Cheryl? While you were snoring on the sofa, I was saving your job. Chet recommended that we cut our losses and fire your ass," he lied. "Now, I'm not so certain I should have stood up for you."

"I don't understand. I thought I was protecting us," she began to tear up.

"Go home. Don't talk to the police, and get your shit together so you can go to Bangor next week. If that's too much to ask, I'll accept your resignation right now."

Scalded by his anger and ultimatum, she had no choice but to leave. "I'm going, and I'll go to Bangor," she replied as she marched out of his office, too proud to show him that she was barely holding it together.

Once out of his office, she went directly to the women's washroom, just in time to vomit a corrosive stream of blood-tinged whiskey into the toilet. Followed by uncontrollable sobbing punctuated by wrenching, spasmodic dry heaves. When no more bile or tears could be expelled, Cheryl put herself together as best she could. Furtively exiting the washroom to her car, she heeded Asa's advice and went home.

Meanwhile, Dr. Sheridan's interaction with Cheryl had him worked up, and he called Chet Humphreys in for an update. The moment Chet walked in the door to his office, the barrage began.

"Where do we stand on notifying the Maine AG and scrubbing the website?"

"I just got off the phone with the AG, and it went well. I don't think we'll have a problem with them," he said reassuringly, recognizing that Asa was at his tipping point.

"Good. And the website?"

"I've talked to IT, and they're getting it done," trying to hide the fact that it wasn't going to get done as quickly as he had hoped.

"When? When will she be off of the website?" he pressed, well aware that IT was not their most accommodating or efficient department.

"She should be off the website by tomorrow," Chet replied, fully expecting what came next.

"Tomorrow!" Asa blew up. "That's too fucking late. It should have been done hours ago. Go. You have one hour to get it done, or you and the IT Director can find somewhere else to work. Understand?" he raged, looking for something to throw or break.

"I'm on it," Chet replied as he quickly exited. He wasn't three steps out the door when a series of shattering crashes occurred.

Chet, who was passing by Dr. Sheridan's assistant's desk, felt compelled to apologize to her knowing that she would have the burden of coordinating the clean-up.

"Oh, it's not your fault, Chet. I could tell he was working his way towards this all day. I have the cleaning service on speed dial," she replied, which sounded like a joke, but was the absolute truth.

"I hope he knows how lucky he is to have you."

"He doesn't, but thanks anyway," she called to him as he exited on his way to the IT Director's office.

Not finding the IT Director in his office, Chet's usually calm demeanor was being sorely tested. By the time he found the Director, who was chatting up a pretty young associate in the finance department, all diplomacy was out the window.

"I need you in my office now," he commanded, interrupting their conversation.

Fully expecting the Director would accompany him back to his office, Chet exploded when he looked back to see the Director still at the young lady's desk.

"What the fuck do you think NOW means?" he yelled.

This not only lit a fire under the IT Director but caused all staff within earshot to halt their work and cautiously look to see who was involved in the skirmish. Everyone knew that Chet Humphreys had a long fuse, so on those rare occasions when he would get angry, it got people's attention.

When Chet finally had the IT Director in his office, he had worked himself into a lather. He slammed the door with such force that it shook the wall. The IT Director quickly decided that expressing his indignation about how his boss had addressed him in the Finance Department wasn't a good idea. Instead, he shrunk into a chair, awaiting the storm he knew was about to intensify.

"What were you doing with that girl who's young enough to be your daughter?"

"She had an issue with her computer," he said defensively.

"You have staff in your Department to do that. Don't bullshit me. You already have a couple of complaints in your personnel file about getting too handsy with young ladies."

"I…"

"I don't want to hear it. That's not why I called you in here. You have precisely 38 minutes to get Cheryl Baker off our website, or you can find a new job."

"That's not possible."

"Why?"

"That part of the website refreshes overnight. We'd have to take the entire website down, scrub the information, and reboot the system, which would take 2-3 hours. It would disrupt some of our eCommerce functions."

"I don't care. Take it down, then. You've got 37 minutes."

"But," he started to protest. Only to be cut off.

"36 minutes. Get out of here. And if you're not back in my office with good news before the clock runs out, I'll have Security help escort you off the premises."

The IT Director didn't need any further convincing. He walked out of Chet's office, made a phone call, and knocked on the Chief Legal Counsel's office door 2 minutes after exiting it.

"The website is down," he reported.

Not trusting him, Chet got on his computer and clicked on the link to the external website. When he received a screen announcing that the site was down for maintenance, he looked up at the IT Director, who was standing restlessly in front of his desk.

"Now, was that so hard? Now get to work scrubbing it, and get the website back up. And if I ever catch you sniffing up some young girls' skirt again, you're out. Understand?"

"Yes, sir."

After the IT Director left, Chet walked over to Dr. Sheridan's office only to learn that he had left for the day with strict instructions not to be bothered. Concerned for the security of his job, Chet texted Asa confirming that the company website was down. Now he hoped it wasn't too late. They may have dodged a bullet, but he knew that the battle to keep the Buffalo PD out of their business had just begun. As he was walking out, a cleaning crew was walking in. Chet turned back and, catching the eye of Dr. Sheridan's assistant, remarked, "You weren't kidding about speed dial, were you?"

"Nope," she replied, smiling.

"You should get hazard pay."

"That will be the day. Maybe I should come to work for you."

"And miss all this excitement? You'd be bored stiff."

"Yeah, right," she chuckled. "Boredom sounds pretty good right about now!"

"I'll let you know when I have an opening, but you didn't hear that from me," he said, smiling as he turned and exited the office.

CHAPTER 18

Maine's Attorney General Lewis Talcott, anxious to follow-up on how to best engage the FDA and FBI in their investigation of AlzCura, was fortunate to know Clark Ainsley, Deputy Attorney General at the U.S. Department of Justice. They had met on their first day in law school, and from the moment they introduced themselves to each other, they knew they were fated for friendship. Lewis, hopelessly lost on the unfamiliar campus, had approached Clark, hoping to get directions to the building that housed his first-hour class. He learned that Clark was similarly lost and trying to find the same class. When they discovered their first names combined to form the famous explorers Lewis and Clark, they set off together on their first expedition to find their class. The rest, as they say, is history.

"Lewis, what an unexpected pleasure," Clark greeted after his assistant had transferred AG Talcott's call into his office.

"Hi, Clark. It's been too long. How are things at the DOJ?"

"Oh, it's a laugh a minute, just as I'm sure your job is," he replied sarcastically. "Listen, I don't mean to rush you, but I have a meeting in 5 minutes. What can I do for you?"

"I'll get right to the point then. We're working on a case that involves a potential murder made to look like a suicide and a series of unreported deaths related to an Alzheimer's vaccine. The weight of the evidence is pointing towards a pharmaceutical company in Buffalo. We have representatives from the FDA meeting with us next week, but I think we should also involve the FBI. What I was wondering was,"

"You're wondering how to engage both agencies without ruffling any feathers. That or losing control of your investigation in the quagmire of the federal bureaucracy or some interagency muscle-flexing contest," he interrupted.

"Exactly," AG Talcott replied.

"The good news is that I have authority over the FBI. The bad news is that the FDA is under the purview of the Secretary of the Department of Health and Human Services. While there have been occasions the FBI and FDA worked together, that usually only occurs after the Office of the Inspector General gets involved. The OIG is a Department under the same authority as the FDA. They would usually investigate criminal activity related to HHS programs."

"So, by meeting with the FDA, will they automatically engage the OIG if it's warranted?"

"Hopefully. Ideally, that's how things should work."

"I'm not getting a warm fuzzy feeling from your response, Clark."

"I know. I'm sorry. I have a hard enough time getting the offices in the DOJ to play nice together. I can't speak for HHS. Who are you meeting with from the FDA next week?"

"Dr. Woodson Shearlow and Dr. Elizabeth Harder from the FDA's Center for Biologics Evaluation and Research."

"Hmm, those names don't ring a bell. I would recommend meeting with them and seeing how it goes. If they don't escalate the investigation as you think appropriate, or you're getting caught up in bureaucratic bullshit, there are plenty of resources above their paygrade that could intervene. If necessary, I could talk to the Secretary of HHS and have her run interference."

"Thanks, Clark. I know you have to run. Let's chat again when we have more time."

"Yeah, wouldn't that be great? More time. Good luck, my expedition buddy," evoking a reference from their law school days.

Armed with a better understanding of the Federal bureaucracy and reassured that he had an ally willing to step in, AG Talcott felt more comfortable meeting with just the FDA representatives. As he was about to pick up the phone to call DA Wydman, his assistant poked her head in and informed him that he had only 5 minutes to get across town for his next appointment.

"You're right, Clark. It's a laugh a minute," he thought to himself as he hurried out the door to the meeting he had mistakenly thought was taking place in his office.

* * *

Inspector Adams wasted no time setting up a web conference call with Detective Farest. He was frustrated at how difficult it had been to collect sufficient evidence to bring charges against AlzCura. He hoped this call would be the break they needed to bring things to a head. After they made introductions, they quickly got down to business.

"First things first," Theo led out, "Do you have a photo of Alexis Baker that you can share so we can determine if Alexis and Margo are one in the same person?"

"I do," Brent replied as he shared an autopsy photo on the screen.

"That's definitely our Margo," Theo confirmed after consulting the photos of Margo with Dr. Caron in his case file. "Thanks for that. Job one complete."

"I'd like to share the suicide note with you," Brent offered. "It was a bit cryptic to me at first, but I've learned a few things since that may clarify it," he commented as the note appeared on Theo's computer screen.

"Well, I certainly can confirm her reference to screwing doctors. We found graphic pictures of her with Dr. Caron on his office computer when he was found hanging in his office from an apparent suicide."

"And her reference to selling drugs?" Detective Farest asked.

"She was here in Maine as a pharmaceutical representative for AlzCura. So I would think she was referencing the Recallamin vaccine she was marketing for AlzCura rather than illicit drugs."

"Thanks. I already learned from AG Talcott that she was expected to come to Maine as a person of interest. What about her reference to the baby? Any clue what that might be about?"

"No clue," Theo replied, but then something occurred to him. "Why would she write 'that baby'? Is she referencing having had a baby, or is she referencing someone else's baby?"

"Good question," Detective Farest replied. "I'm having our medical examiner determine if Alexis has been pregnant in the past. We didn't find anything in her apartment to suggest that a baby was living there, ever."

Then it came to Theo in a flash.

"Wait. Could she be referencing Jackie's baby that was abducted a couple of weeks ago?"

"Oh my God, that woman's baby who was abducted from the park in Nora and returned two days later. How did I not think about that?" Detective Farest asked rhetorically, feeling suddenly like an idiot.

"Yes, that baby," Theo confirmed.

"That's a good theory, but I guess until I get all of the lab's results, I still don't have any evidence yet to confirm it. But wait, how did you know about Jackie and the abduction?"

"Jackie has been working with us on our case against AlzCura. She told us about her baby being abducted and returned."

"OK, but I'm still confused. Why would you be working with her on your case against AlzCura?"

"Jackie used to work for AlzCura as their pharmaceutical representative here in Maine. Margo, or Alexis as we now know, was employed as her interim replacement during her maternity leave. Jackie thinks that AlzCura was behind her baby's abduction as well as a break-in at her house."

"OK, now the puzzle pieces are starting to come together. I didn't know that Jackie had worked at AlzCura."

"We wouldn't have known about her if it wasn't for a guy whose wife was murdered last year. We think her murderer may have been driven to his actions after receiving AlzCura's Recallamin vaccine."

"Do you mean that big murder case where the murderer torched that home and subsequently died in that psych hospital?" Detective Farest asked, recalling all the media attention the horrific case had received and reported even in the Buffalo area.

"Yes, the Darius Scott case. Curt Barnes is the guy we're working with, and he actually introduced us to Jackie."

"Wait, now I'm really confused again. How did he and Jackie connect?"

"You know, I really don't know that, but what I do know is that they have a vested interest in seeing justice served. Jackie's husband died after receiving the Recallmin vaccine. He died of liver failure and a brain aneurysm, which is the same way 19 patients here in Maine died after receiving the vaccine. We're meeting with two doctors from the FDA next week. In addition to the deaths, there is evidence that some adverse events from the vaccine may have gone unreported. We also believe AlzCura may be falsifying test results to hide adverse events."

"So this could be much bigger in terms of adverse impact. The vaccine is being used across the United States, right?"

"Actually, I think they distribute outside the U.S. as well. So yes, this could be huge in terms of the number of lives affected. Have you determined who Asa is and what he may have done to earn Alexis' wrath?" Theo asked, shifting gears to the last unexplained portion of the note.

"I believe so. When I found Cheryl Baker on the AlzCura website, I also found Dr. Asa Sheridan, who is the President and CEO of the company. I haven't interviewed him yet, but it's highly likely he's the one she's referencing."

"Did you find any other evidence in her apartment?"

"Our CSI team dusted for prints in her apartment and car, but I haven't received those results back yet. She did have welts all over her back when we found her. Our medical examiner thinks that they were likely part of sex play a day or two before her suicide."

"OK. Let me know when you get the print results back. We have two sets of unidentified prints from Dr. Caron's office. I entered the prints into the Unsolved Latent File in IAFIS, so your lab should be able to detect any matches. One set of those prints have been found at two other crime scenes here. I'd like to be able to find the owners of those prints."

"I bet you would," Detective Farest said emphatically. "I will let you know as soon as I hear back. As a matter of fact, I'll check with them after our call. Our Forensic Lab is great, but they aren't always quick about releasing results."

"I hear ya. Our Forensics Lab is the same way," Theo replied, recalling his frustrating interaction trying to squeeze information out of Lab Analyst Evan Mercer.

"I guess I'm wondering how to best proceed given your investigation and meeting with the FDA," Detective Farest pondered.

"I want to follow up on why Cheryl Baker would hide her employment with AlzCura. I also need to understand Dr. Asa Sheridan's role in all this. Alexis' death is looking like an actual suicide. So the only concerns I have now are what AlzCura may be hiding, which is likely related to the crimes you're investigating. I don't want to step on your toes or tip AlzCura off prematurely if you guys have a bigger plan."

"I appreciate that, Brent. I know our AG is exploring the possibility of also getting the FBI involved, so if you could hold off on interviewing them, that would be good. I will know more after I brief my boss and the AG on our chat."

"As long as the autopsy and fingerprint evidence doesn't raise any concerns about a potential crime, I can sit on my follow-up for a while. Good working with you. I'll let you know when I have the print evidence."

"Thanks, Brent. It's good working with you too."

Theo felt encouraged by the call and was happy to finally solve the mystery of Margo. Alexis's suicide and suicide note probably told him more than he would have gleaned from interviewing her. Now he just hoped that the fingerprint evidence would produce some additional answers.

Fifteen minutes later, he received a text from Detective Farest.

"No print evidence yet. They say tomorrow. Sorry."

"Thanks," Theo texted back while muttering, "Hurry up and wait" under his breath, frustrated that the old saying about the wheels of justice turning slowly now felt like an understatement.

As Theo was about to head out the door, he received a call

from Dr. Preston Slack.

"Hello, Inspector Adams. I wanted to get back to you about the patients I had retested at an independent lab."

Theo had almost forgotten about this potential source of additional evidence that he had unearthed during his visits to Dr. Slack and Dr. Mason's offices. In Dr. Slack's case, he had 6 patients with elevated AST and ALT levels in their liver function tests. AlzCura had claimed that 4 of the 6 patients were erroneously elevated due to a glitch in their lab system that inadvertently doubled the actual values. Both Dr. Slack and Dr. Mason had agreed to have their patients retested through an independent lab to confirm the corrected levels that AlzCura had supplied.

"Hello, Dr. Slack. Good to hear from you."

"Well, I'm afraid I have concerning information to share with you. AlzCura's corrected values on my four patients are a bunch of hooey. Three of the four had lab values that were comparable to AlzCura's original values."

"So, they're trying to hide the unfavorable values."

"Yes, and while this concerns me, another one of my patients was found to have nearly double the liver function test values as initially reported by AlzCura. When I called the patient to see how he was doing, I reached his wife. She had just returned home from the hospital. Not only is her husband now on a ventilator and not expected to live, but before he was hospitalized, he inexplicably beat his wife senseless. The husband and wife were transported to the hospital in separate ambulances yesterday morning. She was discharged today, and while her face is badly bruised and she has a couple of broken ribs, she'll be alright."

"That's awful," Inspector Adams intoned.

"That's not only awful, but it's also criminal. Now I don't know what results I can trust from AlzCura's lab. What I'm concerned about is how many more of my patients may be headed down the same path. You need to call Dr. Mason. She has similar concerns. I have half a mind to call the FDA and FBI myself."

"I can appreciate your anger and concern, Dr. Slack, but before you make those calls, would you consider joining us when we meet with the FDA representatives?"

"Who's us, and when is the meeting?" Dr. Slack asked bluntly.

"I'm sorry. Attorney General Talcott, District Attorney Wydman, and I are scheduled to meet with two physicians from the FDA's Center for Biologics Evaluation and Research next Friday. I can't imagine they wouldn't want you there since the entire meeting is about unreported adverse event reports."

"I can see how that might be more effective than my making kneejerk phone calls. I'm so angry right now. I just felt I needed to do something. Please, ask your superiors and see if I may join your meeting. In the meantime, I can determine if there are any more Recallamin patients of mine that are in danger. I plan on retesting every one of them."

"I will let you know about the meeting. I will also take your advice and call Dr. Mason. Perhaps she will want to join us too."

"I should think she will. When I spoke to her earlier today, she was pretty exercised."

"Thanks for the call, Dr. Slack. This information may give us sufficient evidence to finally bring charges against AlzCura."

"I hope so. People are dying because of their greed and fraudulent practices. It's unconscionable."

Theo, concerned that Dr. Mason may also be thinking of calling the FDA and FBI, wasted no time in calling her as Dr. Slack had recommended.

"Dr. Mason, I'm glad I was able to reach you. I just spoke

with Dr. Slack about his retesting results, and he mentioned you have similar concerns. Do you have time to talk to me now?"

"I was just about to pick up the phone and call you, so impeccable timing on your part. Yes, I can definitely talk now. I, like Preston, found that the letter AlzCura's Lab Medical Director sent me with the so-called corrected values was not correct at all. All three of my patients had liver function test results from the independent lab comparable to the initial values reported by AlzCura, not the corrected ones."

"Have any of the three had any adverse symptoms or been hospitalized?"

"One of them is in the hospital and doing alright. I certainly don't have any cases resembling the case Preston told me about this morning. That's frightening, and believe me, I'm retesting all of my Recallamin patients as Preston is."

"I can't say I blame you," Theo replied. "I am wondering if you'd like to join Dr. Slack when AG Talcott, DA Wydman, and I meet with two physicians from the FDA's Center for Biologics Evaluation and Research?"

"I'd be happy to. When is it?"

"Next Friday morning. Once I confirm with my boss that it's OK to invite you, I can send you the specifics of the meeting."

"Sounds good."

"You haven't by any chance called the FDA or FBI about this, have you?"

"No," Dr. Mason laughed. "I know Preston was pretty hot about calling them. But as concerning as falsifying lab values on three of my patients may be, I only intended to call you."

"OK, thanks. I just think it will be more productive if we present our evidence together when we meet with the FDA representatives."

"I agree. Thanks for calling Inspector Adams. I look forward to hearing more about the meeting."

Between the information he obtained from Detective Farest and the two physicians from Portland, Theo felt their case against AlzCura gaining momentum. The tipping point could definitely be reached at the meeting with the FDA. Anxious to share the information he had gleaned, Theo called DA Wydman, who summarily approved inviting Dr. Slack and Dr. Mason to their meeting with the FDA. The wheels were in motion, and the train was heading down the track and picking up speed.

CHAPTER 19

The last thing Cheryl Baker expected or wanted to be doing was making arrangements for her daughter's funeral. But she had no choice. She had no one that could help her. Certainly not Asa after the lack of compassion he had shown. Nor her sons, who had trouble enough just managing their own lives. And never mind her ex-husband, who she was convinced contributed disproportionately to her twin son's Neanderthalic genetic makeup. Reluctantly, she fired up her computer to search for a mortuary.

The first shock in Cheryl's series of surprises about the process of arranging a funeral was the star ratings next to each mortuary on the list. It just struck her as vulgar, like burying a loved one was akin to finding the best burger in town. Nevertheless, she found herself filtering out the mortuaries with less than 5 stars and then chose the Grace and Mercy Funeral Home, which had the highest volume of excellent ratings. She wasn't enthused about their overdone holier than thou name but called them anyway.

A gentleman with a calm, syrupy sweet voice answered the phone. "Good morning, Grace and Mercy Funeral Home. This is Richard Grace. How may I help you?"

It was all too real, and Cheryl's resolve to get this done melted away into despair. All that Richard Grace heard over the phone was a grieving woman sobbing.

"I'm so sorry for your loss," he interjected, pausing to allow her to cry a bit more before offering another supportive comment. "I understand how hard this is."

When Cheryl just continued to cry, he continued his telephonic grief counseling. "My wife Mercy and I are here to help you through this."

Somehow the sudden realization that the funeral home's name was derived from the names of its proprietors and not some sappy attempt to pander to religious zealots struck Cheryl as funny. Momentarily stopping her sobs.

"Really?" she managed to blurt out.

"Yes, we're here to help you," he repeated.

"No, I mean, your names are Grace & Mercy?"

"Ah, yes. My last name and my wife's first name," he replied, not expecting that their names would be the intervention that would turn off the caller's waterworks. "May I have your name, ma'am?"

"I'm sorry, I didn't expect to fall apart like that. My name is Cheryl Baker. My daughter," she paused, unable to find the words.

"Your daughter has passed?" Richard offered.

"Yes. I need to," Cheryl paused again. "I'm sorry. I wasn't prepared for this, and I don't even know what to do or ask."

"I understand. I can help you through the process. Maybe you would find it easier if you came in and met with us?"

"Oh, I'd rather not."

"OK. Then let's start with your daughter's name."

"Her name is Alexis," she replied.

"And what type of arrangements do you want to make for Alexis? Burial or crema,"

"Burial," she uttered before he could even finish his last word, which made her shudder just thinking about it.

"Do you already have a cemetery and plot picked out?"

"No," she replied once again, losing her resolve and wishing there was an easier way. "I'm sorry, I really can't deal with all these questions," she began to cry. "Do you offer anything where I don't have to make all these decisions? I just want my daughter to be in a nice place."

"Yes, we do offer a comprehensive package of services, but I will need a couple of pieces of information if you want us to manage all the details."

After Cheryl answered his questions and made financial arrangements, she hung up, relieved not to talk about it anymore. This didn't prevent the torture of the thoughts that kept seeping into her consciousness over the next few days before Alexis' burial. That and expecting her to fly to Bangor the day after the funeral weighed like a millstone around her neck. The only comfort she could find in the days preceding the funeral was in the bottles of whiskey she drank. And only then, when she had consumed enough to pass out, wake up, and do it all over again. She could not reconcile the loss of her daughter except to blame herself, causing her already unhealthy drinking habit to exacerbate.

The afternoon of Alexis' funeral arrived, and Cheryl, weak, wan, and wobbly from a 3-day liquid diet, didn't have the will to attend. Had she not arranged to have Asa drive her to the cemetery, she wouldn't have made it. They were a mile into their trip when she vomited. The acidic phlegm burned her throat and sinuses, creating a stench that even open windows couldn't purge.

As they entered Grace & Mercy Memory Gardens Cemetery, Cheryl was unprepared and not in any shape to appreciate the splendor of the arrangements. Alexis' burial plot was under a large sycamore tree shading an ornate antique white casket adorned in a blanket of white roses and lavender blooms. Since she had declined any type of graveside service and only invited family. Cheryl and Asa were joined by her twin sons, Anthony and Andrew, and her ex-husband. Asa was dressed in an expensive black suit while Cheryl donned a black mourning dress, now slightly stained from vomitus. To Cheryl's disgust, her sons and ex-husband wore jeans and t-shirts that looked like they had just gotten up off the couch from munching on chips and drinking beer while watching a football game. Without a minister to facilitate a solemn ceremony, the ragtag group stood in uncomfortable silence until Anthony spoke up.

"Aren't we supposed to say something?"

For a long time, no one responded. Asa broke the silence.

"What would you like to say, Anthony?"

Before Anthony could respond, Cheryl spoke up.

"Oh, no. We're not going to do this and spoil my baby's funeral. There is nothing anyone of you can say that will do her justice. Let's just be quiet, and you can think whatever thoughts you want."

"She was my baby too," her ex-husband replied.

Cheryl didn't even speak but instead shot him a glance that communicated that if he dared to say one more word, she'd bury him there too.

Cheryl's ex-husband and sons left shortly after that, leaving only Asa and Cheryl graveside. A yellow butterfly flitted around, landing first on one of the roses, then was aloft again landing on Cheryl's shoulder. When the butterfly finally left Cheryl's shoulder, the symbolism of what had just occurred made Cheryl fall to her knees and wail for her daughter not to leave her. She was inconsolable, and the demonstration of her grief lasted longer than Asa could bear. Leaving her graveside, he walked to his car, removed a flask from his inside jacket pocket, took a sip, and waited while Cheryl made her peace.

When she returned, he hugged her, handed her the flask, and told her she didn't need to go to Bangor in the morning.

"Come back to work when you're ready," he said.

"But what about Bangor?'

"We don't need Bangor. If we place a physician in Portland and open up the Recallamin 3 trial in other regions, the Board will be too busy lining their pockets to worry about the Northeast Region."

"Thank you, Asa. I miss her, and I feel like it's all my fault."

"Nonsense. She loved you. If anything, I blame myself."

"Why?"

"I think my decision to send her to Maine to speak with the police pushed her over the edge."

"I can't believe that. If she weren't comfortable with that idea, she would have told me."

"I guess we'll never know. Let me take you home," Asa concluded, uncharacteristically opening the passenger side door for her.

They drove home in silence. Each was waging their own internal battles with what they may have done or not done to contribute to Alexis' decision to commit suicide. Little did they know about the suicide note that Detective Farest was holding in evidence. Nor the findings he was about to receive from the Forensic lab, which would greatly intensify the spotlight on them and AlzCura.

CHAPTER 20

Inspector Adams' revelation about the baby reference in the suicide note was just what he needed to compel the Forensics Lab to prioritize the fingerprint evidence they were sitting on. The lab had missed its promised delivery date for the results, and Detective Farest almost blew a gasket, save for the Lab Medical Director's quick intervention. When the Detective informed the Medical Director that the evidence could contribute to solving an open child abduction case, priorities in the lab were quickly realigned.

"Hi, Detective Farest. This is Constance from the Forensics Lab. I have our preliminary findings from the fingerprint and hair follicle analysis."

"Wait, what? Hair follicle evidence?"

"Yes, we received three sets of prints and four hair samples that were found in the car of the deceased. As well as four sets of prints and four hair samples found in the apartment."

"OK. I wasn't aware of that, but proceed."

"As could be expected, one set of prints and a hair follicle sample matched the deceased in both the car and the apartment. But that's the only expected finding."

"What do you mean?"

"Interestingly, one of the hair follicle samples appears to be that of an infant found in both the car and the apartment. Yet, the report from CSI's investigation of the apartment did not turn up anything you would commonly find in a home with a baby. One set of fingerprints in the apartment are likely the baby's prints."

"Why only likely?"

"Without a comparison sample of DNA or fingerprint, I can't rule out that one baby contributed the hair while another baby contributed the prints. It's unlikely but possible."

"What else did you find."

"We found prints in the apartment belonging to Asa Sheridan and Cheryl Baker. Their prints are in IAFIS due to their employment with AlzCura Pharmaceuticals, and neither have criminal records."

"Cheryl Baker is the deceased's mother," Detective Farest added, which didn't generate a response from Constance, who was content to continue her report.

"We found three sets of prints in the car that matched prints in the ULF."

"The ULF?"

"The Unsolved Latent File in IAFIS," Constance clarified. "The deceased's prints match a case involving a suspicious suicide in Maine. Another set of prints matches an unsolved break-in in Nora, NY. The third set of prints match unsolved crimes in Maine, the suicide, a threatening note left after a failed abduction, and a murder case. Unfortunately, and amazingly if you ask me, these two individuals don't have criminal records, so we still cannot identify them. They were obviously known to the deceased."

That's very helpful, Constance. Is there anything else?"

"We still need to validate our preliminary findings and put together our official report. I don't anticipate any changes, but there's always a chance."

"I understand and appreciate that. Thank you for your

work on this, Constance."

"You're most welcome, Detective Farest. Let me know if you have any questions when you receive the official report."

"I will, thanks."

No sooner than Detective Farest hung up when Medical Examiner Dr. Twyla Potter appeared at his office door.

"Have a minute or two?" she asked.

"For you, I have all the time in the world," he said sarcastically.

"Well, aren't you sweet and full of shit?" she countered.

"What ya got for me?"

"Hopefully, answers to all your questions," as she entered his office and sat down in the chair across from him. "First, she never had a baby."

"Good. That supports my theory."

"Not that it's any of my business, but what's your theory?"

"Well, it's not my theory, really. I'm working with a detective in Maine who suggested Alexis may have been the woman who abducted that baby a couple of weeks ago."

"OK, interesting, but I'm not even going to ask why a detective in Maine would know that."

"Good idea. It's a long story."

"I'll go on then. As for the rest of the autopsy results, no findings suggestive of someone assisting her suicide. No drugs. No injuries or signs of force except for the welts, which I will get to in a minute. As I noted before, she died from asphyxiation by hanging. Her neck wasn't broken, so it probably took about 5 minutes before she died. She lost about a liter of blood from her lacerations, which in the grander scheme of things was of no real consequence except to make for a more sensational crime scene. The media is having a heyday with that, aren't they?" she asked rhetorically.

"What about the welts?"

"I stand by what I told you the other day. The welts occurred 1-2 days before her suicide. There was also evidence of semen in her anal canal consistent with coitus corresponding to the time she received the welts. Rough sex play, not coincident with her suicide."

"OK. Anything else?"

"Nope. That's all I've got. You'll get all the gory details in my report, of course."

"Thanks, Doc."

"My pleasure."

As the Medical Examiner exited, Detective Farest couldn't believe how things were finally coming together. Capitalizing on the barrage of information he had just received from the Forensic Lab and Medical Examiner, he picked up his phone to call Inspector Theo Adams.

"Theo, we received a match on your unidentified fingerprints," Detective Farest stated after the two had traded greetings.

"Good to hear, Brent. What did you find?"

"One set from your suicide case was Alexis' prints - your Margo. And we found a set of prints in her car that match the prints you found in all three cases you listed in the Unsolved Latent File. We don't know who the prints belong to, but we can definitely say that they were known to Alexis."

"OK, well, that gets us down the road a bit."

"Oh, that's not all, my friend. We have fingerprints and hair follicles that may help us confirm that the baby referenced in her suicide note is Jackie's baby, as you suggested."

"Really?"

"Yep. And there's more. One of the prints found in the car match prints found at Jackie's house after the break-in.

"That's great. Very promising."

"Yes, it is. Now let's discuss how I should proceed. I know you said to hold off on my investigation until after you met with the FDA. I think I should at least get Jackie's permission to obtain a fingerprint and follicle sample from her baby. If we can confirm Alexis was involved in the kidnapping, we have cause to investigate whether she had any accomplices. It could lead us to one or both of the individuals we haven't been able to identify."

"I agree. I'll call Jackie and tell her to expect a call from you."

"That would be good. And since you have her contact info, can you send it to me?"

"Sure."

"What about our two remaining mystery prints? If Alexis knew them, perhaps her mother knows of them as well," Detective Farest posited.

"Or her mother may have hired them. From what little I know of Alexis, she didn't sound like the type of person who would organize all this chaos. And what motive would she have had on her own? AlzCura has its reputation and profits to protect. Now they have a motive."

"Good point. Do you think Cheryl Baker might have other kids or family members that are working for the business, so to speak? It's easier to control people when you keep it in the family."

"Hmm, that's an interesting thought. See what you can uncover without alerting her."

"Will do."

"Whoever our two mystery people are, they weren't very meticulous. I can't believe that their luck avoiding the law can continue much longer."

"Yeah, but maybe they're related to a highly-placed executive of a big, profitable pharmaceutical, who can afford to give them cover that your everyday criminal doesn't enjoy. For all we know, they may have had brushes with the law but also the legal firepower to avoid prosecution."

"You may be right. Hey, one more thing," Theo said, suddenly remembering another facet of the potential action against AlzCura of which Detective Farest was not aware.

"What's that?"

"There's an attorney here that is working with a woman named Celeste Boulanger. He is working with her on a lawsuit against AlzCura. Her husband died after being given the Recallamin vaccine. Someone subsequently broke into her home and decapitated her dog, killed a TV reporter, and sexually assaulted her. In that order, mind you."

"What a sick fuck. Pardon my French," Detective Farest exclaimed.

"No offense taken. Those are my sentiments exactly. The reason I tell you this is that I expect the lawsuit to be filed in the next two to three weeks. AlzCura will use its legal resources to make every step of the way in our investigations hard. Once they receive that shot over their bow, it will only get more complicated."

"We need to proceed without tipping AlzCura off and allowing them to shore up their defenses, go underground, and destroy evidence before the cavalry arrives."

"I knew you'd understand. Frankly, I would like to see the Feds storm the place, take the principal executives into custody, and confiscate all the evidence. But I'm not going to hold my breath. The words federal government and quick are not commonly associated with one another."

"Tell me about it. Not that I can brag that my employer is always as swift as I would like."

"Yes, perhaps I shouldn't be casting stones. One of Maine's

mottos is 'life in the slow lane,' after all. Used to even have it on a sign after you cross the Piscataqua River Bridge when you enter Maine.

"You're joking?"

"I'm as serious as a heart attack. They took the sign down a while back, but it's no less true, I'm afraid."

"Then I guess we better get down to business," Detective Farest concluded.

"Let's. Thanks for the update, Brent."

After their conversation, the two detectives briefed their superiors and gained support for the follow-up actions they had discussed. Their investigations were at a critical juncture. Success in bringing the pharmaceutical giant to justice would depend not just on the evidence they were accumulating but clear communication and coordinated actions. Not something considered a forte for separate and distinct law enforcement agencies.

CHAPTER 21

Jackie, Ashley, and Barrett were just driving out of the airport parking lot after seeing Sunny off when Jackie's phone announced Inspector Adams was calling.

"Hi, Jackie. I hope I didn't catch you at a bad time."

"Not at all, Theo. I just dropped a friend off at the airport and am headed home."

"OK. I just wanted to call and tell you to expect a call from Detective Brent Farest of the Buffalo PD. He may have found the person who abducted your baby."

"Really?"

"Yes, but to confirm the evidence, he is going to need Ashley's fingerprints and a sample of her hair."

"OK. That won't be a problem. Did he say who it was?"

"Maybe I shouldn't tell you if you're driving."

"I'm not. I'm a passenger. Why?"

"Remember Margo?"

"You're kidding. Margo, who took over for me at AlzCura?"

"Yes, but Margo is an alias. Her real name is Alexis Baker. The young woman committed suicide in Buffalo just a few days ago. You may have heard about it?" he asked.

Jackie was happy that Theo had confirmed she was not

driving because she was absolutely stunned. "I'm afraid I haven't been watching or listening to the news. I hadn't heard a thing about her suicide," prompting Barrett to look over, recognizing now what she was talking about.

"She was the daughter of Cheryl Baker. Wasn't Cheryl your boss at AlzCura?"

Jackie could hardly breathe, let alone form words in response. She had always suspected AlzCura was behind the break-in, the spray-painted threat, the surveillance equipment, the abduction. Knowing she could possibly confirm that fact somehow made it more real, more frightening.

"Jackie? Are you there?" Theo asked when he didn't get a reply.

"Yes, yes, I'm here, Theo. Sorry, I just blanked out there for a second. I can't believe it. This is a lot to take in."

"Well, before you get all worked up, talk with Detective Farest, and he can arrange to collect the prints and hair from Ashley."

Jackie quickly transitioned from mortified silence to wanting to know the truth immediately. Finding her voice, she made a proposal.

"You know, Theo. I'm in the car with Ashley and Officer Barrett Todd from the Nora PD. Could he collect the prints and hair? Or since we're in Buffalo, could we stop in to see Detective Farest and get it done now? I'd rather get this done sooner rather than later."

"Let me do this. I will text you Brent's number, and you can call him. I'm sure he's just as anxious as you to find out."

"Thanks, Theo."

"You're welcome, Jackie."

Disconnecting from the call, and before she received Theo's text message, Barrett chimed in.

"Were you talking about that young woman who committed suicide that has been all over the news?"

"Yes, but apparently, I have been living in a cave. I never heard about it. Turns out, she may have been the one who abducted Ashley, and she's the daughter of my former boss at AlzCura."

"No shit," Barrett exclaimed but then quickly caught himself. "Oops, I'm sorry. I forgot the baby was in the back."

"I'll forgive you if you do me a huge favor."

"Collect Ashley's fingerprints and a hair sample?"

She looked at him, momentarily stunned, "How?" she paused but then realized how he knew. "Right. I did say that out loud, didn't I? For a second there, I thought you had magical powers."

"Well, I am a cop," he said with false bravado. Making Jackie laugh.

Her phone pinged, signaling an incoming text from Theo.

"I have to call a Detective Farest and see if he wants me to come in with Ashley. Is that OK?"

"Of course," Barrett replied. "I knew you were going to ask that," placing his fingertips to the side of his head as if he was receiving telepathic messages. "I am Oz, the great and powerful," imitating the Wizard from the Wizard of Oz, causing Jackie to chuckle again.

"OK, thanks, oh great and powerful one," she replied with a smile while pressing the hyperlinked phone number in Theo's text to initiate her call.

"Detective Farest, Buffalo Police Department," he answered.

"Detective, this is Jackie Deno. I just spoke with Inspector Theo Adams. He gave me your number. I hope I'm not catching you at a bad time."

"Ms. Deno, thanks for calling. No, I'm happy to hear from you. Did Theo tell you why I'm interested in speaking with you and seeing your daughter?"

"He did, thank you. I just happened to be in town with Ashley and was wondering if you would like us to come in now."

"Yes, that would be terrific. Do you know where our office is located?"

"I don't, but I'm actually with a friend who is a police officer," she said, looking over to Barrett. "I imagine he might know where your office is located," Barrett nodded affirmatively. "OK, he knows how to get there."

"Great. I will meet you in the lobby. How long do you estimate it will take you to get here?"

"Hold on," Jackie replied, looking once more at Barrett. "He wants to know how long before we get there."

"Fifteen minutes," Barrett replied.

"Did you hear that?" Jackie asked, and Detective Farest confirmed.

"I'll see you soon then," Detective Farest said, ending the call.

Detective Farest couldn't believe how everything was falling into place. It's not every day that the Forensics Lab, the Medical Examiner, and a key person of interest just show up at your door in coordinated succession. He called to arrange for a CSI agent to come to his office and then left his office to meet Jackie, Ashley, and Officer Todd in the lobby.

"You must be Jackie," Detective Farest said as the trio entered the lobby.

"I am. And this is Ashley," who looked at the Detective warily from her mother's arms.

"Hi, Ashley," he replied in an enthusiastic tone, which did nothing to change Ashley's timidity.

"Hi Detective, I'm Officer Barrett Todd, Nora PD," shaking the Detective's hand.

"Well, thank you for coming in," he replied, leading them through a security checkpoint on their way to his office.

"So, how did you and Theo connect?" Jackie asked as they entered the elevator.

"I wish I could tell you. Let's just say that a case I'm working on led me to learn about Theo, and we discovered we have a mutual interest in working together."

"I understand," Jackie replied. "I keep forgetting you're not able to talk about active investigations."

"That's alright, there is plenty we can talk about when we get to my office. With your permission, I'm having someone come to my office to collect a hair sample and take fingerprints from Ashley."

"You have my permission," Jackie replied.

"Great. I'll have you sign a consent form when we get to the office. How do you two know each other?" he asked Jackie and Officer Todd.

"Oh, Barrett has been my savior on several occasions. I'm afraid I've been the target of someone's wrath since leaving AlzCura, and each time Barrett has been there."

"I was one of the officers that responded when Jackie's house was broken into and when Ashley was abducted," Barrett added.

"Well, I'm sorry you've had to go through so much misery, but I'm glad Officer Todd was able to help and that you got Ashley back. What a blessing."

"Thank you," she replied as they filed into Detective Farest's office and took seats around a small table.

Detective Farest outlined the plan for their visit. After some paperwork, a CSI agent arrived equipped to take Ashley's fingerprints and a hair sample. Ashley was not enthused about this and clung desperately to her mother, making fingerprinting her near impossible. Jackie had the brilliant idea of making Ashley believe they were trying to engage her in a new activity - finger painting. Before long, Ashley had left a collage of fingerprints on a sheet of paper which the agent decided would have to suffice. Collecting the hair sample was much more manageable, as the agent quickly yanked out a couple of strands from the back of Ashley's scalp as Jackie distracted her.

"So, how long will it be until we know if these match the fingerprints and hair found at Margo's apartment?" Jackie asked as the agent was about to leave.

"You mean Alexis' apartment."

"Right, sorry, I knew her as Margo."

"I'll ask the lab to expedite this. Hopefully, by the end of the day, I will be able to tell you."

"That would be great. I've had nothing but questions. It would be good to have some answers."

"I imagine it would. Speaking of questions, can we transition to some questions I have for you concerning Alexis, Cheryl, and others at AlzCura?"

"Sure," Jackie replied.

"Are you comfortable having Officer Todd here with you? If not, I can interview him separately."

"No, he can stay here."

Detective Farest proceeded to ask Jackie about how she first came to know Alexis and what she knew about how she performed her job.

"I don't know of any specifics about what she did while covering for me. All I know is that when I returned from maternity leave, my clients were pleased I was back. They didn't tell me why they didn't like her. They just told me she wasn't very helpful."

"When was the last time you saw Alexis, and what was her state of mind at the time?"

"I last saw her six months ago when I returned from maternity leave. It was only a brief meeting. She was supposed to update me on my clients – a kind of hand-off to let me know about any issues I needed to follow up on with the practices in my region. She really didn't have much to say. She seemed fine emotionally."

"And you haven't seen her since?"

"No. I didn't expect to. Cheryl told me she was a temp. I thought maybe she was either from a temporary agency or perhaps from one of AlzCura's other regions."

"Did you know that Alexis was Cheryl's daughter?"

"No, I didn't know that. Cheryl never told me."

"Do you know if Cheryl has any other children?"

"No, she never really talked about her life outside of work. Nor did I ever ask. We didn't seem to have that kind of relationship."

"Tell me about Dr. Asa Sheridan. What was your relationship with him like?"

"Other than the internship I did for him when I was in college, I didn't have a lot of contact with him when I worked as a pharmaceutical rep. During my internship, he was kind but demanding. He didn't seem to deal with stress very well. While he never got angry with me, I saw him get furious with others. It wasn't pretty."

"Did you know if Dr. Sheridan knew Alexis?"

"No, but I think Cheryl probably would have told him she was covering for me."

"So, there weren't any rumors floating around about Dr. Sheridan and Alexis?"

"No, but there were plenty of rumors about Dr. Sheridan

and Cheryl. Many people thought Cheryl slept her way to her position at AlzCura. I never saw evidence of it, but many people were convinced they had a thing going on."

"Before you left AlzCura, were you aware of any illegal or fraudulent practices the company may have been involved in?

"I wasn't until near the end of my time with AlzCura. Dr. Steven Caron, who was AlzCura's Regional Investigator in Central Maine, told me about the company hiding patient deaths and adverse event data. They also participated in some questionable financial and marketing practices. Unfortunately, he committed suicide before we could learn specifics."

"We?"

"I'm sorry, Dr. Caron met with me, Curt Barnes, and Maine District Attorney Wydman one evening. That's when we learned about the concerns about AlzCura and agreed to work together to expose the truth. Curt Barnes is," Jackie began but was interrupted by Detective Farest.

"I'm sorry to interrupt you, Jackie, but you don't have to explain any further. Inspector Adams told me about Mr. Barnes and the work the two of you are doing with Maine law enforcement."

"Oh, OK."

"Can we shift gears to the break-in that occurred at your house?"

"Yes, that was the night I first met Barrett," she began nodding towards him. "If catching me as I fainted can be called a meeting! Maybe Barrett would be better able to describe what they found after the break-in."

"I'd be happy to," Barrett replied. "My partner and I were called to the scene and found the perp had entered through the back door. The contents of the house were tossed, but the following day Jackie confirmed that nothing was missing. The perp did spray paint "Goodbye baby" on a wall in Ashley's room. We dusted for prints and found one set we couldn't identify through IAFIS. I entered it into the Unsolved Latent File," as Barrett paused, Jackie picked up.

"I'm afraid I wasn't very helpful the day Barrett and I went through the house. When I saw that spray-painted message, all I could think of was that someone from AlzCura had done it. They broke in when I was in Maine to meet with Dr. Caron, Curt, and DA Wydman. I was pretty sure it was a message from my former employer. I never told Barrett that, nor my parents. I'm sorry, Barrett," she said as tears brimmed her eyes.

"That's OK, Jackie. Past history," he said, reaching over and squeezing her hand to console her. Propped up by his gesture, she continued.

"I called a security company shortly after that to assess my house for a security system, and that is when we found out that whoever broke in had installed a surveillance system to spy on me."

"The perp had installed a Network Video Recording system with hidden cameras," Barrett added. "We obviously missed this on our sweep of the house after the break-in. Now it's my turn to apologize, Jackie. If we had done our job, we would have found this before they had a chance to spy on you."

Barrett's admission surprised Jackie, but she could not hold it against him, given all the times he had rescued her.

"I guess it's my turn to say past history, and it's OK," she replied, reaching out her hand to grasp his.

"So, who do you think at AlzCura is behind all this?" Detective Farest asked, moving the interview along.

"Before you told me that Margo was Alexis and Alexis was Cheryl's daughter, I couldn't imagine who at AlzCura would do this. Now I'm pretty sure that Cheryl must have had something to do with it. Why else make your daughter use an alias? I could understand not divulging that Alexis was her daughter, but using an alias just makes it shady, in my opinion."

"Is there anything else you'd like me to know about Alexis, Cheryl, or anyone at AlzCura?"

"No, not that I can think of. I'm glad you're working with Theo. It has been a difficult time since leaving AlzCura."

"I can't imagine, Jackie. Thank you so much for calling me. This has been very helpful," he concluded while pushing his business card towards her. "Hopefully, I will be calling you later today regarding the fingerprints and hair sample, but this is for you. Call me anytime as you need."

"Thanks, Detective Farest."

"My pleasure, Jackie."

With that, Jackie, Ashley, and Barrett made their exit and drove back to Nora. Along the way, Jackie and Barrett talked more about Sunny than about the meeting they had just had with Detective Farest. When Jackie arrived home, she put Ashley down for her nap, fixed herself a cup of coffee, and took her favorite place on her living room sofa. Despite being in the comfort of her own home, the knowledge that Cheryl Baker may be the mastermind behind all the chaos she had endured was discomforting. Alexis was gone, but Cheryl was still out there. Jackie realized she had not followed up with Jerry from the Security company about installing a security system. She rummaged through her desk and found the assessment and recommendations he had sent her, and made the call.

CHAPTER 22

Attorney General Talcott greeted DA Wydman and Inspector Adams as they entered his office in advance of their anticipated meeting with Dr. Harder and Dr. Shearlow.

"Welcome, gentlemen. I had hoped to have Drs. Slack and Mason call in for this meeting, but both are tied up with patients. I'm not too worried about their part in the meeting, so we'll proceed without them. I'm anxious to share some information with you. I know you probably have information from your collaboration with Detective Farest in Buffalo, Theo. Why don't you begin."

"Thanks. Well, first of all, I confirmed that our Margo was Alexis Baker's alias while at AlzCura. They also found fingerprints in Alexis' car. They match the unidentified fingerprints we found in Dr. Caron's office, on the note left on Curt's door, and in Celeste Boulanger's trailer. One set of prints in Dr. Caron's office was Alexis' prints."

"So presumably, Alexis knew the perpetrator?"

"Yes, but we still can't identify the perp. Since Cheryl Baker employed her daughter, Detective Farest is working on determining if Cheryl Baker has other family members who may have been involved. He is also trying to confirm that Alexis may have been the woman involved in the abduction of Jackie's baby."

"Wow, how did he discover that?"

"Well, actually, I suggested the possibility. Alexis left a suicide note that mentioned not being able to care for a baby. I thought the wording sounded odd, like it wasn't her baby she was trying to take care of. He's in the process of obtaining Ashley's fingerprints and a hair sample to see if my theory holds water."

"Good work. I knew putting you two together would pay off," AG Talcott said. "Any chance he will have the findings before our meeting tomorrow?"

"I'm not sure, but he knows I'm waiting and that we have a meeting with the FDA, so he will call me as soon as he knows."

Anything else?"

"Just that Cheryl Baker apparently tried to hide the fact that she worked at AlzCura. When Detective Farest asked her where she worked, she claimed to be a day trader. She also said Alexis worked for an Italian clothing company."

"Nothing like making yourself look guilty," DA Wydman remarked.

"Nice work. That should help us convince the Feds that AlzCura is dirty," AG Talcott added. "I spoke to a friend of mine. He works for the Department of Justice. He told me that legal matters concerning Departments, like the FDA, under the purview of Health and Human Services most frequently go through the Office of the Inspector General rather than directly to the FBI. So hopefully, our friends who will be visiting us tomorrow give us some assurances that they will involve the OIG."

"What if they don't give us that assurance?" DA Wydman asked, still chafed from his initial contact with Dr. Shearlow and skeptical about how much of a friend he would be in this process.

"Well, then my friend will help us escalate the issue to a

different level."

"Who is this friend of yours, if I may ask?"

"Clark Ainsley. We went to law school together."

"Deputy Attorney General Clark Ainsley?" DA Wydman asked, somewhat shocked.

"The one and only. Our classmates called us the Lewis and Clark expedition because we always seemed to be on a journey together. Mostly involving the search for the best late-night clubs to dance and party with the fairer sex. But that's a story for another time."

DA Wydman and Inspector Adams both laughed, not accustomed to the AG sharing tales from his personal life.

"OK, let's wrap it up, gentlemen. I have a meeting with the Governor. Best not be late for that," he said, causing DA Wydman and Inspector Adams to double-time it out of his office.

* * *

Detective Farest's hopes to get same-day results from the Forensic Lab to determine if Ashley was the baby referenced in Alexis' suicide note were dashed. Constance had called to tell him he wouldn't get the results until the following day. The call ended what had been one of the most productive days in his career. Despite the progress made, it still felt like the cherry was left off the ice cream sundae. He had hoped to have a definitive answer, not only for the sake of the case that was building against AlzCura but also for Jackie's peace of mind. Reluctantly, he picked up his phone to call Jackie.

"Hi, Jackie. This is Detective Farest," he greeted unenthusiastically.

"Hi, Detective," she replied, anxious about what he might say.

Jackie had time to think since their meeting earlier that day. While she had told him that she wanted answers to Ashley's abduction, she realized that regardless of the response, it would not provide the closure she sought. If Alexis had taken Ashley, then Cheryl Baker had orchestrated it, and who knew what she might be plotting next. If Alexis didn't take Ashley, then Jackie would be back to square one, wondering who had done it. In some respects, that was worse. If she couldn't confine her concern to Cheryl and AlzCura, then every stranger became a potential suspect. Everyone who looked at her or Ashley a little too long or who showed an unusual interest, or maybe just lingered in their general vicinity. That would be unnerving.

"I wish I could give you the results, Jackie. Unfortunately, our lab tells me it won't be until sometime tomorrow. I'm sorry."

"That's OK. I've waited this long. What's another day?" she sighed, somewhat relieved as she didn't feel prepared to wrestle with the emotional impact of the answer.

"I'll call you tomorrow as soon as I know something, OK?"

"OK. Thanks for calling, Detective."

"Have a good evening, Jackie," he replied, despite feeling bad about disappointing her.

Detective Farest could not end his day this way. Instead of going home, he decided to stay late and see if he could squeeze some more juice out of the day – his target, Cheryl Marie Baker. For the next two hours, Detective Farest combed through social media and people search sites hoping to learn about AlzCura's Vice President of Operations. Searching for clues as to why she felt compelled to lie about her employment.

It was an exercise in frustration, and the fruits of the first half of his day were quickly rotting from the dearth of information. He tried the same searches for Alexis Baker and Dr. Asa Sheridan with the same results - nada. Peeved, he revisited the AlzCura website to find the name of another executive to search on, wondering if all of their leaders were internet ghosts. Although he found the name of AlzCura's Chief Legal Counsel, Chet Humphreys, it was what he didn't see on the website that struck him. Cheryl Baker was no longer pictured, and he could find no references to her anywhere on the site.

There seemed to be only one explanation. Not only did Cheryl have something to hide, but AlzCura was complicit. Usually, efforts to protect personal or proprietary information would be considered prudent. The vigor of Cheryl's and AlzCura's efforts, under the circumstances, raised nothing but suspicion. Detective Farest knew if Ashley's prints came back a match to prints found in Alexis' apartment, he would need to expedite his investigation.

CHAPTER 23

Cheryl marched into Dr. Sheridan's office to find him already in conversations with Chet Humphreys.

"Well, look who's here? Welcome back!" Asa greeted Cheryl enthusiastically.

"Thanks, Asa. And thanks for not sending me to Bangor. I needed the last few days to get my act together."

"Well, you look much better than the last time I saw you."

"Welcome back, Cheryl," Chet chimed.

"Thanks, Chet."

"Sorry to jump right into it," Chet prefaced, "but did the police try to contact you while you were out?"

"No, not a peep," Cheryl replied.

"They haven't tried to contact me either," Asa exclaimed, anticipating Chet's question.

"Why would they contact you?" Cheryl asked, surprised.

Asa realized that he had not told Cheryl about being at Alexis' apartment the night before she committed suicide. Cheryl had been passed out on his office couch when he had confessed to Chet that he had a somewhat sadomasochistic session with Alexis. While Cheryl was well-acquainted with his predilections, he by no means wanted to divulge this to her on her first day back to work after burying her daughter.

"I visited her apartment the day before," Asa began. "Chet believes the police may have dusted for fingerprints, and if so, they would likely find some of mine."

Cheryl looked at Asa suspiciously. "Why didn't I know about this? And why would they dust for prints for a suicide?"

As Asa struggled to find words, Chet tried to rescue him. "We don't know that they did, Cheryl, but we'd rather be prepared than surprised."

"And do you have anything to worry about? What did you do over there?" she asked and then thought better of waiting for the answer as the look on his face told her everything. "Never mind, I don't want to hear what it was you did."

"She seemed fine, Cheryl. And nothing we did had any bearing on what she did the following day," Asa replied.

"So, no news is good news then?" Cheryl replied.

"Or the calm before the storm," Chet countered. "We can't let our guard down yet. Just to be safe, Cheryl, we took you off of the company website in case they do an internet search. We didn't want them to find you worked for us when you said you worked from home as a day trader."

"OK."

"Can we get down to the real business at hand?" Asa asked, frustrated. "Let's talk about what we can do to make sure the Board doesn't ream us all new ones at the next meeting."

"It sounded to me that you already made up your mind about that when you told me I didn't have to go to Bangor," Cheryl replied. "What's there to talk about?"

"Well, Cheryl, I haven't told Chet yet, and part of my idea will take a level of support from our regional labs that we haven't required of them before."

"OK, quit talking in code. What's your idea, Asa," Chet interjected.

"The first and easiest part of my idea is to hire a physician for the Portland market. Since Dr. Slack and Dr. Mason have elected not to prescribe Recallamin any longer, we put a physician in that market who will."

"The only problem I see with that is the Board only approved placing a physician in Central Maine, "Chet replied. "We already have Dr. Kit Carson under contract, and she's expected to start in about 6 weeks."

"I don't need the Board's approval. Sure, it would be nice. But if we get a physician who can preserve or expand the use of Recallamin in the Portland market, do you think the Board is going to care?"

"OK, what is the other part of your idea?" Chet asked.

"We expand the Recallamin 3 trial to regions outside the Northeast region. In fairness, Cheryl suggested this to me a while back, so it's really her idea."

"That's a risky move. We're already having trouble keeping a lid on the deaths and adverse events we see in the Northeast region."

"To be blunt, I think that is because Muckland mucked that up. If he had been on top of the lab results they were getting, he would have prevented the types of concerns that Dr. Caron and those Portland doctors had."

"Yes, but do we have the kind of Regional Lab Medical Directors who, how shall I say this? Have the moral flexibility to do the type of data gymnastics that Dr. Muckland is willing to do?"

"Money talks, Chet. We have a few that I think can be convinced to be more flexible, as you put it."

"What regions are you thinking about, Asa? I have to make sure we have adequate pharmaceutical rep coverage to get the word out and push the vaccine."

"I'm thinking Gulf Coast and West Coast for starters.

They're a bunch of wild Cajuns, cowboys, and cowgirls out there. Might as well use that independent, pioneering spirit to our advantage."

"Why not the Midwest region?" Chet suggested.

"From a potential patient volume standpoint, that makes all the sense in the world, Chet. Unfortunately, those Midwestern folks are rule-followers and not as quick to adopt novel approaches, if you know what I mean. The Lab Medical Director there is as straight-laced as they come. It would be a hard sell. I say we get a bump from the Gulf Coast and West Coast, and then see where we stand."

"And when do you want to go live?" Cheryl asked.

"As soon as possible."

"It will take me at least 3 to 4 weeks to hire some reps," Cheryl replied.

"We don't have that much time. Can't you shift resources from other regions?"

"Well, that's not popular with the reps. Every time I do that, I seem to lose a couple because they think they need work-life balance."

"I don't care. We need this. Get the Gulf Coast and West Coast regions covered by the end of the week. We go live there next week."

"And the Lab Medical Directors?" Chet asked.

"I'll take care of them. One call, a promise of a 25% raise, and an orientation call with Muckland, and they'll be ready to roll."

"I hope you're right," Chet replied doubtfully. "Won't they need to ramp up lab staff to handle the increased volume?"

"Yes, but that volume won't hit all at once. It will be incremental. They will have plenty of time. Are we all in on the plan?" Asa asked.

"Do we have a choice?" Chet asked facetiously as he and Cheryl began to chuckle.

"I'll take that as unanimous consent then. Thank you very much, lady and gentleman," he announced while rising from his chair, signaling the end of the meeting. "Please close the door on your way out. I have some calls to make to a couple of Lab Medical Directors."

CHAPTER 24

J erry pulled the Security company van up to the curb in front of Jackie's house, and before he was halfway up the porch stairs, Jackie opened the front door to greet him.

"Hi, Jackie," he called, "How did you know I was here? Did you install my competition's system?" he joked.

"Hi, Jerry. No, I was just watching for you. I just brewed a fresh pot of coffee. Do you want a cup before you get started?"

"That would be great, thanks," he replied as he arrived at the top step and followed her into the house to the kitchen.

"I'm sorry it's taken me so long to get back to you. I've been busy."

"I understand, but I feel like I should be the one apologizing. I usually make follow-up calls after I do an assessment, but when I heard someone stole your baby, I didn't think you'd appreciate a sales call. Then I told my wife that I wanted to call you just to see if there was anything we could do for you, but she didn't think it was a good idea. We have a daughter, a little older than Ashley, and I can tell you, my wife and I both offered up many thoughts and prayers for you."

"Aww, that's so sweet, Jerry. Thank you," she said, putting her coffee cup down and giving him a hug.

"Where is Ashley, anyway?" Jerry asked.

"Taking a nap."

"I remember those days. Now my little Daisy runs around non-stop. By the time I get home from work, Maria is exhausted and ready for me to take over."

"Yes, well, Ashley is walking now, and even with her nap, I get exhausted."

After they shared stories of their kids and finished their coffee, Jerry toured Jackie around the house, explaining the security features of the system she had selected. As if on cue, Ashley announced the end of her nap upon completion of their tour.

"Mama," she repeatedly called until Jackie opened her bedroom door to see her daughter standing in her crib.

Jackie changed her daughter and got her ready to go to the park. She called and invited her mother to join them, but she was busy helping a friend and couldn't. Leaving Jerry to install the security system, Jackie decided to abandon the use of the stroller and let Ashley walk with her to the park. They made it halfway to the playground when Ashley used the toddler's universal signal for wanting to be carried. Raising her arms and, with a look of desperation on her face, pleaded, "Ehh, Ehh." Accommodating her daughter's request to be airlifted the rest of the way, she bent down, and mid-hoist was interrupted by her phone announcing an incoming call. With the skill that only a mother could perform, she found and answered the phone while carrying a squirming infant in one arm, a large handbag with the other, while traversing a grassy slope.

"Hi, beautiful!" Curt greeted her enthusiastically.

"Hi, handsome!" she responded in kind. "Hold on a sec, OK?" she asked, arriving at the playground and setting Ash down before she returned to the call. "OK, I'm back," she announced.

"Is this not a good time? I could call back later."

"No, no, this is a great time. I just had to put Ash down. We're at the playground," she said while sitting on a bench, unloading her handbag, and watching her daughter navigate toward a colorful plastic play structure with stairs and a slide.

"I wish I was there with you."

"Well, you will be in a couple of days, right?"

"Right! And it can't get here quickly enough. The kids are driving me crazy. Caitlin already has her stuff all packed."

"Aww, how sweet."

"Yeah, but when I say all, I mean ALL! In addition to her clothes, she has packed up a big box full of all her horses, horse stable, and gear, as well as her dummy steer head and rope. I've tried to negotiate with her not to bring her entire collection of things, to no avail. She is determined to share everything she owns with you."

"Then let her bring as much as your car will allow. I have a big house, and I'm sure Ash would love to play with all the horses."

"I can see you're not going to be a big help in my negotiations with Caitlin. Or in curbing my tendency to spoil my children," he replied.

Curt was fully aware that his generosity in accommodating his kids' wishes was what created the dilemma of Caitlin's menagerie of horse-related toys in the first place.

"Not in the least," Jackie laughed. "I'm a first-time Mom, remember? If anything, I am going to spoil them rotten while they're here."

"We're creating monsters, you know that, don't you?" he asked. Immediately conscious that the question may have sounded to her like he had elevated their relationship to mutual responsibility for parenting his kids.

"Caitlin and Cade don't seem like monsters to me. They seem well-loved and cared for by their father. I'll be honored to be a co-conspirator in spoiling your children," she replied. "Ashley, I'm afraid will be suffering the same fate," she added as she rose from the bench and walked to oversee Ash's ascent of the four stairs that led to the slide.

"Thanks, Jackie. I sometimes worry about being too much of a Disney Dad. Too heavy on indulging them in things they want and too light on disciplinary matters," he confessed.

"Ya know, I picked up a bunch of books about parenting before Ash was born, and after reading the third one, I had to stop. I was beginning to over-think things. So I put the books away. I realized that my parents had already given me a pretty good model of parenting. Maybe not perfect, but I think I turned out alright."

"I think you turned out much better than alright."

"Well, thanks. And your parents must have done a great job parenting you because you're definitely better than alright."

Jackie and Curt continued their conversation about parenting, both relishing the opportunity to bounce their hopes, fears, and opinions on parenting off of each other. As single parents, they had lost not only their spouses but also their co-captains, anchors, and navigators in the often unpredictable, uncharted, and turbulent seas of raising children.

Meanwhile, Ash finally mounted the four stairs and, with her mother's assistance, slid down the short slide, erupting in gales of laughter.

"Someone sounds happy," Curt announced.

"Yeah, Ash just slid down the slide. She loves this slide," she said, righting her daughter and pointing her in the direction of the stairs. Where, once again, Ash began her slow ascent under her mother's close observation and her occasional assistance.

"I can't wait to see you," Curt admitted.

"Then leave now. You told me Caitlin is all packed. Get to it, Professor. Your poor lonely student, could use some late-night tutoring."

"Oh, you are the devil, aren't you?" he exclaimed while weighing the possibility of taking her up on her offer.

"Now that you mention it, professor, I am feeling a bit hot."

"That sounds serious, young lady. I'll be there at 11 p.m."

"Really?" Jackie asked, leaving her southern belle student persona for a moment.

"Well, you did say leave now. Is that OK?"

"OK? It's great. Oh, Curt, please be careful."

"I will. I love you, Jackie.

"I love you too, Curt. See you soon."

Jackie hung up just in time to assist Ash down the slide once more, causing the same infectious laughter. After one more circuit up the stairs and down the slide with predictable results, Jackie picked Ash up and started for home despite a brief protest from her daughter. When they had crossed the street, Jackie put Ash down to let her walk the remaining distance home. Seeing the porch steps, Ash excitedly tackled them with the confidence and bravery reinforced by her experience at the slide. As excited as Jackie was to see her daughter's development, there was always that niggling counter emotion of fear and concern about her growing independence.

Jerry was finishing up the installation of the security system and oriented Jackie to its features. In addition to the door, window, and motion sensors, external security cameras were installed at the front and back of the house. Jerry reviewed the control panel with Jackie, teaching her how to arm the system and pointing out two panic alarms that could be initiated manually. One panic button was an audible alarm producing a high-decibel siren, while the other was a silent alarm. Both were transmitted to the Nora Police Department. A remote control unit allowed Jackie to arm or disarm the system or initiate an audible or silent alarm from anywhere in the home. After Jerry's training session, they set up and tested the system, confirming that Nora PD had received the alert. Despite Jackie covering Ash's ears for the brief audible alarm test, she was startled by the piercing sound and started to cry. Only until Jackie consoled her and found Monty Moose for her to hold.

Thanking Jerry and seeing him out the door, Jackie excitedly prepared the house for Curt and the kid's arrival that evening. Despite the system that Jerry had just installed, it was Curt's company that really gave her a sense of security. While doing the household chores, she replayed their private moments together at the Rockland Resort in her head, which only served to make her more impatient. Unfortunately, there were not enough house preparations to fill the hours before their arrival, and the time continued to pass torturously slow.

CHAPTER 25

Detective Farest pounded his fist on his desk in frustration. As clockwork as the evidence had come to him yesterday, today was the exact opposite. The day began when he had to disappoint Inspector Adams. Theo had called, hoping to obtain information on whether Alexis was involved in the kidnapping of Jackie's baby before they met with the FDA. Now, as the day drew to a close, and there was still no word from the lab, he feared he would have to disappoint Jackie a second time after promising he would call with results today. Just as he was about to write the day off as a bust, his phone rang.

"Hi, Detective Farest. This is Constance from the lab. We got a positive match on the Deno baby," fitting her greeting and report into her opening salvo in an attempt to thwart Detective Farest's ire with the delayed report.

"So Alexis was likely the woman who helped kidnap the baby," he replied, as Constance's strategy succeeded in having him swallowing the tirade he had wanted to unleash.

"Yes, and I suspect that one or both of the other fingerprints in the car were accomplices."

"That's right. She distracted the grandmother while someone else grabbed the baby. I don't suppose we have any additional leads on those unidentified prints?"

"No, we don't, unfortunately. And I'm sorry for the delay in getting our report to you. We were swamped today. I got to it as soon as I could," employing the next step in her strategy to disarm Detective Farest's anger.

"Thanks, Constance. I guess better late than never applies here," he said, as Constance celebrated invisibly with a fist pump on the other end of the line.

There was a reason the lab had Constance support Detective Farest's cases. She was the only lab analyst whose obsessive-compulsive attention to detail and deft interpersonal skills could assuage Detective Farest when his expectations weren't met.

Wanting to end his otherwise frustrating day on a positive note, he called Jackie to make good on his promise.

"Hi, Detective Farest," Jackie answered while powering down the vacuum cleaner in the midst of killing more time before Curt and the kid's arrival.

"Hi, Jackie. I wanted to get back to you about Ashley's fingerprints and hair sample."

"And?" she said, planting herself on a nearby chair in anticipation of hearing the results.

"And it's a positive match. Alexis was involved in the kidnapping and had your baby in her apartment."

While not surprised at hearing the results, it was almost as if a dark gray storm cloud had suddenly obstructed her sunny disposition.

"So, what now?" Jackie asked.

"Well, we still need to find her accomplice or accomplices. We have two unidentified sets of prints, one of which matches the prints Officer Todd supplied from your break-in. We also need to determine what AlzCura and Cheryl Baker's involvement in all this may be. I am coordinating our investigation with Inspector Adams, who I will be calling after we get off the phone."

"OK, thanks. I won't keep you then."

"To the degree that Inspector Adams and I can keep you in the loop, we will."

"I appreciate that," she replied, knowing full well the limitations both had in briefing her on open cases.

Detective Farest hung up and immediately selected Inspector Adam's name from his contact list.

"Hi Brent," Theo answered. "I hope this means you have good news for me."

"I do. I just hope it's not too late."

"No, I called this morning to see if you had any information because I was meeting with the AG and the DA. Our meeting with the FDA isn't until tomorrow morning."

"Oh, good. We now have evidence that positively identifies that Jackie's baby was in Alexis' apartment. As for any accomplices she may have had, we're still left with those two sets of unidentified prints."

"That's great. At least we've narrowed the search. Did you ever determine if Cheryl Baker had any other family members who could be involved?"

"No. Get this, not only is she a ghost on social media and personal identification sites, but AlzCura took any photos or references to her off their website."

"Wow, talk about making yourself look guilty."

"I know, right? The problem is," he began, but Theo interrupted.

"You can't delay your investigation any longer."

"You read my mind."

"Well, I think we're in the same boat here. Two doctors from Portland will be joining us for our meeting with the FDA tomorrow. I've invited them because they have caught AlzCura and their Regional Lab trying to hide elevated liver function test results."

"No kidding? Hey, if I could get there and my boss was supportive, do you think I could join you for that meeting with the FDA? Since AlzCura and their lab are in my jurisdiction, I'd like a seat at the table. If the FDA acts on your findings, I want them to coordinate their efforts with ours."

"Makes sense. I don't see why you shouldn't be invited. They told us to invite anyone who may be able to provide information."

"When is the meeting tomorrow?"

"9a.m."

"Yikes, well, I better start working on getting the OK and finding a flight then."

"Sounds good. Text me if you're coming so I can give folks here a heads up."

"Will do," Detective Farest replied.

They ended the call, and Detective Farest immediately walked to his boss' office to brief him on the status of his investigation and ask permission to fly to Maine.

"We don't have the budget for that. Why do you need to go to Maine? Couldn't you just call in?" his Chief asked.

Detective Farest used the most effective strategy he knew of to convince the Chief Detective of the importance of his being at the meeting in person.

"Listen, if we're not at the table with the Feds on this, they could just march in here tomorrow, not involve us, and potentially prohibit us from pursuing witnesses. Being physically at the table will send a strong message that while we're happy they're involved, we need them to coordinate their activities with our investigation."

"Alright, I get that. I'll brief the Commissioner. See my

assistant. She can help make your travel arrangements. And I want a full report first thing Monday." he called as Detective Farest exited his office.

That hurdle cleared, Detective Farest stopped at the assistant's desk as the Chief had recommended and made arrangements to fly out of Buffalo that evening. As his flight would not get into Portland until late evening, he arranged to lodge there and drive his rental car to the meeting the following morning.

CHAPTER 26

Curt had an hour after his call with Jackie to pack and load up the car before picking up his kids at school. They were leaving for their trip to Nora a day earlier than initially planned. Caitlin had already completed her packing, so he started by packing her luggage and box of toys. Knowing Cade would expect quid pro quo treatment, he lifted Cade's scooter into the trunk, leaving only enough room for Cade's small suitcase. Curt used a portion of the back seat for his bag and to hang a few shirts assuming that his kids would continue their tradition of fighting over who sat in the front seat. Hoping to curb the times they would have to stop, he packed a plastic grocery bag with a selection of snacks and beverages. With only minutes to spare, he locked up the apartment and drove to the school. On the drive, he fought back the inevitable feelings that he had forgotten something in his rush to pack.

Arriving at the school, Curt uncharacteristically got out of the car to meet Caitlin and Cade as they exited.

"You guys can hop in the car," he instructed them. "I just need to speak to Principal Taylor for a sec," as both kids eyed him with suspicion and remained firmly planted in place.

"But we haven't done anything wrong," Cade pleaded.

Rolling his eyes, he invited them to approach Principal Taylor, who had taken his customary place near the school bus to supervise the children's boarding process.

"Hi, Mr. Barnes," Principal Taylor called, seeing him approach with Caitlin and Cade in tow.

"Hi, Principal Taylor. I just wanted to let you know that Caitlin and Cade will not be in school tomorrow. We're taking a brief trip to upstate New York."

No sooner than the words were out of his mouth and Caitlin and Cade turned and ran to the car, finally assured that their father's conversation with the Principal was benign.

"I guess they're excited about the trip," Principal Taylor laughed.

"You have no idea," Curt replied. "Caitlin was packed two days ago!"

"Thanks for letting me know. I'll let their teachers know. Have a safe trip."

"Thanks, they'll be back at school Monday," he called as he turned and walked towards the car where Caitlin had uncharacteristically claimed the backseat.

As Curt slide into the driver's seat, the inevitable barrage of questions began without the opportunity for him to answer. Once they had exhausted their opening salvo, he calmly replied.

"Yes, Caitlin, I packed your box and your luggage. Yes, Cade, I brought your scooter. "Yes, we're going to stop to eat along the way, but I've got a few snacks in that grocery bag in the back. And finally, about 8 hours, referring to Cade's question about how long it would take to get to Jackie's.

"I thought we were going tomorrow. Why are we leaving today?" Cade asked, opening the second round of questioning.

"Well, I could change my mind if you guys would rather go to school tomorrow," he replied, to an immediate emphatic chorus of no's.

"Jackie suggested we leave today," Curt answered. "It will give us more time to visit."

"Can I get some of my horses out of the trunk so I can play with them?"

"Yeah, and can we move that stuff so I can play in the back with Catilin?"

"Yeah, we could move that stuff to the front," Caitlin suggested.

Curt thought he was in some alternate universe. First, Caitlin took the backseat without prompting, and now they wanted to play together? He wasn't going to look that gift horse in the mouth.

"I have to stop and get gas. We can get your horses and re-arrange the luggage then. OK?"

Their affirmative responses, without whining about need-ing immediate gratification for their requests, confirmed that aliens had taken over his children and were controlling their personalities. Since he had no objection, he welcomed the aliens to continue their magic.

After a gourmet meal of burgers and fries at the Kennebunk Turnpike Service Plaza, it was relatively smooth sailing until Boston. Enduring an hour of stop-and-go traffic and the occasional Masshole drivers that Mainers loved to hate, traffic eased as he turned onto I-90. The combination of the monotonous hum of the freeway and the sun making its exit stage west was all the sleep aids Caitlin and Cade needed. Curt drove the last 3 hours of the trip in blessed silence.

Pulling into the driveway of Jackie's house just after 11 p.m., she emerged from the house. She was dressed in her typical bedtime attire. A South Temple University ensemble of gym shorts and t-shirt clung desperately to her body, accentu-ating her most exceptional features. Curt had all he could do to try and concentrate on extracting his children and the luggage from the car. Once the kids were snug in the beds Jackie had prepared for them in the spare room, she led Curt to her bedroom to finally give him a proper welcome.

CHAPTER 27

Detective Farest grabbed a second cup of coffee from the free breakfast bar at the airport hotel before checking out and hopping in his rental car for the one-hour drive to the meeting with the FDA representatives. Unlike his law enforcement colleagues in Maine, who had been working the AlzCura case for months, he had had a whirlwind 10 days. It started with a suicide that quickly evolved to produce evidence of kidnapping, corporate fraud, and possible connections to a series of other crimes in Maine, including murder.

Meanwhile, Inspector Adams walked into the kitchen to find Celeste in one of his t-shirts and barely-there panties, putting the finishing touches on his breakfast. She set the plate with two poached eggs blanketed in hollandaise sauce, accompanied by bacon and home fries in front of him. Then sauntered back to the counter to pour coffee into his favorite New England Patriots mug.

"Want anything else?" she asked, setting the steaming mug down and unconsciously shifting her hip. A move that made her question sound more suggestive than she intended.

"Yes, I do, but I'm afraid I don't have time for it," he quipped, flipping up the hem of the t-shirt with his finger.

"Well, we will have all weekend for that. I hope your meeting with the FDA goes well."

"Me too," he said, shoveling a forkful of egg and home fries into his mouth.

"Attorney Dryer hopes to file my case against AlzCura next week. The timing couldn't be better, don't you think?"

"Depends," he replied, taking a sip of coffee. "If the FDA agrees we have a case and escalates it as we hope, yeah, the timing couldn't be better."

"But?" Celeste said, anticipating his next words.

"But if the FDA doesn't escalate it, then your case may tip AlzCura off before we file our charges."

"Why wouldn't they escalate it? You've said yourself that you have a mountain of evidence."

"Yes, but it's an entirely different ballgame when working with the Feds. They seem to have their own rules. What seems obvious to us may not be so obvious to them."

"I don't get it. Isn't the FDA there to make sure that drugs and vaccines are safe? How could they not act on the information you're going to share with them?"

"Well, I hope they do. I just know that the federal bureaucracy is very complex. I'm afraid that in the past, I've been more often amazed at how the Fed doesn't act."

"Well, I hope you're wrong," she said, bending down to kiss him on the cheek.

Theo introduced another forkful of his breakfast into his mouth as if he hadn't eaten in days.

"What's this sauce? It's incredible. And what kind of eggs are these?" he managed to say with his mouth still half-full.

"You're kidding, right?" Celeste replied, shocked. "You mean to tell me you've never had poached eggs with Hollandaise sauce? Eggs Benedict ring a bell?"

"Nope," he responded while heaping another helping of eggs and potatoes dripping with sauce into his mouth.

"Then, you have led a very sheltered culinary life, Mr. Adams."

"My breakfast is usually a cup of coffee or two," he said, wiping his lips and chin with a napkin and pushing away from the table.

"Didn't your mother ever teach you that breakfast was the most important meal?"

"Yes, she did. And had she also told me that breakfast would be served by a half-naked, ravenous beauty, I may have paid attention," he said, slipping his hands under her t-shirt and drawing her in for a hug and kiss.

"Wish I could stay for dessert, but duty calls," he said, breaking their embrace.

"Oh, I'll keep dessert warm for you," she said suggestively, grabbing his keys and making for the door before he caved to her tempting feminine persuasion.

The 20-minute drive to the State Office Building, where the meeting was to be held, gave Theo plenty of time to transition from thoughts of his temptress to the business at hand. As luck would have it, he ran into Drs. Slack and Mason in the lobby, who were both wearing that disoriented, I-don't-know-where-I'm-going look people have when in an unfamiliar place. Relieved to see a familiar face, the physicians followed Theo onto the elevator and to the conference room across from Attorney General Talcott's office. District Attorney Wydman was already there helping his assistant place table tent name placards strategically around the conference table along with a meeting agenda. A pad of paper and pen were placed at each place setting, and a side table offered bottled water and coffee.

Just as Dr. Slack and Dr. Mason got settled into their assigned seats, Theo's phone announced a text from Detective Farest, who was in the parking lot. As Theo left to escort Detective Farest up, DA Wydman thanked the physicians for coming and gave them a brief overview of the meeting agenda.

"Brent?" Theo called to a man in the lobby who eerily could have passed for Theo's older brother. Not only were they of similar stature and body types, but both wore khaki pants with plaid oxford shirts and sport coats.

"Theo!" he called back, confirming Theo had guessed correctly.

"Glad you could make it on such short notice," Theo replied as the two shook hands.

"Yeah, me too. Jeez, it looks like we coordinated our clothing choices today," Brent exclaimed.

"Well, since this is my only sports coat, there's not much to coordinate," Theo laughed.

"Really? Me too," Brent replied, joining in Theo's amusement.

"Not much call for fashion in the line of work we do, I guess," Theo remarked.

As the two made their way to the meeting room, AG Talcott's assistant passed them in the hall and announced that Dr. Harder and Dr. Shearlow from the FDA were in the lobby, and she was on the way to retrieve them.

As Theo and Brent entered the conference room, everyone, including Attorney General Talcott were present. With only a matter of minutes before Dr. Harder and Dr. Shearlow made their appearance, the group made quick introductions. AG Talcott then made his expectations for the outcome of the meeting known.

"Thank you all for coming today. I think we all share the same concerns about AlzCura Pharmaceuticals and its Recallamin vaccine. My goal is to convince our friends from the FDA to join us in prosecuting AlzCura executives for a series of crimes. These offenses include failing to report deaths related to Recallamin, falsifying test results to hide adverse events associated with Recallamin use, misrepresentation of the side-effects of Recallamin, as well as principles or accessories in the murders of Calli Barnes, Dr. Steven Caron, and Leslie Anderson. I also have assurances from a highly-placed colleague in the U.S. Department of Justice that if the FDA does not escalate this matter to the OIG, we have recourse. So while I hope for a good outcome today, this is not our only option. In short, let's make our objective clear to our friends at the FDA, but we don't need to burn any bridges if they don't want to play. Any questions?"

Hearing none and with heads shaking in the negative, AG Talcott announced that DA Wydman would be facilitating the meeting. As DA Wydman was acknowledging that much of the credit for arranging this meeting belonged to his assistant, the conference room door opened. Dr. Elizabeth Harder and Dr. Woodson Shearlow entered.

The first impression of this duo from the FDA was the striking array of contrasts they presented that was somewhat unsettling. Dr. Elizabeth Harder was a tall, husky woman whose face could best be described as horse-like but not in a good sense. She had wide-set eyes and a long nose with pronounced flaring nostrils leading to a too gummy smile with misshapen teeth in an oversized mouth that at best could be described as hideous. A mane of long, straight, wispy strands of brown hair hung down off her head, completing her equine look. To cast one's eyes upon Dr. Shearlow offered the viewer no relief. His petite, effeminate 5-foot frame was adorned by a head of greasy black hair punctuated by psoriatic white flakes that cascaded onto the shoulders of his rumpled sports coat. His face was the polar opposite of Dr. Harder's. Tiny narrow set eyes, a button nose, and a small mouth with slender uncommonly red lips. In other words, a face one would expect to see on a 7-year old girl who applied too much of mommy's red lipstick, not the face of a 37-year old man. They were such an odd conglomeration of unappealing physical attributes that those around the table, ironically, found it hard to look away.

As they took their assigned seats, DA Wydman commenced his duties as the meeting facilitator.

"Good Morning. I'm District Attorney Will Wydman. I'd like to welcome our colleagues, Dr. Harder and Dr. Shearlow, to Maine," he opened, trying to strike a friendly, collegial tone. "I've put together an agenda," he continued but was interrupted by Dr. Shearlow, whose head barely rose above the conference table.

"DA Weedman, since we called this meeting, we will be supplying the agenda. And Dr. Harder has asked me to facilitate," Dr. Shearlow announced, producing a sheaf of papers containing his intended agenda. "I must say, I find it disturbing that you completely disregarded my prior correspondence outlining the agenda for this meeting."

Caught completely off-guard, DA Wydman replied, "What previous correspondence?"

"The correspondence my assistant sent you earlier this week."

DA Wydman looked at his assistant, who shrugged her shoulders and shook her head in a manner indicating that they had not received such correspondence.

"My apologies, but we apparently didn't receive your correspondence, Dr. Shearlow."

"Well, it seems, to be a pattern with you folks here in Maine. You can't send adverse event reports in a timely fashion, and you can't keep track of the correspondence you receive from the FDA. Now is Ms. Klatz here?"

"Who?" asked DA Wydman abruptly, irritated at Dr. Shearlow's allegation.

"Ms. Klatz. Rebecca Klatz, the office manager who submitted the adverse event reports out of compliance with our timeliness requirements."

"I'm sorry, no, we didn't invite her."

"We specifically asked for her to be present. What about

your Director of Licensing and Certification?"

"I'm sorry, Dr. Shearlow, but why would you want the Director of Licensing and Certification at this meeting?"

"Because your Licensing and Certification Department is presumably responsible for enforcing the rules about timely reporting of adverse events that keep patients safe. In this instance, your Licensing and Certification Department has failed miserably."

The meeting had gone sideways before it even began. AG Talcott, recovering from the shock of Dr. Shearlow's unfair assumptions and allegations, spoke up.

"Hold on, Dr. Shearlow. I take issue with your assumptions and allegations. Had we received your"

"And who might you be?" Dr. Shearlow interrupted as DA Wydman never got the opportunity to get to the Introductions portion of his intended agenda.

"I am Maine's Attorney General Lewis Talcott. I'll be damned if I'm going to let you come in here and ride roughshod over my District Attorney. Now we have assembled a"

"With all due respect, maybe we should reschedule this meeting," interrupted Dr. Harder.

She was concerned about the direction Dr. Shearlow had taken the meeting and not sure how to delicately redirect him. She had coached Dr. Shearlow on how she wanted him to facilitate the meeting, but he had gone off the rails completely.

Unbeknownst to the gathering around the table, Julie, DA Wydman's assistant, had stepped out of the room. She had contacted Dr. Shearlow's assistant, who, upon checking her records, confessed that she had failed to send the meeting agenda. Returning to the conference room just as Dr. Harder was making her suggestion to reschedule, Julie spoke up.

"Excuse me," Julie said, trying to gain the group's attention but failing. "Excuse me," she said louder, this time finally winning their attention.

"And who might you be?" Dr. Shearlow asked, looking at her as though she didn't have the right to breathe the same air that he did.

"I'm Julie, and I just spoke to your assistant, who said she forgot to send the agenda. Next time you cast aspersions on the quality of my work or organization, Dr. Shearlow, you better double-check the facts before opening your mouth. As for you, Dr. Harder, if you're going to use the phrase with all due respect, then why not show some. Don't interrupt our Attorney General in the middle of his explanation."

You couldn't have scripted a worse way to start a meeting. The timely and brutally honest response from DA Wydman's assistant served to put Dr. Harder and Dr. Shearlow in their place and saved the meeting from a premature end.

You could hear a pin drop as Dr. Shearlow and Dr. Harder looked as though they had just been scolded by their mothers. The rest of the group sat in uncomfortable silence, waiting for their response. Dr. Shearlow seemed to be sinking even lower in his chair. Dr. Harder had wilted back into her seat, recognizing her intervention had failed. The tension in the room was too much for Julie, who turned and left the room, fearing she had just ensured that today would be her last day as DA Wydman's assistant. Shortly after Julie's exit, DA Wydman left the room not to counsel but to comfort his assistant. Finally, Dr. Harder found words that obviously didn't come easily or naturally.

"I, I, don't know what to say. Dr. Shearlow, perhaps we can proceed as Attorney General Talcott had suggested, and we will try and get our questions answered in the process. I apologize that you didn't receive Dr. Shearlow's correspondence," she offered tentatively. She turned to look at Dr. Shearlow, hoping that he would respond in kind and support her suggestion. But no such response from him was forthcoming.

"I accept your apology Dr. Harder," AG Talcott replied, "but I believe Julie is the one who most needs to hear apologies from both of you. If you're willing to provide those apologies to her, we can proceed with the meeting."

Dr. Harder readily agreed to the AG's suggestion, while Dr. Shearlow looked like he had just been asked to eat a shit sandwich.

"Woodson," Dr. Harder looked at him sternly when his assent to apologize was not forthcoming. "You need to do this."

He had gone pale and, without uttering a word, nodded his head.

DA Wydman discovered that his assistant had taken shelter in the women's restroom. He asked AG Talcott's assistant to check on her and encourage her to come out to speak with him. Before Julie emerged from the bathroom, AG Talcott left the conference room to brief DA Wydman on Dr. Harder's apology and their consent to use their meeting agenda. As the two chatted, Julie exited the bathroom, eyes red from crying and expecting the worst as both the DA and AG were waiting for her.

"Julie, you're a superstar. I really admire what you did in there," AG Talcott began to her surprise.

"Yeah, I know how great you are, and you even surprised me," announced DA Wydman. "Remind me never to get on your bad side," to which she laughed as relief washed over her from their positive responses.

"I've asked them to apologize to you before we proceed with the meeting. Do you think you can come back in?" asked AG Talcott.

Her face told the story before she even opened her mouth.

"I know. Frankly, I wish I didn't have to go back in there," quipped AG Talcott. "But you saved the meeting, Julie. You've taught them a lesson, and everyone in that room has nothing but respect for you. We'll all be there to support you."

"OK," she said reluctantly. "But if we ever have to schedule another meeting with them, promise me that you'll have your assistant do it."

"That's a deal," AG Talcott said, laughing.

As the three filed back into the conference room, Dr. Harder stood and walked over to Julie and apologized and thanked her for calling her out on her rude behavior. It was heartfelt, and when Julie teared up, Dr. Harder placed a hand on her shoulder and reassured Julie that she had nothing but respect for her. Returning to her seat, she prompted Dr. Shearlow to make his apology.

"I'm sorry you didn't receive our correspondence," he said, looking somewhat in Julie's direction but not making eye contact.

When it appeared that was going to be the extent of his apology, Dr. Harder nudged him with her elbow.

"And I'm sorry I didn't verify that my assistant sent it."

"Woodson," Dr. Harder said impatiently.

"What? I apologized. Twice," he protested.

"Julie, would you kindly refresh my colleagues' memory of what he said to you that he now needs to apologize for?" Dr. Harder asked, to Julie's surprise.

"He said I couldn't keep track of the correspondence I received from the FDA."

Dr. Shearlow's eyes were shooting daggers at Dr. Harder, and without taking his eyes off of her, he tried again to apologize.

"I'm sorry I said that about you," he said through clenched teeth.

"Now look at Julie, and this time, say it like you mean it," Dr. Harder returned his glare with a steely-eyed scowl of her own.

Dr. Shearlow withered in his chair. Overcome with anger and embarrassment, he jumped down off his chair, breezed past Julie without a glance, and exited the room in a huff.

"I'm sorry, Julie. Dr. Shearlow is an excellent analyst, but he sometimes struggles with interpersonal communications," a response that was undoubtedly the biggest understatement any of them would hear that day.

"I appreciate the effort, Dr. Harder. I hope the rest of your meeting goes more smoothly," Julie replied. Capturing the hopes of everyone at the table who were uncomfortable witnesses to the spectacle that had nearly ended the meeting.

The torturous first 30-minutes of their two-hour meeting behind them, Dr. Harder graciously deferred to DA Wydman, who expertly led the group on the evidence that they had amassed. Dr. Shearlow returned to the meeting. Slipping into the room while Inspector Adams was articulating the reason behind the delay in Dr. Caron's office reporting their adverse events. Adams divulged AlzCura's curious policies around event reporting, noting that the FDA's concern about Dr. Caron's delayed reports was likely only the tip of the iceberg. In turn, each of the meeting participants shared their experiences and concerns with Dr. Harder and Dr. Shearlow.

If Dr. Shearlow had any issues with what was presented, he didn't raise them. For the remainder of the meeting, Dr. Shearlow sat quietly next to his colleague with a smirk on his face that seemed to suggest he knew something that they didn't. Dr. Harder was aghast when she heard about the crimes in Maine and in New York and was grateful that DA Wydman had the foresight to invite Detective Farest to the meeting.

You wouldn't have predicted a positive outcome for the meeting based on its dysfunctional start. In the end, it achieved the desired results. When AG Talcott asked Dr. Harder about whether the evidence they presented rose to the level of engaging the Office of the Inspector General, she responded honestly.

"I can't go directly to the OIG with these concerns. I can assure you that I will file a report and speak with the Commissioner about your request to involve the OIG. I certainly think she'll agree to the OIG's involvement."

"Much appreciated, Dr. Harder," AG Talcott replied. "I don't want to sound pushy, but do you have any idea how long before we might know if the OIG will get involved? We have some time-sensitive matters that we're holding on to."

"I'm afraid I can't. My report will go to the Commissioner sometime next week, and I doubt she'll be able to meet with me for a week or two after that. As to whether the OIG would consider this worthy of expediting an investigation, I really can't say. Not in my wheelhouse and well above my pay grade, I'm afraid. I'm sorry. I know that's not the answer you wanted to hear."

"I appreciate that. Please let me know if there is anything I can do to expedite the process. I'd be happy to get on a call with the Commissioner if that would be helpful," AG Talcott offered.

"And I'll second that offer in the name of Buffalo Police Department," Detective Farest chimed in. "AlzCura is in our backyard, and my Chief Detective is anxious to address this sooner rather than later."

"Thank you. My apologies for the unfortunate misunderstanding earlier," Dr. Harder replied. Pausing and chancing a glance at Dr. Shearlow, who wasn't compelled to join her in expressing any apologies or gratitude.

"You've all been very gracious and helpful. I look forward to sharing your concerns and requests with the Commissioner," Dr. Harder concluded.

Dr. Shearlow wasted no time leaving the meeting as Dr. Harder shook hands with DA Wydman and AG Talcott. As Dr.

Harder exited, she nodded to the others around the table, who all offered words of thanks or farewell. AG Talcott asked the remaining participants to stay back for a moment to debrief.

"Well, that was certainly a roller-coaster of a meeting," exclaimed AG Talcott, to chuckles of acknowledgment from those around the table. "And what's with Dr. Shearlow? I think if he had his way, there wouldn't have been a meeting. Thanks, Will, and thanks to all of you, you did a fantastic job presenting our concerns and our case. I had my doubts about Dr. Harder, but she really came around there in the end."

"I agree," DA Wydman offered. "And we definitely owe my assistant kudos. Julie saved this meeting by standing up to that little shit."

"Julie was amazing," AG Talcott added. "I think you should go back to your office and give her the rest of the day off with pay."

"I'd be happy to, Lew. As you might recall, I'm leaving here to take the wife to Quebec to celebrate our anniversary. No reason for Julie to sit in an empty office."

"That's right, Happy Anniversary, Will! Weren't you going to stay in a castle up there?"

"Yep. I'm treating Queen Marge to the royal treatment she deserves for putting up with me all these years," he laughed.

"Well, have a great time."

"Thanks, Lew."

"Any thoughts or concerns about the meeting from the rest of you around the table?" AG Talcott asked.

"I'm not sure we can wait a few weeks for the OIG to potentially come onboard before commencing our investigation," Detective Farest posited.

"I hear ya," AG Talcott replied. "While I'm optimistic that the FDA and OIG will eventually join us, I think we're in the same boat as you, Detective."

"Also, Attorney John Dryer expects to file a civil suit against AlzCura in the name of Celeste Boulanger next week," Inspector Adams stated. "I think we need to act before or at least at the same time as that suit gets filed."

"You're right, Theo. I think we need to act fast. Detective Farest, what are the chances that we could conference call with your Chief and perhaps your Attorney General in the next few days. I'd like to coordinate filing expedited charges against AlzCura?"

"Well, you know as well as I do that the wheels of justice don't always move as quickly as we might like, but I think it's worth a shot. I'm low man on a huge totem pole. In addition to my Chief, we have a Police Commissioner and an Assistant Attorney General in Buffalo to convince before we get the State's Attorney General involved."

"You're right. New York's legal structure is far more complex than ours here in Maine. See what you can do when you get back to Buffalo."

"I will," Detective Farest confirmed.

"What about asking Jackie and Curt to consider filing civil suits?" DA Wydman asked. "If Celeste is filing suit for the wrongful death of her husband, wouldn't it make sense for Jackie and Curt to consider doing so?

"That's an excellent point," AG Talcott replied. "Jackie definitely is in the same boat as Celeste. Curt's case is a bit more complicated, but we should at least ask him to consider speaking to Attorney Dryer. The more attention given to this, the more pressure we apply to compel the feds to join the party."

"Since King William will be catering to his Queen in Canada, I'll be happy to call Jackie and Curt," Inspector Adams offered. Needling his boss at the same time.

"Thanks, Theo," AG Talcott said with a chuckle.

"Yeah, thanks, Jester Theo," DA Wydman added sarcastically, causing laughter from all around the table.

With their plans in place and the week ending on a favorable note, the meeting members made the rounds shaking hands and thanking each other for their contribution to the cause before disbanding. Momentum was building, and with any luck, a cascade of federal, state, and civil actions would soon be choreographed to bring justice to AlzCura Pharmaceuticals.

CHAPTER 28

Jackie woke up cradled in Curt's arms as a ray of sunshine found its way through a gap in her bedroom curtains. Not anxious to leave the comfort and contentment of their cocoon, she listened to Curt's slow rhythmic breathing and basked in how natural his body felt next to hers. There had been a time when Jackie could never have imagined a world without Stu. Then, when he died, she could not imagine her life with another man. Yet fate and a familiar foe had forged a flourishing friendship with Curt, fostering fathomless feelings, filling the void left by her loss.

Jackie heard little feet padding down the hall and Caitlin's attempt to hush Cade.

"Shhh, they're probably still sleeping, Cade. Let's go downstairs," she heard Caitlin say, followed by footfalls like drumbeats down the staircase.

Curt stirred and, waking to find Jackie in his arms, squeezed her a little tighter.

"Good morning, beautiful," he whispered. "Or am I just dreaming this?"

Turning in his arms and snuggling her body up tight against his, she gave him the answer with a kiss.

"Mmm, it's a dream," Curt sighed. "No way I could be this lucky."

"I love you, Curt," she whispered. "I'm the lucky one."

"Did I hear the kids just now?"

"Yes, they just went downstairs."

"So what are we going to do today? Assuming we can't stay just like this for the rest of the day."

"Well, I was going to make breakfast, and then I thought we'd go to the park for a bit. My parents want to take us out to dinner tonight."

"Sounds good. Wanna take a shower together? Save some water?"

The drumbeat of Caitlin and Cade's feet coming back up the stairs made Jackie veto Curt's tempting suggestion.

"I admire your environmental consciousness, but maybe I'll go make breakfast and entertain the kids while you shower," she replied.

They kissed, reluctantly threw back the covers, and went their separate ways. As Curt closed the bathroom door behind him, he heard the kid's excitement as Jackie emerged from the bedroom to greet them. When he appeared in the kitchen 30 minutes later, Ashley was in her highchair, and Caitlin and Cade were helping Jackie with breakfast.

"Daddy!" Caitlin and Cade yelled in unison and ran to hug him. "We're helping Jackie make breakfast," Cade said proudly.

"And I helped Jackie dress Ash this morning," Caitlin added.

"Yes, they have been very helpful," Jackie confirmed. "How was your shower?" she said, winking at him.

"Delightful but not as environmentally friendly as it could have been," he shot back.

"Why wasn't it environmentally friendly?" Cade asked, putting Curt on notice that he might have to curb his quips in the presence of tiny ears.

"Well, Cade," Curt began as Jackie covered a laugh and turned away so the kids wouldn't see the amusement on her face. "I'm afraid I took a long shower and used more water than I had intended. Water is an important resource, and I usually try to be better at conserving it."

"Oh," Cade replied simply, seemingly satisfied with his father's response without needing to ask the usual parade of follow-up questions for which he was famous.

On his way over to Jackie, Curt bussed Ashley on the cheek, causing her to giggle instead of cry like the first time they had met. When Curt joined Jackie at the stove and out of earshot of the kids, he whispered, "I should have just told Cade it was because you refused to shower with me."

To which she couldn't hold back her laughter any longer, which of course demanded another explanation, this time to both Caitlin and Cade.

Breakfast preparations completed, they sat down at the table. For the kids, including Ashley, it was a simple exercise of eating. For Jackie and Curt, who looked contentedly at each other from across the table, it offered not just physical but emotional sustenance. Apart they were two incomplete units. Together they felt like a family. A family not accidentally cobbled together by the mistaken assumption at a restaurant hostess station, but a family with an unbreakable bond and a mutual purpose.

Clearing the table after breakfast, Jackie and Curt shared a quick kiss when they met to deposit dishes into the sink. If the kids saw it, it didn't spur a response, not that they would have cared. Something about the breakfast they just shared had elevated their relationship, and neither of them wanted to stop the upward trajectory.

Ashley walked all the way to the park, hand-in-hand with Jackie and Caitlin. Caitlin reveled in being able to play big sister to Ash, who, unlike Cade, didn't give her any push-back. Something about the addition of Ash had changed the nature of Caitlin and Cade's interactions. They were much more tolerant of each other and more cooperative in general. They still had their moments, but the change was noticeable and welcome. Jackie was unaware of this change, and Curt didn't trust it. As Caitlin and Cade teamed to assist and play with Ashley on the playground, Jackie kept on commenting on how well-behaved they were. Meanwhile, Curt kept waiting for the honeymoon period to end and his kids' true colors to show.

They decided to walk around the park instead of taking the shortcut across the park to Jackie's house. Curt put Ashley on his shoulders when she got tired, and to Jackie, Caitlin, and Cade's great amusement, Ash grabbed two handfuls of Curt's hair like she was holding the reins of a horse. Jackie pointed out her parent's house along the way, and as they approached Jackie's, Curt lifted Ash from his shoulders and put her down. This brought a considerable protest from Ash, who indicated she wasn't ready to come down from her lofty perch. Returning Ash to his shoulders, she grabbed the two hanks of Curt's hair that now stood out like horns from her previous ride. He hadn't been there 12 hours, and Curt was already beginning to wonder how he would ever be able to leave come Sunday.

Back at the house, it was Curt's turn to supervise the kids while Jackie took her shower. As Caitlin and Cade continued to behave like model children, they engaged Ashley in activities in the living room. Curt washed and dried the dishes from breakfast by hand, occasionally peeking in to check on the kids.

Jackie came down refreshed and transformed, causing a chorus of exclamations of awe from the kids that had Curt rushing out of the kitchen. Jackie couldn't understand what all the fuss was about, but Curt's stomach did the flip-flops that she always seemed to cause. Unembellished, she was already beautiful. With the barest hint of make-up, coifed hair, and figure-friendly clothing, she was simply stunning. But it was more than her physical appearance. It was the way she carried herself. It screamed of humility, confidence, and strength. An approachability that had always made people comfortable in her presence.

As the kids swarmed her, she looked at Curt and shrugged, oblivious to the impact she could have just when she walked into a room.

"Jeez, kids, it's only Jackie. I don't know what you're all excited about," Curt said facetiously, turning to go back into the kitchen. Followed by Caitlin's vehement protest when she didn't realize her father was joking.

"Dad! Don't you think she's beautiful?"

Curt poked his head out from the kitchen, took a quick look at Jackie, and replied matter-of-factly to his daughter.

"Eh, she's alright, I guess," and returned to the kitchen, to Caitlin's even more vigorous protests.

Before his daughter decompensated entirely, he re-appeared. As if to prove to her he was joking, he took Jackie in his arms.

"Jackie, you're not just alright. You're the most beautiful woman I've ever known," kissing her tenderly.

When he looked back down at his daughter, she was beaming with happiness. Even Cade, usually adverse to displays of affection, was smiling. And Ashley, anxious to join in the action, held out her arms and called "Mama."

"Alright, NOW, can I go back to my dishwashing?" Curt pleaded with his daughter, who nodded her approval.

A few minutes later, Jackie, holding Ash in her arms, joined Curt in the kitchen.

"You did the dishes by hand?" she exclaimed. "I have a dishwasher, you know."

"Yes, but doing them by hand saves on water and energy,

and you know me, Mr. Environmentally Conscious!"

"OK, OK, if I promise to take a shower with you tomorrow, can we use the dishwasher next time?"

"We have to wait until tomorrow? What if we get dirty later today?"

"It's doubtful since I'm just alright looking."

"True, but I'm feeling exceptionally generous today. You know you have to give back to the less fortunate."

"I have always depended on the kindness of strangers," Jackie parroted the famous Blanche Dubois line from A Streetcar Named Desire, complete with a southern accent.

As Curt went to embrace and kiss her, both were stopped in their tracks when Ashley interrupted.

"Dada"

Floored, both looked at each other as tears brimmed Jackie's eyes. All Curt could think to do was hug her, which she returned with quiet desperation as tears soaked his shirt. But Ash was not finished and grabbed a hank of Curt's hair and repeated, "Dada, Dada." This time, her insistent and enthusiastic proclamations had a counter-effect on Jackie and Curt. Both started to laugh through their tears and turned their attention to Ash, who was obviously proud and enamored with her new word.

"She must have learned that listening to Caitlin and Cade," Curt posited as Jackie wiped tears from her cheeks and smiled at her daughter.

"Yes, my little girl is just a big sponge, isn't she?" Jackie said in motherese while moving to nuzzle Ash's cheek with her nose, causing Ash to let go of her grip on Curt's hair and giggle.

Caitlin and Cade's example probably did help spur the increase in Ash's vocabulary, Jackie thought. She considered whether to tell Curt about her routine of showing Ash a wedding picture of her with Stu that sat on Ash's dresser. Even be-

fore Ash was old enough to talk, Jackie made a point of showing Ash the picture. She would systematically point to Stu and
say "Daddy" and point to her image and say, "Mommy." At first,
it was her way of keeping Stu alive as much for her as for Ash.
After she came to terms with losing Stu, it was more for Ash's
benefit, wanting to be sure she knew who her Daddy was. Now
that Ash had actually said "Dada," she worried about Ash's potential confusion.

Realizing that she was overthinking it and having been
burned by keeping secrets in the past, she told Curt about her
tradition.

"Let's go do it now," Curt suggested.

"Do what?" Jackie asked, not following.

"Let's go up to her room and show her the picture and have
her say the words," Curt said excitedly.

Jackie then recognized the brilliance of Curt's idea. As they
tramped through the living room where Caitlin and Cade were
playing, Jackie spread the news of Ash's new ability, making
sure to give them proper credit. After that, there was no choice
but to include Caitlin and Cade in the reveal of Jackie's formerly
private tradition. As they climbed the stairs, Jackie began to
waver on how she felt about having Caitlin and Cade included
in this activity. She was comfortable having Curt there. She
and Curt had talked frequently about their spouses and the
pain of their losses. She was less certain about how prepared
Curt's kids were for this reality. With no way to delicately dis-
invite them, she soldiered on to Ash's room.

As tradition would have it, Jackie took the framed picture
off of Ash's dresser and sat with her daughter in the corner
rocking chair. This time with Curt, Caitlin, and Cade gathered
around as first-time witnesses. As Jackie pointed to her image
in a beautiful, white wedding gown, Ash immediately said
"Mama" to the delight of her entire audience. When Jackie
pointed to Stu in a smart-looking tuxedo, Jackie prompted Ash

like she had done many times before with "Daddy." When Ash didn't parrot her prompt, Jackie began again, pointing to her image and getting Ash's immediate response. This time, when Jackie pointed to Stu, Ash got it and said, "Dada." While Curt, Caitlin, and Cade cheered, Jackie crumbled into a sea of tears. Curt and even the kids recognized the poignancy of the moment. They abbreviated their celebration to prop Jackie up with hugs and words of support. But it was Ash's irrepressible enthusiasm and pride that ultimately pulled Jackie out of the dark place and into the light of a new day. A day when her daughter began to recognize her father and the two people whose love brought her into this world. Any fears that Jackie previously had about her daughter's confusion were erased. She realized that Ash would come to understand the complexity of life and love and adapt to it just like everyone must.

As it was close to Ash's nap time, Jackie put her in the crib with no return protest. Caitlin and Cade returned to the living room, leaving Jackie and Curt alone.

"Let's go sit on the porch," Curt suggested. "I'll make us some coffee and bring you out a mug."

She couldn't resist the offer, and at the bottom of the stairs, they parted ways, temporarily. As she sank into one of the four padded wicker chairs, a housewarming gift from her parents, and looked out upon the park bathed in the summer sunshine. Her eyes went to the place where Ash had been abducted, and she counted her blessings once more.

Her reverie was interrupted by a call from Inspector Adams.

"Good afternoon, Theo," Jackie greeted.

"Hi, Jackie. I hope I'm not catching you at a bad time."

"No, no, I'm just sitting on my porch enjoying a beautiful summer day."

"Good. The reason I'm calling is that we just got out of our meeting with the folks from the FDA."

Jackie suddenly realized that Curt and the kid's visit had caused her not to think once about the AlzCura crusade or the critical meeting with the FDA.

"Oh, right, how did it go?"

"Well, it started out pretty rough. To make a long story short, Dr. Harder from the Center for Biologics Evaluation and Research feels optimistic that the OIG will get involved. She needs to run it by the Commissioner, so, unfortunately, it's unlikely that the FDA or the OIG will move as quickly as we would like."

"Well, better late than never, right?"

"Right. One of the things we discussed is a wrongful death lawsuit that an attorney who is representing Celeste is about to file. The group wanted me to talk to you and Curt about considering file similar lawsuits."

As if on cue, Curt made his appearance on the porch carrying two steaming mugs of coffee.

"Well, you're in luck, Theo. Curt just happens to be here visiting and just joined me. Can I put you on speaker?"

"Sure. That would be great."

Jackie put her phone on speaker and accepted a mug from Curt, who took a chair next to her.

"Can you hear us, Theo?" Jackie asked.

"Loud and clear."

"Hi, Theo," Curt said, taking a sip of his coffee.

"Hi, Curt. This is great. I needed to speak to both of you."

"Yeah, we figured that Theo. So I drove down here to save you a call," he joked.

"What a guy," Theo replied, laughing. "Well, I don't want to take up too much time from your visit, so let me get to the point. Jackie can fill you in on what we just discussed, but what

I need both of you to consider is whether you would be interested in filing lawsuits against AlzCura. As I told Jackie, Celeste is filing a wrongful death lawsuit through her attorney John Dryer. If you're interested, Curt, I'm sure he would be happy to discuss your situation."

"OK," Curt said tentatively. "Why now?"

"Good question, Curt. All along, we've been sensitive about wanting to coordinate our investigations and actions against AlzCura. We're trying to align the charges by the States of Maine and New York, as well as any civil lawsuits, so they occur at the same time. Not only will that give us the element of surprise, but we feel that the weight of all those legal actions might compel the FDA and OIG to act more quickly to support us."

"OK, that makes sense. I can talk to Attorney Dryer when I'm back in town next week."

Meanwhile, Jackie sat pensively, sipping her coffee. While she understood the rationale for Theo's request, she was having a hard time feeling motivated to pursue it. She wasn't sure if it was just the fact that Curt and the kids were visiting, or if she didn't want to dredge up the past, or a little of both.

"What about you, Jackie? Do you think you could look into the possibility of filing a lawsuit?" Theo asked as if he knew she was wrestling with the decision.

"I guess," she said tentatively. "I'd have to find a lawyer," she added.

"That's fine. I understand it would be a big step for both of you. As for a lawyer, perhaps Detective Farest or your cop friend in Nora can advise you," Theo offered, trying to be as helpful as possible.

"Thanks. That's a good idea, Theo," Jackie replied.

"OK, I'll let you guys go if you don't have any questions for me."

Curt looked at Jackie, who non-verbally transmitted that she had no questions.

"We're good here, Theo. Thanks for the call."

"And thanks for driving all the way down there to save me a call," Theo closed, leaving them all laughing as they ended the call.

Jackie didn't have to say anything for Curt to see the internal chaos Theo's call had caused.

"Let me guess," he began, "You're not certain you want to go there. That is, file a lawsuit."

"How did you know?" she asked, wondering if he was some sort of mind-reader.

"Because I'm in the same boat. As much as I want to see AlzCura brought to justice, I'm not sure that I want to jump into filing a lawsuit right now. I would have in a heartbeat 8 months ago, but now? I'm not so sure."

"That's exactly how I feel. Plus, I'm enjoying this too much," pointing back and forth between herself and Curt. "I've moved on."

"Well, let's not think about it for now. We have the weekend. Let's continue to enjoy it."

"Here, here," she said, raising her mug and getting up to go sit on his lap.

Cradled in his arms, sipping their coffees, they talked about anything and everything except AlzCura.

CHAPTER 29

C heryl Baker received a 911 text from Dr. Sheridan. She dismissed it as just another bout of Asa's much ado about nothing anxiety, which had become more pronounced since the last Board meeting. She took her time to finish an email to a prospective candidate for Jackie's position. Only to be surprised to find Dr. Simon Rosenthal, AlzCura's Board Chair, sitting with Dr. Sheridan and Chet Humphreys when she finally arrived at Asa's office. She immediately regretted her decision not to drop everything when she received the text and took her place at the conference table, fearful for her job.

"I'm sorry, I was in the ladies' room," Cheryl lied to cover her delayed appearance.

That explanation seemed to appease the Board Chair, but Cheryl could almost see the steam emanating from Asa's ears.

"Thank you for meeting with me on such short notice," began the Board Chair. "I just received a call from my nephew, and I'm afraid our effort to thwart Maine law enforcement investigations failed. In fact, I learned that Maine law enforcement was at the table with the FDA along with two doctors from Portland and a detective from Buffalo."

Asa looked like death warmed over, while Chet and Cheryl looked like they were out in left field.

"Simon, you will need to bring Chet and Cheryl up-to-speed. They don't know anything about our previous discussions," Asa interjected.

"Oh, I'm sorry," the Board Chair replied, "I thought you would have told them."

"No, I had hoped our plan would have worked, and I wouldn't have to bring you into this," he said dejectedly.

"OK, well, I appreciate that, Asa, but now we have some serious concerns," he replied. Cheryl and Chet sat on the edge of their seats, waiting to be brought into the loop.

"As you know, I'm the former Commissioner of the FDA," he began as Cheryl and Chet nodded in acknowledgment. "My nephew, Woodson Shearlow, is the Associate Director for Vaccine Safety in the Office of Vaccines Research & Review at the FDA's Center for Biologics Evaluation & Research. In the past, Woodson has been instrumental in helping us gain approval for the Recallamin clinical trials by, how should I put this, some creative analytics? Recently, he called me when his Director caught wind of some unreported adverse events in Maine."

Both Cheryl and Chet could not hide their shock. They knew about Dr. Muckland's data gymnastic efforts to scrub unfavorable data and present a favorable picture of Recallamin outcomes. They had no idea that the Board Chair had someone doing the same on the inside at the FDA. As the Board Chair continued, their shock about the company's inside connections and the depth of the deceptive practices only deepened.

"Asa and I talked about this, and Woodson was going to try to shift the focus away from Recallamin. Woodson was hoping to sell the delayed adverse event reporting as an idiosyncratic failure by one physician's office and a laissez-faire regulatory attitude by the State's Department of Licensing of Certification. Unfortunately, a snafu with communications between Woodson's office and Maine's DA and Woodson's boss' involvement in a meeting that occurred this morning all served to unravel our plan. What Woodson heard at the meeting is frightening. If he's correct, and I have no reason to doubt him, major law enforcement actions are imminent, and multiple lawsuits are about to be filed against us. Also, his Director will be going to the Commissioner in the next week, seeking to get the Office of the Inspector General involved. That could result in the feds swarming our operation and looking to shut us down."

"So, we're sitting ducks?" Asa asked.

"Well, I still have some strings I can pull with the current FDA Commissioner. But I'm afraid that Maine and New York, as well as at least one civil lawsuit, will proceed even if I'm successful at quashing that Director's report."

"Well, keeping the feds out of this would be huge," Chet finally found the courage to join the conversation. "Without the feds, we can employ some legal tactics to obfuscate and delay the state actions and civil suit. They can't just walk in here like the feds and confiscate computers and shut us down. We could drag this out over several years as other pharmaceutical companies have done."

"OK, I'm feeling a bit better about that," Asa responded. "Is there anything else besides Simon pulling strings at the FDA and your legal stalling strategies that we can do?"

"I can't think of any," Chet replied.

"Cheryl? Anything?" Asa asked his Vice President of Operations, who had been uncharacteristically quiet.

"I'm curious, did your nephew mention who was bringing the civil suit against us?" she directed to the Board Chair.

"He just said it was someone who had retained an attorney in Maine."

"So that is probably either Curt Barnes or Celeste Boulanger," Cheryl stated.

"Yeah, so what are you thinking?" Asa pushed impatiently.

"One civil suit is not good, but most pharmaceutical company's don't get into real hot water until there are multiple civil suits. Isn't that right, Chet?"

"She's right about that. What are you suggesting? We're in enough hot water from actions we decided to take involving your sons."

"No, I'm not suggesting using them. God no," she said with emphasis. "Jackie is still our biggest potential liability. If she was involved in influencing those Portland doctors to discontinue the use of Recallamin, she has the potential to influence many other physicians across the Northeast Region. Should we consider going after her legally for breach of her separation agreement?"

"Hmm, that's an interesting thought," Chet replied. "Asa, what do you think?"

"I'm not sure. I suggest we sleep on that and revisit the idea next week."

"Sounds good," Chet replied.

"I can live with that," Cheryl added.

"Anything else?" Asa asked with no responses. "Well then, thank you, Simon, for your support. Should we consider weekly Friday afternoon meetings for a few weeks just to make sure our strategies are aligned and working?"

"I would like that," Dr. Rosenthal replied, which made Cheryl and Chet's thoughts on the matter superfluous.

As Dr. Rosenthal said farewell and left Asa's office, the three AlzCura executives all had the same idea. Asa went to his office bar and returned with a bottle and three crystal tumblers.

CHAPTER 30

J ackie and Curt's porch retreat was just what they needed while Ash napped, and Caitlin and Cade occupied themselves playing in the living room. It had been an emotion-laden morning with Ash's language development and Theo's early afternoon call asking for them to consider taking legal action against AlzCura. Refreshed and with three kids to get cleaned up and dressed in preparation for their dinner with Jackie's parents, they devised a divide and conquer strategy.

"Girls in the master bathroom, boys in the guest bathroom?" Jackie proposed.

"Sounds good to me," Curt replied.

"Did you pack anything girly girl for Caitlin?"

"I told her to pack the dress her mother bought her. Hopefully, it still fits."

"OK. And shoes that match?"

"Yes, I think so. But in all honesty, Caitlin packed her bag, so I'm not really sure."

Jackie looked at him with a face that he couldn't misread.

"I know, I know, I'm not someone who can help Caitlin with being a girly girl. That's why I have you," he said defensively.

Jackie laughed, gave him a kiss, and said, "OK. One girly girl coming up."

Curt and Cade made quick work of getting ready for dinner and took up residence on the porch to wait for Jackie, Caitlin, and Ash to join them. It gave Cade a unique opportunity to talk to his father alone.

"Dad, do you miss mom?"

"Of course I do, Cade. Why do you ask?"

"I don't know. I've just been thinking about her more."

"I usually think about her more when I'm doing something fun or special with you and Caitlin," Curt replied.

"Do you love Jackie more than you loved mom?"

The question was a good but difficult one for Curt to answer in a way his nearly 7-year old son would understand.

"No, Cade, but I don't think of my love for Jackie as being more, or less, or the same as my love for your mother. Your mom was the love of my life. That's why I married her. I'll always love her and what we had together. Nothing and no one can replace what we had. Can you understand that?"

"Kinda," he said unconvincingly.

"How do you feel about Jackie?" Curt asked.

"I really like her, but," he paused as tears welled up in his eyes.

"But what, Cade?" Curt asked as he picked his son up and put him on his lap.

Cade could only cry in response. It reminded Curt of a session that he had with Counselor Timothy Darling when he was struggling with having lost Calli and his growing feelings for Jackie.

"Are you afraid that if you love Jackie, it means you don't love your mom?" he asked, taking a page out of his own emotional battles.

Cade nodded, confirming that his father had correctly

diagnosed the emotional storm that was brewing in him. He buried his head in his father's shoulder and sobbed. Curt held him until he quieted enough to continue.

"You can love Jackie and love your mother, Cade. Jackie could never take away the love you have for your mom. Nor would she want to. Don't you think mom would want you to be happy?"

"Yes," he snuffled, raising his head and wiping the tears from his eyes.

"Well, then you can love Jackie and love your mom if that's what makes you happy."

"Thanks, Dad."

"You're welcome," he replied, hugging and kissing his son, who subsequently got off his Dad's lap and returned to his own chair, relieved of the burden that he had been carrying.

When the girls made their appearance 30 minutes later, it was as if three angels appeared before them. Caitlin was beaming, transformed from an 8 going on 9-year old cowgirl to a mini-Jackie and a picture of femininity. Jackie, holding an equally radiant Ashley, was smoldering in a flattering red dress complimented by the diamond necklace and earrings that Stu had given her. Before Curt could find his voice, Cade spoke up.

"Wow, Caitlin, you look beautiful," getting up from his chair and approaching them.

"Thanks, Cade," Caitlin replied genuinely, still not accustomed to having her brother say nice things about her.

"You're beautiful too," Cade directed at Jackie and moved to hug her.

"Oh, boy, and I get a hug too?" Jackie asked. Looking at Curt quizzically as she bent down to accept a hug from Cade, who had not previously been demonstrative of his affection.

"Yes, you all look stunning," Curt confirmed, getting up from his chair and walking over to join Cade, who was all

215

smiles and looking like a weight had been lifted from him.

"We better get going," Jackie announced, "we can take my car, so we don't have to move Ash's car seat," handing Curt her keys.

"Ah, I get to drive milady's chariot?" Curt asked, affecting a servile tone and bowing.

"Yes, my good sir, but crash it, and it will be the gallows for thee," she smiled.

Jackie got Ash situated in her car seat, and Caitlin and Cade piled in the back seat next to her. Curt opened the passenger door for Jackie and then proceeded to the driver's side, adjusting the seat slightly to fit his frame. On the way to Danielle's Restaurant for dinner, Cade, always the curious one, asked what a chariot and gallows were and why his Dad always opened doors for others.

"Well, Cade. My parents always taught me to be polite, and opening doors for people, especially women, is a sign of respect."

"Why don't other people do it then? Don't they respect women?"

Curt shot Jackie a glance that communicated how challenging it was to answer Cade's questions. They were perfectly reasonable but not necessarily easy to respond to in a way a 6-year old could understand. Before he formulated his answer, Caitlin came to the rescue.

"Not everyone grows up learning the same rules, Cade. You'll learn that when you get to my grade. They're called customs, and they're different depending on where you grow up."

"Thank you, Caitlin. That was an excellent answer," her father said with gratitude.

"But why aren't the rules the same? Wouldn't it be easier if they were the same?" asked Cade, another reasonable set of difficult to answer questions.

This time Jackie took a stab at it.

"It might be easier if all the rules were the same, Cade, but I think it's our differences that make life interesting."

"I think it's just confusing," Cade replied.

"Part of growing up is learning to be sensitive and appreciative of people's differences, even if it's sometimes confusing," Curt chimed in.

"I love that your Daddy opens the door for me," Jackie stated.

The barrage of answers from his sister, Jackie, and his father seemed to satisfy Cade, at least temporarily. Which was a good thing because they were pulling into the restaurant's parking lot.

Jackie's parents were waiting outside the restaurant, and introductions were made before they proceeded to the door. Doris and Jack Selaney were well-aware of Curt and his kid's horrific past, having been previously briefed by their daughter. Jackie, true to her promise not to keep secrets, had also told them about the bond she had formed with Curt and the kids. As they approached the restaurant door, Cade ran ahead. As Cade struggled but finally held the door open as the group arrived at the entrance, Curt looked on with pride and wonderment. His little boy was growing up.

"My, my, what a fine young gentleman you are, Cade," Doris Selaney exclaimed as Cade smiled.

Seating around the table had to be negotiated as Caitlin and Cade both wanted to sit next to Jackie. Doris saved the day by gladly having Ash's high-chair placed next to her chair, allowing Caitlin and Cade to bookend Jackie while Curt took the seat between Cade and Jack Selaney. No sooner had Ash been located next to Doris when she said "Nana," shocking Jackie for the second time that day.

"You didn't tell me she had learned, Nana," Jackie said

accusingly.

"I told you I was going to teach her. I was hoping she'd surprise you some time by saying it when I wasn't there."

"Who's keeping the secrets now?" Jackie exclaimed as her mother nuzzled Ash's neck, causing her to giggle infectiously.

Dinner conversation was kept light, with most of the focus on the children. At one point, Ash said, "Dada," which returned the favor and shocked both Doris and Jack Selaney.

"Me and Cade taught her that," Caitlin said proudly, if not grammatically correct. Curt bit his tongue and didn't correct her, deciding it was better to let her have her moment of joy.

"Well, isn't she growing up before our eyes," Doris stated while nuzzling her again with predictable results that caused everyone at the table to laugh with her.

At the end of the meal, the reason for Caitlin and Cade's seating requests became apparent. While the adults passed on dessert, Caitlin and Cade order their traditional desserts, making sure that they offered the first bite to Jackie, who, although full, didn't disappoint them. Caitlin and Cade then launched into the story about how the tradition came to be when the hostess at the Farrisport Inn had mistakenly thought they were a family needing a table for four.

"What an incredible story, and what a wonderful tradition," Doris exclaimed.

Jackie and Curt then filled in the gaps in the kid's rendition. Adding the story of Monty Moose and how Curt's use of the back of his business card for the note accompanying their gift had allowed Jackie to contact Curt.

"Wow, that is quite a story," Jack Selaney chimed. "If that hostess didn't make that assumption. If you hadn't used your business card. God is alive and well in your relationship."

"The Lord gave, and the Lord hath taken away; blessed be the name of the Lord," Doris quoted from the Bible.

"Amen," Curt and Jackie replied in unison, causing their eyes to connect instantly and intensely.

"Well, I'm sorry to break up the prayer meeting," Jack Selaney interrupted. "Doris and I were hoping to take you all to the Palace Theatre to go see Kung Fu Panda."

Caitlin and Cade's immediate expressions of delight pre-empted any reservations Jackie or Curt may have had. As they made their way to the theatre, which was just a two-block walk away, Jackie realized that the last movie she had seen at the Palace Theatre was "Catch and Release" with Stu. Her emotions roiled inside her, alternating between sadness and amusement. Sadness because the plotline of a husband who keeps secrets and dies had replayed themselves in her marriage. Amusement as she recalled Stu calling her Jennifer Garner's younger and prettier sister. Thankfully, she felt reasonably confident that the plotline of Kung Fu Panda would not come back to haunt her in the future.

The movie was a hit with Caitlin and Cade and passable entertainment for the adults. While Ash, pushing the boundaries of her bedtime, found a way to sleep through most of it. The night ended with an agreement to meet for church and brunch on Sunday before Curt left for their trip back to Maine.

With the kids put to bed and fast asleep, Curt and Jackie wasted no time heating up the bedroom. Everything about the evening had been an affirmation of their special relationship. The decorum they needed to exercise in front of the children, and Jackie's parents now gave way to an abandonment of all propriety. Torridly moving to satisfy their appetite and hunger for one another. Reprising a line from the movie and taking some poetic license, Curt kissed his way down Jackie's body.

"Yesterday is history," he said, kissing her gently on the lips. "Tomorrow is a mystery," as he kissed her on the side of her neck. "But you are a gift," kissing her breasts. "That's why you are a present," he concluded as his lips traveled to her navel and beyond. It may not have been Kung Fu, but both put moves on each other that night designed purely for each other's pleasure. After achieving the apex of their private performance, they lay in each other's arms sated and fell asleep.

The next morning, Jackie and Curt saved water in the shower and dedicated the rest of the morning to a visit to the Buffalo Zoo for the kids. Caitlin and Cade ran excitedly from one exhibit to another, and Curt and Jackie took turns pushing Ash in her stroller. Just as they would catch up to Caitlin and Cade, they were off to the next display like an advance team. This pattern repeated itself for nearly three hours as both Jackie and Curt marveled at the kid's boundless energy and excitement. Eventually, Caitlin and Cade hit the wall and complained vociferously of being tired. So tired, in fact, that they didn't even ask to buy anything as they exited through the aptly named gift shop "Zootique." They gave in to Caitlin and Cade's request for fast food on the way home, and by the time they were turning into Jackie's driveway, Caitlin and Cade's eyes were at half-mast, and Ash was asleep. Jackie put Ash down for her nap, and Caitlin and Cade retired to the living room couch, where both quickly fell asleep watching TV.

Curt and Jackie, who had not ordered fast food, made sandwiches instead and took them out to the porch to enjoy in the same two chairs they had occupied the previous day. Both had the same thing on their mind, but Curt expressed it first.

"How am I ever going to be able to leave here tomorrow?"

"What? You're reading my mind now?" Jackie replied. "I was just thinking about how I'm going to miss you and the kids."

"Not only am I beyond happy, but the kids are too. They haven't fought once, and they obviously love you."

"Caitlin asked me if I loved you while I was doing her makeup."

"What did you say?"

"I told her I loved you very much. But then she dropped a bomb."

"What's that?"

"She asked me if you and I were going to get married."

"Oh, that must have been a bit uncomfortable. What did you say?"

"I told her I didn't know. But she's too smart for that answer, so she asked me if I wanted to get married to you."

"Uh-huh," Curt said, waiting for what her answer to that question would be.

"You're going to make me tell you, aren't you?"

"Of course," he replied.

"What did you think I said?" she responded, turning the tables. "Let's see just how compatible we are."

"OK, in that case, I think you said, of course, are you fucking kidding me? I'd be a fool not to marry that stud."

"Amazing, that's exactly what I said to her," Jackie replied, leaning over to give him a kiss.

"Well, while you were having your little talk with Caitlin, Cade was asking me if it was OK to like you."

"Really?"

"Yep. The poor boy really loves you, and I think he was worried that if he expressed his affection for you, that it would mean he didn't love his mom anymore."

"So, that's the reason he gave me a hug when I walked out on the porch."

"Yep, that or the fact you looked smoking hot, and he's the first 6-year old boy to reach puberty."

"Well, thank you, but I think both of your kids are desperate to have a mother figure in their lives. What did you tell

Cade?"

"I told him that he could love you and that it didn't take anything away from the love of his mother."

"That's pretty astute, professor."

"Not really. I had the same conversation with my counselor about 3 months ago when I was struggling with my feelings for you."

"Three months ago? Really?"

"Yes, and frankly, I fell for you hard the first time we met."

"At the Farrisport Inn? You hardly said a word. I almost thought you didn't like me."

"I didn't say much because I couldn't fit a word in edgewise with the kids occupying your attention. My stomach was doing flip-flops. I couldn't believe the most beautiful woman I had ever seen was sitting across the table from me."

"Oh my God, Curt. I never knew."

"I know, and at the time, I wouldn't have wanted you to know. You were still," Curt paused, not knowing how to proceed.

"I was still married to Stu," Jackie completed the sentence for him.

"Yes," Curt replied sheepishly.

Jackie put down her plate and went to sit in Curt's lap, just like she had done almost 24-hours to the minute the day before. They held each other for a long time in silence. Knowing all that mattered was that they were together, and as her parents had said, a higher power had a hand in their union.

After a 3-hour respite, the kids woke up ready to go again. Jackie took the girls out shopping while Curt pulled Cade's scooter out of the trunk and followed him to the park. When Jackie returned, Curt helped unload the car carrying the bounty from their shopping trip, which included an assortment of clothing and grocery bags.

"Wow, is there anything left in the stores?" he cracked.

"Well, I was just doing my duty, making sure Caitlin has some girly-girl things. I also picked up some things for dinner tonight."

"Daddy, you should see what Jackie bought me. They're so pretty. And she bought me some make-up too," she said excitedly.

"I hope that's OK," Jackie said, looking at Curt with some concern.

"In matters of girly-girl, you're the expert. Of course, it's OK," he replied, changing Jackie's look of concern to one of delight.

While Jackie and Curt worked in the kitchen to prepare an Italian feast, Caitlin entered and exited the kitchen like a model, systematically showing off her new clothes to her father and Cade.

"After dinner, Cade, I'm going to take you out shopping, OK?" Jackie announced in between one of Caitlin's entrances.

Cade's face lit up. "Really?"

"Yep, as long as your Dad can watch the girls," she said, shooting Curt a look that communicated she was sorry she hadn't OK'd her idea with him beforehand.

"No problem," Curt replied, happy that Cade would get individual time with Jackie and surprised that Cade hadn't already sulked over Caitlin's shopping spree.

Cade excitedly ran out of the kitchen to tell Caitlin, giving Jackie a chance to thank Curt for his understanding.

"I'm sorry, I should have asked you first," she said while moving to hug him.

As he willingly pulled her in for a hug and kissed her, he said, "I'm actually happy you didn't, you don't need my permission to do loving things for the children. Not that I mind you coming over here and apologizing," he said as his hands began to wonder.

"Dessert is for later," she announced, kissing him and turning out of his arms to resume cooking, just in time as Caitlin made her entrance in one of her new dresses.

"What do you think, Daddy?"

"I think it's beautiful, honey. Have you thanked Jackie?"

"Only like a hundred times," Jackie replied before Caitlin had an opportunity.

With dinner almost ready and Caitlin's modeling show completed, Jackie asked Caitlin and Cade to set the dining room table. They did so without question or complaint to Curt's continued amazement. You would have thought Jackie was an Iron Chef by how the kids reacted to the simple spaghetti dinner with salad and garlic bread, followed by store-bought cannolis. Jackie could do no wrong in the kid's eyes. As happy as Curt was for them, he began to dread the emotional storm that was certain to accompany their departure the next day.

Curt offered to clean up after dinner, allowing Jackie and Cade to go on their shopping adventure. Afterward, Caitlin suggested they give Ashley a bath before her bedtime, having witnessed how Jackie had bathed her before dinner the day before.

"You know, Caitlin, I have bathed two babies before," her father said as Caitlin was becoming a little too bossy in her supervision of the process.

"But that's not how Jackie does it," Caitlin said defensively.

"OK, well, then show me how Jackie does it," Curt replied, making room for Caitlin to take over.

Surprised and a bit apprehensive, Caitlin slowly approached the tub but stopped short.

"You know, I don't think it matters that much. You're

doing fine," she backpedaled.

"Well, thank you, Caitlin," he replied sarcastically.

"Dad?"

"What, honey?"

"Are you going to marry Jackie?"

Curt continued to bathe Ash, not entirely surprised by his daughter's question since being tipped off by Jackie of similar questions asked of her by Caitlin the day before.

"Do you think I should?"

"Yes."

"Why do you think that?"

"Well, she loves you and Cade, and I love her."

"Well, that's a good start. I love Jackie, too, but marriage is a big step. It's a life-long commitment, and you don't just jump into it."

"I know that, but you both were married before. Can't you tell if you love each other enough to be married?"

"It doesn't quite work that way, Caitlin. We were married to different people, and every relationship is unique. While Jackie and I love each other very much, we haven't had a lot of time together. Plus, it's not just about us. We have to consider what is in the best interest of our children. Listen, I'm happy that you love Jackie and think I should marry her. That means a lot to me. Let's just continue to enjoy our time here with her and let things take their course, OK?"

"OK," Caitlin said, only partially satisfied with his answer.

After Curt dressed Ash for bed and Caitlin read her "Goodnight Moon" in the rocking chair, they put her down in her crib. As Ash looked up at Caitlin and Curt, she said, "Dada," causing Curt to tear up.

"She loves you too, Dad," Caitlin said as if adding evidence to the marry Jackie file.

Jackie returned with an excited Cade and an armful of bags from clothing stores. Rather than model the purchases, Cade displayed the array of shirts, pants, and socks on his bed in the spare bedroom. The four started to watch a movie on TV, but Caitlin and Cade quickly faded, and Curt and Jackie carried them up the stairs and tucked them into their beds.

"I have an idea," Jackie said.

"What's that?"

"A surprise. Why don't you go unload the dishwasher, and I will come and get you when the surprise is ready."

"Your wish is my command, milady," Curt replied, reprising his role as her servant.

Ten minutes later, Curt had unloaded the dishwasher and scrubbed every surface in the kitchen clean. As he was looking for another chore to perform, Jackie reappeared in the kitchen doorway clad only in her bra and panties.

"Ready?" she asked salaciously.

"Not as ready as you it appears, but yes!" he replied excitedly.

Climbing the stairs behind her was an exercise in restraint for Curt. By the time they arrived at her bedroom, he had unbuttoned his shirt and was loosening his belt. She led him into the bathroom, dimly lit by candlelight emanating from a handful of tea lights ringing the bathtub. While he looked on, Jackie sensually removed her undergarments and stepped into the warm bubbly, and fragrant bathwater. Curt couldn't get the rest of his clothes off fast enough in a process that was more frantic than sensuous. Joining Jackie in the tub, their skin slick and sensitive from the warm wet soapy water enhanced the pleasure produced by where their bodies met. Periodically adding hot water to extend their luxurious soak, their physical and verbal communion felt spiritual. An hour later, both emerged not bathed but baptized in each other. Slipping into bed, they fell asleep with their bodies hopelessly and blissfully entwined.

Sunday arrived too soon, and time was moving too fast when Jackie and Curt finally rolled out of bed. With a 9a.m. church service only an hour away, they rushed to get themselves and the kids ready, barely arriving before the bells at St. Paul's Church tolled the start of the service. Fortunately, Doris and Jack Selaney had reserved space in their pew, which was entirely too close to the front for Curt's comfort. As they made their way down the center aisle, Curt couldn't help but feel the entire congregation was making value judgments on their near-tardy arrival. If that wasn't bad enough during the service, Father Woznewski, more than once, cast a glance in their direction, causing Curt to become paranoid. The gospel, as luck would have it, was from I Corinthians 13, and as Father read the gospel, Curt found Jackie's hand and squeezed it as Father read,

"Love is patient; love is kind; love is not envious or boastful or arrogant or rude. It does not insist on its own way; it is not irritable or resentful; it does not rejoice in wrongdoing but rejoices in the truth. It bears all things, believes all things, hopes all things, endures all things."

By the time Father read, "And now these three remain: faith, hope, and love. But the greatest of these is love," tears were streaming down both Jackie and Curt's faces. If Father hadn't been looking at them before, he surely was now, but Curt had moved from feeling paranoia to a place where nothing or no one could touch him. As they sat down to listen to Father's sermon, all the pain, loneliness, fear, and uncertainty in Curt and Jackie's lives over the last year had lifted. Curt, however, was not prepared for the reception he and Jackie would receive as they exited the church. Joining Father Woznewski was Clara Himber and a small but mighty cadre of parishioners that started to sing when they emerged from the church.

What was foreign to Curt and his kids was familiar to Jackie and Ashley, who giggled with delight. As the German children's song ended and the parishioners broke out in applause, the spotlight shifted to Jackie, who immediately handed Ash over to Clara.

"Thank you so much, and what a great surprise," Jackie began. "I'd like to introduce you to some very special people in my life who I'm sure are very confused by all this fanfare. Curt Barnes and his two children Caitlin and Cade who visited me all the way from Maine."

As the crowd once again rose in applause, Jackie quickly briefed Curt that Clara was the woman who had discovered Ash in the church. As Jackie was about to comment further, Father Woznewski indicated that he would take over.

"Jackie, Curt, Caitlin, Cade, and Ashley, we are delighted that you joined us for our service today. I could tell that today's gospel has meaning in your lives and relationship. If I may speak for the entire St. Paul congregation, we want to extend our prayers and best wishes for your continued health and happiness."

Father's words were met with another round of applause and a few amens. To say that Curt and the kids were shocked at this outpouring of kinship was an understatement. While he felt he should make a statement, he was too overcome with emotion to find the words.

Doris and Jack informed Jackie and Curt that Clara would be riding with them and joining them for brunch. Since Ash seemed content in Clara's arms, Jackie suggested Clara keep Ash for the ride to Momma's. As the table for eight assembled, Clara purposefully took a seat close to Curt, wishing to learn more about the man in Jackie's life. After everyone had their fill of Momma's famous carrot cake pancakes and the hour was fast approaching for Curt and the kids to make the long drive back to Maine, they said their farewells.

Predictably, on the way back to Jackie's house, Caitlin and Cade pleaded to extend their stay. Jackie, who could do no wrong in the kid's eyes, quickly snuffed out their whining.

"Let's not end our visit like this, OK? I've already decided that Ash and I are going to come to Maine to visit in a couple weeks, so let's celebrate all the great things that we shared over the last couple of days."

Although Curt knew nothing of Jackie's plan to visit, he wasn't going to argue, as he needed her pep talk as much as the kids did. As they pulled into Jackie's driveway, Jackie had the kids catalog all the good things that happened on their visit. Including Ash learning to say "Dada," the movie, the visit to the zoo, playing in the park, the shopping trips, and their meals together. Curt and Jackie could have added a few more things had their audience not required G-rating content.

There were hugs and kisses all around and a few tears as their time together ended. As Jackie and Curt came together just outside the driver's side door, they shared a prolonged hug and kiss. Meanwhile, Caitlin and Cade sat in the car, hopeful that their father might change his mind and elect to stay.

"I'm in love with you, Jackie. Leaving you is one of the hardest things I've ever had to do."

"I know. I'm in love with you too. I don't want you to go. I hope you don't mind me inviting myself to Maine.

"Are you kidding? Hop in right now."

"I wish I could. Call me when you get home, OK?"

"So, you want me to call you right now? Because you're my home."

"In that case, call me when you get to your apartment in Maine."

"I will," he said, giving her a final hug and kiss before feeling the pain of letting her go and getting into the car.

The ride home was bittersweet but filled with more stories

of hope and happiness than despair. The magic that Jackie had worked in transforming Caitlin and Cade's relationship held fast, as they played cooperatively until both fell asleep as they crossed into Maine. After arriving home and putting the kids to bed, he unpacked his suitcase. He found the pair of panties that Jackie had worn when she had enticed him into taking a bath with her. He reached for the phone, and as it rang, he held the panties to his nose, wondering why in the hell he had left her.

CHAPTER 31

F DA Commissioner Dr. Lynn Franklin hung up the phone. There was precious little time to act before it would be difficult to unwind a potentially sticky situation. She stuck her head out of her office door.

"I need you to set up an emergency meeting with Dr. Elizabeth Harder and a representative from the Office of Human Capital Management. ASAP," she said to her assistant.

While she waited for the meeting to be arranged, she re-read the written complaint that was on her desk and formulated a plan.

Dr. Elizabeth Harder was drafting her report on her visit to Maine when she received a call to come to the Commissioner's office to attend an emergency meeting. Emergency meetings with all the FDA Office Directors weren't rare. She hoped that whatever the emergency was, it wouldn't involve her office and wouldn't significantly delay the completion of her report. She was surprised when she was directed to the Commissioner's office for the meeting instead of the conference room – where emergency meetings were usually held.

"Elizabeth, thank you for coming on such short notice," Dr. Franklin greeted. "Please make yourself comfortable," which Dr. Harder found challenging to comply with, recognizing that a representative from the Human Capital Management department was also in the room.

"I've asked Richard from Human Capital Management to join us because they will be instrumental in supporting your promotion to a new position."

"A new position?" Dr. Harder asked, relieved to hear she wasn't being let go even though she had a spotless employment record.

"Yes, I am promoting you to Director of the Office of Special Projects, and Richard here will be your contact in terms of staffing the new Office. Unfortunately, until the next budget cycle, you will only be able to hire an assistant and an analyst this year."

"Who will take over the Office of Vaccine Research and Review?"

"We have someone in mind for the office, but I need you to get up-to-speed immediately on your first project. As you might already know, with the new Food and Drug Administration Amendments Act last year, we are placing more emphasis on opioid safety. Recently, one of the larger drug manufacturers requested an expansion of their drug's indications to include patients with non-cancer breakthrough pain. I need you to head up the investigation and consideration of that request."

"What about the cases I'm working on in my current position. I was just about to draft my report from our visit to Maine. I think"

"I don't want you to worry about those cases, Elizabeth," Dr. Franklin interrupted. "I will see to it that the person we place in your former position follows up on those cases."

"But,"

"No buts, Elizabeth. Now my assistant will get you the details on that drug manufacturer's request, and Richard will start sourcing candidates for the positions you need to fill. I'll need your recommendation on the request by the end of the week, OK?"

"OK."

"Good. Thanks, Elizabeth. Richard will show you to your new office space."

The whirlwind meeting left Dr. Harder's head spinning. The Commissioner's instructions were clear. She had to let go of any professional obligations to complete unfinished work in her previous job and transition immediately to her new job and new focus.

As Richard and Dr. Harder exited Dr. Franklin's office, the Commissioner breathed a sigh of relief. She shredded the complaint that was on her desk and called the individual that would be taking Dr. Harder's former position.

"Dr. Shearlow, how would you like to be promoted to Director of the Office of Vaccine Research and Review?"

Receiving his affirmative response, she added, "You may start immediately. Do we need to discuss what needs to be done with Dr. Harder's pending case in Maine?"

"No, I think I have a good handle on what needs to be done," Dr. Shearlow replied.

"Good. Congratulations on your promotion," the Commissioner concluded.

"Thank you, Lynn," he replied, his casual use of her first name grating on her. She despised Dr. Shearlow. She saw him as nothing more than an entitled little shit who suffered from small man syndrome. Only aspiring to his lofty position because the former Commissioner, Dr. Simon Rosenthal, happened to be his uncle. If she weren't indebted to Dr. Rosenthal for getting her the job as Commissioner, she would have dispensed with Woodson Shearlow a long time ago. He wasn't even a medical doctor but acted like he was.

"That's Commissioner Franklin to you, Woodson Shearlow, Ph.D. in Anthropology. Got it?" she replied, skewering his lack of appropriate medical credentials.

"Yes, ma'am," he responded, but she had already hung up.

Undaunted, he got up from his desk and removed his nameplate from the outside of his cubicle. He walked over to Dr. Harder's former office, replaced her nameplate with his, and threw hers in the trash. Then, he walked into his new office, picked up Dr. Harder's file entitled "Maine," and deposited it into the office's industrial-sized shredder. Proud of his day's work, he packed up and went home to celebrate his promotion, although it was only 11a.m.

CHAPTER 32

C hief Detective Lester Gains, who went by Les, was a 20-year veteran at the Buffalo Police Department. Many felt he was heir-apparent to replace Police Commissioner Dirk Sorenson, who announced he would be retiring from his post at the end of the year.

Les Gains had a reputation in law enforcement circles for unmatched perseverance, toughness, and success. He was fond of saying that he owed his success not only to his parents but to the bullies who ridiculed him mercilessly growing up. As the story went, a group of grade school bullies frequently made fun of his first name and chanted "Lester the Molester" or "Short Bus Les." Taunting him by saying his parents named him Les Gains because he was a retard. He was surprisingly patient with their ridiculing and took their mocking with an eery silence and calm that only made the bullies goad him more. He never complained to his teachers or his parents, thinking that they would eventually tire of their antics. When their bullying persisted, he changed his strategy. The next day, when their taunting continued, he picked out a bully two grades ahead of him and nearly twice his size, and with a blindingly quick punch, knocked him out cold. He was never bullied again.

Detective Farest didn't waste a minute in reporting to Chief Detective Gains' office Monday morning. He knew that his boss had gone out on a limb to approve his trip to Maine, and

Brent was anxious to prove the benefit was worth the cost. Knocking on his boss' office door, Chief Detective Gains invited him in.

"Good morning, Chief. Do you have time for me to update you on my visit to Maine?"

"I don't know, did you bring me my lobster?" he replied with a seriousness that made Detective Farest wonder if he had missed his boss' request.

"I'm joking, Brent. Relax," he laughed.

"God, you scared me," Detective Farest laughed, joining in the joke.

"What did you learn up in lobsterland?"

Detective Farest told his Chief about how the meeting was almost short-circuited by one of the FDA physicians. Then summarized the additional evidence that had been presented by his counterpart and the other meeting participants.

"So, is the FDA onboard?" Chief Gains asked.

"Yes, and the lead FDA physician at the meeting will be talking to the FDA Commissioner about engaging the OIG. Unfortunately, she couldn't give us assurances about timing, and her best guess was that it would take a few weeks."

"Well, that's not good. We need to act sooner rather than later."

"That's what Maine's Attorney General said. He suggested we try to arrange a conference call this week to coordinate our next steps."

"Who does he want to be involved from our side?"

"He wanted to get the State's Attorney General involved, but I suggested that we start with you, the Commissioner, and perhaps our Regional Assistant Attorney General."

"Phew, that's still going to be a tough group to get together on short notice, but I agree those are the right players. I'll see what I can arrange."

"What was the Commissioner's reaction when you briefed him on my trip?"

"He was fine with it once I laid out all the evidence we had. He'll be even more anxious to get rolling on this with the information you shared with me. Do me a favor and write up a summary of what you told me."

"Already done. I'll send it to you when I get to my desk."

"Well, look at you," Chief Gains exclaimed. "One step ahead of me."

"No, sir, I knew you'd need a report to communicate this up the chain of command, and time is of the essence."

"If you're not careful, you might work yourself into my job someday," Chief Gains replied.

"Thank you, sir."

"And how often do I have to tell you, you can call me Les instead of sir?"

"I'm sorry, sir, I mean Les. It's hard to break old habits."

"I understand. I have the same problem addressing the Commissioner," he laughed. "I'll get back to you later today on potential dates and times for a conference call, OK?"

"Sounds good, Les."

"Bravo, you did it!" Chief Detective Gains said, applauding him for effect.

Detective Farest left his boss's office inspired and energized. The rumors of his boss potentially taking the Commissioner role had weighed heavily on him, worried about who he might have to report to in the aftermath. Now he realized that if he continued to play his cards right, he might be up for a promotion. He fired up his computer, and despite a large backlog of emails from being out of the office, he immediately sent the report of his meeting in Maine to his boss.

* * *

Attorney John Dryer was surprised when Inspector Adams walked in with Celeste Boulanger for his 10a.m. meeting to discuss her wrongful death lawsuit.

"Good morning. I wasn't expecting both of you," Attorney Dryer exclaimed.

"I know, I'm sorry," Theo apologized, shaking the attorney's hand. "I promise this will only take a minute, and I'll be out of here."

"No worries, Theo. What's on your mind?"

"I just wanted to let you know that we had our meeting with the FDA, and while it looks favorable that they will get the OIG involved, it will likely take a few weeks before we see any action."

"OK, that's good. Are you asking me to postpone filing Celeste's suit?"

"Not at all. But I did talk with Curt Barnes to consider speaking with you about filing a lawsuit as well."

"OK, I appreciate the potential referral. Mr. Barnes' case would be significantly different from Celeste's. I'd have to see the evidence," Attorney Dryer replied. Wondering to himself if his brief stint representing Darius Scott would disqualify him from representing Mr. Barnes on the grounds of conflict of interest.

"I can tell you right now, it's problematic. Darius Scott's autopsy, which is now a matter of public record, showed physical signs consistent with those people that had the vaccine and died from brain bleeds and liver failure. However, AlzCura claims Darius didn't get the vaccine."

"Hmm, that does complicate matters, but if AlzCura execs

are as shady as it appears, we shouldn't bank on anything they claim."

"Lastly, the AG, DA, and I are setting up a call with our counterparts in New York to coordinate the next steps, which may include bringing charges against AlzCura."

"So you're OK with my filing Celeste's lawsuit this Thursday, then?"

"I don't think I really have a say in the matter, but since you ask, yes. Someone needs to go first, and with any luck, Maine and New York will right behind you."

"If it's any consolation, it will be a few days after we file before AlzCura is served with the summons and complaint. So they probably won't know until sometime next week. And if Maine and New York join the party, that's fine by me. It would certainly be a helluva 1-2 punch if it occurred. We'll proceed then if you're still willing, Celeste," Attorney Dryer asked.

"Oh, I'm more than willing," Celeste replied.

"OK then, thanks, Theo. But Celeste, if you could stay a bit longer, I'd like to go over the court filing and process with you."

"We drove separately," Theo replied. "And I have to get back to work. Thanks, John," he said, getting up from the chair, shaking the attorney's hand, and giving Celeste a peck on the cheek as he was exiting.

After Theo left, Attorney Dryer went over the court filing with Celeste, which was important but not as crucial as managing her expectations regarding how long the legal process could take.

"OK, I know we went over this before, but I want to be sure you understand just what we're potentially in for by filing this lawsuit."

"I know it could take a long time."

"It could take years. It's like the longest marathon you can imagine, and while you won't have to do much while you're waiting, it's the emotional toll of having this drag on that wears on people. I've seen it before, and I just want to be sure you have adequate support systems."

"I've got Theo, and as long as the media leaves me alone, I'll be alright. Thanks for your concern."

"Alright, I'm just a legal counselor, but I know other people who've had to endure these lengthy legal processes often find it helpful to talk to someone. It doesn't matter whether they're a priest, a social worker, or a psychologist. I know you have Theo, and he's a great guy, but consider whether you always want to lay any burdens you may be feeling on him. It's sometimes better to talk with a professional."

"I see what you mean. For a legal counselor, you're pretty smart about emotional matters."

"Let's just say, I've learned the hard way. I've seen too many clients win their legal cases, but in the process, lose other things near and dear to them. I don't want that to happen to you."

"I'll seriously consider your advice."

"Good, because I want to join you and Theo out at the cabin some weekend for those beers he promised."

"Oh, so that whole spiel about my having support systems was not out of concern for me, then? I get it now," she said sarcastically, as both erupted in laughter.

Their meeting concluded, each knowing that the first domino was about to fall in what both hoped would cause a cascade of falling dominoes aimed at bringing AlzCura to justice.

CHAPTER 33

Everything about Monday morning felt foreign and out of sync for Jackie. Waking up alone. Showering alone. Not hearing the thunder of Caitlin and Cade's feet storming up or down her stairs. It was as if she had a massive hangover whose only cure was to imbibe once more in what had caused it, but, sadly, she couldn't. Instead, she padded around the rooms with the ghosts of the happy experiences from the weekend haunting her. While preparing some coffee in the hopes of infusing a cure to her sluggishness, her phone rang. Hoping it was Curt, she was uncharacteristically disappointed to see the name "Sunny."

"Hi, Sunny," she said, trying to sound chipper but failing.

"Hi, girlfriend. Did I catch you at a bad time? You sound down."

"No, just a bit tired," she lied, not ready to have a conversation about Curt and the kids with her friend just yet. "I haven't had my coffee yet."

"Well, I won't keep you. I wanted to talk about the plan we made for when I come out there this Friday."

Jackie had completely forgotten about her offer to put Sunny up in her house during her internship that was starting in one week. An offer she had been excited to make at the time, but one that potentially posed a barrier to future visits by Curt and the kids.

"OK," Jackie replied tentatively.

"I'm afraid you're not going to like what I have to say," Sunny began.

"Why do you say that?"

"Well, Barrett called me, and he wants me to stay with him. I know this is sudden, but we haven't stopped talking to each other since I left. Would you hate me if I didn't stay with you? We'll still see each other, obviously."

"No, of course not, Sunny. I understand completely," as her voice regained the liveliness that it lacked when she answered the phone.

"Are you sure? Cuz,"

"Yes, I'm sure, Sunny. I'm so happy for you. Barrett's a great guy."

"He is. Do you know that he almost flew out here this weekend? As much as I wanted to see him, I told him to save his money. I don't want to jinx it or anything, but I think he just might be the one."

"I'm so excited for you, Sunny," Jackie said. Even though she was probably more excited that this now opened up the possibility that she would receive more visits from Curt and the kids.

"Thanks, Jackie. I'll have Barrett swing by and pick up Big Bird sometime this week, OK?" Sunny said, referencing the humongous yellow piece of luggage she had left at Jackie's from her visit.

"Sounds good, Sunny."

"I love you, girlfriend. I still want to see you and the snugglebug sometime this weekend, OK?"

"OK. Love you too, little one," tossing in a friendly jab at her petite friend.

Sunny's call, more than the coffee she was sipping, had done more to cure the funk she had been in. Hearing Ashley stirring upstairs, she climbed the stairs, reminded of her sensuous lingerie-clad ascent that weekend as a preface to bathtime fun with Curt. While getting Ash ready for the day, she committed to calling him later to schedule the visit to Maine she had spontaneously decided upon and promised the kids.

As she fed Ash, she suddenly remembered the other unfinished business that she and Curt had from the weekend - a decision on whether to file lawsuits against AlzCura. As passionate and instrumental as she had been in the efforts to expose the truth about her former employer, she had to admit to herself a desire to be done with it. The crusade was nearing the one-year mark and had introduced nothing but chaos and personal risk into her life. The past weekend with Curt and kids, excepting Theo's call, had been like an oasis in a vast desert of fear and uncertainty. She could almost feel the relief just thinking about moving on. Almost.

One thing stood in the way of washing her hands of the crusade - Stu and the countless numbers of other people she knew were being harmed. Her conscience would not let her move away from what she had started. If she did, she would be haunted forever with the thoughts of those already harmed and those that would continue to be harmed by AlzCura's greed and reckless practices. She could not walk away now. To do so would make her feel as much a criminal as the executives she used to work for. With Ashley fed and playing contentedly in the living room, she couldn't put off calling Curt any longer.

"Good morning, beautiful," Curt answered, "and thanks for the gift you left in my bag."

"Good morning, handsome. Glad you like my present."

"Like? I almost jumped back into the car and drove back there."

"Then, I accomplished what I intended. I miss you, Curt."

"And we miss you. I could hardly get the kids out the door to school today. They both cried. They literally cried because they missed you and Ash so much. I felt like the worst person in the world when I dropped them off at school. Thank God you said you'd be visiting. It was the only thing I could use to motivate them."

"Aww, that's actually one of the reasons I wanted to call you. The other reason is that we need to talk about what Theo asked us to consider when he called us this weekend."

"Oh, yeah, that. I totally spaced that out."

"I did too, but let's talk about my visit first."

"Fine with me. How about you leave now, and I'll have a late dinner prepared for you when you arrive?"

"You don't know how tempted I am to take you up on that suggestion."

"You already have some clothes here, so you wouldn't have to pack much."

"Aren't you a comedian? As much as I'd like to be there right now, I have a proposal. Something that will motivate both of us."

"I'm plenty motivated to see you already. I don't think I need any more."

"I mean motivated to do what we need to do so that we can do what we want to do," Jackie clarified.

"What does that mean?" Curt asked, intrigued.

Jackie told Curt of the emotional wrestling match she had fought in her head just before the call that led to her decision about filing a lawsuit against AlzCura. She was not surprised to hear that Curt felt similarly.

"So here's my proposal. We both explore our options for filing a lawsuit. When we have both retained attorneys or in your case, if that attorney Theo mentioned determines you don't have a case, I will come out. If we get it done this week, I'll see you this weekend."

"So we have to eat our spinach before eating dessert," Curt said dejectedly.

"Yes, if you want to put it that way. It's the right thing to do, but won't we both enjoy dessert?"

"That we will. You're right. We need to see this through."

"I love you, Curt."

"I love you, Jackie. Let's talk later when the kids are home. I know they'd love to hear your voice."

"I'd like that. Now call that attorney," she commanded.

"I'm on it," Curt replied, hanging up and immediately doing a search for Attorney John Dryer's contact information.

CHAPTER 34

The enthusiasm that Detective Farest felt after his early morning meeting with Chief Gains waned little by little throughout the day. While away on his trip to Maine, a blizzard of emails, reports, and new cases had accumulated that consumed his day. By the end of the day and near the end of his rope, his boss appeared in the doorway.

"Good news, Brent. Both the Commissioner and the Assistant Attorney General agreed we need to expedite the AlzCura case. I've found 30 minutes on Friday at 2 p.m. when they could conference with our colleagues in Maine if that works for them."

"That's great. I'm sure they'll want to make it work," he replied, rubbing the back of his neck.

"Everything alright," Chief Gains asked, "you look like hell."

"Yeah, I've just been staring at this screen all day trying to catch up with the backlog."

"That's what you get for being a superstar and kicking back in Maine," his boss joked.

"Oh yeah, it was nothing but a party arriving in Maine near midnight only to wake up at 6 a.m. to drive to the meeting. Then catching a 3 p.m. flight back that got delayed in Newark, so I could arrive home at 2a.m. Saturday."

"I know. In all seriousness, the Commissioner and Assistant Attorney General see the AlzCura case as a priority. If you need to off-load any of your work, let me know. You're a victim of your own success, Brent. When people want something done, you're the go-to guy."

"Thanks, sir," he replied and immediately saw his boss's disapproving look. "Thanks, Les," he corrected himself.

"That's better. Now go home and get some rest."

"I will after I call my counterpart in Maine."

Re-energized, he tapped the last call entry to Theo on his phone to call him with the good news.

"Hey, Brent."

"Hi, Theo. I just wanted to let you know that 2 p.m. this Friday works for us if your folks are available."

"That's great news. I'll check with them and get back to you."

"Yeah, well, the sooner, the better. My boss just said our Commissioner and Assistant Attorney General see this as a priority. I'm sure you're even more anxious to get rolling as long as you've been working the case."

"You're right about that. I'll call our DA and AG's assistants now and text you right back."

"Sounds good," Detective Farest responded and ended the call.

Taking Chief Gains' advice to heart, he powered down his computer and called it a day. On the way home, his phone announced an incoming text. Checking it while he was stopped in the interminable rush hour traffic, he was pleased to see Theo's affirmative response to the Friday meeting time. As the stop-and-go traffic continued, he texted Chief Gains the favorable news. He received an immediate text response.

"Great. Now go home."

To which Brent responded.

"On my way, but now I know why I work until 7 p.m. TRAFFIC SUCKS!"

Moments later, he received his boss's response.

"Just be happy you don't have to go to the Commissioner's Council meeting tonight until 9 p.m. Your day will come," the last four words making Brent smile.

"On second thought, I'm lovin' this traffic! Thank Les," he texted in return, earning him a smiley face emoji from Chief Gains in response.

CHAPTER 35

With the FDA mess being handled by his Board Chair, Asa was anxious to implement his plan to get physician coverage in Portland and expand the Recallamin 3 trial to the Gulf Coast and West Coast regions. He had done his part and only needed to confirm that his VP of Operations and Chief Legal Counsel had come through on their part of the plan.

Although the sun had barely cracked the horizon on the new work week, he fired off a text asking them to convene in his office in an hour. For Chet, who was typically an early-riser, the hastily called meeting didn't pose a problem, as he was already on his way into work. For Cheryl, on the other hand, her phone had to ding incessantly, announcing she had a message before she forced herself to reach for it. Then, bleary-eyed, she had to rub the sleep from her eyes a couple of times before she could even make out the message. When she finally did, she grumbled some very choice words for her boss and rolled out of bed. Forgoing a shower, she threw on some clothes, spritzed on some perfume, and ran a brush through her hair, taming most but not all of her bedhead. She grabbed her make-up bag on the way out, hoping to apply some at the stop signals along the way. She would rather arrive at the meeting on time, looking like death warmed over, than risk being late again.

"I'm sorry, ma'am, but I think you must be lost. We're

expecting Cheryl Baker to join us," Asa joked as she stormed through his office door with a minute to spare. Seeing that the Board Chair wasn't in the room and not appreciative of his disparaging comedy routine, she bluntly made her feelings known.

"Go fuck yourself, Asa."

"Oh, I'm sorry, did I inconvenience you on go-live day?"

She looked at him, confused.

"Remember? You were supposed to make sure we had the resources in place to go live with expanding Recallamin 3. Ring any bells?" he replied sarcastically, as a dark and disturbing look transformed his face. Cheryl knew she was on thin ice, and what she said next would dictate whether she kept her job or would be invited to leave and go back home permanently.

"I've got coverage for both the Gulf and West Coast regions, and I revised the physician notice about ReCallamin 3 that we used in this region to fit those markets. All I need is your go-ahead, and we'll be rolling," she said confidently.

Knowing that, in fact, she only had one region covered and hadn't done anything to recast the notices. What he didn't know wouldn't hurt him, she thought. More importantly, she knew that he was unlikely to check the validity of her statements.

"See, that wasn't so hard, now was it?" he responded mockingly, causing Cheryl's face to flush with anger as she fought the urge to give him a piece of her mind or haul off and smack the smug look off his face.

"So, I can pull the trigger on those notices?" Cheryl asked, even though she was thinking of a different type of trigger she'd like to pull at the moment.

"Yes, pull the trigger," he confirmed.

"Gladly," she replied as she tried to burn holes in him with an intense, fiery stare.

If he noticed, he didn't let on, moving instead to Chet, who received more respectful treatment.

"And Chet, have you been able to modify the riders on Dr. Carson's and the two Lab Directors contracts?"

"I have," he replied, pushing a manila folder in Dr. Sheridan's direction.

"Good, so we're done here," Asa said as he pushed back from the conference table only to have Cheryl ask, "Wait, what does Dr. Carson have to do with this plan?"

The last Cheryl had heard, Dr. Kathleen "Kit" Carson had been employed by AlzCura to take over Dr. Caron's vacated office practice in Central Maine.

"Oh, I didn't tell you?" Asa replied. "Dr. Carson will be covering both the Central Maine and Portland markets now."

"How in the hell is that going to work?" Cheryl couldn't bite back how impossible and idiotic the plan sounded.

"I'm hiring a receptionist, medical assistant, and a Physician Assistant to staff an office in Portland, and Dr. Carson will spend one day a week there. In between times, the PA will see patients and attend to their needs. I'm also consolidating Dr. Carson's Central Maine practice at the Dracut-Campion office and selling the Namahoe and Ramsey offices."

"And why didn't you think to involve your VP of Operations in all of these operational changes?" Cheryl asked in a challenging and irritated tone.

"Because I needed to get them done. Let's face it, Cheryl, you haven't been on your game since," he paused momentarily, looking as if he was searching his memory bank. "Ah, since you canned Jackie frankly. What has that been? Six months? You haven't even filled her position yet."

"That's not fair, Asa," Cheryl teared up. "I've worked my butt off for you and this company."

"Yes, you've been a good little soldier Cheryl, but what have you done for me lately?"

"You son of a bitch, I lost my daughter."

"Yes, but our challenges don't pause to allow us to grieve her loss. If it weren't for having Simon on our Board, the Feds, Maine, and New York would be crawling up our ass, and the three of us would probably be marched out of here with matching silver bracelets. I don't know about you, but I'd rather buy my jewelry from Tiffany's than get it free from the FBI!"

"So, what? You're going to fire me?"

"Oh, no, no, no. And let you get out of all of this fun and excitement? No, I am sending you to Los Angeles."

"Los Angeles? Why in the hell would you send me there?"

"Because I know you haven't filled the pharmaceutical rep position in the West Coast region, contrary to what you just told me. And I bet if I asked you to produce the notices you claimed to have revised, you wouldn't be able to do it."

"You fucking..."

"Careful how you choose your next words, Cheryl," he interrupted. "You should consider yourself lucky that I'm not terminating your employment and equity shares in the company for substandard performance. Believe me, you're only here because I stood up for you last week when Simon suggested I cut you loose. Don't make me regret my decision. Now, lay off the booze, get on a plane, and start pulling your weight. Last chance."

Cheryl felt like she had been run over by a stream-roller. She had no choice but to do what Asa said and got up to leave his office, not wishing to suffer any further embarrassment.

CHAPTER 36

J ackie was fast-growing frustrated combing through a list of local attorneys when her search was interrupted by an incoming phone call from Officer Todd.

"Hi Barrett," Jackie answered. "You have impeccable timing."

"Hi, Jackie. Why is that?"

"I was just trying to find a lawyer, and there are so many to choose from. Do you happen to know a good one?"

"Well, first, let me ask you what do you need the lawyer for?"

"I'm thinking about suing AlzCura Pharmaceuticals for Stu's death and wrongful termination. Also, I'm sure they were probably involved in the break-in and kidnapping Ash."

"Nunzio Scarletti," Barrett replied.

"What?" Jackie replied.

"Not what, who. Nunzio Scarletti," Barrett repeated.

"I need an attorney, Barrett. Not a mobster."

"He is a lawyer, Jackie," Barrett laughed. "Best guy in these parts for personal injury and wrongful death cases."

"Really?"

"Really."

"Huh, OK, thanks for that," she replied, not totally convinced by his recommendation.

"You good? Because I called to ask,"

"Oh my God, Barrett. That was so rude of me," she interrupted him, realizing that she had totally hijacked his call with her search for an attorney.

"We're all good," Barrett replied. "Now, I need you to solve a mystery for me."

"Quid pro quo, huh?"

"Yeah, something like that. Sunny asked me to pick up Big Bird at your place," he responded. "Does she really have a Big Bird stuffed animal at your place?"

"You didn't ask her about Big Bird when she asked you to pick it up?" she laughed.

"No, I didn't."

"It's her big, yellow suitcase. And when I say big, I mean huge," she said, laughing again.

"Oh, thank God. I was beginning to worry that she had some kind of strange Sesame Street obsession."

"Not that I'm aware of, Barrett. But an obsession with carrying around a lot of clothes, most definitely, though."

"Well, that I can deal with. Are you home this afternoon? I was hoping to drop by and pick it up."

"Yeah, I'm home. Come by anytime."

"And I hope you don't mind that I asked Sunny to stay with me. She told me you had offered to put her up."

"No, not at all, Barrett. I'm happy you guys hit it off. And besides, I'm anxious to get her collection of Sesame Street characters out of my house," she said deadpan.

"Now you're just messing with me," Barrett replied, laughing.

"I don't know? I haven't checked what's inside that big, yellow suitcase," she said mysteriously.

"I'll take my chances," Barrett chuckled. "See you later, Jackie."

"Bye, Barrett."

With the name of an attorney, but not entirely comfortable with just Barrett's recommendation, she decided to call Tara Newman, Nora Community Hospital's Chief Executive Officer, her former boss for a day. The day Ash had been abducted. Tara had been kind enough to encourage Jackie to call her if she could ever be of assistance. She had also indicated that if and when Jackie wanted to rejoin the workforce, she would hire her back.

"Jackie, I'm so pleased you've called me. How are you doing?" Tara answered enthusiastically after Tara's assistant had connected her call.

"I'm doing great, Tara. Thank you."

"And how is little Ashley?"

"Not so little anymore. Walking, talking, and an absolute joy."

"Oh, I'm so happy for you. Now tell me you're calling because you want to come back to work for me."

"I'm sorry, Tara. I will have to disappoint you on that account. I'm still working on bringing AlzCura to justice. That's actually the reason for my call."

"OK, well, I'm heartbroken, but how can I help you?"

"I'm exploring filing a wrongful death lawsuit, and that police officer you met the day Ash was kidnapped recommended Nunzio Scarletti. I just wanted to know your thoughts on Mr. Scarletti or have other recommendations."

"I think your police officer friend nailed it. Nunzio is a bulldog and very good at what he does. Our hospital attorney is frequently on the opposite side of personal injury cases brought against the hospital. I know he would be the first to tell you that Nunzio is the attorney he respects the most and likes the least on the plaintiffs' side. I would go to him in a heartbeat if I thought one of my family members had been harmed."

"Thanks, Tara. That's really helpful. I should have trusted my friend, but I couldn't get past visions that he was some mobster."

"Well, if and when you see him, be prepared. I wouldn't want to meet him in a dark alley, or a well-lit alley, for that matter. He cuts quite an imposing figure, so I'm afraid your image of him as a mobster won't be tamed. Flashy dresser for a big guy – he likes his Italian suits and shoes. Let's grab lunch sometime when it's convenient for you."

"I'd like that. I will call you."

"And next time, just call my cell. You don't have to go through my assistant. OK?"

"OK, Tara. Thanks again."

Jackie's call with the dynamic CEO of Nora Community Hospital left her feeling oddly inspired and guilty at the same time. Tara just had a way of communicating that was not only supportive but which made you want to elevate your game. On the other hand, Jackie couldn't help but feel guilty on two accounts, not trusting Barrett's recommendation and having resigned from her job at the hospital after one day. Her reverie was interrupted by Ash, who walked up, grabbed her hand, and started pulling while pointing to the front door with her other hand.

"Yes, Ash, we can go to the park. Just let mommy make one more quick call, OK?" she asked her daughter.

Ashley was an expert at making her wishes known, but her tolerance for delayed gratification was limited.

As Jackie scanned the directory of attorney's on her phone in search of Nunzio Scarletti, Ash once again pulled at her mother's arm. The increased decibel level of her verbalizations, which consisted of "Mama, Ehhh," while pointing at the door, made it clear she was on the verge of an all-out tantrum.

"OK, OK, mommy will make the call from the park," giving in to her daughter's persistent demand. Jackie knew that at some point, she would have to set boundaries. But she also saw the benefit of rewarding her daughter's initiative. She wanted her daughter to grow up being able to stand up for what she wanted. It was the typical parental dilemma, when and how much to reward or correct your child's behaviors. But she couldn't be bothered by such existential concerns at the moment, so she got up from the couch and took her daughter's hand, and walked out the door on their way to the park. She'd call Nunzio Scarletti while her daughter entertained herself climbing and sliding on her favorite play structure.

* * *

Attorney Dryer had just escorted Celeste Boulanger out of his office after their meeting when his assistant announced he had a call from Curt Barnes.

"OK, thanks, give me a minute to get back to my office and send the call through," he replied, turning to head back to his office.

"Good morning, Mr. Barnes. How can I help you?"

"Good morning, Mr. Dryer. Inspector Theo Adams suggested I call you. I'm the husband of Calli Barnes, who was"

"Excuse me for interrupting, Mr. Barnes, but I know who you are, and I am well aware of the tragic circumstances of your loss."

"Oh, OK, well then, let me get right to the purpose of my

call. I've been involved with a group of people, one of whom I believe is your client. Celeste Boulanger?"

"Yes, as a matter of fact, I actually just met with Celeste before your call. Are you calling about AlzCura Pharmaceuticals?"

"Yes. Inspector Adams recommended I speak with you about a potential lawsuit against AlzCura. I feel there's a chance that Darius Scott took the actions he did because of the effects of AlzCura's Recallamin vaccine."

"Hmm, well, that raises a red flag for me, Mr. Barnes. Not that I don't want to help you, but I was assigned to Darius Scott's case, so I have to be careful about conflict of interest here."

"I had no idea."

"I suspected as much, and Inspector Adams probably wasn't aware either. While your lawsuit would be against AlzCura, the evidence and the content of your legal argument would pertain to a client I represented, even if only briefly. I think it would be in your best interest to work with an attorney who could claim total objectivity. I'd be happy to recommend several attorneys for you."

"I appreciate that, but let me ask you a question first. Based on what you know about my situation, do you think I even have a case?"

"Well, I'm not sure I should even comment. I will say that people who can prove that they or their loved ones have been directly harmed by AlzCura's vaccine definitely have a case. Those who may have been indirectly harmed will have a more difficult task. I'm not saying it's not worth exploring or even filing a lawsuit. It will just be harder to prove. Another attorney could best advise you. Would you like me to send you that list?"

"I'd appreciate that, Mr. Dryer. Thanks for taking my call."

"You're welcome, Mr. Barnes."

After Attorney Dryer took down Curt's email address, they ended the call. Curt let out a long sigh, not sure that he even wanted to go down this path. His life had finally turned the corner for the better. His kids were happy, doing well in school, and not fighting with each other like they used to. He was in a meaningful relationship with Jackie that he wanted to focus on and continue to develop. Filing a lawsuit, especially one that Attorney Dryer said would be difficult to prove, would just take time and attention away from his kids and Jackie. The more he thought about it, the less he was willing to make such a compromise.

While he sat there convincing himself not to pursue a lawsuit, his phone signaled an incoming email. Seeing it was the list of attorneys that Attorney Dryer had promised, he filed it away in a folder without opening it.

CHAPTER 37

D
r. Elizabeth Harder was livid when she learned of Dr. Shearlow's promotion to her previous post of Director of the Office of Vaccine Review and Research. Despite her boss's advice to focus on her new job and not worry about the pending cases she had left behind, she couldn't let this go without saying her peace. She was not known to be assertive or outspoken. If anything, she was more often criticized as being too timid and needed encouragement and support before you could draw out her thoughts and feelings. That is why Dr. Lynn Franklin was stunned when Dr. Harder barged into her office, fuming.

"You promoted that little weasel to my old job? Have you lost your mind, Lynn?" she spat while leaning ominously over her boss's desk.

"Whoa, whoa, whoa, Elizabeth. I will not have you speak to me in that way. Cool your jets, or today will be your last day with the FDA," she fired back.

"Well, maybe it should be," Dr. Harder challenged. "I took Woodson on as a favor to you despite his lack of qualifications. I mentored him as you wanted me to, and for the last year, you know the misgivings I've had about keeping him on. I thought we were on the same page about moving him out, and now you promote him? How does that make sense?"

"Listen, Elizabeth. Not that it's any of your business, but

I've put him in the Director position on an interim basis. I fully expect he will fail miserably, and then I'll have the ammunition I need to move him out. In his analyst position, he was represented by the Union. You know how hard it is to take disciplinary action against people in positions represented by the Union. Now, as the Director, he's no longer protected by collective bargaining, and I can do what I need to. Does it make sense to you now?"

Dr. Franklin's explanation was understandable and had tamped down the intensity of Dr. Harder's anger, but she still had concerns.

"Yes, that makes all the sense in the world, but I'm concerned about the damage he could do before you get to take that action. Has he told you about what happened in Maine?"

"No, he hasn't."

"Well, I'm not surprised. Excuse my French, but he almost fucked it up royally. I think we're going in there to investigate the safety of the Recallamin vaccine, and he starts blaming the State's Attorney General and District Attorney for lackadaisical regulatory practices. He almost blew up the meeting before it was even over. It was embarrassing," she said with a shudder, recalling how uncomfortable she had been.

"Oh, how awful that must have been," Dr. Franklin replied. "Well, more reason to take the action I did then. Now I have him in a position where I can do something."

"Yes, but I'm concerned he won't tell you all the details about what we learned in Maine. I'd really appreciate the opportunity to send you my report. I don't trust him."

"I understand, Elizabeth, but let's do this. I will set up a meeting with Dr. Shearlow to discuss the Maine visit. Afterward, I will share with you what he told me. If he left anything significant out, that could be the first nail in his coffin. Sound good?"

"Yes, but please do it soon. The Maine Attorney General is hoping you will see fit to contact the OIG. Maine and Buffalo PD would like to move ahead with their investigations in co-ordination with the OIG."

"Yes, I will meet with him very soon. Thank you for that," she replied. "Now, can we put this issue to rest so that you can focus on the opioid safety project?"

"Yes, Lynn. I'm sorry I barked at you. I'm not usually that blunt."

"All is forgiven. We'll talk soon, OK?"

With that, Dr. Harder left Dr. Franklin's office happy that her boss had a plan for dispensing with Dr. Shearlow. He was a thorn in her side and a threat to the effectiveness of the Office.

Meanwhile, Dr. Franklin waited until Dr. Harder left her office before she picked up her phone and made a call.

"Simon, I think we're going to have a problem with Dr. Harder," she said to her former boss and current AlzCura Pharmaceuticals Board Chair.

CHAPTER 38

As Ashley waddled to the steps of the play structure on her way to her favorite slide, Jackie punched in the number for Nunzio Scarletti's law office.

"Scarletti Law Office, this is Marsha. How may I help you?" she greeted pleasantly.

"Hi, Marsha, this is Jackie Deno. I've been referred to Mr. Scarletti and would like to set an appointment to see him."

"Great, I'd be happy to assist in setting up a consultation appointment. Consultation visits with Mr. Scarletti are scheduled for 30 minutes and are free of charge. The earliest Mr. Scarletti could see you would be next Tuesday at 10a.m. Would that work for you?"

"Yes, that would be fine," Jackie replied, looking at Ash, who giggled as she slid down the slide and immediately went to mount the stairs to repeat the experience.

"May I ask who referred you? We like to thank those who provide us referrals."

"Sure, I'd be happy to. Officer Barrett Todd from Nora PD recommended Mr. Scarletti."

"Thank you for that. Is there anything else I can help you with?"

"No, I'm good. Thanks for your help."

"Then we look forward to seeing you next Tuesday at 10a.m. Have a great day, Ms. Deno."

"Thank you, Marsha, you too."

Having fulfilled her part of the bargain with Curt, Jackie wished she didn't have to wait until later that day to speak with him and the kids. She was anxious to schedule her visit to Maine and hoped she could visit this coming weekend.

As Ash slid down the slide for a second time, Jackie got up to join her daughter, redirecting her to a series of spring rider animals. Jackie helped Ash onto the spring rider horse, but she was losing interest until Jackie helped make the horse rock. Then Ash shrieked with glee and was hooked. As soon as the horse would stop rocking, she'd look to her mother, who would oblige her and make the horse rock again, which would produce another round of laughter. This continued for 10 minutes, all the while Jackie reveling in her daughter's joy. Eventually, the rocking motion appeared to make Ash drowsy, and her mother picked her up and carried her home. Ash was asleep before they reached the door. Putting her sleeping daughter down in her crib, Jackie busied herself cleaning the house, too restless to sit still and frustrated at how slowly time was passing.

By mid-afternoon, her home was spotless, and Ashley was up from her nap. She made a cup of coffee and sat down on the couch with her daughter, determined to teach her the names of the three people she couldn't take her mind off. Grabbing her phone, she scrolled to a picture of Curt, Caitlin, and Cade she had taken at the zoo. With Ash in her lap, she pointed to each of the three in succession, saying their names. When she pointed to Curt, Ash, instead of trying to say, Curt, said "Dada," bringing tears to Jackie's eyes. Switching to a picture of just Caitlin and Cade, Jackie tried unsuccessfully to get Ash to say their names. Ash's lesson was abbreviated by the long-awaited call from Curt.

"Hi, Jackie," Caitlin and Cade sang in unison on speakerphone.

"Hi, Caitlin and Cade," she replied enthusiastically. "I am so happy to hear your voices. I miss you."

"We miss you too," Caitlin replied. "When are you going to come here?"

"Well, that's something I hope to discuss with your dad. Hopefully, soon."

"Yayyyyyy," Caitlin and Cade cheered in unison. "We go on summer break after this Thursday. You should come out on Friday. I want you to see me ride my horse," speaking as though she owned the horse her father paid to have her ride a few hours a week.

"I'd love to see you ride, and Ash too. She rode the rocking horse at the playground today."

"Really? I remember that rocking horse," Caitlin replied.

"Me, too," chimed Cade, not wanting to be left out of the conversation.

"Well, is your father there? The sooner I talk to him, the sooner we can decide when I'm coming out."

"Yeah, he's right here," Caitlin responded, handing the phone to her father and telling him it was Jackie.

Taking the phone, Jackie heard Curt suggest to the kids that they go play on the playground. After some minor pushback from the kids who wanted to listen in on their conversation, they relented, and Jackie heard their exit.

"Hi, Jackie. Sorry about that. I didn't want them hovering over me while we talked."

"Hi, Curt. No problem, they are pretty excited about my visit."

"We all are. I love you, by the way."

"Well, I love you too. This day has gone so painfully slow

today, but I have some good news.

"What's that?"

"I scheduled a meeting with an attorney next week."

"That's great. I'm afraid I wasn't as successful," he replied and launched into why Attorney Dryer couldn't represent him and the difficulty his circumstances presented in the way of a lawsuit against AlzCura.

"Hmmm, so what are you going to do?" Jackie asked.

"Honestly, I'm leaning towards not pursuing a lawsuit. And it's not only because it would be a difficult case to prove."

"Why else?"

"Well, I'm afraid of the time and attention it would take aware from the kids and my ability to spend time with you. They're in a great place right now, and this past weekend only made me appreciate more just how important you are to them and to me."

"Oh, Curt. You don't know how much I love hearing that. I feel the same way."

"Then, I have a suggestion. A little change in plan," Curt replied.

"What's that?"

"Since you have an appointment with an attorney next week and the kids are off of school, I could take some vacation time, and we could drive down there Thursday after school. That would give us about 10 days together. How does that sound?"

"I like that idea. No, I love that idea," Jackie corrected herself. "But what about Caitlin? Won't she be upset that she won't be able to show me how she rides her horse?"

"I think she'll get over it knowing we'll be spending 10 days with you. Besides, maybe we can find a place down there where she can ride a horse. They do have horses in New York, don't they?"

"Hmmm, maybe," she replied facetiously. "Oh, Curt, I'm so excited. Is it Thursday yet?"

"Not quite. So you're good with that plan?"

"I'm ecstatic with that plan."

"Alright, I'll go tell the kids. Oh, how is Ash doing?"

"She's great. I tried to teach her to say all your names today."

"I'm sure that was an exercise in frustration," Curt replied.

"Why do you say that?"

"Because the k-sound in our names is difficult for infants and toddlers to learn. For the longest time when Cade was a baby, he called his sister 'Atin' because he couldn't pronounce the K or the L in her name. I think he was almost 3 before he was able to say her full name."

"See, that's why I need you around. You know all these things about kids that I haven't learned yet. I thought I was just a bad teacher."

"So that's the only reason you want me around, huh? To give you the inside scoop on parenting?"

"Well, there may be one or two other reasons why I want you around."

They said their goodbyes, each ending the call excited about the plans they had just made. When Curt told Caitlin and Cade about the change in plans, the only thing Caitlin said was, "I have to start packing." She ran from the playground up to her room to begin the process even though their departure date was still three days away.

CHAPTER 39

Attorney General Talcott had purposely scheduled 15 minutes into his jam-packed Tuesday schedule to make a follow-up call to Dr. Harder. While the Friday meeting had left him optimistic, he knew how things worked, or more often perhaps didn't work, in dealing with Federal agencies. Taking Dr. Harder's business card out of the top drawer of his desk, he punched in her number. As he waited for her to answer, he hoped that she had at least filed her report with the FDA Commissioner.

"Office of Vaccine Research, who are you trying to reach," said the receptionist curtly.

"Ah yes, this is Maine Attorney General Talcott. I'm calling for Dr. Elizabeth Harder."

"Dr. Harder doesn't work here anymore. Would you like to speak with the new Director, Dr. Shearlow?"

AG Talcott nearly fell off his chair and paused too long for the impatient receptionist on the other end of the line.

"Would you like me to connect you to Dr. Shearlow now or not?" she said gruffly.

"No, thank you. That won't," he began to reply but heard the call drop before he had even finished his sentence.

He wasn't sure whether he was more stunned by Dr. Harder no longer working there or by the rude treatment he had just received from the woman who had answered his call. Regardless, what mattered most was whether Dr. Harder had the opportunity to file her report and speak with the Commissioner before she had left. Given his lack of faith in Dr. Shealow, AG Talcott decided to call the FDA Commissioner's office directly.

"Good morning. Commissioner Franklin's office. How may I help you?" answered a woman who clearly could give the previous receptionist lessons on how to do her job.

"Good morning. This is Maine Attorney General Talcott. I was hoping to speak with Commissioner Franklin. Is she in?"

"May I ask what your call pertains to?"

"Sure. I'm following up on a meeting I had with Dr. Harder last week about concerns with the Recallamin vaccine."

"Thank you. May I place you on hold while I check Dr. Franklin's availability?"

"Sure," he replied, relieved that he had reached someone courteous and professional.

"Thank you. Please hold."

AG Talcott's ears were assaulted by a loud screeching sound that was presumably supposed to be introductory music followed by a series of announcements. The female voice may have been pleasant in real life, but it was garbled on the recorded message as if she was talking underwater. Holding the phone away from his ear to preserve his hearing and sanity, he didn't have to wait long before the pleasant receptionist returned to the line.

"I'm sorry for the wait, Mr. Talcott," she apologized with sincerity. "Unfortunately, Dr. Franklin is not available at the moment. I'm afraid that her schedule this week is full, but I may be able to find something on her calendar next week. Would you like me to check on her availability?"

"Please," he said, hiding his growing disappointment.

"Hmm, it looks like next week isn't good either. There is some time towards the end of the month. Will that work for you?"

"I'm sorry, I really was hoping to speak with the Commissioner this week. Is there anyone else I can talk to? Dr. Franklin's assistant or someone else?"

"If you don't mind holding again, I can check on that for you?"

"Please do."

"Thank you. Please hold," she said again, as AG Talcott moved the phone away from his head to avoid the ear-shattering screech and unintelligible announcements sure to follow.

"Thank you for waiting, Mr. Talcott," she returned to the phone shortly. "Dr. Shearlow, the Director of our Office of Vaccine Research, may be available. Would you like me to transfer you to his office?"

No amount of courtesy and professionalism by the woman he was speaking with could prevent the absolute frustration AG Talcott felt at that moment. He declined her offer, thanked her for her efforts, and hung up, knowing his next call would be to his buddy Deputy AG Clark Ainsley at the Department of Justice. Unfortunately, the call would have to wait until tomorrow, as his schedule for the rest of the day was non-stop meetings. Before he ran off to his next appointment, he sent a text to Clark.

"On FDA merry-go-round. I'll call you tomorrow. Your expedition partner Lewis."

CHAPTER 40

When Dr. Sheridan strolled into his office Tuesday morning and found Dr. Simon Rosenthal seated in his desk chair, he knew it wasn't good news.

"Asa, we have a problem," Simon said predictably. "The Maine AG was nosing around trying to contact Commissioner Franklin yesterday."

"That is a problem. Did she speak to him?"

"No, no, her assistant was able to put him off, but I'm afraid it's only a matter of time before Maine and New York take action, with or without the FDA. Not to mention the civil lawsuits we heard we could anticipate."

"Maybe I should get Chet in here for this conversation," Asa suggested.

"Yes, good idea."

While they were waiting for Chet to join them, Simon addressed another concern he had.

"What did you decide to do with Cheryl?"

"I'm sending her to LA to hawk Recallamin to the docs in the West Coast region."

"Well, I still think she's a liability, but I suppose she can't do much harm out there."

"No, I think I put the fear of God into her. She'll do fine out there," he replied, trying to reassure his Board Chair as Chet made this entrance.

"Chet, I was just telling Asa that we need to be prepared for Maine and New York law enforcement actions as well as at least one civil lawsuit, if not more. I don't think we have to worry about the FDA jumping into the fray, but Maine's AG is getting too bold for my taste. Do we have an airtight plan if Maine and New York knock at our door?"

"We do," Chet responded confidently. "As long as the Feds stay out of this, some type of legal process would need to be followed. That could be everything from a subpoena requesting records or to interview someone to filing formal criminal charges against the company. In either case, we would have options to delay and prepare."

"And if the Feds get involved?"

"It depends on what agency you're talking about. The worst-case scenario will be if the FBI, DOJ, OIG, or GAO catch wind of anything amiss. They could walk in unannounced, confiscate any evidence they see fit, and suspend our operations. As long as those agencies don't have any reason to believe that the FDA is compromised in some way, it would be more likely that they would ask the FDA to perform an audit. Which, of course, would not be a problem given your connections."

"So you're saying that the worst-case scenario is unlikely?" the Board Chair asked.

"Extremely unlikely. Federal agencies don't spend a lot of time worrying about or investigating the integrity of their sister agencies. So as long as the FDA doesn't raise any red flags, it's unlikely any of the other agencies would get involved. That's not saying that outside influences can't try to compel the FBI or others to get involved."

"Outside influences like a State Attorney General?" Simon replied.

"Right. So you might want to rethink your strategy with Maine's Attorney General and have Commissioner Franklin try to appease him."

"That's smart. I'll ask her to reach out to him. OK, let's not let our guard down. Is there anything we can do to make sure if that worst-case scenario happens, they won't find any incriminating evidence?"

"Doubtful. The Feds typically have access to far more data than we have. To the degree that we can protect ourselves through our current creative data management practices, I'd say we've done that. However, that doesn't prevent the Feds from collecting other data outside of our control."

"What other data are you talking about," Simon asked.

"Data from hospitals, physician practices, insurance companies, you name it. And, of course, the data from the FDA that your nephew and the Commissioner have been keeping under wraps."

"Huh, OK, let me put it this way. Is there anything we should be doing now that we haven't done to protect us if the worst-case scenario occurs?"

"We can audit our processes to see if our data management practices are still being followed and effective. I'm more concerned about the outside data we don't know about."

"Why can't we just delete any of the data we have that could come back to bite us?" Asa questioned.

"Because the data we would need to delete is attached to how we get paid, and if the Feds do audit us and find we got paid but can't produce evidence that we supplied the service, guess what?"

"Fraud," Asa replied.

"Bingo."

"OK, I think I've taken up enough of your time, gentlemen," Simon stated while getting up out of Asa's desk chair. "You can have your chair back, Asa. It's getting a little too hot for me," he joked.

"Glad to take it back. You had me concerned for a minute when I walked in and saw you sitting in it."

"Only a minute? Shit, I must be losing my touch," he replied, laughing.

As the Board Chair exited Asa's office, Chet and Asa looked at each other and let out a collective sigh of relief.

CHAPTER 41

A ttorney General Talcott could not get to his office fast enough Wednesday morning in anticipation of his call with Deputy AG Clark Ainsley. His law school buddy had responded to his text the previous day with a short but tantalizing response.

"Call me at 8a.m. Have some interesting info for you."

AG Talcott's morning commute from his home in Manchester was usually a 10-minute trip. Today, of all days, a tree had fallen across the tree-lined Pond Road, causing a fairly significant back-up and delay. Fortunately, this was Maine, and nearly half the vehicles in the backed-up traffic were trucks with occupants that either cut wood for a living or to heat their own homes. As AG Talcott was considering whether to turn around and take a more circuitous route to his office, a cadre of burly Mainers, armed with chainsaws, went to work on the fallen tree. Within 10 minutes, the road was cleared, and he was on his way.

Arriving at his office right at the appointed time to make his call, his assistant handed him a coffee as he breezed through the reception area.

"Thanks, you're a life-saver," he called to his assistant as he closed his office door behind him.

Settling into his chair and leaning back to kick his feet up, crossing them on the edge of the desk, he took a sip of coffee and punched the number to call Clark Ainsley.

"Lewis, my man," Clark answered. "So you're having fun on the FDA merry-go-round, I hear," he joked, referencing AG Talcott's text from the previous day.

"Hardly, but thanks for the suspenseful response to my text. It kept me up all night."

"Well, I hope you went to the Emergency Room if it kept you up longer than 4 hours," he replied, laughing.

"Funny guy, now what do you have for me?" AG Talcott asked.

"Well, after we spoke last time, I decided to do a little digging on those doctors you were meeting with. Dr. Elizabeth Harder looks like a straight arrow. Strong background and education. A lifer at the FDA who worked her way up the ranks."

"Yeah, she wasn't the problem. Once we got the meeting on the right track, she was very supportive and helpful. Dr. Shearlow was the problem."

"Not surprised," Clark replied. "Interestingly, Dr. Woodson Shearlow is a Ph.D. doctor in Anthropology, which I found to be odd for the FDA. I dug a little deeper into him, and he was hired when Dr. Simon Rosenthal was the FDA Commissioner. And guess what else I discovered?"

"I have no idea, Clark."

"Dr. Shearlow is Dr. Rosenthal's nephew."

"So we have evidence of nepotism. Not unheard of in government, or the private sector for that matter."

"Oh, but wait, there's more. Much more."

"Well, get to it already. You're killing me here, Clark."

"OK, I'm sorry. Yes, a little nepotism, but it's much deeper than that. Dr. Rosenthal left as FDA Commissioner to work in the private sector. That's not uncommon, but he left to become AlzCura Pharmaceuticals Board Chairman."

"Holy shit," AG Talcott exclaimed.

"Oh, wait. There's even more."

"When Dr. Rosenthal left, he recommended Dr. Lynn Franklin to take his place. She was his Director of Vaccine Research and Review. When AlzCura was submitting requests to run their Recallamin vaccine clinical trials, Dr. Rosenthal was AlzCura's Board Chair. His hand-picked replacement Dr. Franklin was FDA Commissioner, and his nephew, Dr. Shearlow, was Associate Director for Vaccine Safety. Are you getting the picture?"

"All too clearly, I'm afraid. What do you suggest I do."

"Well, as of right now, it only looks suspicious. I haven't dug deep enough to produce any evidence of favored treatment, collusion, or kick-backs, but that would be my concern. It wouldn't be the first time a former government official used their connections to profit illegally. But I would need a valid reason to dig deeper."

"What if I read you in on all the evidence we have against AlzCura? Could that be a way to get the DOJ or the FBI to join the party and allow you to explore potential corruption and collusion in the FDA?"

"Hmm, I'd want to be sure not to step on the Secretary of Health and Human Services toes. The FDA is one of her departments, and she should be supportive of taking any action. If I contact her and she's willing, could you arrange for both of us to be briefed on the AlzCura evidence?"

"Absolutely. As a matter of fact, we have a joint meeting on Friday at 2 p.m. with the Regional Assistant Attorney General, Buffalo Police Commissioner, and their Chief Detective to discuss our respective investigations and next steps. Maybe we could arrange to have you join us by teleconference."

"That sounds like a good plan. I'll call the Secretary of HHS. No promises. For all we know, she may know something we don't."

"I'll wait to hear from you then before setting it up."

"I'll try to get back to you today."

"Thanks, Clark."

"The Lewis and Clark Expedition rides again," Deputy AG Clark Ainsley announced as his closing salutation.

AG Talcott broke into a broad smile as the call ended, thankful that he had friends in high places. Clark's revelations could be the impetus for the DOJ or the FBI to join Maine and New York in taking action. Something about AlzCura Pharmaceuticals had always smelled off. Now there was a full-fledged stench that could no longer be neglected. The source of which ironically could lead back to the government agency whose mission is to protect public health by ensuring the safety and efficacy of vaccines and medications.

AG Talcott's day may have started out with an obstacle in his path, but the rest of his day following his call with Clark was a blur of back-to-back meetings. When he finally returned to his office late in the day, he looked forward to a little free office time before calling it a day.

"Did you even have time to grab lunch today?" his assistant asked when he trudged in wearily.

"Lunch? What's that?" he replied sarcastically.

"Well, there's some leftover Chinese food in the breakroom fridge from a meeting this afternoon. Do you want me to fix you a plate?"

"No, thanks. If I ate now, I wouldn't be hungry for dinner. I promised my wife I'd take her out tonight so she doesn't have to cook."

"Why don't you just take the Chinese food home? It will be like eating out without the hassle of having to go out. You look exhausted."

"You know, that's a great idea. I'll do that. Have I ever told you how much I appreciate you?"

"Never," his assistant said, feigning indignation followed by a smile. "Only about every day."

"Well, I'll try to be better," he smiled and retreated to his office.

No sooner had he sat down and his assistant knocked and poked her head into his office.

"I have a call for you. It's the FDA Commissioner, Dr. Franklin."

Shocked, he instructed his assistant to transfer the call.

"Attorney General Talcott, this is Dr. Lynn Franklin, FDA Commissioner. I'm sorry to call you out of the blue, but my assistant told me you had called yesterday wanting to speak to me urgently."

"Well, thank you for calling back, Dr. Franklin. I can appreciate how busy your schedule must be," he replied.

"Not any busier than yours, I imagine. I understand from Dr. Harder that you didn't have the best start to your meeting last week. I apologize for that. Is that what you were calling me about?"

"In part, although Dr. Harder was very helpful, and I think the meeting was productive in the end. I had actually tried to call Dr. Harder first to follow up on our meeting but was told she doesn't work there anymore."

"Well, that's not exactly true. I promoted Dr. Harder to another position within the agency. I want to assure you that she did brief me on your meeting, and I'm expecting her full report in the next day or two."

"So she talked with you about getting the OIG involved?"

"Oh yes, and I've already given the Deputy Inspector General at the OIG a heads up about needing to meet once Dr. Harder sends me her report. Dr. Harder was very clear about your wish to get them involved, and I'm trying to respect that."

"Thank you for the effort, Dr. Franklin. I appreciate that very much."

"Is there anything else I can help you with?" Dr. Franklin asked.

"No, you've answered all the questions that I had. I look forward to hearing from you after you meet with the OIG."

"Glad I could be of assistance. Have a good evening," the FDA Commissioner said, ending their conversation.

All of a sudden, AG Talcott felt like maybe he had jumped the gun by running to Clark and escalating this beyond the FDA. He was somewhat relieved by Dr. Franklin's call but not sufficiently reassured to unwind what he and Clark had in the works. Although he toyed with the idea of calling Clark to update him on Dr. Franklin's call, it was late, and he was exhausted. All he wanted to do was go home, eat dinner with his wife, and go to bed. As if on cue, his assistant knocked on his door.

"I packed up the Chinese food for you. It's in two bags in the refrigerator. Is it OK if I leave now? My daughter has a soccer game, and I promised her I'd be there this time."

"Go, go, and make sure that my crazy schedule isn't a reason for you to miss any of your daughter's functions in the future. You're indispensable, but I'll be happy to bumble along without you. Family first, OK?"

"Yes, sir. Thank you, sir," she replied, leaving his office and closing the door behind her.

His advice to his assistant was the sort of guidance that falls under the rubric of "do as I say, not as I do." His all-consuming job compromised time with his family more often than he cared to ponder. The concept of work-life balance may have been lost on him, but what he couldn't or wouldn't do for himself and his family, he tried to encourage in those who worked for him.

He could hear the Chinese food calling to him from the refrigerator amidst all the thoughts about the AlzCura case still swirling in his head. Uncharacteristically, he forced himself to leave the things he still had to do in service to his work for the things he could do in service to his wife. He got up, flicked off the office lights, grabbed the food from the breakroom refrigerator, and hoped his in-home dinner date with his wife would improve his good fortune.

CHAPTER 42

D A Wydman sauntered into his office, feeling like he had been gone for weeks, not the three and a half days he had actually been out.

"Welcome back! How was the castle in Canada?" his assistant Julie greeted him.

"Thanks! Marge absolutely loved it. So, as they say, happy wife?"

"Happy life," Julie finished. "That's great. I'm afraid your schedule is pretty crazy the next couple of days."

"Oh, I anticipated that. The punishment for having the audacity to take time off! Thanks for holding down the fort. Any fires I need to know about?"

"Not that I'm aware of, but AG Talcott's assistant told me that things are starting to pop with the AlzCura case. I don't know the details. She just said that she knows that the AG has been speaking to some highly placed people in from the Department of Justice and the FDA."

"Do I have any time with the AG on my schedule?"

"Yes, tomorrow morning."

"Good, after that crazy meeting on Friday, I was worried about where things were headed. Once again, I can't thank you enough for saving that meeting. Here," he said, handing her an envelope.

"What's this?"

"A little token of our appreciation. It's from the AG and me."

"You shouldn't have?"

"Oh, go on already and open it. Hopefully, you'll like it."

With the practiced hands that opened dozens of letters a day in the office, she deftly opened the envelope, pulling out a thank you card containing a gift certificate.

"A spa day?!" she exclaimed excitedly, shooting her boss a look of astonishment. "I've always said I'm going to do this one day, but never have."

"Now you can," DA Wydman replied. "And when you do redeem it, it will be a paid day off that won't be deducted from your paid time off bank."

"Wow, I, I don't know what to say," she said, looking like she was close to tears. "Thank you so much," she said, hugging him.

"Well, you deserve it. Enjoy it," he said as she released her hug, and he retreated to his office to prepare for the busy day ahead of him.

* * *

Celeste Boulanger's life was finally turning a corner putting all her losses in the past few months and the suffocating media attention behind her. Her relationship with Theo, founded mainly on her desperate unfulfillable needs, was now built on mutual love, respect, and purpose. Theo may have been her white knight in the beginning, but now there was little need for rescue, and when the need arose in one or the other, they could rescue each other.

It took three full weekends of work, but Theo and Celeste successfully relocated her trailer to a clearing on Theo's property. Theo had spent the better part of the first weekend just ridding her trailer of any signs of the carnage that had occurred there. It mattered little. The experience of walking into even her sanitized trailer was traumatic for Celeste. Not because of the lack of carpeting or furniture or even the horrors that transpired there. More the memories of Sophie that were like ghosts occupying the trailer.

"Can we get a dog some time?" she cried into Theo's shoulder towards the end of her emotional reunion visit to her trailer.

"Whenever you want," he replied, kissing her on the top of her head.

Celeste had also started going back to work full-time. Thankfully, she was no longer badgered by the Maine media that had found some new sensation to cover.

Theo's investigations related to AlzCura, while still technically open, no longer required much of his time. His current caseload was more representative of the infrequent petty crimes that were more typical in Maine. Not only did he welcome the more manageable workload, but any concerns he had been feeling about taking up a relationship with Celeste had all but evaporated.

* * *

The days leading up to Friday's joint meeting between the principal law enforcement officials from Maine and Buffalo PD dragged on interminably for Detective Farest. It wasn't for lack of things to do. But rather that he had Cheryl Baker and Dr. Asa Sheridan in his cross-hairs and couldn't pull the trigger on making them squirm in one of his interrogation rooms. It had been his experience that nothing good ever came from delaying action when you had definitive evidence. Yet, there he was, delaying action on two individuals in his own backyard – individuals responsible for heinous corporate crimes and likely involved in capital crimes in Maine. Getting antsy, he went to see his boss.

"Got a minute, Les?" he said, poking his head into the office of Chief Detective Les Gains.

"Let's see," Les paused, looking at his computer calendar. "Looks like I have six minutes for you. What's on your mind?"

"The AlzCura case. Don't get me wrong, I'm glad you set up the meeting with the Commissioner and Assistant AG, but"

"But you're worried what might happen in the interim with those two shady AlzCura executives free in the breeze," Chief Detective Gains helped finish Detective Farest's thought.

"Yeah, how did you know?"

"Don't forget, I was in your shoes before. I didn't get here by sticking a thumb up my butt when the evidence told me to act," he said graphically.

"So, what can I do?"

"You're not going to like my answer. Wait."

"You're right. I don't like that answer."

"Listen, if it makes you feel any better, we can go ahead and get a warrant to detain and question Ms. Baker and Dr. Sheridan. We can exercise those warrants as soon as possible after our meeting. I know that's little comfort, but it's something."

"I'd appreciate that."

"OK, write it up, and I'll get the sign-off."

"Thanks, Les."

Detective Farest left Chief Detective Gains's office feeling only slightly better about waiting but tremendously better that Chief Detective Gains shared his impatience.

CHAPTER 43

AG Talcott dragged into the office, looking like death warmed over.

"Jeezum," his Maine-born assistant exclaimed. "I don't mean any disrespect, sir, but you look like crap. Did you get any sleep last night?"

"I didn't. But the Chinese food was a hit with my wife, so the night wasn't a complete bust. I have you to thank for that. She slept like a baby, while I just tossed and turned."

"Well, I'm happy to hear that. It wasn't the food that kept you up, was it?"

"No, no, the food was delicious. I just couldn't shut off my brain. It's an occupational hazard I have yet to conquer."

"I'm sorry. If it's any consolation, your schedule is pretty light today. Maybe you can knock off a little early," she suggested trying to be helpful.

"That's what I like about you. You're an eternal optimist. When I see a light schedule, I wonder what crisis is going to erupt to fill in my free time."

"Did you open your fortune cookie last night?"

"What? No. Why?" he asked, confused.

"Don't you know it's bad luck not to open your fortune after you eat Chinese food? No wonder you didn't sleep. Did your wife open hers?"

"Yes."

"See, and she slept like a baby. You said it yourself. I have an idea," she said as she marched off to the breakroom, leaving him standing there in wonderment. When she returned, she handed him a fortune cookie.

"Here, open this. It will change your luck," she demanded.

"You're kidding, right?" he said skeptically.

"Open it!" she repeated her demand.

Too tired to argue, he unwrapped the cookie, broke it in half, and read the message aloud.

"You already know the answer to the questions lingering inside your head," he said matter-of-factly and then suddenly looked like he had been struck by lightning. His assistant's instructions to open a fortune cookie had led him to the resolution of the internal debate that had caused his insomnia.

"So?" his assistant asked.

"You're amazing. I have to go make a call," he said as he rushed energetically into his office and closed the door.

"See, I told you," his assistant called after him, wondering what revelation the fortune cookie had prompted.

AG Talcott had wrestled all night with whether to trust the information Dr. Lynn Franklin had shared with him or to proceed as he and Clark had discussed. Now he knew that the only way he could resolve the conflict in his head was to go back to the source - Dr. Elizabeth Harder. If she was still at the FDA, maybe he could track her down and either confirm or refute the information that Dr. Franklin had shared. After being bounced around several times, he finally reached Dr. Harder.

"Good morning, Dr. Harder. This is Lewis Talcott. We met last week. I hope I didn't catch you at a bad time."

"Attorney General Talcott, what a pleasant surprise. No,

this is a fine time. What can I do for you?" she asked, somewhat shocked that he had been able to find her.

"Well, I received a call from Dr. Franklin last night, and I guess I'd first like to congratulate you on your promotion."

"Why, thank you. It was all very sudden."

"No kidding. When I called your office, they told me you didn't work there anymore and that Dr. Shearlow was the new Director."

There was a long pause.

"Dr. Harder?" AG Talcott asked, wondering if their phone call had been disconnected.

"I, I, I'm sorry. I'm here." Dr. Harder said, swallowing the anger she still felt about Dr. Shearlow's promotion but not wanting to air her dirty laundry with Maine's Attorney General.

"I also wanted to call to thank you. Dr. Franklin assured me that you had conveyed the findings of your visit and that she was going to be meeting with the OIG after you submit your report. So, thank you for that."

After another long pause, AG Talcott once again asked if Dr. Harder was still on the line.

"I'm sorry, AG Talcott. This is hard for me. I never spoke with Dr. Franklin about the findings from my visit or the urgency of getting the OIG involved. She never gave me that opportunity and specifically instructed me not to file my report but to leave that to my successor."

"I don't understand. Are you telling me that Dr. Franklin lied to me?"

"I don't want to say that. Perhaps Dr. Shearlow met with her. How else could she have found out that you wanted to get the OIG involved? Someone had to tell her. It must have been Woodson."

"Good point. But I still don't understand why Dr. Franklin would say you told her."

"I don't know what to say, AG Talcott," Dr. Harder replied, starting to feel like she was between a rock and a hard place.

"I'm sorry, Dr. Harder. I understand this puts you in an awkward position. I just don't have a lot of confidence that Dr. Shearlow could effectively advocate for us with the Commissioner after his bizarre performance at our meeting on Friday."

AG Talcott was almost certain now that his call from Dr. Franklin had been a ruse and thought about thanking Dr. Harder and ending the call. Instead, sensing that Dr. Harder could be a potential ally, he decided to take a calculated risk.

"Dr. Harder, let me ask you this. Did you know Dr. Simon Rosenthal?"

"I know he was the FDA Commissioner before Dr. Franklin, but I can't say I really knew him per se."

"Would you be surprised to learn that Dr. Rosenthal left the FDA to become the Board Chair of AlzCura Pharmaceuticals? That he had a hand in putting Dr. Franklin in the Commissioner position? And that Dr. Shearlow is his nephew?"

The silence at the other end of the line screamed her response to AG Talcott even before Dr. Harder was finally able to articulate an answer.

"I didn't know that. I'm stunned. How did you find that out?"

"Let's just say I have friends in other federal agencies that have access to an unusually large amount of information."

"Now, I understand why Dr. Shearlow was upset with me."

"How's that, Dr. Harder?" AG Talcott asked, wondering what she was referencing.

"Before we received those late adverse event reports from Dr. Caron's office, his office manager Rebecca had called our office. I happened to get the call, and the poor woman was absolutely beside herself. She tearfully explained why she was late in submitting the adverse event reports of a series of mortalities. I tried to calm her down and reassure her that there would be no repercussions for the delay. About a week later, when I hadn't heard anything about the reports, I asked Dr. Shearlow about them. Dr. Shearlow was responsible for receiving all adverse event reports and notifying me of any that resulted in death. He had received the reports the same day I had spoken with Rebecca but hadn't notified me. When I asked him why he hadn't notified me, he became defensive and angry. To make a long story short, he shared the reports with me, and I became concerned because Recallamin deaths had not been on my radar previously. I asked him for a report on all Recallamin mortality reports over the past 6 months, and the only thing that stood out was the deaths in Central Maine. That's when I asked him to set up a meeting with Rebecca, which was intended to review the patient's medical records to determine why they were such an outlier in terms of mortality. Now I'm wondering if the 6-month mortality report Dr. Shearlow gave me was accurate."

"Is there a way for you to check? I hate to say it, but I have little confidence in Dr. Shearlow and Dr. Franklin at this point."

Dr. Harder hesitated to respond, and before she could, AG Talcott recognized what he was asking of her and tried to convince her it was the right thing to do.

"I know doing so would put you in an awkward and uncomfortable position. However, if Dr. Shearlow is hiding data, and Dr. Franklin is a party to it, think of all the people that may be dying or harmed."

"Oh, I am fully aware of what's at stake here," Dr. Harder finally replied. "I just didn't wake up today thinking I would need to consider potentially becoming a whistleblower. I'm shocked."

"I'm sorry, Dr. Harder," AG Talcott apologized, feeling like he was putting a burden on her that she couldn't or didn't want to carry.

"No, no need to apologize. I can access the Vaccine Adverse Event Report database. Do you mind hanging on the line while I pull up the data? It shouldn't take me more than a few minutes?"

"I'd be happy to wait."

"OK, let me just get out of this program and get into the VAERS database," she said, leading him verbally through the clicks of her mouse. "Hmmm, let me try that again. Huh, why would that be?"

"What's the matter?" AG Talcott asked.

"It says my access is denied. That doesn't make sense."

"It does if they don't want you to uncover what they may be hiding," AG Talcott offered. "Do you need access to it in your current job?"

"No. I only need access to MedWatch, a completely different system. That's the program I was in before trying to get into the VAERS database."

"So maybe they changed your access?" AG Talcott asked.

"I'd be amazed. The difficulty and delays of gaining access to programs are only surpassed by how long it takes to restrict access to programs. I'm afraid IT is woefully under-resourced."

"So, that means someone had to pull some major strings to get it done this quickly."

"Yes, and now I'm worried that they may be able to see that I tried to access it. What would I tell them?"

"Force of habit from your previous job?" AG Talcott suggested, now worried that he had put her in an even more uncomfortable position.

"That would be a hard sell. I didn't access it that much.

That was Dr. Shearlow's job. Now I wish I had. I do have someone who might be able to get me the information, but it might take me a day or two."

"Dr. Harder, I think I have imposed on you enough. If your conscience leads you down that path, so be it, but I think there's enough smoke here for me to escalate this to other federal authorities. Thank you for your help."

"I'd say it was my pleasure, but I'd be lying," Dr. Harder replied, uncharacteristically cracking a joke. "I will let you know what I learn. I know too much now to let this go. I need to see it through."

They ended the call, and AG Talcott immediately texted Clark Ainsley.

"Need to chat ASAP."

* * *

Likewise, Dr. Elizabeth Harder took immediate steps after the call, worried that her attempt to access the VAERS database may spur unwanted attention if not sanction. Fortunately, her colleague from the Center for Drug Evaluation and Research was not only in the same building but was also in her office and available.

"Oh, thank God you're here, Janet," Dr. Harder greeted the Center's Director, Dr. Janet Sullivan.

"Elizabeth, good to see you. What's the matter? You look flustered."

"Oh, it's my computer. I'm working on an important project, and in the middle of everything, it shuts down to run an automatic upgrade."

"Oh, I hate that when they do that. Doesn't IT know that we actually have work to do during the day? How can I help you?"

"I just need some data from the VAERS database. A simple listing of Adverse Reports resulting in mortalities in the last year by State for a vaccine called Recallamin. Could you run it for me?"

"Absolutely," Dr. Sullivan replied, pulling up the database as Dr. Harder looked on, hoping against hope that her fears would not be realized.

After setting up the search criteria as Dr. Harder specified, she hit the "Run Report" button. Within 30 seconds, her request was processed, and the report scrolled on her screen.

"Whoa! Now I can see why this is an important project," exclaimed Dr. Sullivan as a queasy feeling lodged itself in the pit of Dr. Harder's stomach.

"How many?" Dr. Harder asked.

"A total of nearly 6,000 deaths in the U.S. over the last year. Five thousand nine hundred and forty-seven to be exact."

Dr. Harder suddenly felt dizzy as all the blood drained from her face.

"Are you sure those are the mortality cases and not all the adverse event reports?" she asked hopefully.

"Nope. It shows right here 5,497 cases of a total of 9,326 adverse event reports. Almost 64% of all reports are mortality cases. Isn't that unusually high?"

"Yes, it is. Could you print that report out for me?"

"Sure. I could email it to you if you'd like."

"No, that won't be necessary," she replied, not wanting an electronic trail of evidence that might get flagged that she would have a hard time explaining.

Dr. Harder knew that some portion of those mortality cases were likely deaths due to natural causes and unrelated to the vaccine. However, the total number of occurrences far exceeded the amount she would have expected, given the reports Dr. Shearlow had supplied her. She was now sure that Dr. Shearlow had been hiding this data from her. What was even more frightening to Dr. Harder was that adverse event reporting from the field was not 100%. There was a good chance of a higher number of deaths attributable to Recallamin that wasn't accounted for in the database.

"Thank you so much, Janet. You're a life-saver," Dr. Harder said as Dr. Sullivan handed her the hefty hardcopy report of the data.

"Happy to help, Elizabeth. Don't be a stranger," she called as Dr. Harder was exiting.

"I won't," she replied despite feeling like her employment with the FDA was in grave doubt. To Dr. Harder, it seemed like everyone was looking at her suspiciously as she made her way back to her office. In fact, no one was paying attention to her. It was just the document in her hand and the plan in her head that was making her paranoid.

Arriving back at her office, she fully expected to be accosted by Security and unceremoniously led out and banished from the FDA for life. Instead, all was just as she left it, and no one was waiting for her. Closing the door, she logged into her computer, navigated to a website, clicked on the green "File a Complaint" button, and completed and submitted OSC Form 14.

Dr. Elizabeth Harder had just notified the U.S. Office of Special Counsel of the wrongdoing she was aware of and put her faith in the Whistleblower Protection Act of 1989.

* * *

When AG Talcott's phone rang, he expected Clark was responding to his text. Instead, he was surprised to see it was Dr. Elizabeth Harder calling him back.

"Dr. Harder, I wasn't expecting to hear from you so soon," he answered.

"Well, I managed to get the mortality data on Recallamin, and it was far worse than I thought. Nearly 6,000 deaths nationwide. I have filed a complaint with the Office of Special Counsel reporting Dr. Shearlow and Dr. Franklin's involvement in hiding the data. I imagine when the OSC assigns one of the investigating agencies to the case, they will find that all the clinical trial data was fudged as well. I feel sick to my stomach. I should have never trusted Dr. Shearlow. Were you able to reach your federal agency friend?"

"No, not yet, but perhaps given I have you on the line, maybe I can conference him in. Would you be opposed to that?" AG Talcott asked.

"Not at all," Dr. Harder replied enthusiastically, her only motivation now being on righting the wrongs perpetrated by Dr. Shearlow and Dr. Franklin.

"I'll have to put you on hold for a minute, OK?" AG Talcott said, getting up from his desk to get his assistant to help him navigate the phone system. When Dr. Harder heard AG Talcott return to the line, he took roll-call.

"Dr. Harder, are you there?"

"Yes, I'm here."

"Clark, can you hear us?"

"Loud and clear, Lew."

After introducing Dr. Harder to Clark Ainsley, AG Talcott asked Dr. Harder to recap for Clark what she had just told him five minutes earlier.

"Thank you, Dr. Harder," the Deputy Attorney General said after she had finished. "You did the right thing reporting this to the OSC. I'm sure it wasn't an easy thing to do, but it should help expedite corrective actions."

"Well, I hope so. I can't believe this happened under my

watch."

"Clark, were you able to speak to the Secretary of HHS?" AG Talcott asked.

"As a matter of fact, I just got off my call with Julia when you called," Clark replied, referring to HHS Secretary Julia Ramon-Perez. "All I can say is that I wouldn't want her angry with me!" he exclaimed.

Ms. Ramon-Perez was a petite, attractive woman of Latino origin who grew up tough as nails in the Bronx, New York. Behind her delicate appearance was a fierce and determined tigress. She learned to stand up for herself, growing up with four older brothers who, while protective, also challenged her constantly. An attorney by training, Julia had held several jobs as General Counsel in the healthcare industry, including with a prominent hospital corporation and later a multi-national pharmaceutical company, before arriving at the Department of Health and Human Services. After 5 years as Deputy Secretary at HHS, she was appointed as HHS Secretary by the President. Her background and never back down determination were perfectly suited for the task of uncovering the corruption in the FDA, one of the operating divisions under her purview, and also for bringing AlzCura Pharmaceuticals to justice.

"So you told her about Dr. Rosenthal, Dr. Franklin, and Dr. Shearlow?" AG Talcott asked.

"You bet I did, and hoo, hoo, you should have heard the blue streak of Spanish that came out of her mouth. I don't even know Spanish, but I could tell it probably wasn't something I'd ever dare say in front of my mama!" Clark replied, chuckling.

"So, how did you leave it with her?"

"She thought we should immediately set up a multi-agency task force which she and I would co-lead. Now that the OSC has been notified, we'd have to coordinate our plan with them."

"And would this task force include representatives from Maine and New York law enforcement?"

"Absolutely."

"So were you thinking we'd do this Friday at 2 p.m. at the joint meeting we have scheduled?"

"Yeah, I told Julia about that, but she doesn't want to wait that long. She wants to do it later today."

"Jeez, alright. I can't speak for my New York colleagues, but I'm sure I can rearrange my schedule."

"You needn't worry about New York. I have already given Blair Johnson, the New York Attorney General, a call. He will see to it that he and the assistant AG in Buffalo and the proper authorities in the Buffalo PD are available. We're shooting for 4 p.m."

"What about me?" Dr. Harder asked. "Do you want me on the task force call?"

"Well, that's entirely up to you, Dr. Harder," Clark replied. "You can choose to remain anonymous now that you've filed your complaint with the OSC. Or you're welcome to join the team. I'm sure you have valuable information you could share."

"I'd like to be involved."

"Then welcome aboard," Clark responded. "I'll have my assistant contact both of you after our call. Lew, if there are others on your team that you'd like involved, give their names and contact information to my assistant, OK?"

"Will do. One more question," AG Talcott stated before Clark ended the call. "I appreciate the urgency of the meeting, but I'm concerned about any further delays in taking action."

"Don't be, my friend. Julia and I have a plan of action. As long as the representatives at the meeting are willing to support it, shock and awe could occur as soon as tomorrow morning," the Deputy Attorney General replied. Invoking a wartime phrase in his response to emphasize the depth and breadth of their proposed actions.

"Thanks, Clark. I appreciate your help."

"And I thank you, Dr. Harder," Clark responded. "The information and actions you took today only strengthened Julia and my plans."

"Why, thank you," Dr. Harder replied, surprised to receive praise when all she had been feeling most of the morning was guilt.

After the conclusion of the call, AG Talcott asked his assistant to set up an emergency call with DA Wydman and Inspector Adams.

"You already have a call with DA Wydman in a half-hour. Do you just want me to have Inspector Adams join the call?"

"Yeah, that works. Thanks!"

"You're welcome. Now, what do you think about fortune cookies?" his assistant asked.

Causing him to look at her funny until he realized that it was the fortune cookie she had given him that had led him to call Dr. Harder.

"They're amazing. Just like you!" he replied, smiling before returning to his office to prepare for his meeting with DA Wydman and Inspector Adams.

He had just enough time to infuse his third cup of coffee to stave off near exhaustion before the call. DA Wydman provided a brief summary of his anniversary weekend in Canada. AG Talcott followed by updating the DA and Inspector Adams on the revelations about AlzCura's Board Chair and the complicity of Dr. Franklin and Dr. Shearlow in the cover-up. The AG also outlined the extent of the harm caused by the Recallamin vaccine nationwide.

"I don't know whether to be happy or concerned that all of this was accomplished while I was on vacation," DA Wydman exclaimed.

"Relax, Will. It was the months of groundwork that you and Theo did that made this all possible," AG Talcott replied.

"Well, thank you for that, Lew," DA Wydman replied. "Theo deserves the lion's share of that credit."

"Thanks, but I was just doing my job," Theo responded humbly.

"Ironically, if I didn't have a connection in the Department of Justice and if we had never met Dr. Harder, we probably wouldn't be having this conversation."

"Yeah, there are so many what-ifs in this case. If any of them had not occurred, we might have never gotten to this point," DA Wydman exclaimed.

"Or discovered their accomplices in the FDA for that matter," added AG Talcott.

Now about this inter-agency meeting later today. Should we be asking Jackie, Curt, and Celeste to join the call?" DA Wydman asked.

"Yeah, good question, Will," AG Talcott replied. "They have been so instrumental in getting us to this point, I almost think we should. But then again, we'll likely be talking about taking law enforcement actions, so I'm leaning towards not including them."

"I agree," replied DA Wydman, quickly followed by Theo's agreement.

"OK, it's settled then. Just us, and maybe we can set up a call with Jackie, Curt, and Celeste sometime after the fact," AG Talcott proposed.

"Sounds good, Lew," DA Wydman replied.

AG Talcott wasn't sure whether his second wind was the coffee or the excited anticipation for the inter-agency meeting with Clark Ainsley and HHS Secretary Ramon-Lopez. It didn't matter. Things finally seemed to be lining up, and the ideal and all too infrequent reality of a coordinated Federal and State action seemed imminent.

CHAPTER 44

C heryl Baker put the finishing touches on the Recallamin 3 trial physician notices she had erroneously claimed were ready for the Gulf and West Coast region campaigns. She had never felt so humiliated as when Asa had exposed her recent failings in front of Chet Humphreys. That and the realization that Dr. Rosenthal, the Board Chair, had recommended her dismissal had done more to sober her up than any other type of intervention could have. Despite the new lease on life, the last thing she wanted to do was fly to LA and do the grunt work of a pharmaceutical rep for the next few weeks. Her reverie was interrupted by her assistant, who poked her head into the office.

"I have your itinerary for your trip to LA," she announced as Cheryl waved her impatiently into the office.

"Just what I wanted a 3-week sentence to the hell ironically called the city of angels," she said, reaching for the travel information.

"I booked you on the first flight out Thursday morning," her assistant replied. "I was able to get you into the Beverly Wilshire if that's any consolation."

If Cheryl thought it was a consolation or not went unspoken. Her assistant exited the office feeling that familiar twinge of lack of appreciation and respect that was the hallmark of working as an executive's assistant in the hell called

AlzCura Pharmaceuticals. If the money weren't so good, she would have left long ago, so she swallowed her pride and the choice words for her boss that were screaming to be let out and quietly went back to her desk.

Although it was only 10a.m., and despite her very tenuous job status, Cheryl was already thinking about going home and pouring herself a drink. If it weren't for the candidate interview for the vacant Northeast Region Pharmaceutical Rep position, she would have acted on that desire. Losing Alexis had stripped her of any desire to continue, not just her job but with life in general. She was left with her twin sons, Anthony and Andrew, who were more often an embarrassment and a liability than sources of parental pride and fulfillment. Even her relationship with Dr. Sheridan, which offered some semblance of companionship and emotional support in the past, died with Alexis' passing. Prompting a feeling that Dr. Sheridan only showed interest in her as a way to gain access to her nubile daughter to satisfy his unique sexual tastes.

The intercom beeped, and her assistant announced that the pharmaceutical rep candidate had arrived.

"Send her in," Cheryl replied.

After Cheryl and the candidate exchanged introductions, Cheryl asked her first question.

"If you were on a sales call and the doctor agreed to prescribe our vaccine as long as you agreed to sleep with him, would you?"

The candidate was shocked and unable to formulate an immediate response.

"It's a simple yes or no question. Would you?" Cheryl pressed the candidate impatiently.

The flustered candidate blurted out her answer, "No!" shifting uncomfortably in her chair.

"Thank you, we will get back to you in the next week or two

with our decision."

The previously flustered candidate was now rendered incredulously paralyzed, unable to believe that the interview was over and equally unable to utter any words in response.

"You can go now. Thank you for your time," Cheryl said, standing and extending her arm out, not to shake the candidate's hand but to point her in the direction of the door.

The stunned candidate got up and tried to walk out of the office with at least a shred of dignity and confidence she walked in with. Stopping at the door, she finally found her voice.

"Do you mean to tell me that no was the wrong answer to that question? Because if that's the case, that's really fucked up."

"Actually, no was the right answer, but the question and my responses were designed to see how you would function under pressure. You failed. Better luck next time."

"You're crazy, lady," the candidate replied.

"See, you just proved my point. You can't deal with pressure. Now get out of my office and stop wasting my time," Cheryl barked.

The candidate left Cheryl's office and could be heard screaming profanities in her wake.

Five minutes later, Cheryl exited her office and told her assistant she was headed home to prepare and pack for her trip the next day. Both Cheryl and her assistant knew that a good part of that preparation involved a bottle and a glass.

CHAPTER 45

HS Secretary Julia Ramon-Perez introduced herself and thanked those on the call for their flexibility in accommodating the hastily scheduled meeting. Deputy Attorney General Clark Ainsley followed, echoing the Secretary's sentiments and asking those on the call to briefly introduce themselves. In addition to the law enforcement officials from Maine and New York and Dr. Elizabeth Harder, leaders from the U.S. Office of Special Counsel, Federal Bureau of Investigation, and the Office of Inspector General were also in attendance.

"Let me get straight to the point," HHS Secretary Ramon-Perez began. "We believe that AlzCura Pharmaceuticals pushed their Alzheimer's cure while not only downplaying the risk of harm but hiding the adverse events from discovery. Their executives, along with FDA leaders, engaged in racketeering and conspiracy, misleading not just the general public but doctors, insurance companies, and government programs such as Medicare and Medicaid. I don't mean to dismiss the evidence those of you on the call may have regarding AlzCura Pharmaceuticals or the complicity of the FDA. In time, we hope to work with you to understand the full depth of your concerns. For the sake of efficiency and the limited time we have today, Deputy AG Ainsley and I would like to lay out a plan. We hope that this plan will not impinge but rather help facilitate the legal actions you may still need to take. I ask that you listen to our plan and reserve your questions or concerns until we ask for your thoughts. Deputy AG Ainsley will take it from here. Clark."

"Thank you, Madame Secretary. In short, the evidence we have on AlzCura Pharmaceuticals executives and two individuals at the FDA are sufficient to issue arrest warrants for a series of fraudulent activities. The criminal charges include: misrepresenting the safety and efficacy of the Recallamin vaccine, failure to report deaths and other serious adverse events related to its use, and collusion by both private individuals and public officials to profit from these activities. In addition to these warrants and criminal charges, Secretary Ramon-Perez is proposing additional steps. Julia."

"Thank you, Clark. Our most significant concern is the safety of the public. We have evidence that Recallamin likely contributed to a substantial number of deaths. A far higher proportion than were reported in the clinical trials on which the vaccine's approval was based. Now, with evidence of compromised leadership at the Food & Drug Administration, I will impose an immediate suspension of the manufacture, distribution, and prescription of the Recallamin vaccine. That suspension will remain in place until a full and thorough analysis of the vaccine's real efficacy and safety can be completed. We will conduct a full and thorough audit of all FDA actions during Dr. Franklin's tenure to ensure these fraudulent activities didn't extend beyond AlzCura's Recallamin vaccine. OK, we've talked enough. I want to be sure that Clark and I have an opportunity to answer your questions."

After a momentary pause, AG Talcott spoke up.

"This is Attorney General Talcott from Maine. First, I'd like to thank you for arranging this call and formulating the plan you just shared with us. While I am delighted to hear your plan, I have two immediate concerns. When are you planning to take these actions? And will your actions prevent us from pursuing criminal investigations related to individuals subject to your warrants?

"I'll take that," Deputy AG Ainsley replied. "We're taking these actions tomorrow, and the warrants explicitly include language that obligates them to cooperate with any additional legal actions that may be brought by other jurisdictions. In point of fact, these warrants should only strengthen your ability to pursue the investigations or actions you may need to take. Does that answer your questions, AG Talcott?"

"It does. Thank you, Deputy AG Ainsley," AG Talcott replied, not used to referring to his law school buddy by his formal title.

"I have a question," Chief Detective Les Gains spoke up. "Will the individuals be taken into custody when the warrants are issued?

"Good question, Chief Detective Gains," Deputy AG Ainsley replied. "We believe the seriousness of the crimes and the financial means of those involved represent a potential flight risk. We have every intention of recommending to the judge that they are held in custody."

"Can we know who you plan to issue warrants to?" Chief Detective Gains asked in a follow-up question.

"Sure," Deputy AG Ainsley responded. "Right now, we have drawn up warrants for the following individuals: Dr. Simon Rosenthal, Dr. Asa Sheridan, Cheryl Baker, Dr. Lynn Franklin, and Dr. Woodson Shearlow."

"Excuse me, this is Inspector Adams from Maine. Have you considered AlzCura's Regional Lab in your plan? I know that some of the erroneous data about Recallamin are from their Regional Lab in Buffalo."

"Thank you, Inspector Adams," Deputy AG Ainsley replied. "We had not considered that. Good catch. Do you happen to know who at the Regional Lab would be responsible for the erroneous data?"

"The letters I saw containing erroneous information were from Dr. M. David Muckland, the Lab's Medical Director."

"Great. We will have to draft a warrant for Dr. Muckland then," he replied and then asked someone in the room with him a question.

"Bill, do we have the manpower to include AlzCura's Regional Lab in Buffalo in our raid tomorrow?"

In the background, the individuals on the call heard Bill respond that he would work on getting the necessary resources.

"Alright, any other questions," Deputy AG Ainsley asked, returning to the call.

"This is Dr. Elizabeth Harder. I have a question for Secretary Ramon-Perez."

"Go ahead, Dr. Harder," Secretary Ramon-Perez replied.

"I was wondering how I might be of assistance. I feel terrible this happened right under my nose while I was Director of the Office of Vaccine Safety. I would like to be part of the team that sets things right," she said hopefully.

"Well, Dr. Harder, I was going to speak to you privately, but since you asked. I was hoping that you would agree to lead the team to re-analyze the Recallamin data and audit the activities of the FDA."

"Really?" Dr. Harder responded in disbelief.

"Really," Secretary Ramon-Perez responded. "I intend to remove Dr. Franklin and Dr. Shearlow from their posts first thing tomorrow and name you as interim FDA Commissioner. Can I count on you?"

After a moment of shock, Dr. Harder realized that the HHS Secretary was waiting on her response.

"Of course. I would be honored, Madame Secretary," Dr.

Harder responded. Shocked to be going from a guilt-ridden whistleblower to interim FDA Commissioner on the same day.

"That's great. And you can call me Julia. You and I will be spending a lot of time together cleaning up this mess," the HHS Secretary replied. "Are there any other questions from the group?"

"Yes. This is Police Commissioner Dirk Sorenson from Buffalo PD. When is this all going to go down, and how can my Department assist?"

"Thank you, Commissioner Sorenson," Deputy AG Ainsley replied. "I am going to have Director Bill Steig from the FBI's Inspection Division contact you after this call. The two of you can coordinate what resources you may need to provide. I appreciate your offer. As excellent a shop as the Buffalo PD is, I know you're not sitting over there, twiddling your thumbs looking for things to do. So I expect that the FBI will be supplying most of the necessary resources."

"Thank you, sir. I appreciate your kind words and look forward to speaking with Mr. Steig."

"Any more questions?" Secretary Ramon-Perez asked.

When no more questions were forthcoming, the HHS Secretary provided some final thoughts.

"OK, I'd like to thank you all again, but I don't want us to think for one minute that the steps we are about to take will magically result in a quick or easy path to justice or healing. You can bet that AlzCura will lawyer up and exercise every legal tactic to rescind the suspension and evade or delay being held accountable. Likewise, the revelations about the complicity of our FDA leadership will shake the American public's confidence in our ability to ensure their safety. Most importantly, thousands of families will learn that their loved ones died as a result of corporate greed and our failure to ensure fail-safe protections. Undoubtedly, there will be a tidal wave of legal actions, all perfectly reasonable given the facts, but nonetheless, challenging to coordinate and resolve as quickly as the aggrieved parties deserve. It will take our coordinated and concerted efforts to stay the course. I am painfully aware that our Federal and State agencies historically have not been the model of communication, coordination, and teamwork. For that reason, I am proposing that this not be our one and only meeting. Would this group be open to at least monthly touch-base meetings?"

To which the call participants gave their enthusiastic and unanimous support.

"Good. Then Deputy AG Ainsley and I will work with all of you to find what dates and times works best for these meetings going forward. Clark, do you have any final thoughts?"

"Yes, thank you, Julia. I will also be working to create a confidential portal where the State Attorney General's office can share communications on an as-needed basis. While this only applies to Maine and New York, we anticipate that over time, other states will join in taking legal action and be able to benefit from this communication vehicle."

"Alright, thank you, Clark. My clock shows we've used 28 of the 30 minutes we allotted for this meeting. Who says government can't be efficient?" she said, ending on a light note, which caused a smattering of laughter as people disconnected from the call.

AG Talcott, who was sitting in his office with DA Wydman and Inspector Adams, looked up and had only one thing on his mind.

"Gentlemen, it's time for the State of Maine to bring charges against AlzCura Pharmaceuticals. If you two put together the complaint, I will get the case on the court docket, so we can file our complaint tomorrow."

"Will do," DA Wydman replied enthusiastically. "Do we include the murders of Dr. Caron and Leslie Anderson in the complaint?"

"No, hold off on those for now. We can always file an amended or new complaint if we identify that last set of fingerprints, and they implicate AlzCura."

"So then the wrongful deaths, deceptive marketing practices, and fraudulent practices related to their vaccine's safety and efficacy," DA Wydman recited.

"Yes, and also before I forget. Let's set up a call with Jackie, Curt, and Celeste for Friday morning, if possible. I'd like to brief them before they hear it on the news."

"I can do that," DA Wydman replied. "I think they will be thrilled to hear that all their suffering and efforts finally paid off."

After DA Wydman and Inspector Adams exited, AG Talcott breathed a sigh of relief, leaned back in his office chair, and felt the full measure of his lack of sleep. Despite the handful of unopened emails that were calling to him from his computer monitor, he logged out and, for once, took his assistant's advice and left the office early. Tomorrow would be a big day, and he needed to be on the top of his game.

CHAPTER 46

C heryl Baker was startled awake by her phone alarm, and it took her a minute to orient herself to why she was getting up so early. When she finally realized that she needed to go to the airport to catch her flight to Los Angeles, she grumbled a few choice words and trudged to the bathroom. An hour later, filled with dread, she was on her way. Sending her to LA to schmooze physicians felt like cruel and unusual punishment.

To her chagrin, even the express precheck line was backed up, adding to her growing frustration. When the person in front of her fumbled through her purse for her driver's license and then scrolled interminably through her phone to find her ticket, Cheryl thought she was going to scream. Even the check-in agent looked annoyed. To make matters worse, she just stood in place after the agent waved her through. Taking time to return her driver's license to her wallet, store her wallet in her purse, fumble with her phone, and finally drag her carry-on past the agent.

Cheryl, the model of efficiency, handed the agent her driver's license and placed her phone on the reader resulting in an almost immediate recognition and green indicator light. As the agent was inspecting her driver's license and checking some information on the computer monitor, Cheryl couldn't resist commenting on the person who had preceded her in line.

"I can't understand how that lady could wait in an express line and not be prepared when she got up here. I mean, if you have all the time in the world, go through the regular check-in line, right?" she asked rhetorically.

When the agent didn't immediately wave her through or respond to her comments, she asked.

"Is everything alright?"

He looked up and replied, "It will just be a second. I need to confirm something with my supervisor," as he turned and waved to another agent to come to his station. As the two inspected her driver's license and computer screen again, Cheryl was beginning to believe it was just going to be one of those days.

"Ms. Baker," said the supervising agent, "I'm going to have to ask you to come with me."

"What? But I have a flight I need to catch," Cheryl exclaimed in disbelief.

"Please just come with me," he said matter-of-factly, betraying no sense of what the possible concern could be.

As she followed the agent, she tried to extract some information or even just a reaction from him.

"Is this some kind of random check process I'm not aware of? Was there something wrong with my flight information? I can't miss my flight. I have important business in LA."

None of her questions or comments spurred a response from the agent who led her down a narrow hallway to a locked door that opened when he swiped his ID badge. Entering, all Cheryl saw was a windowless room with a table and two chairs.

"Please take a seat, Ms. Baker, and someone will be in shortly to speak with you."

"I don't think you understand. My flight leaves in 45 minutes. I checked bags through to LA. If I miss my flight," she started to say before the agent interrupted her.

"Ms. Baker, someone will be here shortly. I'm sure arrangements will be made if you happen to miss your flight."

Reasonably reassured, the agent left, leaving Cheryl to stare at the stark walls. After five minutes, which felt like an hour to Cheryl, the walls seemed to be closing in on her. Anxious, she got up, went to the door, and found it locked. This only contributed to the suffocating feelings that were creeping over her.

"Hello," she yelled. "Is there anyone there? I have to go to the bathroom." Hoping that her pleas might spur a response and an opportunity to get out of the room at least temporarily.

When no one responded, she sat back down in a huff and decided to call Asa. Retrieving her phone, she made the call only to be thwarted by no cell phone reception. Just as her anxiety had grown to the point that she was about to start screaming, the door opened, followed by two beefy police officers.

"It's about time," Cheryl said at the height of her frustration.

"Ms. Baker, we're here to transport you to the Buffalo Police Department for questioning," said one of the officers.

"On what grounds, and what about my business trip to LA?"

"We have a warrant for your arrest and detention on charges related to your involvement in fraudulent practices by AlzCura Pharmaceuticals. I am now going to advise you of your rights."

As the officer recited her Miranda rights, Cheryl's mind swirled.

"Ms. Baker. Do you understand each of these rights I have explained to you?" the officer repeated a second time when she failed to respond to him the first time.

"Oh, yes. Yes, I do," she said, absently realizing that she had not heard a word he had said.

"With these rights in mind, do you wish to talk with us now?"

"No. I want to call my lawyer."

"You will be allowed to call your lawyer once we get to the station. Please come with us."

As Cheryl silently walked between the police officers trailing her carry-on bag behind her, it seemed like a long walk of shame. Dozens of travelers gave them a wide berth and stared at her like she was some kind of terrorist as they made their way through the airport terminal. The officers confiscated her bag, purse, and cell phone before depositing her in the back of their cruiser.

❋ ❋ ❋

Chet stormed into Asa's office with the news.

"Security just called me from the front desk. The FBI's here. They have warrants to serve, and they're asking for you," he blurted out, clearly flustered.

"What should I do?" Dr. Sheridan asked, equally rattled by the news as he fumbled with his hands thinking there must be something he could do before their arrival.

"We wait and do nothing until we see the warrants. They're on their way up."

"They?" Asa asked. "How many are there?"

"I think only two agents are on the way up. However, Security says there are at least a dozen more FBI agents waiting in the lobby."

"A dozen? Jesus, Chet that can't be good. I should try to call Simon and warn him," he said, picking up his phone just as his assistant knocked on his office door.

"The FBI is here. They need to speak with you," his assistant said.

Putting his phone down, he told his assistant to escort the agents in.

"Dr. Asa Sheridan, I am Lead FBI Agent Kyle Dixon. We have a warrant to detain you for questioning. We also have a warrant to search the premise and confiscate evidence related to the marketing, efficacy, and safety of your Recallamin vaccine," he said. Handing the warrants to Dr. Sheridan, who immediately gave them to Chet.

"May I ask why you need to detain Dr. Sheridan for questioning?"

"I'm sorry, and who are you?" Agent Dixon asked.

"I'm Dr. Sheridan's attorney."

"Well, I think you will find all the details of Dr. Sheridan's questioning and our search contained in the warrants."

"Can we have some privacy while we review these?" Chet asked.

"No, we will wait here while you review them," Agent Dixon replied. "And while you're at it, you will want to review this additional order from the FDA requiring you to immediately suspend all manufacturing, distribution, and prescribing of the Recallamin vaccine."

Dr. Sheridan was too stunned by what the agent said to pass the order along to Chet.

"The FDA is also in the process of recalling the entire stock of distributed vaccines in the U.S.," Agent Dixon added. "As for vaccines distributed to other countries, the FDA is working with their counterpart agencies to inform them of the suspension and recall."

"On what grounds?" Chet blustered. "That will put us out

of business."

"It's all detailed in the order," Agent Dixon replied.

As Asa and Chet took the warrants and FDA order to the conference table, Agent Dixon and the other agent stood by patiently. Chet's look of determination, anxious to find vulnerabilities and loopholes to exploit, slowly changed to a look of resignation. After fifteen minutes, he whispered to Asa.

"These are bullet-proof, I'm afraid. We have no choice but to comply."

Dr. Sheridan had never known Chet to be at a loss for coming up with some kind of evasive maneuver.

"Why do they want to question me? Is it about Alexis' suicide?" Asa asked.

"No. This warrant is for federal charges related to fraud, conspiracy, and falsification of records related to the efficacy and safety of Recallamin. It says that you are to be transported to and detained at the Buffalo Police Department. So, I wouldn't be surprised if Buffalo PD doesn't have another warrant waiting for you there."

"Jesus Christ, Chet, isn't there anything you can do to postpone this?"

"I'm afraid not, Asa. As a matter of fact, I'm surprised they've given us this much time. Our best bet now is to cooperate and wait for our day in court."

"Gentlemen," Agent Dixon stated, "unless you have any questions, we need to proceed."

Both Chet and Asa reluctantly got up from the conference table, and Chet fired a final salvo in desperation.

"I'd like to have AlzCura representatives present during the search and seizure of evidence."

"I'm afraid that's not allowed," Agent Dixon replied and immediately turned to the other agent. "Go and tell the team to get started."

As the agent left to execute Agent Dixon's instructions, Dr. Sheridan started to plead his own case. Realizing that Chet, his Chief Legal Counsel, had resigned himself to the inevitable.

"I have to notify my Board and the rest of my Executive Team," he said, walking over to his desk and picking up the phone.

"Put down the phone, Dr. Sheridan," Agent Dixon commanded. "We already have your Board Chair in custody as well as Cheryl Baker. We also have agents at your Regional Lab facility. As soon as I give the order, they will search that facility and take your Lab Medical Director into custody."

Dr. Sheridan's hair-trigger anger was only eclipsed by a deep and pervasive feeling of helplessness that held his desire to start throwing things in check. He slowly returned the phone's handset to its cradle.

"Then what can I do?" he asked despondently, looking first at Chet and then at Agent Dixon.

"You're coming with me to the Buffalo Police Department," Agent Dixon replied while removing handcuffs from their holder on his belt.

"Now?" Dr. Sheridan asked, taking a couple steps back. "But, I need to confer with my attorney first."

"Yes, now. Your attorney can confer with you at the police station."

"Are those handcuffs really necessary?" Dr. Sheridan pleaded as Agent Dixon moved in his direction.

"Yes, and if you don't come with me cooperatively, I have a team of agents outside your office ready to remove you forcibly if we have to."

"That won't be necessary," Chet answered. "Asa, just go with him. I will come right down to the police station. In the meantime, don't say anything."

Dr. Sheridan took a couple steps forward and, defeated, held out his arms to allow Agent Dixon to apply the cuffs. As Agent Dixon led him out of his office, they were met by a team of two FBI agents and two Buffalo police officers. As Agent Dixon handed Dr. Sheridan off, an officer recited his Miranda rights.

* * *

Dr. Lynn Franklin never got to her office on Thursday morning. She didn't even get to the front desk security station before she was met by two Silver Springs police officers accompanied by two FBI agents.

She knew better than to make a scene by feigning shock and indignation. It would have just called more attention to her in the lobby crowded by employees of the FDA filing through Security on their way to their jobs. An FBI agent informed her of the criminal charges, and a police officer recited her Miranda rights. She was then quietly escorted to a police cruiser for transport to a federal facility. Except for affirmatively answering the officer's question about whether she understood her rights and declining to say anything until represented by her attorney, she remained mute.

All that Dr. Franklin could think about on the ride was her decision to promote rather than terminate Dr. Elizabeth Harder. Dr. Simon Rosenthal had insisted that she sack Dr. Harder. Instead, she chose to keep her in the agency. Convinced that given Dr. Harder's pristine work record, she would have undoubtedly appealed the firing and filed an unlawful termination suit. Now, Dr. Franklin recognized that Dr. Rosenthal had been right. Wrongful termination was clearly the lesser of two evils.

Dr. Shearlow's arrest was likewise executed in the front

lobby. His reaction was quite the opposite of Dr. Franklin's when he saw police officers and FBI agents approaching. He took flight across the hall, squealing like a stuck pig. Had he been a larger man, he would have knocked over several people in his wake. Instead, his diminutive size made him ping-pong off of people like he was a pinball. His escape attempt couldn't have been more obvious or public. When he decided to take up shelter in the Ladies' restroom, the crowd watching the chase collectively broke into laughter.

The police officers and FBI agents eventually emerged from the restroom dragging a sobbing and combative Dr. Shearlow in cuffs. The crowd, many of whom had postponed going through Security to watch the outcome of the show, erupted in applause. To their delight, this just made the little man in custody more animated in his hopeless attempts to break free. Before they exited the building, Dr. Shearlow screamed a profanity-saturated final salutation to his audience, which only made them laugh and applaud more enthusiastically.

CHAPTER 47

C urt arrived at Jackie's house late Thursday evening with Caitlin and Cade sound asleep. After they extracted the kids from the car and carried them to bed, Jackie and Curt decided to reprise their bathtub therapy session.

Before they immersed themselves in the relaxing warmth of the tub, their bodies had other more urgent desires which needed to be satisfied first. While Jackie didn't need to help facilitate these desires, it didn't hurt.

"Why Professor, little ol' me has been starving to be filled with your penetrating knowledge," she drawled. Her tight jeans accentuating one of her finer features as she bent over the tub to start the water running.

"Well, young lady, I don't usually teach at such a late hour. However, I can see you're ripe for an infusion of my wisdom," he replied, grabbing her hips and rubbing up against her suggestively.

"Oh, Professor, I can almost feel your powerful intellect penetrating my ignorance already."

Suffice to say, their bathtub therapy was postponed until some alternate treatment had been enjoyed. Fully reacquainted, they fell into bed and slept soundly in each other's arms until little human alarm clocks woke them early the next morning.

With just enough time to prepare breakfast for Caitlin, Cade, and Ash before the 9a.m. call with DA Wydman, Jackie and Curt worked like a well-oiled machine in the kitchen. Caitlin and Cade spoke animatedly to Jackie about their last day in school and all the plans they had for summer. Even Ashley pitched in with some well-timed mama and dadas from her perch in her highchair. As Jackie and Curt started to clean up, they heard a knock on the front door, followed by a yoo-hoo.

"That's my mother," Jackie said to Curt and the kids. "I'm going to have her take the kids to the park while we get on our call."

"Well, there they are. How good to see you all again," Doris Selaney exclaimed enthusiastically while systematically hugging Caitlin and Cade and busing Ash on the cheek, which coaxed a "Nana" from her.

"Oh, what a good little girl," she said to her granddaughter, giving her another kiss on the cheek.

"Hi, Mom," Jackie said as her mother approached but passed her up to greet Curt.

"Sorry, dear. I'm going to hug this handsome man first," she smiled at her daughter and made good on her promise giving Curt a big hug.

"Good to see you again, Mrs. Selaney," Curt said.

"Well, it's good to see you too, but from now on, you call me Doris or Mom. That's an order."

"Yes, Mom," Curt replied in response.

"That's better. I'm glad you're a quick learner," she said, looking at Jackie, who was rolling her eyes.

"Now, can your daughter get a hug too?" Jackie exclaimed, feigning disappointment that she was passed over.

"Of course, honey. Just remember, the last shall be first," she quoted a phrase from the Bible as she hugged her daughter.

"How is that possible?" Cade asked.

"What's that, Cade?" his father questioned.

"How can the last be first?" he clarified.

"Oh, I will tell you how," replied Jackie's mother. "Let's go to the park, and I'll tell you," she added, setting Caitlin and Cade excitedly in motion. Once Jackie's mother was out the door with the parade of kids, Curt hugged Jackie.

"Your mother is something else," Curt replied.

"That she is. And you, Mister, are something else too."

They kissed and, with the time for the conference call fast approaching, grabbed fresh cups of coffee and retired to Jackie's computer stationed in the living room. Connecting to the video feed before calling in, they saw two new faces on the split-screen in addition to DA Wydman, Inspector Adams, and Celeste Boulanger.

"I wonder who they are?" Curt replied as he punched in the telephone number to connect to the call.

Once fully connected, DA Wydman greeted the group noting his surprise to see Jackie and Curt together.

"Now, is Jackie in Maine, or are you in New York, Curt?"

"I'm in New York," Curt replied. "I see we have some new faces on the call."

"Yes, not only new faces but very special guests," DA Wydman replied. "Let me first introduce Maine's Attorney General Lewis Talcott," he started as the AG put up his hand and gave a brief wave. "Lew, do you want to introduce our other special guest?"

"Thanks, Will, I'd be happy to, but before I do, let me first thank you, Jackie and Curt. It was through your tragic losses and your subsequent dedication that gave birth to this crusade against AlzCura. Without you, none of what we have to report today would have been possible."

"Thank you, sir," Curt replied as Jackie wiped tears from her eyes.

"Now, without further adieu, let me introduce you to my good friend Clark Ainsley. Clark and I went to law school together. Clark aimed a lot higher than I did, and he is now the Deputy Attorney General of the U.S. Department of Justice. I called Clark a week ago, and by doing so, we both learned some very interesting twists to the AlzCura story. I will let Clark fill you in."

"Well, thank you, Lew," crooned Clark in a deep baritone voice. "And let me also express my thanks to all of you. I'm late to this party, and we all owe you a debt of gratitude for all that you have done and endured over the last year. What I can tell you is that today, the Recallamin vaccine is no longer available. Also, the perpetrators of greed and deception that conspired to hide the dangers of the vaccine responsible for the deaths of thousands are all in custody and facing significant federal charges."

"Let me add," AG Talcott interjected, "that both the State of Maine and Celeste, through her attorney John Dryer, filed wrongful death lawsuits against AlzCura Pharmaceuticals."

"And we expect, in the coming weeks and months, many more states and individuals will file suits," added Deputy AG Ainsley.

Jackie and Curt were both awestruck by the news and thirsty for more details.

"I can't tell you how thankful I am to hear this," Jackie exclaimed. "I'm seeing an attorney next week to be one of those individuals hopping on the wrongful death lawsuit bandwagon. You mentioned there were some interesting twists to the story. Can you share the details?"

"I'd be happy to, Jackie," replied Deputy AG Ainsley. "When Lew called me about your concerns, I dug into some intel on AlzCura. I learned that their Board Chair, Dr. Simon Rosenthal, was a former FDA Commissioner. While retiring from public service to join the private sector is not uncommon or illegal, using his previous ties to the FDA for favorable treatment and profit is unlawful. As I dug deeper, I learned that Dr. Rosenthal had hand-picked his successor at the FDA, Dr. Lynn Franklin. She subsequently employed Dr. Rosenthal's nephew, Woodson Shearlow. Lew's investigation and suspicious bank transactions helped us identify the conspiracy. They, along with Alz-Cura executives, fudged clinical trial and adverse event data on the efficacy and safety of Recallamin."

"Wow, so are Dr. Franklin and Dr. Shearlow in custody as well?" Curt asked.

"They are," Deputy AG Ainsley confirmed. "and Dr. Elizabeth Harder has been named interim FDA Commissioner. I'd be remiss not to recognize my colleague HHS Secretary Julia Ramon-Perez here. It was her actions that made the suspension of the Recallamin vaccine possible."

"And for Jackie, Curt, and Celeste's benefit," AG Talcott interjected, "Dr. Harder had visited Maine with Dr. Shearlow a week ago. It was her actions after that meeting that blew the whistle on Dr. Franklin and Dr. Shearlow. Most importantly, here, that we haven't mentioned is the breadth of harm Alz-Cura has caused. When Dr. Harder uncovered the actual harm data, she found that nearly 6,000 people died in the U.S. last year from complications of the vaccine."

"Six thousand?!" Curt repeated.

"Yes, I know. That number shocked me as well," AG Talcott replied.

"What about Recallamin deaths outside the U.S.?" Jackie asked. "I know they had operations in Europe when I worked there and were planning opening operations in Canada and East Asia."

"We don't have that information as yet," Deputy AG Ainsley replied. "However, one of Dr. Harder's first tasks as interim

FDA Commissioner will be to lead a team of experts to conduct a thorough analysis of the actual efficacy and safety of Recallamin. We don't want to throw the baby out with the bathwater if there is evidence that it works for a specific population."

"What about the crimes that have happened to Jackie, Curt, and me? Do we know if these were the work of AlzCura?" Celeste asked.

"Unfortunately, Maine, along with Buffalo PD, still don't have sufficient evidence to charge anyone is these crimes," AG Talcott replied. "We know that Alexis Baker harbored Jackie's baby in her apartment. She also had a relationship of some nature with Dr. Caron, whose death was not a suicide. However, there are still two sets of unidentified fingerprints associated with these crimes. Hopefully, now that we have the principal figures from AlzCura in custody, we can uncover additional evidence. I'm sorry I don't have a better answer to your question."

"So, what's next?" Curt asked.

"Well, it depends upon who you're talking about, Curt," AG Talcott responded. "For Clark, me, and our counterparts in New York, we go to work prosecuting the crimes and continuing to solve the cases Celeste just asked about. For you, Jackie and Celeste, the heavy-lift is over. The tragedies you've had to endure and the blood, sweat, and tears you've had to shed in exposing the truth paid off. The criminals are being brought to justice. Hopefully, the actions we took yesterday to give you all the opportunity to close that painful chapter in your lives and start a new chapter filled with happiness. You all certainly deserve it."

"Thank you for that," Curt replied.

"Let me jump in here," DA Wydman interjected. "It seems like ages ago when Jackie, Curt, Dr. Caron, and I, the original Table for Four, met at the Farrisport Inn where all of this started. At the time, I had no idea how important that meeting would be. As impressed with Jackie and Curt as I was back then, my gratitude and respect for your commitment to this cause have only grown. Without you, none of this would have been possible."

"Thanks, Will," Curt replied. "And I'd like to thank you. I still remember the first time we met, shortly after Calli's murder. I was pleasantly surprised by how much concern you had for the welfare of my kids. Remember? You even recommended that place down in Portland, where my kids could go for grief counseling. Ironically, it was returning home from one of their sessions in Portland when we stopped to have dinner at the Farrisport Inn and met Jackie. So, in many ways, had you not made that recommendation for my kids, the Table for Four would have never occurred."

"Wow, I didn't know that. I'm always amazed when I hear things like that. Like there really is a master plan that we catch glimpses of from time to time," DA Wydman said, waxing philosophical.

"And we mustn't forget Dr. Caron's contribution," Jackie added. Amazed to be the one bringing it up, given the less than pleasant introduction to Dr. Caron she had as AlzCura's pharmaceutical rep. "It was his brave admissions during our Table for Four dinner that really gave us the ammunition we needed to pursue this crusade. He made the ultimate sacrifice."

"Well, hopefully, the coming days, weeks, and months will do justice to the injustices you and many others have had to suffer," AG Talcott interjected. "Thanks for sharing a bit of the backstory that helped to get us to this point. Obviously, a lot of things had to come together, and we're not finished. I expect we will learn much more and hopefully bring to justice those who perpetrated the crimes we still haven't solved."

"Let me second what my colleague just said," Deputy AG Ainsley added. "I especially appreciated hearing about how this all began. While I have no shortage of commitment to this cause, meeting with you, the victims, and hearing about your early efforts add to my devotion to this effort. Thank you. I aim to do you proud."

AG Talcott indicated that he anticipated there would be a wave of media attention, and Jackie, Curt, and Celeste should expect some requests for interviews. He recommended that they be cautious about sharing any information and instead deflect their requests to their attorneys or to law enforcement officials.

Jackie and Curt hugged for a long time after the call. Relieved on so many levels by the actions that had been taken. The most significant of which was suspending the use of the Recallamin vaccine. Guaranteeing no one else would have to suffer the grief of losing their loved ones as they had.

"Ready to start that new chapter?" Curt said, reprising the words that AG Talcott had spoken during the call.

"I feel like we already have," Jackie replied. "It's more like that one dark cloud that was blocking part of our sunshine has finally moved off, but it's not totally gone."

"It's still hanging around because two sets of fingerprints still remain a mystery?" Curt asked, shifting from AG Talcott's book analogy to Jackie's blue sky one.

Jackie nodded to confirm he had correctly guessed what she was thinking. He hugged her tighter and kissed the top of her head.

"Even so," Curt added, "the winds have shifted in a favorable direction, and as long as we're together, it should be clear sailing from here on out. Don't you think?"

Jackie nodded and, looking up at Curt with tear-filled eyes, kissed him.

"Can we celebrate Ash's birthday at the Farrisport Inn?" she asked out of the blue.

"Ah, sure," Curt replied, thrown off a little by her request. "When's her birthday?"

"August 20th, six weeks from now."

"August 20th? Really?"

"Well, yeah. I am her mother, and I was there when it happened!" she laughed.

"No, I didn't mean to suggest you didn't know. It's just that August 20th," Curt paused as his eyes now brimmed with tears.

"Curt, what's the matter?" Jackie said with concern in her voice.

"August 20th is also the day I lost Calli. Two days before Cade's birthday," he replied as a lone tear streaked down his cheek.

"Oh my God, Curt, I had no idea. I'm sorry," she responded, hugging him. "We don't have to celebrate on that day."

"No, no, we do," Curt replied, recovering and wiping the one stray tear from his face. "I am now beginning to understand how intricately woven together our lives have been. We do need to celebrate on August 20th. Yes, let's do it," he said with confident finality. "Now, let's go rescue your mother from our kids at the park," he added, punctuating his command with a kiss.

The call about bringing AlzCura Pharmaceuticals to justice and their plans for celebrating Ash's birthday at the place they had first met buoyed their spirits through the rest of Curt and the kid's visit. Sunny arrived to begin her internship at the Buffalo police department, and Jackie and Curt had dinner with Sunny and Barrett Saturday night. Sunday was reserved for church with Jackie's parents, followed, of course, by brunch at Momma's. Jackie met with her attorney Nunzio Scarletti and began the process for filing her wrongful death lawsuit against AlzCura.

Curt and the kid's extended visit only served to consolidate their relationships. They found a place where Caitlin could show off her horse-riding skills, and Cade had ample time to demonstrate his prowess riding his scooter. Jackie and Caitlin also had plenty of "girl time" together. Cade continued his gentlemanly ways, frequently beating his father in opening doors and pulling out chairs for Jackie. Then basking in hugs and compliments received from Jackie in return. Jackie and Curt also had no shortage of private time, poignant moments, deep conversations, and playtime. None of this made it any easier when Curt and the kids had to pack up and leave.

As Curt drove off with Caitlin and Cade waving frantically out the window, he saw Jackie waving back through the rearview mirror. It was a scene he was determined to never have to repeat again.

EPILOGUE

The media firestorm around the arrests of AlzCura's pharmaceutical company executives and FDA officials and the recall and suspension of the Recallamin vaccine sent shockwaves across the nation. Some people undoubtedly viewed it as just another one of the countless examples of corporate greed and government corruption. They were the minority, however, compared to the millions of individuals with Alzheimer's and their families whose hopes were dashed by the news. Not to mention the anxiety suffered by those who had received the Recallamin vaccine. They now had a life sentence of worry, wondering if and when their liver would fail or their brain would develop an aneurysm that would eventually explode. Some quietly endured these fears, while others flocked to their doctor's offices or hospital emergency rooms at the slightest ache or pain. Many people who actually lost loved ones filed lawsuits, and many States ultimately joined Maine and New York in their own suits against AlzCura Pharmaceuticals.

Health & Human Services Secretary Julia Ramon-Perez and her interim FDA Commissioner Dr. Elizabeth Harder were the lightning rods during these turbulent times. Their job was to assuage the masses and restore the public's faith in the FDA while re-evaluating the real efficacy and safety of the Recallamin vaccine.

Deputy Attorney General Clark Ainsley found himself with the unenviable task of trying to develop a fair and efficient legal process to accommodate the thousands of lawsuits that were filed. Eventually, all the individual suits were organized under one class-action suit, and the number of TV ads from law firms trolling for Recallamin cases exploded.

The FBI's haul from their raid on AlzCura Pharmaceuticals not only revealed the systematic suppression of abnormal lab results and adverse events caused by the Recallamin vaccine but dozens of illegal financial arrangements with physicians across the country, funded through Noreast Regional Bank by AlzCura Board member Easton Arthur, the bank's Executive Vice President. The breadth and depth of the greed, conspiracy, and corruption grew with each new thread of evidence that was pulled. Resulting in criminal charges, convictions, and incarcerations for many more people caught up in AlzCura's web of deception.

AlzCura Pharmaceuticals, with no way to generate revenue and staring at legal settlement costs that would likely be in the hundreds of billions of dollars, would ultimately file for bankruptcy. Dr. Asa Sheridan, Cheryl Baker, Dr. Myron David Muckland, Dr. Lynn Franklin, and Dr. Woodson Shearlow would be convicted of multiple fraud and conspiracy charges, followed by many others, including AlzCura's Chief Legal Counsel Chet Humphreys.

The mystery of the two sets of unidentified fingerprints was eventually solved. Detective Farest, assisted by his summer intern Sunny Day, learned of Cheryl Baker's second home and her twin sons through a review of her financial records. Cheryl Baker wasn't talking, on advice from legal counsel, so Detective Farest obtained a warrant to search the home and question her sons. When a police officer knocked on the door of the house, both Anthony and Andrew tried to escape out the back door, only to be met by the officer's partner. The disgusting photographic evidence of their exploitation of little boys and girls displayed on their walls was evidence enough to detain them. When their fingerprints set off alarms of their involvement in open cases in Maine and an open break-in and child abduction case in Nora, New York, their fate was sealed. Andrew Baker was eventually convicted of murdering Dr. Steven Caron and Leslie Anderson. He also was found to have decapitated Celeste's dog and leaving the note on Curt Barne's door. Anthony was convicted of the break-in and surveillance of Jackie's home and subsequent abduction of Ashley. Both were also convicted of multiple allegations of child criminal exploitation.

Chief Detective Les Gains was promoted to Police Commission as expected. His first act as Commissioner was to make Inspector Brent Farest his new Chief Detective. In turn, new Chief Detective Farest offered his former intern, Sunny Day, his vacated detective position. Sunny's burgeoning relationship with Officer Barrett Todd and her friendship with Jackie only made accepting the offer of employment and move from Arizona that much easier.

For Celeste Boulanger's birthday in October, Inspector Theo Adams brought home a Bichon Frise puppy. Not only was she delighted with the dog, but she was overcome with joy when she discovered the engagement ring Theo had attached to the dog's collar. The two got married pond-side the following summer and welcomed a cute red-headed baby boy nine months later.

Jackie met with her attorney Nunzio Scarletti and filed her wrongful death lawsuit. A few weeks later, she traveled to Maine with Ashley to celebrate her daughter's first birthday with Curt, Caitlin, and Cade. Reuniting at the Farrisport Inn restaurant, where it had all began, was the perfect venue. Everything about their birthday dinner went smoothly until the waiter came over to apologize that they had failed to make the dessert Curt had ordered. Curt took it in stride, and Caitlin and Cade were only too happy to extend their tradition of sharing their desserts with Jackie and their father. After dessert, Caitlin and Cade asked if they could take Ashley to see the moose head in the lobby. No sooner had the kids left when a familiar face approached the table – Brittany, the hostess that had mistakenly thought they were a family of four.

"Mr. Barnes, we are so sorry about your dessert. I hope you don't mind that I'm delivering it to you now," she said, placing a ring box in front of Curt.

"Not at all, Brittany. Perfect timing. Thank you," Curt replied, picking up the box and getting out of his chair.

Jackie was speechless as Curt approached and got down on one knee.

"Jackie Deno, will you marry me?" he asked, opening the box to reveal the diamond ring, his stomach doing flip-flops double-time.

Through tears of surprise and joy, Jackie accepted. The dining room guests who witnessed his traditional on-bended knee marriage proposal erupted in cheers, and Jackie and Curt sealed the moment with a kiss. The kids, who had never left the restaurant but had watched from afar, joined them immediately after. Caitlin and Cade excitedly and repeatedly hugged Jackie and their father. Even Ashley, seeing so much happiness around her, smiled and giggled throughout. Curt had choreographed it all. The missing dessert. The kid's request to show Ash the moose head. Even Brittany's role, which she agreed to do despite it being her day off.

Curt and the kids moved into Jackie's house two weeks later, just in time for Caitlin and Cade to start the school year at their new school. Curt stayed on with Jackson & Barnes Consulting, convincing his partner Sam to take their Maine healthcare consulting company regional. Jackie reached out to Nora Community Hospital's CEO, Tara Newman, and got her Physician Liaison job back. Tara also entered into a consulting engagement with Curt.

While Jackie and Curt had intended to be wed by a justice of the peace at a small family gathering, Doris and Jack Selaney convinced them to do otherwise. The following spring, they were married at St. Paul's Church by Father Woznewski. The wedding party included Caitlin as the flower girl, Cade as ringbearer, Sunny as maid of honor, and Curt's brother BB as best man. The guests in attendance included many of the individuals that were so instrumental in helping Jackie and Curt over the past two years: Barrett Todd, Clara Himber, Tara Newman, Timothy Darling, Sam Jackson, and Loribeth Lacroix. To Jackie and Curt's surprise, Celeste Boulanger, Theo Adams, DA Wydman, and Dr. Preston Slack also traveled from Maine. Hostess Brittany was also there as one of Jackie's bridesmaids. The path of Jackie and Curt's relationship could hardly be described as a fairy-tale. Though it had been punctuated by magical moments from the beginning. It was no less magical when Curt kissed his wife, Jackie, in front of God and the wedding guests.

It took Dr. Elizabeth Harder's team nearly six months to determine the actual efficacy and safety of the Recallamin vaccine and release their report to the public. The good news was that Recallamin was deemed to be effective and safe in people with a specific genetic make-up. People with these particular DNA markers and symptoms of mild or moderate Alzheimer's often experienced no continued decline or adverse events. Some even showed remission of symptoms and restored mental functioning. This, however, only constituted about 10% of the patients who had received the vaccine. The bad news was that for people without those particular DNA markers, the vaccine was shown not to be effective. The worse news was that there were people with a constellation of DNA markers that definitely had a much higher risk of adverse events and death from the vaccine. With millions of people clamoring for an answer to the Alzheimer's scourge, the results offered some hope. Dr. Harder's team estimated that of the nearly 1 million newly diagnosed Alzheimer's cases each year in the United States, approximately 100,000 could benefit from the Recallamin vaccine. The financial reality of this estimate meant one company couldn't manufacture, market, and distribute the vaccine and realize a return on investment.

Recognizing the benefit of the vaccine but the prohibitive

cost, Dr. Harder's study prompted two U.S. Senators, a Democrat, and a Republican, to draft the Alzheimer's Assistance Act. The act sought government support for subsidizing the cost of supplying the Recallamin vaccine. Unfortunately, the bill was mired in the political process, which all too often resembled constipation instead of salvation. The bill eventually passed, and after a request for proposal process, the government awarded a pharmaceutical company permission to restart manufacturing and distributing the Recallamin vaccine. Tight prescribing controls requiring confirmation of genetic testing and proper DNA markers were put in place.

Curt, through Dr. Harder's study of the Recallamin data, eventually learned that Darius Scott had indeed received the vaccine, which likely contributed to his actions in murdering Calli. He chose not to pursue legal action. His days of living in the past and trying to reconcile the unreconciliable were behind him. He was looking ahead.

Jackie and Curt's relationship quickly fell into a comfortable routine. Caitlin and Cade were happy and made many new friends at school. Ashley continued to call Curt her Dada. Curt's stomach still did flip-flops when he looked at Jackie. Jackie continued to tease him by playing the part of the naïve southern belle student hoping to learn from her older and wiser professor.

One morning, Curt sat down for breakfast. Instead of silverware at his place setting, there was a plastic instrument with a window showing two parallel lines.

"Does this mean what I think it means?" he asked, looking at Jackie in shock.

"It does if you're thinking it means you're going to have another child calling you daddy!"

Nine months later, they greeted Hope Barnes into the world.

Hope because Jackie and Curt's relationship had given

them hope in the aftermath of tragedy. Hope, because it was hope that Jackie and Curt never lost in their crusade against AlzCura even when the odds had seemed against them. Hope, because they hoped their daughter would grow up to be a beacon of light in a world too often darkened by deceit, discrimination, and despair. Hope, because hope was still the most effective vaccine for holding on to love and the lifetime of memories love creates.

❀ ❀ ❀

Thank you for reading Memory's Hope. Insert address below in browser to view other books by Chris Bliersbach.

https://readerlinks.com/mybooks/3464

ACKNOWLEDGEMENT

My parents both died from complications of Alzheimer's Disease. Before their downward spiral from this devastating disease, they lived long, productive lives. They endured unimaginable hardships growing up, yet survived and emigrated to America to build a better life for themselves and their children. They instilled in me values for which I will be forever grateful. Thanks, Mom and Dad. This book and the entire *Table for Four* series are for you.

A portion of the proceeds from this book and the other books in this series, including *Table for Four* and *Memory's Hope*, will be donated to the Alzheimer's Foundation of America (AFA). AFA's mission is providing support, services, and education to individuals, families, and caregivers affected by Alzheimer's disease and related dementias nationwide and funding research for better treatment and a cure.

BOOKS BY THIS AUTHOR

Table For Four: A Medical Thriller Series Book 1

A blockbuster Alzheimer's cure. A murder and unexplained deaths. Two aggrieved parties meet by chance. Will they expose the truth, or die trying?

Dying To Recall: A Medical Thriller Series Book 2

A suicide, a break-in, an ominous warning. Is it a coincidence? Or have Jackie and Curt unleashed the wrath of vengeful pharmaceutical executives?

Memory's Hope: A Medical Thriller Series Book 3

The case against AlzCura intensifies until the FDA's shocking response to the data. Will the guilty parties walk, or will they be brought to justice?

Aja Minor: Gifted Or Cursed: A Psychic Crime Thriller Series Book 1

Aja has disturbing powers. She feels cursed, but the FBI thinks otherwise. Will she stop a serial rapist and killer or become his next victim?

Aja Minor: Fountain Of Youth: A Psychic Crime Thriller Series Book 2

Aja Minor goes undercover. The target, an international child trafficking ring. When her cover is blown, the mission and her life are in jeopardy.

Aja Minor: Predatorville: A Psychic Crime Thriller Series Book 3

Solving a surge in assaults and missing children is Aja Minor's next test. But when the hunter becomes the hunted, will she get out of Predatorville alive?

Old Lady Ketchel's Revenge: The Slaughter Minnesota Horror Series Book 1

No one truly escapes their childhood unscathed. Especially if you grew up in Slaughter, Minnesota, in the 1960s and crossed Old Lady Ketchel's path.

Hagatha Ketchel Unhinged: The Slaughter Minnesota Horror Series Book 2

Twenty-four years in an asylum is enough time to really lose your mind. And arouse one to unleash the dark and vengeful thoughts residing therein.

Hagatha's Century Of Terror: The Slaughter Minnesota Horror Series Book 3

What does a crazy old lady in Slaughter, Minnesota, need on her 100th birthday? Sweet revenge, of course.

Loving You From My Grave: A Wholesome Inspirational Romance

He ran from his past. She's held captive by hers. Could love set them free, bridge their differences in age and race, and survive death?

Little Bird On My Balcony: Selected Poems

A collection of poems that speak to the love, loss, longing, and levity of navigating young adulthood.

Adilynn's Lullaby: Poems Of Love & Loss

A collection of poems about love and loss that provide hope and inspiration during some of life's most difficult times.

ABOUT CHRIS BLIERSBACH

Chris Bliersbach is originally from St. Paul, Minnesota, and now lives in Henderson, Nevada.

Follow him on Amazon, Facebook, Goodreads or join his mailing list at cmbliersbach@gmail.com

Made in the USA
Middletown, DE
16 July 2023

35309573R00205